City of Angels Trilogy

By M. Ward Leon

For information, or to order additional copies, please contact:

Beacon Publishing Group
P.O. Box 41573 Charleston, S.C. 29423
800.817.8480| beaconpublishinggroup.com

Publisher's catalog available by request.

ISBN-13: 978-1-961504-04-2

ISBN-10: 1-961504-04-2

Published in 2023. New York, NY 10001.

First Edition. Printed in the USA.

City of Angels Trilogy

For my Joanie & Meghan

*The City of Angels is my homage to Raymond
Chandler, Dashiell Hammett, and all the great
writers of hard-boiled detective novels.*

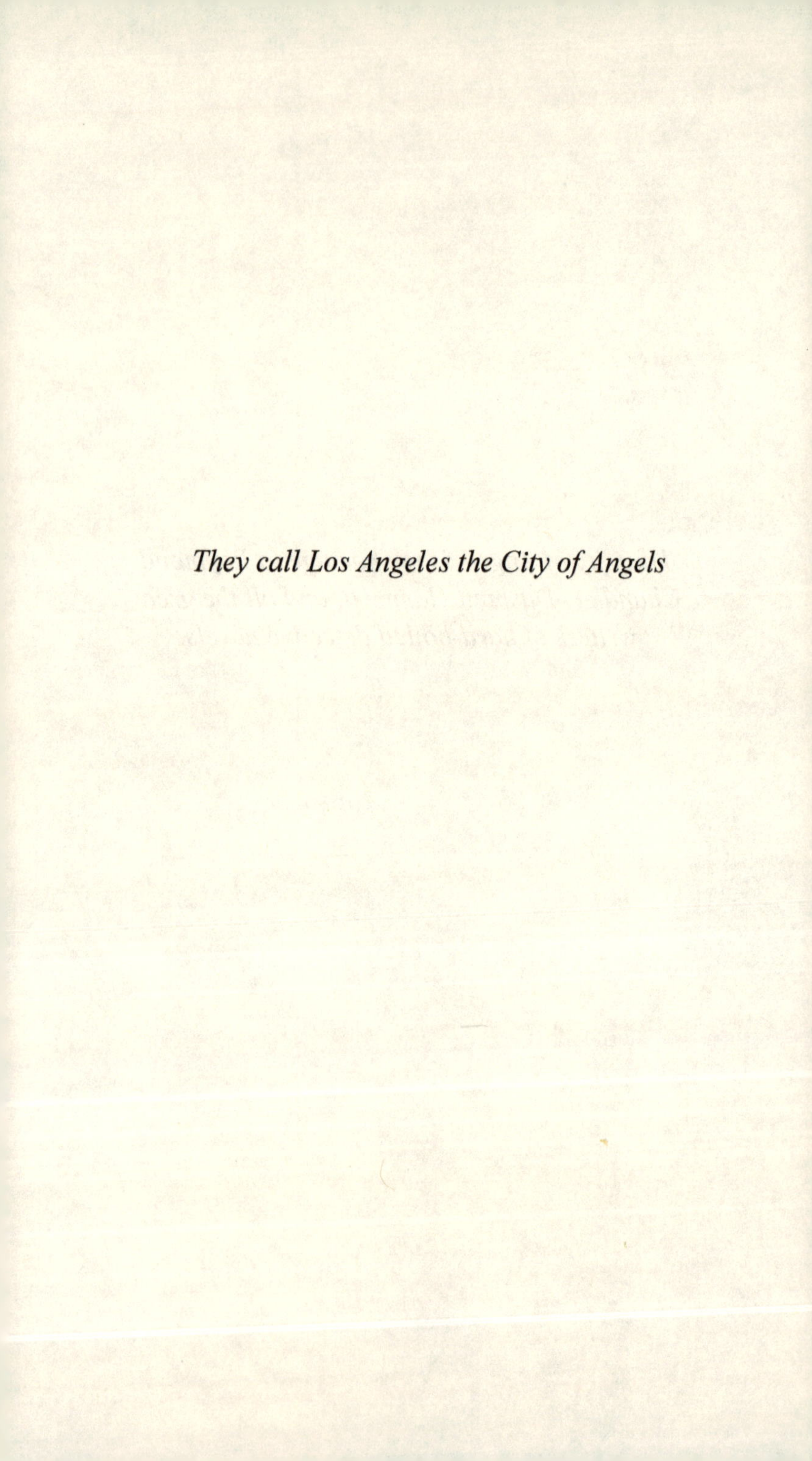

They call Los Angeles the City of Angels

City of Angels Trilogy

Herr Doktor

Only the Good Die Young

The Red Queen

1940s Glossary

German / Nazi Glossary

Herr Doktor

"Sieg Heil! Sieg Heil!" Screamed Walter Miller, right arm raised in the Nazi salute as Aribert Heim took the stage at an underground meeting of the Amerika First Volksbund held at the Murphy Ranch.

The Murphy Ranch was built in Rustic Canyon, Los Angeles, in the 1930s by sympathizers of the anti-Semitic, white supremacist Silver Legion of America, better known as the Silver Shirts.

On December 8th, 1941, the organization was effectively shut down once police called for the open arrest of any individuals associated with the group. That's when the fascist federation went underground.

In the years immediately following the United States defeat of Nazi Germany, the Silver Shirts decided it best to keep a low profile until the anti-German fervor settled down.

Now that Hitler and most of his band of thugs were dead or captured, the U.S. government turned its attention to the threat of communism.

If there's one thing the Nazis hate almost as much as the Jews, it's communists. But, since the commies are taking the heat off them for the time being, they'll go about their business of anti-Semitism undeterred. Of course, most Nazis believe that the International Jewish conspiracy is made up of bankers and Bolsheviks.

Walter Miller, a German-American whose real name is Walter Fritz Müller, has always been a good little Nazi since American Nazi spymaster Frederick Duquesne was recruited in 1937.

Fritz Müller was born to German immigrants in Los Angeles in 1900. Gerhart Müller's father changed the family name when he arrived in America. He was a cobbler who opened a successful shop on the first floor of the Bradbury Building in downtown Los Angeles. His parents worked long hours in the shop, living the American dream. The Müllers had just opened a second shop on Monday, October 28th, 1929.

The following day, October 29th, was Black Tuesday when the stock market crashed. Billions of dollars were lost, wiping out thousands of investors, including Fritz Müller. Thus began the "Great Depression."

Fascism feeds on desperation and fear. And during such times, there will always be someone evil to claim to have the answer, someone to show who is to blame for their misery. Because it can't be your fault, it has to be someone else.

As the world's economies crashed, Adolf Hitler found the perfect scapegoat. The Jews. Who better to take the fall? After all, aren't all Jews greedy, dirty, and conniving? It must be their fault. Damn Christ-killers.

Walter Miller, at 29, was like tens of millions of others who were out of work, hungry, destitute, and angry. For a time, he rode the rails as a hobo. Miller traveled all across the country looking for work and finding none. He stood in line for hours in soup kitchens and bread lines until one day, while walking along a railroad track outside of Wilmer, Texas, he found a .38 revolver hidden under a pile of trash.

On August 14th, 1930, Walter Miller walked into the Bank of Wilmer at Fifth Street and Hickory Street in downtown Wilmer. He walked up to the teller, handed her a raggedy canvas bag, showed her his pistol, and softly said, "Gimme all the money in the drawer, or I'll plug ya."

Alma Sue Hickock, the twenty-two-year-old teller, did as she was told. She filled the bag with almost three hundred dollars, and while she did that, she pressed the silent alarm button on the floor by her right foot.

Walter took the bag full of cash and walked out of the bank into the waiting arms of Wilmer Sheriff Billy Ray Calhoun and six of his deputies.

"Drop the gun!" Calhoun shouted as six double-barrel shotguns were pointed at the surprised and shocked desperado.

"Don't shoot, coppers!" Miller said as he dropped his pistol.

Miller was handcuffed and taken to the Wilmer jail, where he was fingerprinted, mug shots taken, and thrown in a cell with six other prisoners. He stood trial and was sentenced to three years imprisonment to be served at the Texas State Penitentiary in Huntsville.

Walter worked in the textile factory in prison, making blankets for the US Army during the day. At night, he was a voracious reader. Miller read everything that the prison library had. He read books of poetry, classic literature, pulp fiction, biographies, and even an obscure book called Mein Kampf, written by an unknown German author, Adolf Hitler.

Once released from prison, Walter hitchhiked back to Los Angeles. Because of his German heritage, he landed a job at a Biergarten in downtown LA, the Deutsches Haus Tavern. The tavern quickly became a popular hangout for Nazi sympathizers, white supremacists, anti-Semites, xenophobes, thugs, goons, and hooligans.

He was working at the Deutsches Haus Tavern when he met William Didley Pelly, the founder of the Silver Legion of America, commonly known as the Silver Shirts. The Silver Legion of America was an underground American fascist organization headquartered in Ashville, North Carolina. They patterned their uniforms after Mussolini's Black Shirts and Hitler's Brown Shirts, better known as the SS.

Walter Miller joined the Los Angeles branch enthusiastically on the spot. He became one of the more vibrant, exuberant, and fanatical members, rising through the ranks to become Captain.

Things were going famously for Walter until December 7th, when the Japanese bombed Pearl Harbor. Miller was arrested with fifty of the Silver Shirts while hiding out at the Murphy Ranch compound on December 8th, when the FBI conducted a pre-dawn raid.

Walter Miller stood trial and was convicted under the federal sedition act and the Smith Act of 1940.

"Will the defendant please rise?" The bailiff said.

"Walter Miller, having been found guilty, I sentence you to a term of imprisonment of a minimum of no less than five years and no longer than ten years. Goodbye, Mister Miller." Judge Remer said.

"Welcome to San Quentin, ladies," Butch Rumson, the Captain of the guards, shouted to the men filing off the bus. Some of the prisoners were repeat offenders, hardened criminals. Others, first-timers, they looked like a deer caught in the headlights. Having served time for bank robbery, Miller knew what to expect.

They were made to stand side-by-side in a straight line while guards holding carbines surrounded them.

"You are no longer free men; you are now the property of the California State Penal System. From this day on, you will no longer be John Smith, Bob Jones, or Tommy Wilson. You will be assigned a number; memorize it. That is who you are for the duration of your time here. Do you understand?" Rumson stated.

The men in line didn't reply.

"I said, do you understand!" He screamed.

The prisoners mumbled that they understood.

Rumson walked up to the toughest-looking man in the line and proceeded to jam his Billy club into his stomach, forcing him to double over and fall to his knees.

"Do you understand!" Rumson screamed again.

"YES, SIR!" The men shouted.

"That's better. I'm Captain Rumson, that's what you'll address me as, that or Sir. Is that clear?" Rumson said as he began pacing back and forth in front of them.

"YES, SIR!"

"You will address all the other guards as Sir. Is that understood?"

"YES, SIR!"

"Now listen up, you maggots! You will eat at mealtimes, and only at mealtimes.

You will participate in all prison activities.

You will keep the cell clean at all times.

You will not tamper with, deface, or damage any prison property.

You will address each other by number only.

You will be allowed 5 minutes in the showers.

Smoking is a privilege.

Mail is a privilege.

Visitors are a privilege.

Failure to obey any of the above rules may result in punishment. Do you understand?" Rumson said.

"YES, SIR!"

"All right. Guards, get these maggots out of my sight!" Rumson ordered.

The guards marched the men into the administration building to be processed.

Walter Miller walked out of San Quentin Prison on April 14th, 1947, after serving six years, ten months, and thirteen days of his ten-year sentence. Waiting for him outside the prison gates was Wilhelm Kuhn, a now-defunct Silver Shirt.

While Walter was serving time in prison, the Silver Shirts reinvented themselves into Amerika First. They still held all the beliefs and convictions of the original anti-Semitic, white supremacist ideals of the Silver Legion of America. The AF repackaged and rebranded themselves to seem less of a radical racist group and more homogenized.

On the ride down to Los Angeles, Wilhelm Kuhn filled Walter in on the organization and what his leadership role was expected to be.

While in prison, Walter had used his activities productively by forming a legacy, the first white supremacist gang, The Aryan Tribe. He recruited several men from that gang who would be released in the next few years. Men whose criminal skills would be helpful to the growth of Amerika First.

Amerika First was founded a couple of days after Germany surrendered. Tristan Kendrick Wentworth, a New York businessman, was its founder. Wentworth, a wealthy real estate developer, is known for his anti-Semitic and bigoted beliefs. He is a fervent white supremacist who has publicly promoted limiting immigration from what he calls shit-hole countries and called for more immigrants from Ayran countries such as Norway, Sweden, and, of course, Germany.

Wentworth was the commander of New York's Silver Legion of America branch. He also did time in prison at Sing-Sing. Wentworth was sentenced to a one to three-year term; Wentworth did the three-spot. He organized Amerika First after Silver Legion of America when he was released. It became a nationwide sensation.

Wentworth, a master of the media and an eloquent orator and showman used much of the rhetoric and communication techniques of his hero, Adolf

Hitler, to enlist thousands of disenchanted veterans who came home to find their jobs had been filled by someone else.

He used the same scare tactics that Goebbels used, creating a scapegoat. In Germany, it was the Jews; Wentworth used immigrants, blacks, and of course, the ever-popular Jews.

Wentworth was a pathological liar; he took a play right out of Mein Kampf, telling a lie so colossal that no one would believe that someone could have the audacity to distort the truth so infamously.

Whenever someone would challenge him for lying, he would turn it around, accusing them of lying, and if it were the media, he would yell fake news. It's the media that's the enemy of the people. He claimed that he and he alone had the answers, and nobody knew more about anything than he did. He was their savior.

Walter had heard and read all about Tristan Wentworth. He was a big admirer and was ecstatic about meeting and working alongside the great man as his number two.

The drive down from San Quentin was long; they didn't arrive in Los Angeles until after eleven that night. A room had been arranged for Walter at the Heidelberg Inn in downtown Los Angeles.

Wilhelm Kuhn dropped Walter off at the Inn and said he would meet him in the lobby at 9 a.m. the following morning, have breakfast, and meet with the man himself, Tristan K. Wentworth.

"*Gute Nacht,*" (good night) Wilhelm said.

Walter stood nervously before shaking Wilhelm's hand; he smiled and said, "*Gute Nacht und Danke*." (Good night and thank you)

John Marlboro had just finished a missing person case involving a father taking the child away from the mother after losing custody in a divorce. The father tried to take the three-year-old across California state lines into Nevada. Marlboro was able to nab him at a Bob's Big Boy diner just on the other side of Barstow, heading to Vegas. The father was arrested and the little girl safely returned to the mother.

He was planning on taking a couple of days off and heading over to the Channel Islands for a little well-deserved R&R. He was sitting in his office in the Brockman Building, 700 South Grand Avenue in downtown Los Angeles, when there was a knock on the door.

"It's open!" Marlboro shouted.

The doorknob turned slowly, two women, a beautiful young woman in her twenties and an elderly lady with a cane, who looked to be in her sixties, came into his office.

Marlboro stood up, gestured to the two chairs in front of his desk, and said, "Ladies, please, won't you take a seat."

The young woman helped her companion and then took her seat.

"Now, what can I do for you ladies?" Marlboro asked.

The young woman said, "My name is Sarah Stroński, and this is my aunt, Mrs. Zibiah Anielewicz."

"Okay?"

"We're Jews."

"Okay."

"You don't mind that we're Jewish?" Sarah asked.

"No. Why would you think I would?"

"We've been to several other investigators who declined to work for us."

"Ladies, your religion is not important to me. I'm here to help you if I can," Marlboro explained.

"Mr. Marlboro, have you ever heard of Mauthausen-Gusen?"

"I believe it was one of the Nazi's concentration camps in Austria if I'm not mistaken."

"You are correct; it was a death camp. My aunt was a prisoner there for three years," Sarah uttered.

"I'm so sorry," He said.

"Mr. Marlboro, in that camp, there was a man, a doctor. Aribert Heim was known in the camp as Doctor Death and the Butcher of Mauthausen. He was captured after the war but escaped. Heim is one of the most wanted Nazi war criminals in the world. My aunt has seen Heim here in Los Angeles, Mr. Marlboro."

"Have you gone to the police?" He asked.

"Yes, but they showed no interest."

"So, what would you like me to do, Miss Stroński?"

"We want you to find him and bring this monster to justice," She said passionately.

"You want me to track down this Aribert Heim and bring him to the police?"

"No. You must turn him over to the Mossad, the Israeli Intelligence Agency if and when you capture him."

"If I capture him, where will I find the Mossad?"

"The Israeli Embassy."

"Well, if they're here, why don't they capture him?"

"They have no jurisdiction here in the United States. It is against international law," She explained.

Marlboro sat quietly for a few moments, trying to process what this case would involve.

"Will you take the case, Mr. Marlboro?" Sarah asked, looking at him with big brown doe eyes.

"All right, Miss Stroński, I will take the case. So, you know, I get twenty-five dollars a day and expenses."

"That will be fine."

"I will need a lot of information from your aunt. Where did she see him? What did he look like? Was he with anyone? What was he wear…"

"Why don't you and I discuss this privately? My aunt finds this whole matter very stressful and disturbing, as you can well understand."

"Yes, of course. When would you like to get together and discuss some of these details, Miss Stroński?" Marlboro asked.

"Sarah, please. How about this evening over dinner? Why don't you come over to my apartment? I have a lot of documents, newspaper clippings, and photographs that I can share with you. Say seven o'clock."

"All right. And your address?"

"898 Manning Avenue."

"Ah, Westwood."

"Yes. So, I shall expect to see you at seven."

"Thank you. It was a pleasure meeting you both. Mrs. Anielewicz, Sarah, I shall see you tonight."

Aribert Heim, better known as Doctor Death and the Butcher of Mauthausen was the son of a policeman and housewife. He studied medicine in Graz, Austria, and received his diploma in Vienna. Heim joined the SS after Nazi Germany annexed Austria in 1938. In the spring of 1940, he volunteered for the Waffen-SS, where he rose to the rank of Hauptsturmführer (head storm leader).

Heim was infamous for performing operations without the use of anesthesia. Jewish prisoners were poisoned with various injections directly into the heart. He would use petrol, phenol, assorted poisons, and even water to induce death.

Heim use to remove organs from living prisoners without the use of anesthesia, resulting in the deaths of hundreds.

In 1942, he was transferred to serve in the 6th SS Mountain Division Nord in northern Finland as an SS doctor.

In 1945, he was captured by U.S. soldiers and sent to a camp for prisoners of war, where he was released due to a clerical error.

The Butcher of Mauthausen was a free man.

Marlboro pulled his fire-engine red Fleetmaster into the U-shaped driveway of 898 Manning Avenue, Westwood. The house was an off-white California style, one-story home with a grey slate roof that sat back off the street up on a hill. He parked by a short red brick wall that led to the front door.

Miss Stroński was standing at the open door as Marlboro approached.

"Good evening, Mr. Marlboro. Won't you please come in?" She said as she walked him into the living room.

"Beautiful home you have." He said as he entered the house into a spacious living room.

"Thank you. Please have a seat. It's my parents' home."

"Oh, I'd love to meet them. Are they home?" He asked as he took a seat on the sofa.

"I meant to say it *was* my parents' home. Both my parents are dead."

"I'm sorry. The war?" He inquired.

"No. My parents were killed in an automobile accident a year ago up on Mulholland Drive. Drunk driver."

"How horrible," Marlboro said apologetically.

"Yes, it was tragic. My father was Doctor Stroński; he worked on the Manhattan Project."

"He must have been a brilliant man."

"When the Nazis started taking power, my father and mother had the foresight to see the inevitable. They, along with others like Enrico Fermi, Max Born, Marc Chagall, and Albert Einstein, knew what lay ahead."

"What year did you immigrate?"

"1938. The week after *Kristallnacht*. It was the night the Nazis in Germany torched synagogues, vandalized Jewish homes, schools, and businesses. Close to 100 Jews were murdered. Soon after, thirty thousand men were arrested and sent away to concentration camps."

"Thank God you got out."

"Yes, we were very lucky. Unfortunately, most of our family weren't so fortuitous."

"Your aunt."

"Aunt Zibiah is the only survivor from our family. We lost sixteen in all."

"Were they all sent to Mauthausen?"

"For whatever reason, the Nazis sent most of them to Auschwitz. Only my aunt, her husband, and their two children were sent to Mauthausen. She was the only one to survive."

"Is she doing okay?"

"She suffers from survivor's guilt. She survived only by chance. When they got off the train, they asked if she had any trade. She had been a seamstress, so they put her to work in the tailor shop, making and repairing prisoner uniforms."

"Your uncle and cousins?"

"They worked sixteen hours a day in the quarry. They were forced to carry granite blocks weighing seventy-five pounds up 186 steps to the top of the quarry just to throw them down into a ravine. Prisoners called them the Stairs of Death.

Many died on the Mauthausen Stairs of Death every day, and occasionally, those who survived were placed in a horrible line-up at the edge of a cliff called The Parachutists Wall.

Prison guards would point a gun at you; you'd have the option of pushing the prisoner in front of you off the cliff to his death or being shot. That's how my cousins died. They decided to be shot rather than kill another human being. Over a hundred and twenty thousand men died on those stairs.

My uncle was killed when he stopped to help another inmate who had stumbled on the stairs. They made everyone stop and watch. My uncle was strapped to a board and had a large granite block dropped on his head. I understand they intentionally made it, so he didn't die instantly but suffered for hours."

"Goose-stepping bastards," Marlboro sneered.

"Were you in the war, Mr. Marlboro?"

"Yes. I was in the Army Air Corps. I was a tail gunner on a B-25, stationed in Burma, fighting the Japs."

"Did you see a lot of action?"

"A amount," He said modestly.

John Marlboro flew over twenty-six combat missions in all. On his thirteenth mission, their plane, nicknamed "Hell's Belles," was shot down by a squadron of Jap Zeros. All the crew made it out safely. They were captured by the Japanese patrol, beaten, and taken to a prisoner-of-war camp.

Each of them was repeatedly beaten and tortured. The camp was made up of mostly British and Australians. There were only a handful of Americans, all of them airmen.

The commandant, Captain Fukumoto, was a career soldier who was angry that he had to babysit a bunch of POWs and wasn't able to fight on the front lines. So, he took his frustration and hostility out of the prisoners.

The Japanese guards took pleasure in torturing and tormenting the prisoners. Aside from the beatings, they would stake a man out in the midday sun with a glass of water just out of reach or force a man to drink pints of water, being tied to the ground and having guards jump on his stomach.

They were starved of food, and many of the prisoners suffered from cholera and dysentery. The men were so desperate for anything to eat they would eat anything they could find: frogs, snakes, and spiders.

About once a month, the Kempetei (the Japanese version of the Gestapo) would come into the camp and yell ten names of prisoners who would be ordered to dig their own graves, after which they would force the men onto their knees in front of the graves and proceed to shot them in the head.

After three weeks of captivity, Marlboro and his crew decided they'd rather die trying to escape than die a slow and agonizing death.

One night, when there was a new moon, the crew of the "Hell's Belles" waited until three in the morning and snuck out of the hut where they were kept. They crawled on their stomachs to the edge of the barbed wire fence, dug a hole under the fence, and escaped.

They hadn't gotten but a few hundred yards when the Japanese discovered they had escaped. That's when all Hell broke loose. Fifty guards gave chase, shooting wildly into the jungle in all directions, hoping to hit someone. The seven-man crew decided to split up into two groups. Marlboro, the bombardier, and the two waist-gunners went off to the east while the Captain, co-pilot, and radio operator ran to the west.

Of the seven-man crew of the "Hell's Belles," only two men survived: Marlboro and the bombardier, a fella named Mark Powell from Chicago, Illinois. They lost the two waist-gunners to the jungle. Tommy Farmington died from a poisonous snake bite, and Jimmy "Smoky" Jackson was killed while traversing a raging river. He got swept away downstream, hitting his head on some rocks, and drowned.

Marlboro and Powell were eventually found by a scouting patrol of the now-famous Merrill's Marauders. The Marauders were a light infantry assault unit that became famous for its guerilla warfare and deep-penetration missions behind enemy lines, creating havoc and disrupting Japanese forces.

Marlboro and Powell were sent to Hawaii for two months of R&R. Afterwards, they returned to active duty in Burma, each flying with new crews. They were awarded the Air Medal, the Distinguished Service Cross, and the Silver Star.

Marlboro went on to earn the Distinguished Flying Cross and two Purple Hearts for wounds he received on different missions. Marc Powell was killed when his plane was shot down on a bombing run over Rangoon. There were no survivors.

Marlboro discovered the fates of the "Hell's Belles" crew after the war. They were recaptured, brought back to camp, and beheaded by Captain Fukumoto.

After the Japanese surrendered, Captain Fukumoto was captured and tried as a war criminal. He was convicted and hung by the neck.

Sarah had prepared a typical Jewish meal. First, a bowl of chicken soup with matzo balls, then, as the main course, a brisket of beef with a side of potato latkes and roasted carrots. Later, Sarah served rugelach with coffee.

Over dinner, there was no talk of the Holocaust, only small talk about things going on in Los Angeles and themselves.

Sarah told Marlboro about her teaching a course about Women in the Bible and one for Jewish Culture in America at UCLA. And Marlboro told her about his six years in the LAPD and life as a private detective.

After dinner, she told him more about Doctor Death. "There was the time when my Aunt Zibiah was working, repairing some prisoner's uniforms, and she saw Heim approach a small girl, five or six years old, clutching a doll. He asked if he could see it. The child nervously handed the doctor the doll, he then proceeded to take his pistol out of its holster and shoot the child in the head.

Moments later, Heim brought the doll into the tailor shop, pointed at my aunt, handed her the doll, and said, "There is a tear in this dress. Can you repair it?"

She replied sheepishly, "Ja, Herr Doktor."

"That is good. I have a niece that will love this. I will be back in an hour." He said as he walked out of the shop. As he strolled down the street, Heim stepped over the girl's body and walked on as if he was stepping over a pile of trash," Sarah said, starting to sob.

Marlboro could only sit quietly and listen reverently. Having experienced torture and cruelty, he could relate to the extreme pain that Sarah and especially her aunt live with daily.

"There is one more story that I want to tell you about, so you know exactly what you're up against.

Aribert Heim butchered a prisoner who came to see him with an inflamed foot. The young man was an athlete in otherwise excellent health. Aribert examined him and his teeth. He gave the prisoner an anesthetic and then cut him open, castrated him, and removed one of his kidneys to see how long the man would live. The young man soon died. Heim then cut off the man's head, boiled it, and stripped of its flesh.

Heim used this young man's skull as a paperweight on his desk. He said that he wanted the head because of its perfect teeth. Aribert was also known to have removed tattooed flesh from prisoners and used the skin to make lamp shades, which he gave to the commandant of the camp.

Mr. Marlboro, these men have no regard for human life. If Heim is indeed here in Los Angeles, he will be well protected by men who will not think twice about killing anyone they feel threatened by."

"I understand, Miss Stroński," Marlboro said reassuringly.

"Sarah, please. Mr. Marlboro."

"Alright, Sarah. And it's John," He said with a smile.

He looked at his watch and said, "Well, I best be going. I have a friend who works for the government, whom I will contact tomorrow. I want to thank you for a wonderful dinner."

"Thank you for coming, Mr. Marl… John."

"Good night, Sarah."

Two months earlier, Walter Miller and Wilhelm Kuhn met Heim in the parking lot of Nate'n Al's Delicatessen on North Beverly Drive in West Hollywood.

As Miller, Kuhn, and Heim met by Kuhn's car, Miller whispered, "Herr Doktor, do you think it's safe to eat at a Jewish restaurant? Aren't you worried that someone might recognize you?"

"Nein. I've had this beard for over a year and had it colored grey. Plus, most of this Jew scum is too timid to look you into your eyes. Besides, what are the odds that anyone might recognize me? Come, gentlemen, shall we dine?" Hein said with a wolfish grin.

The three men walked into the restaurant like they owned the joint. Hein was dressed in a pin-striped suit and tie; he looked very dapper. Miller and Kuhn were dressed less formally, and their clothes weren't as fine a quality.

The hostess approached them and asked, "Three for breakfast?"

"Yes," Miller replied.

The young woman took the three of them to a table by the window facing Beverly Drive.

"How's this?" She asked.

Miller, feeling unsure, looked at Heim. The doctor smiled and said, "This will be fine, Thank you."

Once seated, the hostess handed them each a menu and said, "The waitress will be with you in a moment. Enjoy."

Heim sat looking out the window, watching the people parade by. He turned to Miller and said, "I will not cower to these kikes. We are the master race, after all. Are we not?"

"Ja, Herr Doktor." Miller answered.

"Walter, Herr Kuhn has spoken very highly of you, as has many others. They tell me you are very committed to our cause."

"Yes, Herr Doktor. I am your humble servant."

An elderly Jewish waitress approached the table asking, "So, have you decided what you'd like, or do you need more time?"

"I believe that we are ready. I'll have the smoked whitefish and scrambled eggs." Heim said.

"I'll have the same." Kuhn concurred.

"Scrambled eggs and ham," Miller added.

"Very good, and something to drink?"

"We'll all have coffee," Heim said as he looked for any dissension. There was none.

"Herr Miller, it is with great honor that I have the privilege to stow upon you the title of Commander of the Los Angeles Chapter of Amerika First. Congratulations." Heim said proudly.

"I am honored, mein Führer." Miller whispered.

"Ah, if only you could have met him, Müller. So few of us were truly blessed to have been in his presence. Now that he's gone, his vision must be carried out. That's why it's important to have men like you carrying out *His* will."

The old waitress brought their meals and coffee, placed them in front of each man, and said, "Now. If there's anything else you need, just let me know."

As they were in the middle of their breakfast, Heim noticed two women walking past the window, looking at him. An elderly woman and her companion, a young woman, both of them looked Jewish to Heim.

They passed by the plate glass window three times, and each time, the older Jewess seemed to be becoming more and more agitated and frantic. Finally, Zibiah Anielewicz stood in front of the window, pointed at Heim, and screamed, *"To on, rzeźnik Mauthausen!"*

The younger woman, Sarah Stroński, tried to comfort her aunt, but the old lady kept yelling, *"To on, rzeźnik Mauthausen!"*, "The butcher of Mauthausen!"

People on the street were beginning to stop and take notice, as were the patrons of Nate'n Al's. The majority of them are Jewish.

Heim threw a twenty-dollar bill on the table, then he, Miller, and Kuhn calmly stood up and walked out of the restaurant and proceeded to get in their cars and drive off in separate directions.

Later that same day, Sarah Stroński called the Los Angeles Police to file a report.

"So, Miss Stroński, your aunt claims to have seen a Nazi war criminal eating breakfast in Nate'n Al's, a Jewish Deli. Is that right?" Sargent Malloy asked sarcastically.

"That's right. Aribert Heim. He was a Nazi doctor in Mauthausen concentration camp. He is a wanted war criminal known as the Butcher of Mauthausen. Heim was responsible for the killing of hundreds of thousands of Jews," Sarah said.

"This Butcher of Mauthausen just happened to be having breakfast at a Jewish deli. A Nazi eating at a Jewish deli. Doesn't that strike you as a little odd?"

"Look, Sargent, would you take me more seriously if I told you he was eating sauerkraut and wiener schnitzel instead of ham and eggs?"

"Lady, all I'm saying is that it sounds a bit farfetched, is all."

"So, you're basically not going to do a damn thing about it," Sarah said caustically.

"I'll make my report and turn it over to my boss. And he'll…"

"Yeah, he'll have a good laugh. And go around telling all the boys in blue, hey, did you hear the one about a Nazi war-criminal having breakfast in a Jewish deli? Thanks for nothing, Sargent," She said as she stormed off.

Under his breath, Sargent Malloy uttered, "Bitch."

Under Sarah's breath, she uttered, "*Manyak!*"

Shortly after her encounter with the police, Sarah contacted Marlboro.

The following day, after dinner with Sarah, Marlboro picked up the phone and dialed Madison-7241.

"Federal Bureau of Investigation. How may I direct your call?" The FBI operator asked.

"Agent James Beck."

"One moment, please."

"Agent Beck."

"James, Marlboro, here."

"John, to what do I owe the honor?"

"I was hoping that you might have some time to help me out with a case that I'm working on."

"Well, I am busy working on a couple of bank robberies at the moment, but I can always spare a few hours for you."

"Great, can you swing by my office sometime today?"

"How about three o'clock?"

"Swell. See you then."

CLICK

Marlboro hung up the phone and walked the few blocks to the Central Library on West 5th Street. He went to the reference desk, where an attractive redheaded young woman with brilliant green eyes was cataloging several volumes of U.S. government publications.

"Anything interesting? "He asked.

"Oh, these are some very stimulating subjects you might find compelling."

"Oh, really. Like what?"

"Well, here's one on the Birds of Kilauea Point, or how about this, a study on the Moose Junction quadrangle."

"Way too exciting for me, I'm afraid," Marlboro said.

"Oh, is there anything in particular that you're looking for?" She said as she pursed her lips.

Marlboro looked her up and down, grinned, and said, "Mmmhmmm."

"Regarding reference materials."

"Nazis," He answered.

"Excuse me?" She said, surprised.

"Nazis. Nazi war criminals, to be more specific. Do you have anything on Nazi war criminals?"

"I'm sure we do. Follow me to the stacks, and we'll take a look."

"Lead on, doll," Marlboro said with a devilish smile.

She tried to hide her simper, but Marlboro, the master shamus, caught it. She led him past the public book displays into the reference library, where the general public was not allowed.

They went to the card catalog file cabinet, where the ginger-haired fox began to sort through the swamp of the Dewey decimal system.

"To be honest, I never could work out the old Dewey decimal system," Marlboro admitted.

"It is really quite simple; the Dewey decimal system is just a way to put books in order by subject. It places the books on the shelf by subject using numbers from 000 to 999. It is called "decimal" because it uses numbers to the right of the decimal point for more detail. For example, 944.1 is for the History of Brittany, see. Each subject has its own group of numbers…"

"You lost me at It's quite simple," Marlboro interrupted.

"Why exactly are you interested in Nazi war criminals, if you don't mind my asking," She queried.

"I'm a private dick working a case involving a possible Nazi criminal."

"Here in Los Angeles?" She asked, amazed.

"So, I'm told."

"Well, it appears that we have several publications on the subject." She said as she closed the file drawer and led him over to the shelf where the publications were located.

"Here you are. Is there anything else?" She asked demurely.

"Dinner?"

"Excuse me?"

"Well, you've been so kind. I'd like to thank you by taking you out for dinner. Whad'ya say, doll?"

"I get off work at six o'clock."

"Say, I never did catch your name."

"I never said it."

"I'm John Marlboro."

"Saoirse. Saoirse O'Callaghan."

"I shall see you at six o'clock, Saoirse O'Callaghan."

"Slán." She said with a wink and a smile.

Saoirse left Marlboro to go through all the government reports related to Nazi war criminals.

He started by reading through the journals of the International Military Tribunal for the trials at Nuremberg, all 48 volumes. Over the next eight hours, Marlboro's research involved hundreds of government documents, photographs, and military reports. By the time he left, he was both physically and mentally drained.

Before heading back to the office, Marlboro stopped off at a liquor store and bought a large bottle of rye.

Tristan Kendrick Wentworth, the leader of the Amerika First Party, had a home in Los Angeles, in the Holmby Hills overlooking Beverly Hills.

The mansion, at 284 Delfern Drive, was modest compared to his neighbors. It was a mere 12,220 square foot home, with seven bedrooms and nine baths. The coveted landmark estate featured four gated entry points, all with armed guards, nestled among mature trees, manicured gardens, with a guest house, putting green, tennis court, pool, and a spa grotto.

Each of the seven-bedroom suites included a sitting room with a fireplace, the living room had a fully stocked bar with a full-time bartender, a formal dining room that sat twenty-four, two movie theatres, a gymnasium, a billiard room, a Chef's country kitchen, cobblestone driveway with a porte cochere.

Tristan considered it more of a cottage than a mansion, like the one he had in Palm Beach on Ocean Boulevard.

Tristan Wentworth had gotten a call from Wilhelm Kuhn wanting to arrange a meeting with Wentworth, Walter Miller, Aribert Heim, and himself to discuss the upcoming private meeting with the Golden Circle members of the Amerika First Party.

Golden Circle members were primarily high-roller donors, business owners, CEOs, captains of industry, and executives who all had one thing in common: they were anti-Semites.

Businessmen who believed, like Henry Ford, used his newspaper, The Dearborn Independent, to promote anti-Semitism by publishing articles such as "The International Jew, the World's Foremost Problem."

Ford was the only American to be favorably mentioned in Hitler's Mein Kampf. Adolf Hitler so admired Ford that he kept a life-size portrait next to his desk. Henry Ford was presented the Grand Cross of the German Eagle on his seventy-fifth birthday by Karl Kapp and Fritz Heller, two German Consuls.

The Reichsführer (commanding officer) of the *Schutzstaffel* (SS protection squad), Heinrich Himmler, described Ford as "one of our most valuable, important and witty fighters."

Since the defeat of Hitler, all of the members of the Golden Circle are closet anti-Semites. While privately prejudiced against Jews and other minorities, they display a face of tolerance to the public. Hell, it wouldn't be good for a business to be labeled a bigot.

Wentworth himself owned dozens of rental properties in and around Los Angeles and New York City. He is a notorious slumlord who has been brought into the courts for cutting off tenants' hot water and heat, allowing rodent infestation in the buildings, not doing any repairs, and not cleaning the building's public areas.

There wasn't anything that Wentworth wouldn't do to get rid of tenants so he could raise rents. He harassed an elderly couple who refused to move. The wife was dying of cancer and plagued with emphysema. Wentworth had construction workers drill hundreds of small holes in their bedroom ceiling from the apartment above theirs so the bedroom would be filled with dust.

At one point, the United States District Court of the Eastern District of New York brought suit against Wentworth for racial discrimination. Wentworth ended up settling out of court, claiming he was innocent. In New York City, he has earned the title of the most unscrupulous landlord…ever.

At noon, a black Cadillac Series 75 Fleetwood Limousine pulled up to the main gate of Wentworth's humble abode.

The guard walked up to the driver's window, holding a clipboard, and asked, "Can I help you?"

The chauffeur answered, "Mr. Kuhn and guests to see Mr. Wentworth."

The guard checked his guest roster and saw that Mr. Wentworth was indeed expecting Mr. Kuhn and guests.

"Yes, sir. If you would proceed up the driveway to the front door," The guard instructed the driver. He walked back to the small guardhouse and stepped on a button inset in the guardhouse that operated the main gate.

"Thanks, Mac," The driver said as he drove up the driveway.

By the time they reached the front door, Tristan Wentworth was standing outside, waiting to greet his guests.

Before the chauffeur could get out to open the door, Wentworth opened the passenger door with a big smile on his face.

"*Herzlich willkommen, liebe Freunde* (welcome, dear friends). Please come in."

Once inside, Wilhelm Kuhn made the introductions. "Tristan, it is my honor to introduce you to Walter Miller and, of course, the esteemed Doctor Heim. Gentlemen, your host Tristan Wentworth."

Wentworth first shook Miller's hand and said, "Walter, it is my pleasure to meet you, and I look forward to working very closely with you."

He then stood erect and gave the Nazi salute towards Heim, "Sieg Heil, Herr Doktor. It is truly an honor to have such a distinguished guest in my house. Please won't you all come in and make yourselves comfortable."

Wentworth led his guests into the living room and directed them to the sofas.

"May offer you something to drink. Herr Doktor?"

"Do you have any *Kräuterlikör* (herbal liqueur)?"

"I have some Jägermeister."

"That would be fine," Heim said.

"Walter? Wilhelm, what can I get you?"

"I'll try what the doctor is having," Miller said.

"I will, too," Wilhelm concurred.

Wentworth turned to the elderly black man standing behind the bar and said, "Leroy, we'll have four Jägermeisters."

"Yes, sir," The bartender replied.

"Ein Rheinlandbastarde?" (a Rhineland bastard) Heim asked, surprised.

"Der Neger macht eien Sklaven gut," Wentworth proudly replied.

Miller turned to Wilhelm and whispered, "What did he say?"

"He said that the nigger makes a good slave," Wilhelm chortled.

As the four of them sat in the living room making small talk, Leroy brought them their drinks. Wentworth, Miller, and Kuhn each accepted the drink presented to them on a tray from the aged bartender. Heim sat with his arms crossed and refused to take the beverage from the tray.

"Just set the glass down, Leroy. Ah, that will be all," Wentworth said.

"Very good, Mr. Wentworth," Leroy said as he bowed slightly, turned, and left the room.

"*Schmutziger Schweinehund,* (dirty bastard)" Hein sneered as he took his handkerchief and wiped down the glass where the black bartender had handled it.

Wentworth stood and held his glass up to make a toast. "*Heil Hitler.*"

An enthusiastic chorus of *Heil Hilters* echoed within the cavernous room.

"Herr Doktor, I can't tell you how excited the members of Amerika First are to hear you speak Saturday evening," Wentworth said.

"*Ich danke dir sehr* (thank you very much), I look forward to it," Heim said as he took a sip of his Jägermeister.

He looked at his host and quipped, "Hmm, that *Neger* makes a damn fine drink."

"Thank you, Herr Doktor," Wentworth said proudly as if he made the drink.

Unbeknownst to Wentworth, Aribert Heim didn't give a toss about him or his pathetic little pseudo-Nazi organization. The doctor desperately needed money and a place to hide until he could arrange for his passage and papers to immigrate to Egypt.

FBI Agent James Beck, the spitting image of Hollywood legend Victor Mature, originally started his career in law enforcement with the LAPD. He and Marlboro went through the police academy together, graduating tops in their class. Beck served three years as a Los Angeles policeman before the war broke out when he joined the FBI and worked in the Special Intelligence Service, a covert counterintelligence branch of the FBI. He was stationed in Argentina.

He was named Vice-President of marketing for the front organization called the "Importers and Exporters Service Company."

Because more than 1.5 million expatriate Germans lived in South America, the area had become a hotbed of Axis espionage, propaganda, and sabotage. President Roosevelt felt the need to monitor these activities.

There were more than 340 undercover agents spread all over South America. By the end of the war, 887 Axis spies had been apprehended, as well as 281 agents of Axis propaganda, 222 smugglers, and more than 100 saboteurs and other operatives.

Marlboro felt that if anyone could help him, it would be James Beck.

At precisely three o'clock, there was a quick knock on Marlboro's office door, and Agent Beck entered.

"John, it's good to see you."

"James. It's been too long. Please have a seat," Marlboro said.

"So, how can I help the famous shamus, John Marlboro?" Beck said, grinning.

Marlboro looked his friend in the eye and said, "Aribert Heim."

The smile melted off of Beck's face.

"Aribert Heim. The Butcher of Mauthausen?" Beck asked with astonishment as he leaned forward in his chair.

"Doctor Death."

"Where is he?"

"Well, that's why you're here. I have an eye witness who spotted him having breakfast at Nate'n Al's."

"A Nazi having breakfast at a Jewish Deli?" Beck said suspiciously as he leaned back into the chair as if he had the air taken out of him.

"Listen, I know it sounds ridiculous, but think about it, where would be the last place you'd expect to see a Nazi war criminal," Marlboro reasoned.

"But, come on, Marlboro, a Jewish deli?"

"My eyewitness was a prisoner at Mauthausen for over three years. It hasn't been that long where time would affect her memory."

"I don't know."

"Can you think of any reason why Heim would come to Los Angeles or who he would reach out to?" Marlboro asked.

"The only thing that comes to mind is there's a small fringe neo-Nazi group called Amerika First that operates out at the old Murphy Ranch."

"That abandoned place out in Rustic Canyon, where the Silver Shirts used to hold rallies before the war?"

"Yeah, we've gotten word that some rich asshole from New York, a guy named Wentworth, has been using the ranch to hold meetings late at night. They dress up in their little Nazi-type uniforms and parade around a bonfire giving each other the Nazi salute and shouting *Heil Hitler*."

"Dangerous?"

"Haven't heard of anything yet. But, with these radicals, it's just a matter of time."

"Amerika First, huh?"

"You thinking of trying to infiltrate?"

"Yeah. Do you think you could phony me up a fascist background?"

"What, dummy up an FBI file on John Marlboro, Nazi sympathizer?"

"Yeah."

"Under one condition."

"What's that?"

"I go with you."

"I thought you were working on some big bank robberies?"

"They pale by comparison for the chance to nab the Butcher of Mauthausen. When do you want to get started?" Beck asked.

"Tomorrow."

"Tomorrow? Why not start now?"

Marlboro gave Beck a sheepish grin.

"Ah. Who's the skirt?"

"I just met her today. She works in the Central Library reference department. Her name is Saoirse O'Callaghan, and she is gorgeous."

"Where are you taking her?"

"Dinner. Any suggestions?" Marlboro asked.

"I know a joint where you can get a mean Sauerbraten Meatballs."

"Sounds *köstlich* (delicious)."

Saoirse O'Callaghan had just walked out of the main entrance of the Central Library, and she spotted Marlboro leaning against his fire-engine red Fleetmaster with the top down. She smiled and gave him a little wave.

"Good evening," He said as he opened her car door for her.

He walked around, got into the driver's seat, pulled away from the curb, and headed west.

"So, do you like German food?" He asked.

"Now, why am I thinking this has something to do with your case," She said with a nod of her head while her red hair billowed like streamers in the wind.

"I knew it; there's no fooling you librarian dolls," He said.

She didn't answer; she just glanced and smiled at him. A smile that Marlboro had seen on many a freckled face, green-eyed Venus flytraps. He knew he had to tread lightly with this alluring colleen, or else.

"So, whaddya say?"

"Only if you tell me about the case."

"You're one tough twist."

"Where I come from, you had to be."

"And where might that be?"

"Belfast."

"Ireland."

"Say, you are a good detective."

"And you, doll, are a bit of an *asal cliste*."

"Where did you learn that?" She said, sounding impressed.

"My old man taught me several curse words in eight different languages."

"Smart ass. Very good. So, what's the story with the Nazis?"

Marlboro drove silently for a few minutes, wondering whether he should bring her into this devil's web. He turned and asked, "Are you sure you want to know?"

"I lost my two brothers fighting the Nazis. Tell me," She demanded.

"I'm searching for a war criminal. The incarnate of pure evil, Doctor Aribert Heim, known as Doctor Death and the Butcher of Mauthausen."

"And you think he's here in Los Angeles?"

"I have an eyewitness, a survivor from the camp who recognized him."

"Why come to you and not the police?"

"They did, but the police either didn't believe them, or were too busy with local crimes to go hunting for Nazis."

She smiled and said, "Gee, I sure could go for some Jägerschintzel and Grüne Spinat Casserole or maybe a side of Spätzle's."

Marlboro pulled up to the valet parking at The Turner Inn Hofbräu, where they were greeted by a young man wearing the traditional lederhosen.

"*Guten Abend*," The attendant cheerfully said as he opened Saoirse's door.

"Good evening," She replied.

As Marlboro came around the car after handing the attendant the keys to the Fleetmaster, he took Saoirse by the arm and asked, "You speak German?"

She held up two fingers indicating a small amount and whispered, *"Ein bisschen."*

Inside was decorated as an authentic Germanic beer hall. There was a high ceiling with wooden beams; at one end of the hall was a raised stage where the German Oompah Band played folk music. Tables with red and white checkered tablecloths surrounded the dance floor which was packed to the edges with Aryan hoofers.

The hostess looked like something out of Richard Wagner's *Die Waiküre*. She would make the perfect *Brünnhilde*, the ideal Germanic female heroic legend that Hitler believed epitomized the glorified Teutonic example of the master race. The woman, who appeared to be in her thirties, wore the traditional dirndl dress.

The dirndl consists of a bodice and skirt or a pinafore dress, a blouse, often low-cut, short puff sleeves, a full skirt, and an apron. All the female staff wore them, and the men were decked out in lederhosen.

She approached them holding two oversized menus and asked, "Two for dinner?"

"Yes, two," Marlboro replied.

"Right this way."

Marlboro and Saoirse followed the fräulein to their table, which was located off to the left of the dance floor. As they were walking to their table, Marlboro couldn't help noticing they were being scrutinized by the locals, because they didn't fit the stereotypical of blonde hair, blue-eyed master race.

Soon after they were seated, a pretty young waitress came to take their order.

"Good evening, my name is Gretchen. I'll be your waitress tonight. Would you folks like something to drink?"

"Gretchen, I think we'll have two beers," Marlboro said.

"Glasses or mugs?"

Marlboro looked around and saw that everyone had ordered large mugs of beer.

"Mugs."

"Very good. I'll go get those and be right back to take your order," Gretchen said.

She returned moments later, placed the brimming mugs in front of each of them, and asked if they were ready to order.

"Ma'am?"

"I think I'll have the Jägerschintzel with Grüne Spinat Casserole," Saoirse ordered in perfect German.

"And for you, sir?"

"I'll try the Rinderroulade and an order of Kartoffelpuffer," Marlboro said, pronouncing his meal phonetically, butchering the pronunciation so bad that both Gretchen and Saoirse broke down laughing.

Marlboro stood up and asked Gretchen, "*Badezimmer* (bathroom*)*?"

She pointed to the other side of the dance floor. He leaned down and said to Saoirse, "Excuse me, I'll be right back."

Marlboro made his way across the dance floor to the entrance of the men's room. As he entered the anteroom leading into the men's bathroom, there was a large bulletin board with various business cards, notices and posters of events. Pinned on top of the heaps of handbills was a notice inviting people to attend a rally for the Amerika First Party at Murphy Ranch on Saturday. Above the invitation copy at the bottom of the notice was a drawing of a rat with a Star of David printed on its back. The headline above the illustration of the rat said, "The Plague Still Exists!" There was a phone number and the name Wilhelm Kuhn to contact for more information.

Marlboro went into the men's room, and took care of business; he came out, he ripped the notice off the board and stuffed it into his suit jacket.

When he returned to the table, he saw a man chatting up his date. The man was in his late twenties, blonde hair, tall and lanky.

Marlboro tapped the man on the shoulder. The young man turned around, gave Marlboro the once over, curled his lip, and sneered, "Yeah?"

"Step back or fall back," Marlboro stated matter of factly.

Marlboro could see the young man going through a series of scenarios in his mind, trying to find one where he would come out victorious. Apparently, he couldn't come up with one, so he excused himself and left.

Marlboro watched as he went back to a table of twenty something's that barely looked old enough to shave. They were gathered around a table, looking like a small gathering of the *Hitlerjugend* (Hitler youth).

Marlboro sized them up as a group of *schlägers* (goons) that he might have to deal with as they left. But for now, he sat down as if nothing had happened.

Saoirse held up her mug towards Marlboro, smiled, and said, "Sláinte mhaith. Good health."

Marlboro reciprocated. He held up his mug, and clinking them together, said, "Here's looking at you, kid."

During dinner, Marlboro kept a casual eye on the young man he dismissed and his friends. They looked as if they were hatching a scheme of revenge.

As he and Saoirse finished their after-dinner coffee and apple strudel, Marlboro leaned into Saoirse and whispered, "I'll be right back."

He walked to the table where the group of *schlägers* (thugs) was sitting, pulled up a chair, and said, "Listen, fellas, I'm not looking for trouble, but I'm not walking away from it either."

Marlboro opened his suit jacket to reveal his shoulder holster carrying his .38 Police Special. Their eyes got as big as saucers as their tough-guy attitude dissipated.

"You a copper?" The man asked.

"Better. I'm a private dick. So, I don't have to play by cop rules. Any you mugs give me any trouble, and I'll fill ya full of lead. Get it?" Marlboro asked the young jobbie.

The young man sat quietly, nodded, and replied, "Got it."

"Good."

Marlboro returned to his table, paid the check, and he and Saoirse left the beer hall.

As they were driving back to Saoirse's home, she asked him, "So, did you find anything in the wolf's lair?"

"I did, as a matter of fact. There is going to be a meeting this Saturday. I'm hoping Herr Heim might be in attendance."

"Can I go?"

"Sorry, doll, It's, how do you say, men only."

"*Es sind nur Männer.*"

"Right. *Es sind nur Männer.*"

"That's a bunch of hooey," Saoirse complained.

"I agree, Nazi hate-mongering could use a bit of a feminine touch."

"Hey, don't kid yourself. There were plenty of tough female Nazi war criminals, Irma Grese for example."

"I know the name, but…"

"Irma Grese, "The Hyena of Auschwitz", was an *SS* guard at the Nazi concentration camps of Ravensbrüch, Bergen-Belsen, and Auschwitz. By the time she was twenty-one, she rose to the rank of *Rapportführer,* the second-highest rank for a female *Konzentrationslager* (concentration camp) warden.

She was only twenty-two when they hung her for war crimes. Irma was one tough cookie."

"I'm impressed," Marlboro confessed.

"By Grese?"

"No, doll, by you."

"Hey, Marlboro, I don't just file reference materials. I read them, too."

"How about helping me get as much information on Amerika First, Tristan Kendrick Wentworth, Wilhelm Kuhn, and Aribert Heim, *aka* Doctor Death and the Butcher of Mauthausen. Would you do that for me?" Marlboro asked.

"No. But, I will do it for your survivor," She said with a snide grin.

Marlboro pulled into the driveway of 4188 Farragut Drive in Culver City. The home was a small one-story, simple grey and white 1000 square foot, three bedrooms, one bath house that sat on a corner lot surrounded by an idyllic white picket fence.

"Well, here we are. Would you like to come in for a nightcap?" She coyishly asked.

"I would love a nightcap."

As they walked up to the front door, Marlboro asked, "This is a very nice house. Do you live here alone?"

"All by myself. Surprised?"

"A little. It's quite the accomplishment for someone so young."

"Not so much of an accomplishment; it's my parents' house. They live in San Francisco; my father is with the U.S. Treasury." She explained.

Inside, the house had a lot of Irish touches, a Celtic Cross, a Trinity Knot wall plaque, a wall tapestry of St. Brigid of Kildare, and a large map of Eire.

Marlboro looked around and said sarcastically, "What, no leprechauns?"

"Ar, ndóigh," Saoirse said.

He stood looking perplexed.

"That means, of course. Marlboro, if we're going to get involved, you better start to learn to speak Gaeilge."

"Are we going to get involved?" He asked innocently.

She pulled him close, loosened his tie, and unbuttoned his shirt.

"Oh, I think so," She smiled and gave him a deep, passionate kiss. Saoirse pulled back, smiled, slapped him hard on his face, and said, "Just remember, Marlboro, blondes are noticed, but redheads are never forgotten."

While agent James Beck sat listening, Marlboro dialed the number on the flyer regarding the upcoming Ameriaka First rally at Murphy's Ranch.

"Hello?" A man's voice answered–a man's voice with a slight German accent.

"Hello, I'm calling about the rally this Saturday night. Is Wilhelm Kuhn there?" Marlboro respectfully inquired.

"Who is this?" The voice asked.

"My name is Madison Wolf, and I saw a flyer posted at The Turner Inn Hofbräu last night about the Amerika First rally this Saturday, and I'm calling to get more details."

"Like what?"

"Well, since I've never been to one of your rallies, is there anything that I should know, or is there something that I should or shouldn't bring?"

"Are you a Jew, spic, or nigger?"

"No! Certainly not!" Marlboro exclaimed.

"Wolf, huh? What kind of name is that?"

"It's derived from the old German Wolfgang meaning the son of."

"*Sprichst du Deutsch*?"

"*Ein bisschen.*"

"A little, huh? I think it's best that we meet. Where you at?"

"Now?"

"Yeah, now."

"I'm downtown."

"How about we meet at The Turner Inn Hofbräu for lunch? Noon."

"Alright. I have a pal who'd like to attend the rally, too. Arlo Presley, is it okay if he tags along?"

"He's not a Jew, spic, or nigger, is he?"

"No. He's a White Anglo-Saxon Protestant."

"Okay. Noon. Ask for Kuhn.

CLICK

Beck smiled and said, "Arlo Presley?"

"Hey, it was the first white bread name that popped into my head."

"Oh sure, I'm Arlo Presley, and you're Madison *Wolf*."

"Well, if you had called, you could have been Madison Wolf. That'll teach ya."

"Yeah. Yeah. Smart guy," Beck sarcastically quipped.

When Marlboro and Beck walked into The Turner Inn Hofbräu, the joint was packed. There was a different hostess, this one not so Germanic.

"Two for lunch?" She asked.

"Actually, we're supposed to be meeting a fella named Kuhn," Marlboro replied.

"Right this way," She said as she started to walk towards the stage but veered to the right and guided them down a hallway that led to a private room hidden behind the stage.

She knocked, waited to be called in, then opened the door, revealing two men seated at a table with three goons placed strategically around the room.

"Come in. Please have a seat. I'm Wilhelm Kuhn, and this is Walter Miller," Kuhn said with absolutely no emotion in his voice whatsoever.

Marlboro, not sensing any attempt on Kuhn and Miller's part to be social, walked up to the table, sat down, and said, "I'm Madison Wolf, and this is my friend Arlo Presley."

"You boys don't mind, but we have to pat you down to see if you're packing or if you're coppers," Kuhn said.

"Knock yourself out," Marlboro quipped.

Two of the goons gave a pretty thorough search of their persons, afterwards one of them said, "They're clean."

"So, why are you interested in Amerika First?" Miller asked.

Beck and Marlboro had decided to go in full racist rather than trying to be coy.

"As Adolf Hitler said, the sacred mission is to assemble and preserve the most valuable racial elements and raise them to dominant position. All who are not of a good race are chaff.

I believe that the Jews and other inferior races are ruining America. It's time to clean house," Marlboro eloquently stated.

"So, you've studied the writings of the Führer?"

"I have, as well as those of Henry Ford and William Pelley, among others."

"And how about you, Mr. Presley? Why are you here?"

"I ain't as well read as Madison. All I know is that I'm just plum tired of them Jews running all the banks, degrading our culture, keeping us good Christian folks down while they have the best jobs and make all the money. Damn kikes!"

"Arlo, you may not be as eloquent as your friend Madison, but I like your sentiment," Kuhn said.

"Were you both in the war?" Miller asked.

"We were both in the Marines; we fought those rice-eating Tojo's at Guadalcanal, Okinawa, and Iwo Jima. And by God, we kicked their yellow monkey asses to Hell!" Beck exclaimed.

"What would have happened if they had tried to send you to fight the *Wehrmacht*?" Miller challenged.

Beck, without hesitation, piped up, "I think I'd either been shot or in prison as a deserter."

"Me, I would have tried for conscience objector if that didn't work. I probably would have ended up sharing a cell with Arlo," Marlboro said with a sly grin.

Kuhn asked, "What do fellas do?"

"A little of this and that," Marlboro answered.

"That sounds a little shady. I like that," Miller said, intrigued.

"Well, you know about us, but we don't know anything about you guys. For all we know, you two might be cops," Beck said.

That brought resounding laughter from Miller, Kuhn, and the three hoods.

"Cops? Us? Hardly," Kuhn said, still chuckling.

"We just have to be careful. You can understand that we have to be vigilant. We don't want the wrong element infiltrating our ranks, Jews, communists, and other scum," Miller grinned. "Am I right?"

"Right," Beck agreed.

"So, what exactly happens at these rallies?" Marlboro asked fishing for details.

"Whad'ya mean?" Miller asked.

"I mean, all we are doing is standing around listening to speeches and shouting *"Sieg Heil,"* Marlboro grilled.

Miller and Kuhn looked at each other with skepticism, suspicion, and excitement.

"So. You boys are looking for some action?" Miller challenged.

"Well, we didn't come here to reminisce about the good old days when you all paraded around a bonfire, burning books, holding pictures of Hitler, and singing *"Die Fahne hoch,"* Marlboro said with a hint of a taunting tone.

Kuhn curled his lip and snarled, "Look! You…"

Trying to calm things down, Miller interrupted, "I can assure you that we are men of action, Mr. Wolf."

"Really," Beck said.

"Did you hear about the fire at the Wilshire Boulevard Temple last year? That was us. Twelve *Jüden* died in the fire," Miller proudly admitted.

Kuhn laughed adding, "They went up in smoke like in Auschwitz."

"That was you?" Marlboro asked.

"Yeah, and the drive-by shooting of those three rabbis in San Pedro a month ago. That was Wilhelm and me," Miller proclaimed with pride.

"Yeah. I clipped two Heebs myself, and Walter bumped off the other Yid (Jew)," Kuhn professed.

"That the kind of action you're looking for?" Miller asked.

"Well, I must admit, I am impressed," Marlboro feigned admiration.

"Me too," Beck said.

"So, you two interested?" Kuhn demanded.

"Count us in!" Marlboro declared.

"Good. To prove yourselves *würdig* (worthy), we will have a little initiation for you," Miller said as he stood up from the table, walked to a cupboard that was situated between two of the thugs standing at the back of the room, and produced two German .9mm Lugers.

"Here," He said as he placed the two revolvers in front of Marlboro and Beck.

"You ever hear of a Jew lawyer named Leon Lewis?" Miller asked.

"No," Beck said.

"No, should we?" Marlboro asked, even though he and Beck knew precisely who he was.

"This kike shylock was the son of a bitch who got people to infiltrate the American Nazi Party and was responsible in numerous arrests of *das Mutterland's* (the motherland's) intelligence officers who were arrested and sent to prison," Kuhn explained.

"We want this *schmutziger Jude* (dirty Jew) dead," Miller sneered with revulsion.

Marlboro took the gun, pulled back the slide to see if it was loaded, dropped the clip out, and examined the mechanical workings. He popped the loaded clip back in, placed the gun on the table, and asked, "What's in it for us besides the pleasure of knocking off this Jew boy mouthpiece?" Marlboro sedately asked.

"You'll be one of us!" Miller proclaimed.

"Well, that's all well and good, but this sounds like a major hit job. Otherwise, you two or one of these gorillas would have done it long ago. Bumping off a couple of old Jewish rabbis and torching a building is one thing, as commendable as that is, but the killing of a national figure is something else. If we get caught, me and Arlo here would be getting the gas in San Quentin, just like those six million Jews," Marlboro said.

"What are you asking for?" Miller asked.

"Five large," Marlboro stated.

"Five thousand. You're crazy!" Kuhn growled.

"Maybe. But we're not stupid. Whad'ya think we are a couple of two-bit gunsels?" Beck modestly said.

"How do we know you won't take the dough and take it on the lam?" Kuhn asserted.

"How about once we set it up, you and your goons can come and observe the show," Marlboro proposed.

"*Großartig*! (great) Half now and half when the job's done, and each of you will receive the rank of colonel."

Beck looked at Marlboro and said, "*Wunderbar*."

Marlboro smiled and asked Miller, "So, what's for lunch?"

When Agent Beck returned to the Bureau, he met with his superiors and reported the details of his meeting with Walter Miller and Wilhelm Kuhn.

They knew about them but were unaware of their latest murderous activities. Beck laid out his and Marlboro's plan to fabricate Attorney Leon Lewis' death to win Miller and Kuhn's confidence.

The plan is to alert Lewis, get buy-in to the scheme, and fake his death by having Marlboro and Beck fire blanks. The FBI would then leak the story of his death to a trusted member of the press announcing his death.

The Los Angeles Bureau Chief called the head of the FBI, J. Edgar Hoover, immediately after hearing about the sighting and Marlboro and Beck's plan to capture Nazi war criminal Aribert Heim.

Hoover approved the plan but wanted some solid evidence against Miller, Kuhn, and, if possible, the big man himself, Tristan Kendrick Wentworth, if, Heim were to escape for some reason.

Marlboro had the idea to bug a safe house with audio microphones and film cameras to capture the payoff for the hit on Lewis and see if they could get Miller and Kuhn to recount their deadly exploits of the synagogue fire and the killing of the three rabbis.

Chief Inspector Callahan selected a house the Bureau had used in the past. Everything was already in place; all the microphones and cameras were concealed in the walls, and they were all set on timers, so no men were needed to operate them. Once the time for the meeting was set up, the agents would prep the gear to start recording ten minutes before the scheduled meeting.

The safe house was located at 6856 Bevis Avenue, Van Nuys, in the San Fernando Valley. It was a modest one-story blue stucco and rock-faced house. The lawn was unkempt; there were cheap broken blinds in the windows, dead plants next to the house, and an old beater of a car sitting in the driveway.

Inside wasn't much better, old shabby broken furniture, several holes in the wall, piles of dirty dishes in the sink, no food in the refrigerator, just beer. Hanging above the sofa was a black and white framed photograph of Hitler at the Nuremberg rally, standing in front of one million people, flanked on either side hung a Nazi flag. The one on the right side of the photograph was the *Hakenkreuzflagge*, the official German National Flag. On the left side hung the *Reichskriegsflagge*, the National Battle flag that was flown on all warships, the Luftwaffe's aircraft, the Army's vehicles, and the building of the armed forces.

In the bedroom, on the floor, were several books written during the Nazi regime: *Mein Kempf, Der Untermensch, Entartete Kunst,* and *Als Flieger in Zwei Kriegen.* Books that the FBI felt would give credence to Marlboro's character. He was given a crash course in Nazi-era art, music, and literature.

When Marlboro walked into the house, he turned to Beck and said, "This house reeks of white supremacy; they'll love it."

Leon Lewis is the first national secretary of the Anti-Defamation League, the national director of B'nai B'rith, the founder and first executive director of the Los Angeles Jewish Community Relations Committee, and a key figure in the spy operations that infiltrated American Nazi organizations in the 1930s and early 1940s. His work as a spymaster resulted in the successful prosecution of multiple American Nazis before and during World War II and prevented many acts of Nazi sabotage and assassinations on the West Coast of the United States. The Nazis refer to Lewis as "the most dangerous Jew in Los Angeles."

"May I help you, gentlemen?" The receptionist at Leon Lewis, Attorney's law office, asked.

Beck flashed his badge, "Agent James Beck, FBI, and this special consultant John Marlboro. We'd like to see Mr. Lewis."

"Do you gentlemen have an appointment?"

"No," Beck answered.

"One moment, please," She said as she left her desk and walked into Lewis' office.

Moments later, she appeared and, holding the door, said, "Won't you gentlemen please come in."

Beck and Marlboro entered the office of "the most dangerous Jew in Los Angeles."

"Mr. Lewis, I'm Agent James Beck, FBI, and this special consultant, John Marlboro. We would like your help."

"Always glad to help the FBI if I can. What can I do for you?"

"We want to kill you. If that's all right with you," Marlboro said deadpan."

Miller and Kuhn pulled up to the FBI safe house at 6856 Bevis Avenue in the Valley at 4:30 pm, accompanied by two of their henchmen in tow.

"What a dump," Miller commented to Kuhn as they got out of the backseat of their black 4-door Packard Clipper.

The four fascists strolled past the broken-down 1938 Nash Lafayette sitting in the driveway, hood up, engine parts laying all around, the right rear was jacked up, and the tire was missing.

Kuhn attempted to ring the doorbell to no avail. Miller banged on the door until Marlboro answered.

He opened the door holding a beer bottle, wearing a wife beater t-shirt, hands covered with grease.

Marlboro took a sip from the bottle, smiled, swung the door open, and said, "*Willkommen, komm rein* (welcome, come in)."

"*Vielen dank,* " Kuhn replied.

As they filed in, Beck came out of the kitchen carrying a six-pack of Blatz Beer.

"Can I get you boys a beer?" Beck asked.

"No, thank you, " Miller said, not asking if any of his group if they would like one or not.

Kuhn asked, "Mind if we look around?"

It was more of a statement of fact rather than a question of permission.

"Sure, go ahead. Knock yourself out," Marlboro quipped as he and Beck sat on the couch and waited.

They could hear their "guests" opening doors, pulling out drawers, and riffling through closets. After ten minutes, Miller and entourage returned to the living room.

"Find what you're looking for?" Marlboro inquired.

"We must be careful, is all. Nothing personal, you understand," Kuhn said, trying to appease Marlboro.

Miller stood in front of the Hitler photograph and flags and said, "Very impressive, Mr. Wolf. Mind if I ask where you got those *flaggen*."

"I traded a buddy of mine for a couple of Jap souvenirs that I got back in the Pacific for those babies."

"*Schön*. Don't you agree, Wilhelm?" Miller asked while admiring the Nazi ensigns.

"Yes, they are quite beautiful," Kuhn responded.

Marlboro took a gulp and said, "Herr Miller, shall we proceed with the business at hand, the *Judenanwalt* (Jew lawyer) Lewis."

Miller looked at one of his Bruno's, nodded, and told him, "Dieter, go get the bag."

Beck held up a bottle to Miller and Kuhn, "You sure you don't want one? They're cold."

Miller held up his hand, "*Nein, danke*."

Dieter walked back into the living room, handed the bag to Walter, then stood almost at attention behind Miller.

"Does he ever speak?" Marlboro asked sarcastically.

The big palooka just stared at Marlboro. If looks could kill, he would be dead.

Kuhn glanced over to the bruiser and just said, "Dieter."

The big bruiser looked around the living room, picked up the yellow pages phone book off the coffee table, which was over three inches thick, and ripped the book into two halves as effortlessly as if he was tearing a single piece of paper.

Beck gave a slow, low whistle, "*TriiiiiiRiiiiew*."

Marlboro, trying to be cool, said, "Impressive. But I'd be more impressed if you could put it back together."

Miller unzipped the bag and dropped a stack of twenty-dollar bills on the coffee table.

"Here's half. Twenty-five hundred, you get the other half when the job is done. So, when do you plan on taking care of Herr Lewis?"

"Tomorrow," Marlboro answered.

Neither Marlboro nor Beck reached to count the money.

Kuhn asked, "Aren't you going to count it?"

"Is it all there?" Beck catechized the SS wannabe.

Marlboro said, laughing, "We trust ya. Hey, if you can't trust a fellow *Sturmtrooper* (stormtrooper), who can you trust. Besides, if you try to grift us, we'll kill ya."

Miller and Kuhn were taken aback by such a bold comment. It stiffened the backs of the two goons, but Miller put the atmosphere at ease when he laughed. He figured, just let these two losers have their fun. Once they kill the Jew lawyer, they'll deal with them if and when they accomplish their mission.

"Alert us when the job is done," Kuhn said as he indicated to his guards that they were leaving.

As Miller walked out the door, he turned, raised his arm in a Nazi salute, and said, "*Viel Glück* (good luck). *Heil Hitler*!"

"*Heil Hitler*!" Miller echoed, returning the salute in a lackadaisical manner.

Leon Lewis had given Mrs. Rosenbaum, his secretary, the morning off. He told her he had a couple of off-sight meetings with clients, so that she could come in later that afternoon.

Marlboro and Beck sat in a forest green two-door Dodge Luxury Liner outside Lewis' office. They were pretty sure that either Miller and Kuhn or someone from Amerika First would be watching. The FBI had placed their people in position the night before. They had an ambulance and agents dressed as LAPD officers stationed nearby so they would get their first.

Lewis arrived at his office every day at 7:30 a.m., just like clockwork. Today was no different. As he entered the Eastern Columbia Building at 849 South Broadway in downtown L.A., Marlboro and Beck followed him into the building.

Lewis walked through the crowded lobby towards the bank of elevators. When he reached the elevators, Marlboro and Beck pulled out their Lugers and opened fire, repeatedly shouting "*Judensterben*!" (death to Jews) and "*Blut und Boden*!" (blood and soil)

Lewis fell to the ground Trin a pool of blood as undercover FBI agents, men, and women swarmed around him to keep everyone away. Within minutes, their ambulance and police officers arrived and whisked the unharmed Lewis away.

Moments after the shooting, Federal agents arrived to take over the investigation. They had brought in a forensic team to collect evidence. The area was cordoned off, keeping the public and newspaper reporters at bay.

By noon, the news on all the radio stations reported Leon Lewis' violent murder.

At noon, KFWB radio broadcasted the following:

"Good afternoon, Los Angeles. We bring you the following news bulletin. Famed lawyer Leon Lewis was brutally gunned down this morning in the lobby of his downtown office. It appears to be the work of anti-Semitic zealots who yelled, what eye-witnesses claim to have heard, anti-Jewish hate chants.

The FBI has taken over the investigation of this vicious murder. Federal officials tell KFWB that this slaying will get the Bureau's full attention.

Lewis was responsible for launching a major anti-Nazi spy ring and intelligence gathering operation that resulted in the successful arrest and prosecution of dozens of American Nazis before and during the war.

Mr. Lewis was pronounced dead upon arrival at Cedars-Sinai Hospital. He leaves behind a wife and two daughters.

And in other news, the city council announced...."

"Well?" Miller asked.

Dieter stood at attention while he reported what he had observed at the Eastern Columbia Building that morning. Sitting next to Miller was Wilhelm Kuhn and the Amerika First leader, Tristan K. Wentworth, at the group's headquarters. The cellar of The Turner Inn Hofbräu.

Amerika First's headquarters was nothing more than a corner in the beer and wine cellar of The Turner Inn Hofbräu. There was a worn-out, tattered cloth couch, a beat-up gray metal desk, six mismatched chairs, a copy machine, and an Amerika First flag hanging behind the desk. The Amerika First flag was identical to the American flag, with the exception that all forty-eight stars had been replaced with swastikas.

Unashamed of their meager surroundings, Wentworth likes to recount the humble beginnings of der Führer at the beginning of the Nazi movement.

"Well, sir, I followed Wolf and Presley from their home in the Valley to the downtown office building of that *schwein* Lewis. They parked across the street from the building while I parked around the corner, but I was still able to see them at all times. They talked to no one, just sitting in their car waiting for Lewis to arrive.

I spotted Lewis walking towards his office at 7:30. I got out of my car and followed him as far as the corner. That's when I saw Wolf and Presley get out of their car and cross the street. They entered the building right behind Lewis.

I quickly walked to the entrance and walked in. I saw Wolf and Presley following Lewis to the elevators, and as soon as Lewis pressed the elevator button, Wolf and Presley pulled their gats and started blasting the Jew bastard.

You should have seen it; it was beautiful. There was blood everywhere and people screaming, running towards the old dying kike. I ran to get a better look. It looked like they must have shot him eight or nine times. He was lying in a large pool of Jew blood.

Then the police and ambulance showed up, as well as the FBI. They locked down the joint, and that's when I split."

"Excellent!" Wentworth said with glee. He stood up and emulated the little jig that Hitler did on June 21st, 1940, the day France surrendered to Germany.

"It is truly a day of great celebration, *Obergruppenleiter* (senior group leader) Wentworth," Kuhn rejoiced.

"What are the names of the two men who did this great service to the cause?" Wentworth asked.

"Madison Wolf and Arlo Presley," Miller replied.

"Now that the deed is done. It's *Oberst* Wolf and *Oberst* Presley," Kuhn said.

"*Jawohl*, that's right," Wentworth said with a big grin.

"I must admit, I didn't think they could pull it off and get away with it," Miller mused.

"Well, we need men like that. Men of action. *Übermensch*, just like Nietzsche said. We Aryans are truly the master race, the *Meisterschaft*," Wentworth proclaimed.

"I guess we should arrange to go see Wolf and Presley and give them the second half of their bounty," Kuhn said.

Still elated by the news that his archrival Lewis had been killed, Wentworth spun around and said, "I'd like to accompany you when you meet with the two assassins."

"Of course, *mein Obergruppenleiter* (senior group leader)," Miller barked.

"Keep me abreast," Wentworth said as he left the basement. On his way out, he stopped, turned around, and gave a snappy Nazi salute, "Sieg Heil!" He roared.

A unanimous chorus sang out, "Sieg Heil!"

When she got home from the library, Saoirse was surprised to see Marlboro sitting on her front porch steps.

"I thought I scared you off," She said.

"You kidding? It takes more than having great sex to get rid of me," He said sarcastically.

"Where have you been?" She demanded, standing upright with her hands on her hips and her foot tapping impatiently.

"Chasing after a gaggle of Nazis," He uttered almost apologetically as he sat on the porch swing.

"In that case, I forgive you," Saoirse said as she plopped down beside him on the swing and kissed him passionately.

"Sorry, doll, I didn't come by sooner."

"I understand. Oh! Did you hear that a famous Jewish lawyer has been gunned down today? They think some Nazis did it; did you know about that?"

"Yeah, I heard about it on the radio. Terrible,"

"I hope these are some of the creeps you're after."

"They are. If all goes well, this should be over in a few days. After I wrap this up, do you wanna go away for a few days? Maybe go up the coast to Monterey?"

"Ew, that sounds swell."

"Great."

"Come on, let's go inside," She said as she stood up, tugging on his hand.

"Can't. I gotta date with a Nazi."

He stood up, pulled her close, and looked deep into those emerald-green eyes; he brushed her lips delicately with his. Her lips were as soft as rose petals. As they pressed their lips together, he inhaled her hot breath. He felt the warmth of her skin as her mouth opened, accepting his tongue as it danced past her clenched teeth to the dewy space within.

Marlboro could feel the blood leaving his head and rushing down his body. He knew they had better stop as their hands began exploring each other's bodies.

He pulled away from her embrace as a drowning man gasping for air. He saw the look in her eyes, begging him to stay. He slowly and gently pushed her away from him and said, "I can't, doll. I'll be back as soon as I can."

"*Bí cúramach.* Be careful," She softly said as she waved goodbye.

Marlboro and Beck were sitting on the couch at 6856 Bevis Avenue, cleaning the Lugers that Miller and Kuhn had given them to assassinate Leon Lewis, when there was a knock on the door.

"Who is it?" Shouted Beck as he slammed the loaded magazine clip back into the Luger. Marlboro did the same.

Marlboro was making his way to the door when Miller said, "It's Miller."

Beck and Marlboro had their weapons ready in case it was a setup. Marlboro grabbed the door handle and glanced back at Beck to see if he was prepared. Beck nodded affirmatively.

Marlboro turned the knob and swung the door open to reveal Miller, Kuhn, and some dumpy-looking guy dressed in a three-piece suit with a Clark Gable mustache, salt and pepper hair, and a Cuban cigar sticking out the side of his mouth. The two henchmen weren't in the group but were waiting in the Cadillac Fleetwood Limousine parked in the driveway.

Miller saw the weapons, held up his hands, and said, "Easy, fellas. We come in peace."

"Sorry, we thought you might have been the cops," Marlboro said.

"Or G-men," Beck added.

"Come in," Marlboro offered.

He and Beck took their places on the couch, leaving the others to find a seat for themselves.

"Who's he?" Beck asked, pointing the Luger at Wentworth.

"This is…" Miller started to say when Wentworth interrupted.

"Gentlemen, I am *Obergruppenleiter* (senior group leader) Tristan Kendrick Wentworth of Amerika First," Wentworth proudly stated.

"Nice to meet ya. Did ya bring the rest of the dough?" Marlboro asked.

Wentworth seemed genuinely heartbroken that these two didn't guffaw over him, but he soldiered on.

"Indeed, we did," Kuhn said.

Miller reached inside his coat pocket and dropped the other half of the twenty-five hundred down onto the coffee table, where the first half of the payment hadn't moved.

Wentworth leaned towards the couch from his chair opposite them, extended his hand, and said, "I want to thank you both for your service to the Amerika First movement. At this moment, I bestow the rank of *Oberst* to each of you. Colonel Madison Wolf and Colonel Arlo Presley welcome to the fight."

Both Marlboro and Beck reached over the coffee table and shook his hand.

"Do you have any more Yids (Jews) you want us to pop?" Marlboro nonchalantly asked.

"Well, not at the moment, but we will," Wentworth admitted.

Miller said, "The *Obergruppenleiter* (senior group leader) wanted me to extend his personal invitation to this Saturday's meeting. We have an honored guest. Someone you might not have heard of, but a great man who has served the *Führer* and the *Reich*, Hauptsturmführer (headstorm leader) Aribert Heim."

"Isn't he the Angel of Death, or was it Doctor Death? I get the two mixed up," Marlboro said.

Wentworth perked up, finally someone who knows something about the history of the glory days and not just a knuckle-dragging thug who wants to yell

"*Sieg Heil*" and kill niggers, spics, and Jews. Although those are necessary fodder to accomplish the mission.

"Mmm, I am impressed; it is Doctor Death. The Angel of Death is the acclaimed Doctor Josef Mengele," Wentworth said with fascination.

"What else do you know about Doctor Heim?" He asked Marlboro.

"Well, if my memory serves me right, he was the camp doctor at Mauthausen-Gusen for a couple of years. Where he earned the nickname the Butcher of Mauthausen.

After the war, he was captured and escaped; the last I read, his whereabouts are unknown. But I guess his whereabouts are now known," Marlboro said.

"Well, I am not at liberty to say at the moment, but he will be our honored guest at Saturday's rally."

"Aren't you concerned for his safety?" Beck asked.

"We have taken appropriate safety precautions and extra measures. This is more than a rally; it's a fundraiser. There will be many important, notable, and influential people attending, even a Hollywood star or two," Miller said, boasting.

"Can we count on you two for your support?" Wentworth asked.

"We are more than willing to do our part. But *Obergruppenleiter* (senior group leader) Wentworth, look around. Let's face it; this place is a dump. We did what we did today because we believe in the cause, but also for the money.

Now, if you could see yourself paying a bonus, of, say, another five grand. Then, if and when the shit hits the fan, Arlo and I would be more inclined to go on offense and take the fight to the enemy rather than play defense," Marlboro explained.

"I think we can afford to pay you a bonus of five thousand," Wentworth said.

"Great," Beck said.

"*Gruppenleiter* (group leader), Miller, give *Oberst* (colonel) Wolf and *Oberst* (colonel) Presley their well-deserved bonus."

"*Jawohl*," Miller said as he reached into his other jacket pocket and produced another stack of cash that he placed on top of the pile of money already sitting on the coffee table.

"If there's nothing else, I think we'll be on our way," Kuhn said.

"There's just one thing, *Obergruppenleiter* (senior group leader). I am curious if you planned those attacks on the synagogue and the killing of the three rabbis?"

"Why do you want to know?" Kuhn asked suspiciously.

"I was very impressed by the planning and the execution of the operations. I was wondering if you were the mastermind because I just wanted to say how excited we are to be working under such a brilliant tactician," Marlboro said, trying to lay praise on thick.

Wentworth puffed up his chest and proclaimed, "Why yes, they were my ideas, but I have to credit

Gruppenleiter (group leader) Miller and *Sturmführer* (storm leader) Kuhn, who successfully carried out the mission."

With that, they said their goodbyes. As Wentworth got outside, he turned to Marlboro and said, "We'll see you Saturday at five o'clock."

"But I thought the rally doesn't start until eight," Marlboro replied.

"True. Eight o'clock is for the troops; you're both invited to the VIP reception; you have to come in to receive your uniforms."

"*Vielen, dank. Heil Hitler*," Marlboro said.

At FBI headquarters, Agent James Beck and Marlboro are seated in interrogation room 2, waiting to report to Chief Inspector Callahan.

Three other agents in the room are working on the case. Agents Andrew Joiner, Michael Freely, and Frank Giustino are all from the counterintelligence unit. A member of the Israeli national intelligence agency, Mossad, was also in attendance Colonel Zvi Yatom.

Back in the Ukraine, Zvi Yatom had a small dental practice in Kiev. When the Nazis rounded up all the Jews, he, his wife, and baby were forced into a cattle car with 140 other Jews, traveling for three days without food or water to the Belżec extermination camp in Poland.

Upon arrival, at 4:30 in the morning, the selection process began to see who would live and who would die. All women and children were sent to the right, all the men to the left.

SS-Sturmbannbführer (major) Christian Wirth, camp Commandant, would stand on the train platform and decide who would die in the gas chambers. A job he relished; he was nicknamed Christian the Terrible.

Men, women, and children were made to strip naked. The women, children, the elderly, and anyone Christian felt was unfit to work were forced to run down a fenced-off path to the gas chambers, leaving them no time to absorb where they were. As they were running, the guards would brutally whip them to create an atmosphere of panic and disorientation.

Zvi Yatom's last memory of his wife and baby girl was seeing them running in terror to their death.

When asked by an SS guard what his occupation was, he answered dentist. An occupation that the Nazis needed. Zvi was sent to the table where he was given a tattoo on his left forearm, a dirty striped uniform with a tattered yellow Star of David sewn on the left breast pocket, a matching striped cap, and a pair of worn-out shoes, two sizes too big.

He was taken to the gas chambers, given a pair of dental pliers, and told to wait. He and three other dentists waited thirty minutes until all the screaming and crying stopped. A group of *Sonderkommandos*

(Special work units made up of camp prisoners, usually Jews) rushed up to open the metal doors, revealing the pile of dead, who, just an hour earlier, was standing on the train platform. The *Sonderkommandos* started removing the dead and piling them in front of Zvi and the other dentist so they could start yanking any gold teeth, bridges, and crowns they found in the dead's mouths. Half a dozen SS guards watched over them, shouting, "*Schnell! Schnell*! (hurry! hurry!)"

Speed was of the essence; there were another 2000 victims just waiting to die. Zvi and the other dentist were ordered only to examine the men and women; the children were taken directly to the furnaces to be burned.

Zvi thanked God that he didn't see his wife and baby daughter. Because if he had, he probably would have gone crazy and tried to attack the SS guards, which would have meant his immediate death.

Zvi worked two years at Belżec before being sent to Mauthausen in Austria, where he saw first-hand the cruelty of Aribert Heim. Luckily for Zvi, Heim was transferred shortly after he arrived. Zvi was assigned two jobs. Since Mauthausen didn't have a gas chamber, the camp killed the prisoners through hard labor; whenever a prisoner died, he would be called upon to extract any value from their mouths.

Because of his medical background, his other labor job was assisting in medical experiments for Bayer AG, a division of IG Farben, one of Germany's largest pharmaceutical companies. They were, among others, responsible for manufacturing Zyklon-B, the cyanide-based pesticide used to kill prisoners in the Nazi death camp gas chambers.

Zvi did what he could to help patients who went through medical experiments, easing their pain and suffering. On occasion, if he could, aid when patients were in excruciating agony, give them an overdose of morphine, resulting in their death. It's something that he lives with every day.

After the war, he immigrated to Israel, where he joined Mossad—working his way up through the ranks to Colonel. Zvi Yatom has become one of the foremost experts in hunting and tracking Nazi war criminals.

Chief Inspector Callahan came into the room and stood at the head of the conference table, looked around the room, and said, "Gentlemen, let me introduce everyone quickly before we hear from Agent Beck. We have Agents Joiner, Freely, and Giustino from the counterintelligence unit. And we're honored to have with us a member of the Israeli national intelligence agency, Mossad, Colonel Zvi Yatom. I'd also like to introduce John Marlboro, a private investigator responsible for this opportunity. One of his clients has given us the lead on the whereabouts of Aribert Heim."

Callahan sat down and turned to Beck.

"Beck," Callahan said.

"Chief Inspector Callahan, gentlemen. Several days ago, John Marlboro came to me for assistance in the tracking down of Aribert Heim, *aka* "The Butcher of Mauthausen," also known as "Doctor Death."

I contacted the Chief Inspector, who permitted me to pursue the lead to ensure it was credible. It is.

Marlboro and I have been able to infiltrate a known neo-Nazi group called Amerika First that will be holding a rally and fundraiser for Aribert Heim, who, from what we have been able to gather, is desperate for money. His intentions are, at this time, unknown.

To gain the group's trust and confidence, Marlboro and I were given an initial assignment to prove our loyalty: the assassination of the famed Jewish attorney, Leon Lewis. Thanks to Mr. Lewis, the Bureau, and dozens of others, we were able to fake Mr. Lewis' death and convince the leaders of Amerika First that we accomplished the hit.

In addition, we have audio and film confessions from the leaders of Amerika First to a series of anti-Semitic crimes, including the arson of a synagogue, which resulted in several deaths, and the murders of three rabbis in the Los Angeles area. In addition, we have evidence for the payment of the assassination of Leon Lewis, as well as their confessions on tape and film.

Because of our killing of Lewis, we have been given commissions as Colonels in the Amerika First Militia Party, which will entitle us to a VIP meeting with Aribert Heim this Saturday.

So, that's where we are at the moment," Beck concluded.

"Mr. Marlboro, is there anything you'd like to add?" Callahan asked.

"Thank you, Chief Inspector. Just one thing: We have been paid a five-thousand-dollar bonus to be part of the security detail for Heim. At this point, we don't know what that entails. We have two days until the rally; I'm afraid that doesn't give us much time. Now, I'm pretty sure that although they say they trust us, these guys are usually paranoid and suspicious of everyone, even each other.

We've taken extra precautions not to be followed, but from now on, we won't know if we will be able to connect with you safely again before the rally. We have to have a prearranged backup plan before we leave."

"Good point," Callahan said.

Senior Agent Michael Freely asked Beck, "Do you think it's possible that we could attend the rally?"

"Hard to say, with such a high-profile guest speaker. One thing I'm sure of is that security is going to be on heightened alert. So, you won't be able to sneak a weapon in," Beck answered.

"Where is the rally to be held?" Agent Joiner inquired.

"The Murphy Ranch house," Marlboro said.

"Rustic Canyon?"

"Right," Marlboro confirmed.

"What if we enter the area late tonight, say three or four in the morning, and hide some weapons," Colonel Yatom suggested.

"That's pretty rough terrain off the roads in there. It would mean hiking in commando style," Callahan said.

"I'm up for giving it a try," Yatom volunteered.

Callahan thought for a moment, "I agree; let's give it a try. I think they should be small caliber weapons, nothing too big, so as not to be discovered. Something that can be concealed once retrieved."

"Besides handguns, might I recommend a new weapon that we Israelis have just developed, an open-bolt, blowback submachine gun. The Uzi," Yatom suggested.

Agent Giustino reacted quickly, saying, "If you don't mind, Chief, I prefer my 9mm Parabellum Browning machine pistol."

"Personally, I don't care what you choose. Just make damn sure it's not detected," Callahan demanded.

"Sir, I think it best that Marlboro and I get back in sight so they don't get suspicious," Beck said.

"Why don't you have somebody come around the house Friday afternoon disguised as an auto mechanic delivering some parts? We have an old beater out front that they've seen us working on. I don't think it will draw undue attention," Marlboro said as they were preparing to leave.

"Good idea, Marlboro. We'll send someone out tomorrow afternoon," Callahan said.

"Make sure the guy's a motorhead, just in case," Beck added.

Although Leon Lewis knew that he was about to be shot, he was still surprised when Agent Beck and Marlboro spun him around and yelled, "*Judensterben*!" (death to Jews) and "*Blut und Boden*!" (blood and soil) When the two of them started shooting him, he had a capsule of fake blood in his mouth and a handful of soft gelatin blood bubbles that Hollywood uses in their gangster films that the actors smash against their bodies to give the effect of gunshot wounds.

Marlboro had advised him to try and land face down on the ground once he was shot. A dozen plainclothes FBI agents would surround him and protect him from anyone seeing that he wasn't really shot.

His wife and two daughters were flown undercover to his family in Chicago the previous day. After the shooting, Leon was immediately taken to a private airport in an ambulance and flown to Chicago to be held incognito until the following Monday for their protection.

By the time he arrived at his family's home, the Chicago Tribune had the story on the front page, just below the fold.

"LEON LEWIS, FAMED JEWISH LEADER, MURDERED"

"Leon L. Lewis, 59, first executive director of the Anti-Defamation League and former national director of B'nai B'rith. He died today from gunshot wounds Wednesday morning while waiting for an elevator in the lobby of his office building in downtown Los Angeles.

Mr. Lewis, a University of Wisconsin graduate who received a law degree from the University of Illinois Law School, moved to Los Angeles in the late 1920s.

He became active in the American Legion and Disabled American War veterans, serving many years as chairman of the DAV Americanism Committee and conducting that organization's first investigation into subversive activity.

From 1933 until his retirement in 1945, he was the executive director of the community relations committees of the Los Angeles Jewish Community Council.

Mr. Lewis leaves his widow, Mrs. Ruth L. Lewis, two daughters, and a sister, Mrs. Al Levy.

Funeral services will be conducted at 11 a.m. Monday in the chapel of Malinow & Simon Mortuary."

Upon reading his obituary, Leon shrugged, smiled, and said to himself, "You only live twice."

Doctor Death was enjoying the gracious hospitality at the home of Jeffery Billingsworth, President of NTD Engineering, located in Long Beach, California. NTD is a subsidiary of IG Farben GmbH, Berlin.

Jeffery Billingsworth was a long-time secret admirer and supporter of the Nazi regime before and during the war. When he was contacted by the ODESSA, a Nazi underground group that helps high-ranking Nazi officers wanted for war crimes, he welcomed the opportunity to shelter the good doctor in his home.

Billingsworth has a secluded palatial mansion up in the Hollywood Hills, tucked away from view on Outpost Cove Drive. He and his wife Betty were honored when Aribert Heim arrived to stay with them for the week leading up to the Amerika First rally and fundraiser.

They held a couple of small informal dinner parties commending all of Heim's work and accomplishments with several like-minded business leaders.

Heim basked in all of the attention and adulation showed to him. But more importantly, he reveled in the donations they bestowed upon him, close to one million dollars.

Heim was about to sit down for breakfast when Billingsworth came in excited to announce that Leon Lewis, the kike shylock, had been assassinated. He placed the copy of the Los Angeles Times down in front of Heim with glee.

"That fucking Jew bastard should have been eliminated years ago." Billingsworth said.

"*Wunderbar!* That is good news." Heim said, laughing.

"What better way to lead into tomorrow night's rally? Well, Doctor, I better be heading to the office; my chauffeur is here. Oh, Betty will be going to her bridge club this morning, so will you be all right here?" Billingsworth inquired.

"I shall be fine. Would it be alright if I tinkered around in your workshop, Jeffery?"

"I would be honored, doctor. I didn't know you enjoyed woodworking."

"Oh, yes, I love the feel of the tools. It reminds me of handling my medical instruments."

"Please feel free and enjoy yourself."

"I'm sure I will."

"Rachel will be here if you need anything, Doctor. Have a good day. *Auf Wiedersehen.*"

"*Auf Wiedersehen.* Jeffery."

Rachel, the Billingworth's maid, brought in Heim's breakfast, bacon sitting on top of pancakes and a cup of black coffee.

"*Speckfannkuchen und Kaffee. Vielen Dank.*" Heim said with a big smile of gratitude.

Rachel returned the smile and scurried back to the kitchen to clean up the morning dishes.

Heim finished his *Speckfannkuchen und Kaffee* and went out the patio door to the guest house in the backyard, which was turned into Billingworth's woodshop.

Heim was very impressed; the woodshop had everything one would ever need. There was a table saw, bandsaw, dual router table, scroll saw, spindle sander, miter saw, and a workbench. Heim was excited to see that his host had a set of *Wohngeist* (living spirit woodworking hand tools) from Germany that included a set of hand-forged chisels, a vintage set of Japanese saws, and a complete set of Palm & Knife. All the blades had been pre-honed to a mirror-like, razor-sharp edge.

Heim went about setting out all the tools he thought he might need for the project. He wanted to make this gift something very special for his host and hostess, who had been so gracious.

Once he had everything prepared, he went back into the house and asked Rachel if she would be so kind as to serve him his lunch in the woodworking shop.

"Yes, of course. What can I make you for lunch?" She asked.

"How do you say. *Körnigsberger Klopse*. Ah, small balls of meat." He said, holding up his hand, forefinger, and thumb, forming the sign of "okay."

"Meatballs?" She guessed.

"Ja, de meatballs *und Dampfkartoffeln*."

Rachel stood shaking her head, not understanding.

Heim went looking around and found and held up a potato.

"Potato!" Rachel said excitedly.

"Ja, potato."

"Boiled, steamed, mashed?"

"Steamed, *Bitte*. Please," He said, smiling as he took her hand and kissed it.

Senior Agent Michael Freely took the point of the squad as they made their way, traveling west from the Sullivan Fire Road parallel to the Old Tank Spur Trail.

It was rough terrain, making traveling at night even tougher. They wore army fatigues, with their faces blacked out. They carried their firearm weapons wrapped in small canvas bags. If they were to engage the enemy, they would rely on their WW2 combat trench knives. The orders were no shots to be fired and to elude the enemy at all costs.

That was the plan, but as any combat soldier knows, you throw the plans out the window when you engage the enemy because they haven't studied your plan. Besides, they have their own plans.

As they were working their way towards the main building of the Murphy Ranch, they eluded several patrols of young men in their twenties wearing Nazi-style uniforms carrying 7.92mm Mauser bolt action rifles, standard Nazi issue.

At approximately 3:30 a.m., the camp patrols had become less frequent. That's when Freely and the men found a secluded area to bury their weapons under a cluster of California sagebrush growing next to a large Lodgepole Pine.

On their way back to the rendezvous point, they came upon a lone straggler who apparently went away from his camp to use the latrine. Zvi, who was a couple of yards ahead of Freely and the others, quickly doubled back and covered the young man's mouth while simultaneously sticking his ten-inch trench knife in the upper left side of the man's back, piercing his heart, causing instantaneous death.

He looked at the others and whispered, "What! Do you want Heim or not?"

Freely said, "We have to take him with us. We can't leave him here."

Yatom carried the dead man in a fireman's carry style. By the time they reached their rendezvous point over two miles away through heavy brush, Zvi hadn't broken a sweat. He put the dead man in the trunk of the car, and they headed back to FBI headquarters.

The ride back was silent until Agent Giustino asked Zvi, "Did you have to kill him?"

"Funny, I've never heard a Nazi ask that," Zvi said coldly.

Marlboro and Agent Beck stopped by 898 Manning Avenue in Westwood to update Sarah Stroński and her aunt Zibiah Anielewicz on their progress relating to Aribert Heim.

Beck and Marlboro walked to the front door and rang the bell. From inside, they heard the muffled sound of Sarah saying, "One moment, I'm coming."

"Who is it?" She asked from behind the locked door.

"It's John Marlboro, Sarah."

The door opened to reveal Sarah dressed as she was going out, and behind her, sitting on the sofa, was her aunt.

"Won't you please come in?" She said, gesturing towards the living room.

"Is this a good time?" Marlboro asked.

"Yes, of course," Sarah replied.

"Sarah, Mrs. Anielewicz, this is Agent James Beck. He is with the FBI."

"Ladies," Beck said as he gave a slight bow.

"I wanted to stop by and let you know where we are with Aribert Heim. Without going into too much detail, I've enlisted the help of the FBI to assist me in the capture of Aribert Heim.

If things go according to plan, we will hopefully have this monster behind bars soon," Marlboro said.

"You realize that we can't promise anything, but we are quite confident," Beck added.

"We understand, and we appreciate all of your help. We wish you *zeyn zikher aun mazldik.* That means be safe and good luck," She said as she gave each man a kiss on the cheek.

"You should be hearing from me very soon," Marlboro said.

She smiled wistfully as she waved, "Thank you for coming by."

After Sarah closed the door, she recounted the conversations with Marlboro and Beck to her aunt in Yiddish.

Her aunt started to weep.

"What's wrong?" Sarah asked.

"I fear that evil will triumph," Aunt Zibiah whispered.

Rachel brought Heim's *Körnigsberger Klopse und Dampfkartoffeln* out to the workshop as he requested.

Heim was spreading sawdust all around the woodshop floor.

Rachel stopped at the entrance of the workshop, surprised to see him emptying the barrels of sawdust on the ground.

"It's for absorption," Heim explained.

Rachel didn't understand the man's logic, so she just shrugged and brought the meal inside.

Heim walked over to a wooden desk in the corner of the workshop. He sat down on a straight-back wooden chair, picked up a Pelican knife, and began sharpening it. A Pelican knife is used for cutting clean, thin slices. It resembles the blade of a scalpel.

"Here's your lunch, sir. I hope it's to your liking."

Heim took a whiff and said, "Mmm. Smells just like my mother's. Rachel, please have a seat for a moment. Tell me a little about yourself."

He pointed to the oak banker's desk chair next to the desk. Rachel sat down, facing him off to the left side of the desk.

"Well, I've been working for the Billingsworths for over ten years," She said slyly.

"No, no. Tell me about yourself. Where were you born, where you're from, are you married? You know, so I can get to know you. Let's start with, what's your last name?" He said with a wolfish grin.

Rachel felt uneasy talking about herself, but his easy manner and pleasant demeanor put her at ease.

"Landon, my last name is Landon. My husband, Michael, works as a driver for MGM Studios. He's worked on all the big movies, like The Philadelphia Story, Thirty Seconds Over Tokyo, Battleground, and On The Town with Frank Sinatra.

I was born in Chicago. My father had a little tailor shop on the southside until the Depression. We moved around and finally ended up here in Los Angeles.

My father joined the army when the war broke out. He was killed at Normandy on Omaha Beach." Rachel stopped, got silent, and was about to get up and return to the kitchen when Heims put his hand on hers and said, "I'm so sorry, Rachel. May I ask what your father's name was?" He said sympathetically.

"Max Felderman."

"Felderman. So, you're Jewish?"

"Yes. Why?" She asked, feeling uneasy.

"Did you know that I am a doctor, Rachel?"

"No. What kind of doctor?"

"A very famous doctor, or should I say infamous. I was the doctor in the Mauthausen concentration camp. I did all kinds of unspeakable things to the Jews. And you know what? Nobody cared then, and nobody cares now," Heim sneered.

Rachel tried to bolt off the chair, but Heim was on her like a spider on a fly. He grabbed her by the neck, forced her up out of the chair, and walked her backward to the six-foot wooden workbench in the middle of the room. The Butcher of Mauthausen lifted her up off the floor and slammed her down onto the bench, hitting her head on a metal vise grip knocking the breath out of her.

She lay seeing stars and was stunned, trying to think clearly. He was running back and forth to both sides of the workbench, tying her arms and legs to the wooden table. As she was about to scream, he stuffed an old dirty rag in her mouth. The more she struggled, the more the ropes tightened.

Heim walked up to her, put his devil's face in hers, and whispered, "It's been too long since I've felt this alive. Oh, how I've missed the suffering, the pain, and the terror that we're going to experience, Rachel.

Now, the more you struggle, the more pain you're going to experience, and the more pleasure I will receive. So, let's get started," He said gleefully.

Heim picked up a large pair of scissors and started to cut off her dress. He sniped off her bra and underwear; as she lay naked, he stood over her, smiling, thinking of all the wonderful things he would do to her. Reaching over to the radial saw next to the bench, he flipped the switch on. The high-pitched whirling blade had the desired effect that he wanted.

Rachel began to cry and shake with fear. Heim leaned down by her ear and cheerfully said, "Don't worry, I'm not going to rape you, you Jewess whore. But just to be sure that you won't have any more Jew bastards, I am going to cut out your fallopian tubes," He laughed as he held up the Pelican knife.

He lightly dragged the knife blade from her breasts down to her stomach. He smiled as he cut open her lower abdomen.

"EEEYYYAAAAHHH!" *"EEAAAHHEEE!"* Rachel screamed as the pain was excruciating. The roar of the radial saw drowned out her muffled screech.

Heim didn't use any anesthesia on his subjects in Mauthausen and saw no reason to now. After all, she was just a Jew.

Rachel passed out from pain five minutes after Heim started the procedure. Not caring, he accidentally nicked an artery as he enjoyed butchering her. She was beginning to hemorrhage internally. Heim laid her intestines on her stomach so he could show her. He did so enjoy seeing the terror in their eyes when he held them up and dropped them on the floor.

To bring her around, he went to get the cup of coffee she had brought with his lunch and threw it in her face. As she slowly began to regain conciseness, she saw the face of Hell smiling, laughing, mocking her. Heim held up her intestines and casually threw them on the floor.

"It's nothing, just garbage like you. Soon, I'll be throwing you away as well," He said nonchalantly.

Rachel's eyes got as large as saucers when she saw the pure evil incarnate pleasure on his face. She gave a mournful scream.

"*EEEYYYAAAAHHH!*"

Heim enjoyed seeing the terror in her eyes. But alas, he decided that since she would soon be dead, the least he could do was show his gratitude to his host by presenting him with a memento of his appreciation.

Heim walked to the wall where Billingsworth kept his set of vintage Japanese saws. He selected a Dovetail Dozuki Saw. He felt that the saw cuts were razor sharp, as sharp as a surgical saw, and was satisfied that it was capable of doing the job.

He went over to Rachel, gazed into her dying eyes, grinned a toothy grin, lifted her head by grabbing her hair, and began to saw.

"Has anybody seen Rolf?" Billy Ray Thompson asked the members of Murphy Ranch night patrol.

The last time I saw him, he went out to take a crap in the woods," Tommy Warner answered.

"That dumb shit probably fell into a ravine," Thompson grumbled.

"Maybe he got bit by a snake and died," Warner said.

"I wish," Thompson moaned.

"I bet he went home to his mommy," Luke Addler quipped.

"Come on, let's see if we can find the dumb son-of-a-bitch," Thompson ordered.

The fourteen members of the night patrolled spent the better part of four hours looking for Private Rolf Henderson but didn't find hide nor hair of the poor private.

"How much longer do we have to look for this dickhead?" Warner sniped.

"All right, let's go back to the Ranch and report Henderson either AWOL or MIA. We'll let Miller and Kuhn figure it out," Thompson announced.

When they returned to the Ranch, Thompson went to Miller's office to report Private Henderson missing. Miller was sitting behind a makeshift desk out of two sawhorses and an old closet door. Thompson knocked on the door.

"Come!" Miller shouted.

Thompson snapped to attention, gave the Hitler salute, and announced, "*Herr Gruppenleiter* (group leader). *Feldwebel* (sergeant) Thompson reporting that *Privat* Rolf Henderson is missing, Sir!"

"Missing! What do you mean he's missing, Sergeant?" Miller's tone was anything but concerned, just angry.

"Sir, he was discovered missing this morning when the night patrol came off duty. His squad tells me that at around zero three-thirty, Private Henderson went off into the bushes to go to the bathroom but didn't return to camp. Sir!"

"And have you searched for poor Private Henderson, Sergeant?"

"Yes, Sir. We spent four hours searching for him. It was thought that he might have injured himself in the dark, maybe falling down a ravine. Sir!"

"Has he done this sort of thing before?"

"No, Sir. He's only been with the outfit for a couple of weeks. I'm thinking that there's a possibility that he may have gone AWOL. Sir!"

"Very well. I'll have a yeoman in admin give his mother a call and see if she's heard from him."

"Yes, Sir!"

"That's all, *Feldwebel* (sergeant) Thompson. Dismissed."

"Heil Hitler," Thompson said, clicking his heels and giving the Hitler salute as he spun around and left the room.

"Heil Hitler," Miller said, returning a half-assed Hitler salute as he pondered the caliber of these recruits.

He stared up at a color photograph of Adolf Hitler and uttered to himself, "Heydrich would turn over in his grave if he saw the bunch of gutless *Stiefmütterchen* (pansies) that we have to deal with."

SS-Gruppenführer (group head) Reinhard Heydrich was the highest-ranking SS and police official during the Nazi era and the principal architect of the Holocaust. He chaired the 1942 Wannsee Conference, which developed and formalized the plans for the "Final Solution to the Jewish Question" – the deportation and genocide of all Jews in German-occupied Europe.

He was ambushed, wounded, and died a week later from an infection sustained during the attack by a team of Czech and Slovak soldiers.

In retaliation, Hitler ordered the towns of Lidice and Ležáky razed, all the men over the age of 16 were murdered on the spot, and the women and children of the towns were deported and exterminated in Nazi concentration camps.

Miller picked up the phone and called Rolf Henderson's home.

"Hello?" A tiny woman's voice, barely audible, answered the phone.

"Is this the Henderson residence?" Miller asked.

"Yes. Who's calling, please."

"This is Walter Miller. May I speak to Rolf, please?"

"Rolf is not here. May I take a message, Mr. Miller?"

"May I ask, is this his mother?"

"Why, yes, it is."

"When was the last time you saw Rolf?"

"Wednesday morning."

"If you should see him, would you have him give me a call? It's very important," Miller stressed.

"Yes, I certainly will."

"Thank you."

CLICK

Kuhn walked in at the tail end of the conversation.

"Who was that?"

"Rolf Henderson's mother."

"What did she want?"

"No. I called her. Rolf is missing."

"Missing?"

"According to *Feldwebel* (sergeant) Thompson, last night when Rolf was on night patrol, he went out into the woods to take a dump and never came back."

"What do you think happened?"

"The stupid twit probably fell down a ravine or wandered off to go home to his mommy," Miller surmised.

"*Dummkopf.* (fool) If he did go AWOL, we'd have to make an example of him. We can't let this sort of thing happen. He'll have to be punished severely!" Kuhn ranted.

"And if he's injured or dead?"

"It will be a good lesson to the other men. This is what happens when you don't obey orders."

"That's right. That's the one thing the Nazis taught us; you must always follow orders."

After Heim went about the Billingsworth kitchen looking for a large enough pot to suit his purposes, he returned to the workshop and finished his lunch. He had to admit that the filthy whore did make a damn good *Körnigsberger Klopse und Dampfkartoffeln.* (meatballs in white sauce and steamed potatoes) And now that his stomach was full, he could get on with the task at hand.

He utilized and put to good use most of the machine saws in the shop. Once he had dismembered

Rachel's body, he went behind the woodshop building and dug a five-foot hole at the base of the structure, behind a thick row of Coyote brush.

Heim then dumped Rachel's remains into the hole and covered her with several bags of powdered lime he found in the gardener's shed before filling the rest of the cavity with dirt.

As he swept up the bloodied sawdust, he got a big smile on his face; he uttered to himself, "See, I told you it was for absorption."

All the while he was cleaning up his mess, Heim had a pot cooking on the stove. Blondi, the Billingsworth's German Shepherd, was pacing around in the kitchen, nose in the air. As Heim went into the kitchen to check on the contents of the pot, Mrs. Billingsworth came home.

"My, my, that smells delicious. What are you cooking, Herr Heim?"

"You'll just have to wait and see, Betty. It's a surprise."

"Ooh, I can't wait?" She said.

"You run along, Betty. I'll call you when it's done."

Betty Billingsworth was so excited that she didn't notice that Rachel wasn't about.

Once she had left the kitchen, Heim took the pot out to the workshop with Blondi close behind. He set the pot on the workbench and opened the lid. Carefully removing Rachel's head, he placed it on the bench. Making three incisions in the back of her scalp, he then proceeded as if peeling an orange. From years of experience, Heim easily removed the face from the skull and casually tossed it on the ground to a waiting and hungry Blondi.

With a long-reach hook and pick tool, Heim was able to remove Rachel's brain through the nasal cavity with no problem.

He sat there holding the skull of Rachel Landon, admiring his handy work. He couldn't wait to present it to Jeffery and Betty as a show of gratitude. It would make a great paperweight in his home office, a real conversation piece.

Marlboro and Beck showed up at the Murphy Ranch an hour before the schedule. They were surprised to see a lot of hubbub and chaos going on. Miller and Kuhn addressed a group of twenty men wearing Nazi-style uniforms.

Miller noticed Marlboro and Beck standing on the front portico, watching. He left Kuhn and the others and walked over to them.

"You boys are early," Miller said, surprised.

"We were in the neighborhood and thought we'd stop in," Marlboro said sarcastically.

'What's going on?" Beck asked.

"One of our younger recruits went missing. We think he may have gotten lost and possibly injured himself, so we're organizing a search party. Care to join in?"

"What? Dressed like this?" Beck said acerbically, pointing to his blue jeans, tee shirt, and sports coat.

Miller was initially put off, then realized Beck was just being cheeky.

"We could use the help, whaddya say?"

Marlboro looked at Beck and said, "What the Hell. We could use a nice stroll in the woods."

"Great," Miller replied.

The search party was broken up into groups of four. Both Marlboro and Beck were surprised to see that several young women were wearing the uniforms and that they were just as fanatical as the men.

Miller approached them and asked Marlboro and Beck if each of them would take charge of a group.

"Sure," Marlboro replied.

"Do we have time to go change into our field uniforms? This is a brand new sports coat." Beck asked.

"Of course. While you fellas go change into your fatigues, I'll have a quick talk with the troops about who you are," Miller said.

"*Achtung! Achtung!*" (attention! Attention) Kuhn shouted.

Everyone who would be involved in searching for *Privat* Henderson was milling around and snapped to attention when *Sturmführer* (storm leader) Kuhn gave the command.

"*Gruppenleiter* (group leader), Miller, wishes to address you. So, listen up," Kuhn ordered.

Miller stood on the porch, held up his right arm, and roared, "*Sieg Heil!*"

Below, staring up at him, were twenty wannabe Nazis returning the salute and shouting, "*Sieg Heil!*" all in unison.

Marlboro and Beck came out of the front door of the main ranch house, all dressed up in their new Amerika First Nazi field uniforms. Miller spotted them as they emerged and gestured for them to come and stand by him.

"Troops, I want to introduce *Oberst* Wolf *und Oberst* Presley. If you don't already know, these two patriots were responsible for the killing of that *Schweinehund Jude* Leon Lewis two days ago. This is the kind of heroism and leadership that our party needs. We are fortunate to have such men of high caliber in our ranks," Miller said proudly.

Kuhn raised his arm and yelled, "*Sieg Heil!*" "*Sieg Heil!*" "*Sieg Heil!*" as all the masses joined in the chorus of cheers.

Marlboro and Beck returned the salute and bowed in acknowledgment. Marlboro couldn't help wondering how many of these poor fools would be dead, wounded or arrested by the end of the day.

Beck and Marlboro each headed up a squad in search of *Privat* Henderson. They had heard from Agent Freely late last night that Henderson had been killed. Freely told them how Rolf Henderson had wandered upon Yatom. How Zvi killed the twenty-one-year-old with a slab into the back, piercing his heart and killing him instantaneously.

And how Yatom carried the dead boy over two miles to the rendezvous point and dumped his body in the trunk of the car. They drove to the coroner's office, placing Henderson under a John Doe until the mission was completed.

For over two hours in vain, the five units searched in and around the areas where the night patrol last remembered seeing *Privat* Henderson. Finally, Miller blew the whistle, signaling that the search was over. The squads headed back to the ranch house to get ready for the rally.

In Marlboro's group were two young women, members of the Amerika First's *Helferinnenkorps* (woman's corps of the SS), the women's branch of the army. Hilda Koch and Ilse Köhler were two blond-haired, blue-eyed college students and two of the vilest, racist people Marlboro had ever encountered. Although he found them both physically attractive, the bigotry and hatred were so revulsive he hardly could bring himself to speak to them.

On the way back to the ranch after the futile search for *Privat* Henderson, they were fawning all over him because he had killed Leon Lewis.

"What was it like to kill the Jew?"

"Did it feel good?"

"How did he die?"

"How many Jews have you killed?"

"Have you ever killed a nigger?"

"Can I come and watch you kill a Jew."

"I find you very attractive; want to screw?"

"Me too. How about after the rally?"

"*Fräuleins*, I am flattered. Let's wait and see how the rally goes first. Then we'll see," Marlboro replied so as not to sound too interested.

Ilse giggled at Hilda and whispered, "I can't wait. Maybe he'll screw us both."

Hilda smiled, "*Jawohl*."

Jeffery Billingsworth's chauffeur dropped him off at home at precisely 5:45 pm every day like clockwork. Rachel's car, a two-tone navy blue and cream-colored Pontiac "Torpedo," was parked off to the side of the driveway where she always parked.

When Billingsworth came through the front door, Rachel was usually there to greet him, take his coat and hat, and present him with an ice-cold martini. On this day, there seemed to be something not quite right: no Rachel, no martini, and an unusual smell wafting from the kitchen.

Betty descended from upstairs, looking like she had just awoken from a nap.

"Hello, darling," Betty greeted her husband with a small peck on the cheek.

"Hello, my dear. Napping?"

"Yes, I had such an exhausting day today; you wouldn't believe it. Silvia's caterer got the dates mixed up, so we had to prepare our own lunch. Can you imagine?"

"How awful. Sounds very inconvenient."

"It was very discommodious."

"Have you seen Rachel? She didn't hand me my martini."

"No, I haven't. When I got home, I went straight upstairs to nap."

"Hmm, that's odd. Rachel!" Billingsworth shouted.

Jeffery and Betty walked into the kitchen. There was no sign of Rachel, and nothing was on the stove or in the oven.

"I did see Doctor Heim in the kitchen when I came home; he appeared to be cooking something that smelled delicious," Betty said.

"I wonder where Doctor Heim might be?" Jeffery mumbled.

They walked through the living room down the hall to Jeffery's home office slash den. There, standing in front of Jeffery's antique rolltop desk was Heim, arms crossed, looking like the cat that swallowed the canary, with a big toothy grin that went from ear to ear.

"*Herr Doktor*, do you know where Rachel might be by chance?" Billingsworth asked.

"Betty, Jeffery, I have a surprise for you. Please sit down," Heim said brightly.

The Billingsworths sat on the leather couch opposite the desk, excited with anticipation. What marvelous gift could this esteemed guest be presenting them with? They couldn't imagine what it could be.

"Jeffery, Betty, you both have been so kind to invite me into your lovely home with such generosity; you've been so gracious. I wanted to do something for you, something special," He said as he reached behind him and revealed a skull that he presented them with.

Jeffery held it and examined it, showing it to Betty, who was beginning to turn as white as the skull.

"It's an Objet d'art. I made it myself," He said proudly.

"You made this?" Betty asked, thinking it might be a carving.

"*Jawohl.*"

"What is it made out of?" Jeffery asked.

"Rachel, your Jew whore," Heim smiled arrogantly.

"What!" Jeffery shouted in disbelief as he dropped the skull on the carpet.

Heim was shocked and confused. "Don't you like it? It took me all day to prepare it, just for you," Heim said, sounding slightly wounded.

"No. No, it's magnificent. We are just so surprised, that's all," Jeffery said, trying not to offend his guest.

He suddenly understood what real fear and terror was. The man standing proudly in front of them had just murdered and butchered their maid, cutting off her head simply to make what he considers an Objet d'art out of a human head.

"I knew you must have arranged to have a Jew maid here for my pleasure. It brought back such wonderful memories of my days in the camps. You're both too kind and thoughtful. This memento is just a small token of my appreciation."

"You're quite welcome," Jeffery said, almost in shock.

Heim picked the skull up and held it, turning it around, admiring it in front of them, saying, "See, isn't a thing of beauty, even for a Jew. Let me set it right here on top of your desk. There. *Prächtig* (gorgeous)!"

"Yes. *Prächtig*, (gorgeous)" Jeffery agreed.

Marlboro and Beck were called in to meet with *Gruppenleiter* (group leader) Miller and *(group leader)* Kuhn to go over their assignments at that evening's rally.

"Come in," Miller said.

"I hope *Privat* Henderson is all right and that he's not lying at the bottom of some ravine that we might have missed," Beck said.

"It is more likely that *Privat* Henderson is sitting at home sucking down a cheeseburger," Kuhn mused.

"He better hope that he is lying in some ravine because if I find out that he went AWOL, I will nail his ass to the wall," Miller growled.

"Is everything on schedule?" Marlboro asked, trying to change the subject.

"Yes, in fact, I wanted to see if you two would consider being part of *der Sicherheitsbeamter* (the security guard)," Miller said.

"The security guard." Kuhn interpreted.

"Sure, so what's the plan," Marlboro asked.

"The three of us will accompany *Herr* Heim from his car when he arrives at the VIP reception that will be held in the main ballroom in the ranch. It will be a meet and greet with notable local businessmen and possibly some Hollywood celebrities.

Once we're in the ballroom, we will just mingle and circulate, but at all times, keeping an eye out for the safety of our honored guest.

When it's time to attend the rally, we will be joined by eight members of *der Sicherheitsbeamter Sicherheitsbeamter* (the security guard), who will join us in escorting Doctor Heim to the stage out back of the main ranch house.

Now, we're expecting as many as 200 people at the rally. As the doctor's security guards, we will be stationed on and around the stage.

We will have dozens of armed, uniformed members and plainclothes operatives roaming among the crowd in search of any troublemakers.

If any disturbances happen anywhere in the crowd, our only priority is the protection of the doctor. Understood?" Kuhn asked.

"Got it," Beck said, nodding.

Agents Andrew Joiner, Frank Giustino, Michael Freely, and Colonel Zvi Yatom were making their way back to the Murphy Ranch in Rustic Canyon. They were all crammed into a sand-colored 1946 Jeep Willys. It was rough going over the rugged terrain up Sullivan Fire Road, much like it was the night before when they came up to the ranch to hide their weapons.

They were dressed in blue jeans, chambray shirts, and army boots. Hoping that wouldn't stick out too much.

There were several cars in front of them and dozens more behind them. When they got to the turn-off point, there were half a dozen men dressed in Nazi-style uniforms armed with *Maschinenpistole 40* submachine guns walking down the line of cars waiting to turn into the destinated parking area, looking for any troublemakers, agitators, rabble-rousers, and anyone who they thought looked Jewish.

As they got to the gate to the entrance, two men approached the car and gave them the once over. The man on the driver's side walked up to the driver, Mike Freely, and said, "Password."

Beck had called Freely that morning with the password.

"*Blitz*." Freely replied.

The guard waved them through. In the rearview mirror, Freely saw that the car behind them didn't know the password. The occupants were dragged out of the car, given a beating, thrown back into the car, and made to go back down the fire road from where they came.

After they parked the Jeep, they followed the throng of people heading to the ranch. As they were getting close to the rally, they spotted the California sagebrush next to the Lodgepole Pine, where their weapons were buried. Unfortunately, there were too many people milling about to retrieve them.

Agent Joiner offered up a plan. He would pick a fight with someone away from the Lodgepole Pine to divert the crowd's attention and allow the others to uncover their weapons. He knew he could sustain significant bodily injury, but there seemed no other way. He knew that once he started, he was on his own.

The easiest way to pick a fight was to make advances on some guy's girl. So, he spotted a woman that could have been the poster child for Aryan perfection. She was tall, had short blonde hair and green eyes, and wore a Nazi officer's dress cap.

"Hey, doll," Joiner said.

Her boyfriend was a bruiser. Joiner figured him to weigh close to two hundred-thirty pounds, but he was soft, and as Joiner would soon find out, he was not in great shape nor a great fighter; plus he was inebriated.

"Hey! Back off, Jack! She's with me!"

"That can't be. This doll is *wunderschönen* (beautiful), and you're a *Schweinehund*," (pig dog) Joiner said, laughing.

"What did you say?"

"I said, that can't be, she's beautiful, and you're a pig."

People standing around started laughing and egging the lunkhead on.

"Come on, doll; you don't want to be with a palooka like this."

The guy could see that he was going to lose his date if he didn't do something. She seemed to enjoy the attention.

"I'm warning you, buddy. Scram."

Paying no attention to the threat, Joiner asked, "Say, doll, what's your name?"

"Ingrid." She said with a wide grin.

"Ingrid. That's a lovely name, almost as lovely as you are, doll."

The boyfriend had had enough. He spun Joiner around and swung a big haymaker. Joiner had anticipated the move. Seeing what was coming, he ducked out of the way and threw an uppercut to the big man's jaw, knocking him backward.

A crowd started to gather around the scuffle, leaving Freely and his men to quickly recover their weapons unnoticed. Several uniformed guards stood by and watched, encouraged, and sniped at the large hooligan to be more aggressive.

Joiner allowed the fracas to continue for a bit longer; although the man was much bigger than him, his pugilistic skills were much to be desired. After a few more minutes of sparring, Joiner laid the brute out cold with a combination of jabs, hooks, and a right cross to the big man's temple, scoring his first street-brawl knockout.

"Come on, doll, let's go to the rally," Joiner said as he held out his hand.

She slapped it away, screaming, "You brute! Just go away."

Ingrid went down to comfort her unconscious fascist friend. He was bleeding from the nose and cut lip. The jeering crowd started kicking and spitting on him as they passed by. There's one thing that Nazis hate almost as much as Jews, and that's a loser.

Joiner was able to catch up with the squad as they tried to make their way towards the front of the stage. They decided to split up and spread their firepower out, giving them maximum coverage.

With the FBI squad mixed within the crowd in front of the stage and Beck and Marlboro somewhere backstage, the plan was that they would have an excellent chance of either capturing or killing Doctor Death.

Aribert Heim was dressed and ready for the limousine to arrive to take him to the rally. Heim was wearing a black suit with his Nazi war medals on full display. There was a blue, white, and gold Cross of Honor, the German Iron Cross with black, red, and white ribbon, the Nazi Party Pin, the German Cross in Silver, the West Wall, Anschluss, and Memel Medals. He wore a German SS infantry commemorative with eagle and skull badge on his left lapel.

The Billingsworths had just come down the stairs when the doorbell rang.

DING-DONG

A man dressed in a Nazi-style uniform was standing at the door. When the door opened, he snapped to attention, clicked his heels, and gave the Hitler salute.

"*Sieg Heil*! Your limo is here, sir. Ready when you are."

Jeffery walked into the living room and announced, "*Herr Doktor*, your limo is here."

Heim strolled to the front door and was taken back that his hosts weren't dressed.

"Aren't you coming with me?" Heim asked.

"No, we'll follow shortly; we still have a couple of things we have to attend to. You go ahead, and we'll meet you there."

"Very well. This is going to be a big night. Come soon," Heim said.

As the driver opened the car door for the honored passenger, he greeted him with a *"Heil Hitler."*

"Heil Hitler," Heim said as he entered the backseat of the limousine.

Jeffery and Betty smiled, waved, and watched the limo drive out of the driveway and down the street; Jeffery closed the door and freaked out.

"Jesus Christ! The man is a lunatic. Killing Rachel and cutting off her head as a present. What are we going to do, Betty?" Jeffery said in a panic.

"I don't know," Betty sobbed.

"What have we gotten ourselves into? We're accomplices in a murder, accessories after the fact, and harboring a known war criminal. My God, we're going to prison!"

"Should we call the police? After all, we didn't know that he was going to kill her," Betty asked.

DING-DONG

"What do we do?" Betty whispered in horror.

"Answer the door."

"But it might be the police!"

"Betty, go upstairs. Let me handle this," Jeffery ordered.

He waited until he heard Betty close the bedroom door before opening the front door.

It was Michael Landon, Rachel's husband, standing on the porch.

"Good evening, Mr. Billingsworth."

"Michael, please come in."

Michael entered the foyer, looked at his wife's employer, and asked, "Going out."

Jeffery was a bit taken aback; he peered down at himself and replied, "Oh, ah yes, yes, we're going to a friend's dinner party. It looks like it's going to be a stuffy affair."

"Is Rachel here?" Michael asked.

Jeffery gave a quick glance around and answered, "Why, no, Michael, she isn't. She wasn't here when I came home at 5:45, and Betty told me she hadn't seen her when she came home from her bridge game around 3:30 this afternoon."

"It's odd that she's gone, and her car is still in the driveway," Michael said.

"I know. We were starting to get concerned as well," Jeffery feigned distress.

"She didn't leave a note or anything?"

"Not that I saw. Why don't you come in, and we'll have a quick look around."

They walked through the kitchen, living room, dining room, and the den, where Rachel's skull sat on top of Billingworth's rolltop desk.

When Michael entered the den, he stopped, walked over to the desk, and looked at the skull.

"Is that a real human skull? Mr. Billingsworth?"

"No, Michael, it's a replica. A friend of mine is a doctor and gave it to me as a lark," Jeffery said.

"I've seen a lot of skull props for the movies, but I've never seen any of them that look that real,"

Landon said as Jeffery was ushering him out of the den and back into the Livingroom.

"I think I better call the police. Something not right," Michael confessed.

"I think you should give it until the morning. Rachel might have gone off with one of her girlfriends and just lost track of time."

"I don't know; it's so unlike her."

"Well, even if you call, the police won't start looking for her unless she's been missing for at least 24 hours. Now, you go on home, and if we hear anything, I promise I'll call you straight away," Jeffery said as he led Michael to the door.

"All right, Mr. Billingsworth, I guess you're right. Let me know if you hear anything."

"I promise. And the first thing I recommend is that you try calling all of her and your friends."

"I will, thank you, Mr. Billingsworth."

Once the front door had closed, Betty came running down the stairs.

"What did he say?" She asked frantically.

"He's very concerned. I did convince him that he had to wait 24 hours before calling the police. We don't have much time, Betty. I think I better call Roger Levine."

"Our attorney?"

"Yes, it's ironic, isn't it? A pro-white supremacist is calling a Jewish lawyer to advise us how to deal with a Nazi war criminal murdering our Jewish maid," Jeffery said as he called his "shyster" lawyer.

When Aribert Heim arrived at the entrance of the Murphy Ranch; two armed, uniformed men got into the limousine. The two men simultaneously said, "*Sieg Heil.*"

Heim gave a small grin as he was having feelings of Déjà vu, reminding him of *der Reich, der führer, und die glorreichen Tage.* (the empire, the leader, and the glory days)

As he looked out upon the crowd assembling and the small unit of paramilitary men and women in uniforms, his memories of the fatherland soon disappeared. These weren't the cracked SS troops that he had been proud to serve with. They were more like cartoon characters, men and women playing dress-up with guns. There was no way this rag-tag outfit would ever be a viable force, never mind an army. They would be no deterrent against even the local police.

Well, it was no concern of his; he was just here to get some much-needed funds. Once he got what he came for, he would be off to Cairo and leave these poor, self-aggrandized tin soldiers to their fate of doom.

The limousine dropped him and his armed entourage at the entrance of the main ballroom, where he was met by his host, *Obergruppenleiter* (senior group leader) Tristan Kendrick Wentworth, and his wife, Mila. Mila was relatively younger than her husband; she was actually his third wife. She was just slightly older than his two sons from the first marriage.

"*Sieg Heil, und willkommen Herr Doktor*. It's an honor to meet you, sir."

"The honor is all mine, *Obergruppenleiter* (senior group leader) Wentworth."

"I'd like to introduce you to my lovely wife, Mila."

Heim gave a slight bow, took her hand, and kissed it, saying, "It's a pleasure to meet such a beautiful lady as yourself."

"The pleasure is all mine," Mila said, blushing.

Wentworth took his guest by his arm and showed him into the ballroom where dozens of Los Angeles' white bigoted elite applauded as *SS-Hauptsturmführer* (headstorm leader) Aribert Heim entered the room.

He smiled his wolf's smile, held up his hands in appreciation, and said, "*Vielen Dank* (thank you). You are too kind. Thank you."

Obergruppenleiter (senior group leader) Wentworth, standing next to the Butcher of Mauthausen, smartly dressed in his dress uniform, a single-breasted white jacket featuring wide lapels. On the right lapel was the insignia of the *SS sig runes* (double SS lightning bolt symbol for victory). On the left was a thin single silver stripe next to three diagonal silver diamonds signifying the rank of *Obergruppenleiter* (senior group leader). On the left sleeve, the swastika armband, worn underneath the jacket, and a white shirt with a light brown tie that matched the trousers.

The riding breeches were worn with black knee-high jackboots and a waistbelt with silver buckles. Connected to the waistbelt was a tightly pulled belt around the tunic. The idea was to give the effect of leanness and power; unfortunately, because Wentworth was fifty pounds overweight, the effect was lost.

Seeing Wentworth dressed up in his make-believe *SS Obergruppenleiter* (senior group leader) uniform made Heim chuckle. Wentworth would have been lucky to have gotten the rank of *Unterwachtmeister* (sergeant), never mind an *SS* officer of such a high rank.

Heim felt that he was being shown off as Wentworth's show dog, but he swallowed his Nazi pride and played the game. He needed the money.

"Ah, *Herr Doktor*, I'd like you to meet Mr. and Mrs. Albert Fitzroy. They own Fitzroy's, the ultra-exclusive high-end chain of department stores; of course, they're restricted. No Jews, niggers, or chinks allowed," Wentworth proudly said.

Heim did a quick bow with a click of the heels, "*Herr und Frau Fitzroy*, it is a pleasure to meet you. I thank you for coming to this evening's festivities."

"It is our great honor, Doctor," Fitzroy oozed.

"What are your plans, Doctor. Do you plan on staying here in Los Angeles?" Mrs. Fitzroy asked.

"Alas, no. I fear that there are many within your government that are being influenced, pressured, and bullied by the international Jewish conspiracy to keep me out of this great country," Heim bemoaned.

"That is a great pity. Keeping a great and renowned doctor from entering our country after all the medical research and the medical advancements that you've accomplished. Well, I, sir, think that it's just a great pity," The *Obergruppenleiter* (senior group leader) interjected.

The dog and pony show with the donors went on for over two hours, plus he had the rally to attend.

Wentworth could see that Heim was starting to fade, so to pick his spirits up, he leaned over at one point and whispered in Heim's ear, "So far, *Herr Doktor*, we have collected over a half a million dollars that has been deposited into the Swiss bank account as you requested. *Ist gut* (is good)?"

"*Jawohl. Ist gut.* (yes, it's good)," Heim said with a huge, reenergized smile on his face. He seemed to have gotten a shot of adrenaline; he slapped Wentworth on the back and whooped, "Let's go to the rally."

Marlboro and Beck went about the VIP gala mingling and keeping their eye always on the Butcher of Mauthausen, never letting him out of their sight. They also were gathering the names of the attendees to be presented to the Senate's committee on un-American activities.

A sweet-looking little old German woman approached Marlboro, pointed to Heim, and asked, "Excuse me, *junger Mann* (young man). Who exactly is that handsome man over there that everyone is making such a fuss about?"

"That is Aribert Heim, a notorious Nazi war criminal," Marlboro replied unabashedly.

"Was he responsible for torturing and killing Jews?" She asked timidly.

"Thousands."

"Really?" She said, surprised.

"Really."

"Ooh, I must meet him!" She smiled and rushed over to engage him in conversation.

Marlboro stood and observed them laughing and joking together. He shook his head and uttered, "It's true you can't judge a book by its cover."

He met up with Beck; they compared notes on the attendees.

"I can't believe how many of these people have been completely under the FBI's radar," Beck confessed.

"These are the types of supporters that Hitler counted on to stay silent until he took control. The ones that backed him got rich, and those who opposed him got killed," Marlboro contemplated.

Beck spotted Miller and Kuhn approaching.

"*Oberst* (Colonel) Wolf und *Oberst* (Colonel) Presley. How's it going?" Kuhn asked.

"Good, sir," Marlboro answered.

Beck nodded in agreement.

"We're getting ready to head out to the rally. Once we're out there, I want you and Presley to be flanked on either side of the stage. Wolf, you take the left side of the stage, and Presley, you'll be on the right. We'll have three men standing behind the speaker's podium.

We're not expecting any trouble, but stay alert. You never know. Any questions?" Miller asked.

"Nope, I think it should be pretty straightforward," Marlboro said.

"Remember, shoot first and ask questions later. We'd rather have a couple of dead fanatics than Doctor Heim injured. Got it?" Kuhn asked.

"Got it," Marlboro said as he pulled out his Luger and checked it to be sure it was loaded, as did Beck. Then Marlboro and Beck each pulled out a .45 Colt automatic pistol they had tucked in their belts, hidden behind their backs under their jackets, and checked them.

"Hope you don't mind? But like you said, you never know," Marlboro mused.

"We like a little good old fashion U.S.A. firepower as backup," Beck said.

Miller looked at Kuhn approvingly and said, "On the contrary, *Oberst* (Colonel), I like your style."

"Now then, *Obergruppenleiter* (senior group leader) Wentworth will go out first to give a speech condemning the Jewish Communism Conspiracy that's going on in America today. Then he'll introduce Doctor Heim, and that's when you and the security forces go out on stage."

"Got it," Beck said.

As they made their way to the rally stage, a mixture of American and German marching songs was being broadcast over the public announcement system.

From America, they played Stars and Stripes Forever, Anchors Away, Semper Fidelis, The Liberty Bell, Marines Hymn, and Yankee Doodle. From Nazi Germany, they played *Die Fahne Hoch, Hitlerleute, Kampflied der Nationaalsozialisten,* and *Deutschland Erwache.* (raise the flag, Hitler's people, the battle song of the national socialists, and Germany awake).

Beck estimated that the crowd size was well over two hundred, which included Amerika First members, VIP guests, and your everyday garden-variety anti-Semites, bigots, and racists. And just about all of them were stinking drunk, which would work out well when the shit hit the fan. Once the shooting starts, the crowd will panic and create chaos, causing the majority of the armed guards to forget any semblance of military training and revert to self-preservation. Their primary instinct is to get the Hell out of there, putting up little or no resistance. There will be. A handful of men who'll fight back; hopefully, Freely and his squad will be able to take care of them.

They arrived on stage moments before Wentworth and his entourage, Miller and Kuhn. Wentworth gave a signal to the audio and lighting team. The music faded, and the lights went off. The crowd started chanting, *"Sieg Heil!" "Sieg Heil!" "Sieg Heil!"*

Suddenly, a spotlight flashed on, revealing Tristan Kendrick Wentworth, leader of Amerika First, all dressed up in his *Obergruppenleiter* (senior group leader) Nazi uniform, holding the Hitler salute.

The crowd went wild, shouting choruses of *"Sieg Heil!" "Sieg Heil!" "Sieg Heil!" "Sieg Heil!" "Sieg Heil!" "Sieg Heil!"*

"Mr. Landon, can you tell me, when was the last time you saw your wife, Rachel?" Officer Dooley asked with pen and notepad at the ready.

"Seven o'clock this morning, as we were both leaving to go to work."

"And what do you do?"

"I'm a teamster at MGM Studios. I drive trucks for movie productions."

"And your wife? Where does she work?"

"She works as a maid for the Jeffery and Betty Billingsworth on 7259 Outpost Cove Drive. She's been with them for close to ten years."

"And has your wife ever taken off like this before?"

"No, never."

"Have you tried calling her friends to see if she might have gone with one of them?"

"Yes. No one has seen her or talked to her today."

"I'm sorry, Mr. Landon, but I have to ask. Was everything good between you and your wife? I mean, is it possible that she might be seeing someone else?"

"Rachel? Never!" Landon said voice raised.

"Okay. Okay, it's just that we have to ask. You understand."

"Of course, I didn't mean to get angry."

"Is there anyone that you can think of that might want to hurt Rachel?"

"No, she was the kindest person that you would ever meet."

"Now, you say her car is still parked at the Billingsworth home, is that correct?"

"Yes, I went there tonight to see why she might be late—an unannounced party, something like that. I spoke to Mr. Billingsworth, and he told me that neither he nor his wife had remembered seeing her after eleven this morning.

He told me that they were going out to a party, so there was no reason why she would have had to stay late."

"Well, Mr. Landon, we don't usually get involved in a missing person case until the party has been missing for at least twenty-four hours.

But I'll tell you what; I'll just swing by the Billingsworth house and give it a quick once over. You say that the Billingsworths will be out for the evening, so I'll stop by again tomorrow morning when someone will be there.

Now, Mr. Landon, try not to worry; nine times out of ten, there's nothing nefarious going on. Soon as I know anything, I'll give you a call or stop by."

"Thank you, Officer Dooley, for your time, and I appreciate all your help. Good night."

"Good night."

Dooley wasn't going to bother going over to check out the car, but as it turned out, it was on his way to the station, so he figured, what the Hell.

He drove up through the Hollywood Hills to 7259 Outpost Cove Drive. The place was well-lit, with lights on in the home and the driveway. There, parked to the right side of the driveway, was a brown 2-door Hudson Hornet.

Dooley got out of his black and white, went to the front door, and rang the doorbell, no answer. He took his flashlight and peered into the Hudson Hornet; he saw nothing of interest inside the car.

As he walked back to his car, a large German Shepherd came around from the back of the house; its tail was wagging.

"Hey, buddy," Officer Dooley said in his friendliest make-nice to the big doggie voice.

The dog strolled over to the Dooley and dropped something at his feet, almost as if he wanted to play with or share whatever it had in its mouth with the policeman.

"Good boy," Dooley said as he petted the dog on its head. He then reached down and picked up the object at his feet.

The lighting was weak, so it wasn't recognizable; it felt wet, slimy, and looked oddly familiar. He turned on his flashlight to examine it. The first thing he recognized on the object sent a shiver down his spine. It was a human ear. The ear was attached to a large portion of the scalp. The hair looked to have been poorly cut short, almost sheared. The hair color looked to be black; part of the left eyebrow was attached, and it, too, looked to be black.

Dooley, a sixteen-year veteran of the Los Angeles Police Department, had seen a lot of horrific things in his career, but this was up there at the top of the heap. He walked over to the bushes by the front of the driveway and puked his guts up.

Once he had emptied the contents of his stomach, he returned to the squad car, picked up his radio, and called the dispatcher.

"Dispatch, this is 1-Bravo-4; come in."

"This is dispatch."

"I need assistance. Possible 187."

"What's your 10-20?"

"7259 Outpost Cove Drive."
"Help is on the way 1-Bravo-4."
"10-4."

"Ladies and Gentlemen, Fellow Americans, American Patriots:

I would like to read to you some parts from the Free America speech that the great American patriot Fritz Kuhn, the leader of the German-American Bund, gave at Madison Square Garden in February 1939. Kuhn was later deported in 1945 by the International Jewish Conspiracy.

I am sure I do not come before you tonight as a stranger.

You will have heard of me through the Jewish-controlled press as a creature with horns, a cloven hoof, and a long tail.

The Jews will surely succeed in their far-reaching ambitions unless you Aryans, Christians, wake up and not only speak out in thunder tones to demand that our government be returned to the American people who founded it but also put your shoulder to the wheel and act understandingly.

We–Amerika First–organized as American citizens, with American ideals, and determined to protect ourselves, our homes, our wives, and our children against the slimy conspirators who would change this glorious republic into a Bolshevist paradise. We must fight to break the hand of the palsied hand of Jewish Communism on our schools, our universities, and our very homes.

Whenever a Jew appears in history, he is worked up by his fellows into a "Personality" who "overshadows" the white man who accomplishes the things for which the Jew takes credit.

It is a standing complaint of the Jews that they are persecuted, though they have the utmost liberty in the United States and are filling more places in public life in proportion to their numbers than all the other racial elements together.

Here are a few of the things we, Amerika First, are actively fighting for:

A socially just, White-Gentile ruled the United States.

Gentile-controlled labor unions were free from Jewish, Moscow-directed domination.

Gentiles to be in all positions of importance in government, national defense, and educational intuitions.

Outlawing of the Jewish Communist Party in the United States, prosecution of all known Communists for high treason.

Immediate cessation of the dumping of all political "refugees."

Cessation of all the fake news media, who are the enemy of the people.

This is what we, Amerika First, believe in. Take it or leave it. If you approve and wish to make your influence felt, join us. If you're tired of feeling powerless, join us. Join us if you're tired of being kept down by the Jews. We are looking for Aryan White Gentile Christians: we shall have victory together.

If the government won't bow to the will of the people, then it is up to every one of us to take advantage of our God-given and Constitutional rights to bear arms and force them by any means necessary to grant us our freedom!

God bless you, and God bless a white America.

Sieg Heil!" Wentworth shouted and raised his hand in the Hitler salute to a roar of hundreds of drunken bigots cheering.

"Sieg Heil!" "Sieg Heil!" "Sieg Heil!" "Sieg Heil!"

He stood there basking in this glory, nodding his head, emulating Benito Mussolini, waiting for the crowd to settle down.

He held up his arms to quiet the multitudes. Slowly, the horde became silent, waiting for something to happen.

"Now, Ladies and Gentlemen, Fellow Americans, American Patriots, it is my honor and privilege to present one of the Third Reich's foremost heroes and preeminent doctors; I give you Aribert Heim.

"Sieg Heil!" "Sieg Heil!" "Sieg Heil!" "Sieg Heil!" "Sieg Heil!" "Sieg Heil!" "Sieg Heil!" "Sieg

Heil!" "Sieg Heil!" "Sieg Heil!" "Sieg Heil!" "Sieg Heil!"

Heim strolled up to the podium, shook Wentworth's hand, gave a short bow to his host, turned to the crowd, and held up the Hitler salute. The crowd went crazy; having an actual Nazi holding up the Hitler salute was a fascist's dream come true. It was the next best thing to Uncle Adolf standing there in person.

Heim looked out over the pathetic rabble of a measly two hundred slovenly and drunken people. Unlike the Nuremberg spectacle of one million strong, it felt like a joke. There, he looked out over *Storm Troopers, the Luftwaffe, the Wehrmacht,* and, of course, the *Waffen-SS*.

Oh, how the mighty have fallen. The Third Reich, Hitler promised it would last a thousand years. It lasted only twelve. Most of the Nazi leaders are either dead, in prison or fugitives like Heim. They are all scattered in the wind, trying to find some kind of sanctuary, a place to hide, driven underground.

Maybe Hitler had the right idea: a bullet to the head. For a soldier, it is a coward's way out. But then again, what kind of life is this? Hopefully, Egypt will be better, although he'll have to convert to becoming a Muslim; that was part of the deal.

He just has to get through this night, and then he's free. Whatever that means.

Jeffery and Betty Billingsworth were hiding in their bedroom. They saw Officer Dooley arrive, ring the doorbell, and wander around the grounds.

They saw Blondi bring the policeman something in his mouth but could not see what it was from peeking out of the plantation shutters.

"I thought you let Blondi in!" Jeffery whispered.

"I thought you did."

"Jesus fucking Christ, what do you think that thing is?"

"I can't tell. But whatever it is, it made that poor policeman throw up," Betty muttered.

They watched as Officer Dooley went to his car and used the radio. It wasn't but minutes that more police cars with lights flashing pulled up into Billingworth's driveway.

"I'm scared, dear. What are we going to do, Jeffery?"

"I guess I'd better go down," He said, trying to muster the courage.

"This isn't going to go down to well at the club," He uttered to himself.

By the time he got downstairs, four black and white with their lights flashing, two plainclothes detectives, the medical examiner, and the boys from the crime lab all had parked in the driveway and in front of 7259 Outpost Cove Drive.

Although it was considered undignified and socially unacceptable, some neighbors did venture out of their stately homes to see what was happening at the Billingworth's residents. A few of the more refined residents sent their maids to observe the goings on and then report back to them.

As the police were searching all around the property, Jeffery Billingsworth opened the door, wearing his dressing gown over a pair of blue and white pajamas, just as Officer Dooley knocked on the front door. Standing behind him was Detective Lawlor from homicide.

"Mr. Billingsworth?" Officer Dooley inquired.

"That's right, officer. What's all this? What is going on?" Billingsworth said, acting incredulous.

"May we come in for a minute, Mr. Billingsworth?" Detective Lawlor asked as he and the Dooley entered the house. It was more of a statement of fact rather than a request.

"Yes, of course. Come in."

"Mr. Billingsworth, why didn't you answer the door when I knocked and rang the doorbell numerous times earlier?" Dooley asked.

"I'm so sorry, officer; you see, my wife and I wear earplugs while we sleep. I'm a bit embarrassed to say that we both snore terribly."

"Mr. Billingsworth, I'm Detective Lawlor. Whose car is that parked in your driveway?" Detective Lawlor asked.

"Why, that's Rachel Landon, our maid."

"Is she here?"

"No."

"Do you know where she is?"

"No. Like I told her husband earlier, Betty, my wife, and I haven't seen her since this morning."

"Has Mrs. Landon ever left her car here before?"

"Not that I can remember."

"Whom all lives here, Mr. Billingsworth?"

"Just Betty and I."

"Do you mind if we have a look around?"

"Can you tell me what this is all about, Detective?"

"We have reason to believe that Mrs. Landon has met with foul play."

Billingsworth's whole life flashed before his eyes, the blood drained from his face, and he got weak in the knees.

"Are you all right, sir?" Dooley asked as he led Billingsworth to the couch.

"Yes, I'm fine. It's just that Rachel has been with us for ten years; she was like family."

Betty Billingsworth had been eavesdropping at the top of the stairs. She came downstairs when she saw her husband being helped on the couch. She also was wearing a dressing gown and pajamas.

"Jeffery, are you all right?" She said as she sat down next to her husband,

"Betty, these policemen think that something terrible has happened to Rachel."

"Mrs. Billingsworth, when was the last time you remember seeing Mrs. Landon?" Detective Lawlor asked.

"I believe it was a little before eleven; I was going to go play bridge at Doris Upson's house. I didn't see her when I returned."

"So, the last time you saw her was around eleven. You didn't see her when you returned?"

"No. I only saw the doctor when I came home."

As soon as it left her mouth, she knew she had made a big mistake.

"Doctor?" Lawlor asked.

"Ah, yes, we have a house guest, Doctor Heim. He has been staying with us for a few days," Jeffery said nervously.

"And where is this, Doctor Heim?"

"He's out for the evening."

"So, he'll be returning."

"Yes, but it probably will be late."

"That's all right. We'll wait," Lawlor said.

Officer Dooley saw that they looked distressed, sitting on the couch huddled together.

"Are you folks all right? Can I get either one of you something to drink?" He asked.

They looked at Dooley, half smiled and shook their heads no.

"Dooley, take a look upstairs, and I'll look around down here," Lawlor ordered.

Officer Dooley went upstairs and began a cursory search into each of the five bedrooms. Three of the bedrooms seemed to be unoccupied; the master bedroom and the guest room seemed very tidy yet lived in.

In the guest room, Dooley found a Chilean passport for Doctor Heim and a second passport with the same photograph issued to Mister Tarek Farid Hussein by the Egyptian government.

"This ain't right," He muttered.

He began to go through the dresser drawers and found a signed photograph of Adolf Hitler with a personal message addressed to Aribert Heim.

"This ain't right, either," Dooley uttered out loud.

He took the two passports and the photograph and went downstairs to show Lawlor.

It was about the time Officer Dooley reached the bottom of the staircase that Detective Lawlor found the skull sitting on top of Billingsworth's rolltop desk.

"Dooley!" Lawlor shouted.

"Yeah?"

"Take a look at this?" Lawlor said, holding up the skull.

"Is that real?" Dooley asked.

"I was with the 6th Armored Division on April 11th when we liberated Buchenwald. I saw thousands of these, and this, my friend, is the real deal," Lawlor said as he picked up the skull and carried it into the living room.

He held it in front of Jeffery Billingsworth and said, "Where did you get this?"

"It was a gift," Billingsworth said slyly.

"From whom?"

"From Doctor Heim."

"Where is Doctor Heim from?" Dooley asked.

"Ah, Germany."

"Interesting. Because according to this passport, Mr. Billingsworth, he's from Chile," Dooley said as he handed Lawlor the two passports.

"Who exactly is this, Doctor Heim?" Lawlor asked.

"You know what. I think I better have my attorney here," Billingsworth stated.

"You know, I think that might be a good idea. Jeffery Billingsworth, Betty Billingsworth, you're under arrest for the murder of Rachel Landon. Book 'em, Dooley, and take them downtown."

"Detective Lawlor, you better come quick!" Roger Niven from the ME's office shouted at the front door entrance.

"I'll be right there. Dooley, keep an eye on these two until I come back," Lawlor instructed.

"Yes, sir."

Lawlor went outside where the ME was waiting.

"What is it?" Lawlor asked Niven.

"We found a body buried behind the woodshop building. It appears that of a woman who has been dismembered, disemboweled, and the head is missing."

"Thanks, Roger. Keep me posted. Do me a favor and have your guys go through that woodshop with a fine toothcomb and see if you can find any evidence from that dismemberment," Lawlor said.

Detective Lawlor walked back into the living room where the Billingsworths were seated on the couch, handcuffed.

"Okay, who's the sick bastard that cut up into pieces and disemboweled Rachel Landon, then buried her body behind your workshop, Billingsworth? Was it you?" Lawlor grilled.

"No! God, no," He said, beginning to weep.

"It was Doctor Heim. We didn't know anything about it until he presented us with her skull," Betty said, sobbing.

"Presented you with a human skull? Why would he do that?"

"He said it was because of our hospitality and because she was Jewish," Jeffery professed.

"What? He kills her and cuts off her head because she's Jewish. What? Is this guy some kind of Nazi?" Lawlor said as the light went on in his head.

"Yes," Billingsworth confessed.

"This guy is a Nazi war criminal. Did you two know that?" Lawlor sneered.

They lied, "No!"

"Get them out of my sight, Dooley. Run them downtown."

"We can't go like this. Can't we change into something more appropriate?" Jeffery asked.

"Get them the Hell outta here, Dooley," Lawlor barked.

"Come on, let's go!" Dooley took them outside and placed them into his squad car.

Lawlor walked up to the black and white, tapped on the window, and said, *"Auf Wiedersehen."*

Aribert Heim held up his hands to quiet the mob; when the crowd was quiet, he said, "I just want to say how it warms my heart to see that our Aryan brothers and sisters are carrying on the tenets of National Socialism. I know that with people like you someday we shall prevail! *Sieg Heil!*"

The drunken horde began yelling, *"Sieg Heil!" "Sieg Heil!" "Sieg Heil!" "Sieg Heil!"*

As the crowd continued to shout, Heim stood watching *Obergruppenleiter (senior group leader)* Wentworth, his wife Mila, *Gruppenleiter* (group leader) Miller, and *Sturmführer* (storm leader) Kuhn came up onto the stage to join their honored guest. They waved to the crowd with big smiles as their photographer took pictures of them and the crowd.

Agent Freely made a mental note to target that photographer to confiscate the film so that the FBI could use it to identify the people attending the rally.

As it appeared that the rally was coming to an end, agent Andrew Joiner drew his Colt revolver. The man fought with earlier had been keeping his eye on Joiner, planning to jump him at the appropriate time, noticed the gun and began shouting, "Gun! He was a gun! Man with a gun!"

There was panic as people started to run in every direction. Armed guards began shooting indiscriminately, striking dozens of people at random. Joiner commenced returning fire. Freely and his squad initiated their mission to capture Doctor Death.

"Let's go!" Freely shouted as he brandished his Ithaca Model 1911 A1 .45 pistol, which he carried from Normandy to Berlin.

Staff Sergeant Michael Freely was with the 116th Regiment of the 29th U.S. Infantry Division that landed on Omaha Beach on June 6, 1944. They slogged halfway across Europe, battled through the Battle of the Bulge, and on to Berlin. And here he was, fighting the Nazis again outside the City of Angeles.

The agents, along with Colonel Yatom, started to advance toward the stage. Due to the utter chaos, they weren't drawing any attention from the armed guards running around on the platform where Wentworth and Heim were.

Gruppenleiter (group leader) Miller and *Sturmführer* (storm leader) Kuhn were the only two who seemed to have some military composure, yelling, trying to get some kind of coordinated attack on armed intruders. Kuhn stayed with Wentworth and Heim, guarding them as they ran off stage, trying to make their escape in all of the confusion.

Marlboro and Beck left the stage running in hot pursuit of the Butcher of Mauthausen.

"Halt or I'll shoot! FBI!" Yelled Beck, holding up his Luger and FBI ID.

Kuhn turned and began to fire, striking Beck in the right leg and taking him down.

Marlboro aimed and fired, hitting Kuhn four times in the upper torso, killing him instantly. Wentworth threw his gun down and his hands up in the air, pleading.

"I surrender, don't shoot. Don't shoot!"

Heim wasn't about to capitulate; he grabbed *Obergruppenleiter* Wentworth's wife, Mila, and held her as a human shield, pressing the barrel of his Spreewerk cyq P38 pistol to her head.

"Don't come any closer. If you try anything, I shall shoot the *Hündin*! (bitch)" Heim sneered as he began to back up towards the stage door.

Marlboro grabbed Wentworth by the collar, spun him around, and forced him to follow Heim and his wife. All the while, he was aiming his Luger at Heim.

Heim was smart; he kept moving behind his hostage's head, making a clean shot impossible.

Miller and the three guards had made their way to join a dozen other fairly well-trained guards to try and mount a counterattack. Even though they had superior numbers, in the end, it was the military experience of Freely and other FBI agents that carried the day, that, and Zvi's Uzi Submachine gun.

Heim eased his way to the waiting limousine outside the main building. As he opened the car door, he and Mila got into the limo and sped away.

Marlboro fired seven rounds at the limo's tires but, to no avail; the limousine disappeared down the ravine's fire road.

He took Wentworth back to the stage to the waiting arms of the FBI reinforcements, who had rounded up *Gruppenleiter* Miller and eighteen members of the Amerika First paramilitary. Among the group of prisoners were the two blond-haired, blue-eyed college students, Hilda Koch and Ilse Köhler of the *Helferinnenkorps* (woman's corps of the SS).

Hilda and Ilse were sitting on the ground, their hair and uniforms all disheveled and crying.

"Stand up, *fräuleins*. You two look like a couple of Pekinese down there."

"What's going to happen to us?" Ilse asked, sobbing.

"Well, you did say that you wanted to screw. Consider yourself screwed, doll," Marlboro snarked as he went to see how Beck was doing.

Beck was being tended to by army medics, as well as scores of other wounded.

"How is he, Doc?" Marlboro inquired after Beck.

"He's lucky. It could have been a lot worse. He'll be up and around in no time," The medic said.

"Heim?" Beck asked.

"He nabbed Wentworth's wife and took it on the lam in the limo. A Nazi war criminal driving around L.A. How hard could it be to find him." Marlboro said sarcastically.

In the end, twelve Amerika First "soldiers" were killed, and fourteen civilians were wounded. Mila Wentworth was found dead later that day alongside the 405 Freeway, with a bullet wound to the head.

EPILOGUE

Aribert Heim was able to contact members of *Organisation Der Ehemaligen Ss-angehörigen* (ODESSA), the organization of former SS members who aided in facilitating his escape to Egypt.

While in Cairo, he worked on a research paper decrying the possibility of anti-Semitism owing to the fact that most Jews were not Semitic in ethnic origin under the pen name of Dr. Youssef Ibrahim. It was never published.

Heim assumed the name Tarek Hussein Farid and lived in Cairo until his death of colon cancer in 1992.

The corpse of the Butcher of Mauthausen was washed and wrapped in a white sheet in accordance with Muslim tradition and placed in a wooden coffin. He was then interred in a common grave anonymously.

In 1947, Heim was tried and convicted in absentia for the brutal murder of Rachel Landon in a Los Angeles Superior Court.

In 1979, he was indicted in absentia by the Baden-Baden state court on hundreds of counts of murder.

Aribert Heim left behind his former wife, Fredi, two sons, and a daughter born out of wedlock in Chile.

Obergruppenleiter (senior group leader) Tristan Kendrick Wentworth, leader of Amerika, First stood trial for harboring a Nazi war criminal, fourteen counts of complicity in the murder of people killed at the Amerika First rally. He was found guilty and sentenced to 30 years in state prison.

After further investigation into the Amerika First movement, it was determined that Wentworth had embezzled $28,000. He was subsequently convicted and sentenced to five years in a Federal prison on tax evasion, the sentence to be served after his sentence in state prison.

Tristan Kendrick Wentworth did serve his entire state sentence and federal tax sentence. He was released from prison in August of 1982 at 76.

Wentworth died homeless and penniless. His body was found at the abandoned Murphy Ranch complex.

Gruppenleiter (group leader) Walter Miller was charged and convicted of fourteen counts of second-degree murder. He was sentenced to life imprisonment without the possibility of parole.

He was sent to San Quentin State Prison, where he helped form his legacy, the Aryan Brotherhood.

Miller was murdered in the "yard" at San Quentin by a group of black and Hispanic inmates. He was 52.

Jeffery & Betty Billingsworth were found guilty of harboring a known Nazi war criminal, obstruction of justice, and accessory after the fact.

Betty Billingsworth was sentenced to 10 years and fined twelve thousand dollars.

Jeffery Billingsworth was sentenced to 15 years and fined eighteen thousand dollars.

The Billingsworths were further ordered to pay compensation to Michael Landon in the sum of eight hundred thousand dollars for the wrongful death of Rachel Landon.

Betty Billingsworth was released after serving seven and a half years of her sentence. She divorced her husband and went to live with her sister in Dubuque, Iowa

Jeffery was involved in an altercation in his fifth year; he was thrown over a third-tier railing, causing permanent paralysis from the waist down.

He lived the rest of his life in a wheelchair. He was released, having served thirteen years. He had a humble pension from NTD Engineering. Since it wasn't a lot, Jeffery found he couldn't afford to live in Los Angeles, so he ended up renting a small apartment in Loma Linda, a suburb of San Bernardino. Light years from the life he once knew.

One day, some neighbors called the police to come and investigate a rank odor emanating from apartment 1C.

Inside, the police found Jeffery Billingsworth sitting in his wheelchair, his right hand clutching a .38 Smith & Wesson revolver, a large hole in the back of his head, and his brains splattered on the wall.

Leon Lewis and his family went back to their home in Pacific Palisades. He returned to his private law practice in Los Angeles. He remained active in the Los Angeles Jewish Community Council and B'nai B'rith. Mr. Lewis died of a heart attack while driving home in 1954 at the age of 65.

Agents James Beck, Andrew Joiner, Michael Freely, and Frank Giustino received FBI Medals of Valor for their work on dismantling the neo-Nazi organization Amerika First.

Colonel Zvi Yatom returned to Israel, where he was involved in the capture of several Nazi war criminals. In 1960, he was instrumental in the capture of Adolf Eichmann. Eichmann was the key facilitator in managing logistics involved in the mass deportation of Jews to ghettos and extermination camps.

Eichmann stood trial, was found guilty of mass murder, and hung in 1962.

Marlboro parked the fire-engine red Fleetmaster in front of 898 Manning Avenue, Westwood.

He was holding a large bouquet of roses when he rang the doorbell. Sarah opened the door, looking surprised at the bouquet, and said, "Please, won't you come in?"

Her Aunt Zibiah was sitting in the living room when Marlboro walked over to her and handed her the bouquet.

"These are for you."

She looked at him with a smile and said, "*A groysn eyshr khkh.*"

He looked at Sarah and said, "I take that to be thank you."

"Very good," Sarah said.

"I'm afraid I have some bad news."

"Please have a seat," Sarah said, gesturing to a chair.

He sat opposite her and her aunt on the sofa.

"What is it?" She asked.

"Well, as you know, I was working with the FBI, and when the opportunity came to capture or kill him, he eluded us. I know it's no consolation to your aunt, but we captured several members of the neo-Nazi hate group, Amerika First. Putting it out of business. I can't tell you how sorry I am."

Sarah looked down, turned to her aunt, and said, "*Zey gegrvut, ober Heim slipt avek.*"

Her aunt sighed deeply and started to weep, leaning into her niece.

"I told her that you tried, but…."

"I know. Here," Marlboro held out an envelope to Sarah.

"What is that?"

"It's my fee. I failed. I can't accept this."

"No. You earned it."

Marlboro gently dropped the envelope on the coffee table, stood up, and said, "*Gat zal eykh bentshn.*"

Sarah smiled, "God bless you, too."

Marlboro pulled the Fleetmaster into the driveway of 4188 Farragut Drive. It was seven o'clock in the evening; the sun was still high in the sky.

He knocked on the door and waited. The peephole popped open, and he saw a bright green eye staring back at him.

"Hey, doll, open the door," Marlboro requested.

The peephole slammed shut. He could hear the muffled sounds of activity and the unlocking of the door. He waited for the door to open. Nothing.

He tried the doorknob, and it turned.

Marlboro slowly opened the door. There was no one there that he could see. He stepped inside, closed the door behind him, and hollered, "Saoirse. Saoirse."

He ambled down the hallway until he got to the bedroom. Marlboro found her lying in bed under the covers, just her head with that mane of brilliant red hair sticking out.

"I thought you were going to make me dinner?" Marlboro asked with a bit of cheek.

"And just what do you think you might be wanting, Mr. Marlboro?"

Marlboro grinned a wolfish grin and said, "A Sheepherders Special."

"And what might a Sheepherder's Special be?"

He walked over to the bed, pulled down the covers, revealing that she was naked, and said, "A piece of ewe."

The End

Only the Good Die Young

On June 8th, 1946, at approximately 5 a.m., the nude body of twenty-four-year-old actress Diana Dawson was found on the Los Angeles River culvert under the 4th Street Bridge Arts District of Downtown LA. A motorist fixing a flat tire on the bridge noticed something unusual and alerted the policeman, who stopped to assist him.

The police determined that Dawson had been beaten, raped, and shot. The medical examiner found that she had lacerations and bruises on her wrists and ankles, indicating that she had been tied up and possibly tortured before someone put a bullet in her head.

The ME estimated that her body had been dumped into the river somewhere up north. It was probably near Chinatown due to the approximate time of death, the location where the body was found, and the rate of the river's current.

Unfortunately, by the fall of 1947, the police had exhausted all their leads, and the case had grown cold. It wasn't due to the fact that they didn't have an abundance of suspects; they did. But they found that when going up against the Hollywood establishment, they were going up against a wall of silence. People were afraid to talk; careers were made or crushed by a nod of the head or the utterance of a single word, "Communist."

Diana Dawson's case was soon forgotten, with over 300 murders per annum in Los Angeles. The Los Angeles Times quoted police Chief William H. Parker, "It's just a question of manpower; we just don't have enough police at this time. However, no case is ever closed."

John Marlboro has been a private investigator for six years, ever since he left the LAPD after ten years on the force under dubious circumstances. The official story is that he resigned after he and a superior officer disagreed over the handling of a suspect's treatment while in custody. Rumors were that an overzealous lieutenant used a phonebook to beat a confession from a black robbery suspect, and Marlboro ended the interrogation with an uppercut to the lieutenant's jaw.

Marlboro fits the stereotypical image portrayed by Raymond Chandler and Dashiell Hammett of the ideal hard-boiled shamus. He's ruggedly handsome, tough, wisecracking, and hard-drinking. Yet, he's morally upright, contemplative, somewhat philosophical, and blessed with a photographic memory. While he's not afraid to risk physical harm, he's not vengeful.

He owns three suits, two gray pin-stripes, and one navy blue, all strategically and slightly too big for him. So, when he's packing a gat, it's not noticeable. He wears the traditional private detective's grey fedora, black wingtips, and brown tortoise sunglasses. Depending on the client and the case, he'll either smoke a Parker Super Bruyere pipe or Lucky Strike cigarettes. He's very conscious of the image that both telegraphs; the pipe says sophisticated, thoughtful, and educated, while the Lucky's communicate no-nonsense, coarse, and street savvy.

John Marlboro felt comfortable working on either side of the street.

The Moniker on the door read John Marlboro, Private Investigator, painted in gold letters of his small one-room office in the Brockman Building, 700 South Grand Avenue in downtown Los Angeles.

The Brockman Building is a twelve-story Beaux-Arts building noted for its early use of multi-colored terra cotta, as well as its pioneering role in establishing West Seventh Street as downtown Los Angeles' premier shopping destination. Designed by Barnett, Haynes, and Barnett, the building features elaborate terra cotta detailing and a copper cornice –

the only one in the city at the time of its construction in 1917.

Marlboro hadn't had a case in weeks, and he'd barely been in the office, spending most of his days at Santa Anita betting on the bangtails. He decided to stop by the office to pick up the mail if there was any. As he entered the office, the phone rang.

"Hello, this is Marlboro."

"Mr. Marlboro, I'd like to make an appointment to stop by and see you today if possible."

"One moment while I check my schedule," Marlboro said as he held the receiver over some papers; he was rustling as if he was checking his calendar.

"Today would be fine, any time after two o'clock. And to whom am I speaking with?"

"My name is Charles Dawson."

"Very good, Mr. Dawson. I look forward to seeing you at two."

"See you then. Goodbye."

"Goodbye."

Marlboro hung up the phone and walked the two blocks to the L. A. Central Library to see what he could find out about Mr. Charles Dawson.

It didn't take Marlboro long to discover that Charles Dawson was the owner of one of California's largest dairy farms, The Dawson Brothers Dairy. Located in San Jacinto, with over 1,200 head of cattle on more than 900 acres, family-owned and managed. Dawson Brothers Dairy has been in continuous operation in Southern California since 1910. Today, with his younger brothers Raymond and David, Charles continues to run the family business as a third-generation herdsman.

He also discovered that Charles Dawson is the father of murder victim Diana Dawson, whose killer the police have yet to find.

After spending the morning sifting through Library files and records on Charles Dawson, he went through newspaper clippings, magazine articles, and public records looking for anything about the Diana Dawson murder.

On the way back to his office, Marlboro stopped for a quick lunch at the Original Pantry Café, one of Los Angeles' oldest restaurants.

"Hey, Johnny, how's it going?" Anne Hoppe, the counter waitress, asked as Marlboro sat down at the counter.

"Everything's Jake."

"Whad'ya have?"

"I'll have a burger with the works and coffee."

Anne turned to the cook and shouted, "Burn one, take it through the garden, and pin a rose on it. And gimme one cup of joe."

A faceless voice from behind the wait station hollered, "Coming!"

As Anne placed a knife, fork, and paper napkin on the counter, Marlboro took a slow 360 spin on the counter stool to check out the clientele. Occasionally, he'd spied some upper-crust, blue blood slumming with John Q. Public. At this hour, most of the people in the joint were on their lunch break, a bunch of working stiffs, nobody of interest.

Anne leaned one elbow on the counter while she waited for the order and slyly asked, "So, Johnny, working anything juicy?"

"Nothing at the moment, Anne, but if I do, you'll be the first to know."

"You know, Johnny, I'm a bit of a peeper myself."

"No, kidding?"

"Oh yeah, I always solve the crimes on Dragnet before Detective Friday does."

"Well, Anne, next time I'm stumped on a case, I just might call you in for a consultation."

"I'd love to work closely with you, Johnny."

"Say, Anne, I think I see my burger."

"Huh? Oh yeah. Be right back."

As Anne set the burger and coffee down, she said, "Hello, Detective Hanson."

Marlboro glanced to his right just in time to see his ex-partner, Detective Jason Hanson, as he grabbed the stool next to him.

"John," Hanson said.

"Jas, been a long time."

"That it has. How're you doing, staying busy?"

"Busy enough, you?"

"Oh, I can't complain."

"Well, you can, but nobody would give a damn."

"True. Say, doll, can I get the tuna sandwich with onion and a coffee with cream and sugar?"

"Yo, cookie, gimme one radio sandwich, make it cry, and one hot blonde in sand."

"Coming up!" The anonymous hash slinger bellowed.

"But, seriously, John, how are you doing?" Hanson asked.

"I'm healthy at the moment. In fact, I have a client coming over at two," Marlboro said as he glanced at his watch.

"Speaking of, I got to get a move on."

"Well, it was good seeing you again, Johnny."

"You too, Jason. You take it easy."

"Later."

As he was leaving, Anne shouted, "Call me if you need me, Johnny boy."

Charles Dawson was patiently waiting outside Marlboro's office, smoking a cigar. Dawson was short and dumpy. He looked to be as tall as he was round. He was sporting a baggy, wrinkled, navy blue pinstriped suit with a matching fedora.

Just by looking at the man, Marlboro surmised that the death of his daughter had hit him rather hard. It was evident that he had given up on life, including his appearance.

Dawson was unshaven, unkempt, stooped, shouldered, and he shuffled as he walked. Still, Dawson did have one point of vanity: his hair. He combed what few strands were left on his head from the left side over to the right.

"Mr. Dawson, I'm sorry to have kept you waiting. I was visiting another client. Please come in," Marlboro said as he unlocked the office door.

"Thank you."

"Please have a seat."

Marlboro hung his hat on the hat rack and walked to his desk, "Can I get you something to drink? Coffee or maybe something stronger?"

"No. No, thank you."

"Now then, Mr. Dawson, what can I do for you?" He asked as he sat behind his desk.

"It's my daughter Diana. She was murdered last June, and the police have yet to come up with anything. I'm sure you've heard about it. It was in all the papers. All I get from the police is the runaround. I got to know who killed my baby!"

"Why me, Mr. Dawson?"

"I hear you're a guy who can get the job done, whatever it takes. I want the bastard who did this caught. And I don't care what it costs. Will you do it?"

"Now, I can't promise anything, Mr. Dawson, but I'll see what I can find out. I'll nose around. I do have some sources that the police don't."

"When can you start?"

"Right away. Do you have access to your daughter's belongings?'

"Yes, they're out at the farm."

"Can I come by tomorrow and go through them?"

"Anything you need. I'll be there all day, so drive on out. It's the Dawson Brothers Dairy. We're out in San Jacinto."

"Mr. Dawson, so know, I get twenty-five dollars a day and expenses."

"As I said, I don't care what it costs," Dawson said as he reached inside his coat pocket, took five one hundred dollar bills, and laid them on the desk.

He stood up and shook Marlboro's hand, "I'll see you sometime tomorrow, Mr. Marlboro."

"Till tomorrow, Mr. Dawson."

"Detective Hanson, speaking."

"Jason, Marlboro, here, got a minute?"

"Sure, whaddya need?"

"I just met with Diana Dawson's father. He hired me to investigate his daughter's murder. Apparently, he's not all that thrilled with the job the LAPD is doing. So, Jason, think I could take a peek at the Dawson file?"

"Whoa, you're tooting the wrong ringer, Johnny boy."

"Jason, come on, man, we used to drink out of the same bottle. Just gimme twenty minutes."

"Fifteen."

"Twenty."

Hey, do you want to see it or not? Fifteen."

"Okay, fifteen. Where?"

"Central Library in half an hour. In the northwest stacks."

"See ya there."

Marlboro was always impressed when he entered the library and walked under the rotunda adorned with David Cornwell's magnificent murals depicting the history of California. He was by no means a connoisseur of art, but some art speaks to the everyman.

He made his way to the northwest stacks, where he found his ex-partner sitting at a table reading the Los Angeles Times.

"What's the rumble? Anything interesting going on in the world?" Marlboro asked.

"Well, Some guy named Chuck Yeager broke the sound barrier, an earthquake in Chile killed 233, there's a camera that gives you a photo in 60 seconds, and the Brooklyn Dodgers will be playing the Yankees in the World Series. So no, nothing interesting is going on in the world."

"Thanks, you just saved me fifty cents," Marlboro said as he sat across from Hanson.

As Detective Hanson slid a manila folder across the table to Marlboro, he said, "You got fifteen minutes."

Marlboro opened the file and quickly scanned the contents: the crime scene photographs, the police report, the coroner's records, and the crime lab findings.

"Pretty skimpy; no wonder you guys haven't solved it."

"Uh, huh, and you think you can do better?"

"Well, one thing's for certain."

"Yeah, what's that?"

"Can't do any worse. Hey, thanks, Jas; I owe ya. I'd better blow," Marlboro said as he left to go back to his office.

The first thing he did when he got back to the office was to write down the names of potential suspects that he had gleaned from the police files. Marlboro had recognized some of the characters and some he didn't.

There were some powerful men of the Hollywood elite, big shots, moguls, and industry leaders. The type of men who have dark secrets and have the gunsels to keep them dark. Gorillas who will beat your teeth out and then kick you in the gut for mumbling.

He made a list of where and who to see first after meeting with the Brothers Dawson tomorrow morning out on the farm.

Marlboro got an early start traveling east out of L.A.; traffic was a breeze at that time in the morning. Everyone was heading west into L.A. to go to work.

Cruising along I-10 in his fire engine red 1946 Chevrolet Fleetmaster Convertible listening to Muddy Waters singing 'Hoochie Coochie Man' on KFWB, Marlboro thought to himself, life is good.

Past the City of Industry, Rancho Cucamonga, Chino, down through Riverside, across the Moreno Valley, skirting along the Mt. San Jacinto State Park, and finally to the farming community of San Jacinto.

Marlboro had little difficulty finding The Dawson Brothers Dairy. It was right off Highway 79 on Record Road. Although he smelled it before he saw it, there's nothing like the smell of the urine and dung of 1,200 cows wafting all around you, traveling at 60 miles per hour with the top down. It was eye-watering. Definitely not for the faint of heart.

Marlboro drove down a dirt road past hundreds of Brown Swiss and Guernsey cattle grazing in fields on either side of the road. At the end of the drive stood the entrance of The Dawson Brothers Dairy; it wasn't what Marlboro had expected.

His preconceived notion of a dairy farm was a large red barn with cows in individual stalls side by side hooked up to a milking machine, all very small-time, homey, mom-and-pop farm. What he discovered was an ultra-modern, sophisticated dairy business, or better put, a dairy factory.

There was the pasteurizer, chaff cutter, calves pen for male and female, dry cow pen, pens for suckling calves, multiple milk receiving rooms, a veterinary dispensary, miscellaneous sheds for milking utensils, agricultural implements, and dairy stores, so much for mom-and-pop farming.

After the grand tour, Charles Dawson invited Marlboro into the house to meet his wife, Margaret, and give the private eye any and all the information about their daughter Diana that might help him solve her murder.

"Mr. Marlboro, this is my wife, Margaret."

"It's a pleasure to meet you, Mrs. Dawson. I'm just sorry it has to be under these circumstances."

"Thank you, Mr. Marlboro. Won't you please have a seat?"

The interior of the farmhouse was warm and cozy. In the living room, there were wooden floors with a large graphic area rug and an overstuffed sofa that almost swallowed Marlboro up when he plopped down on it. The couch faced a stone fireplace with a large oak mantle. On either side of the sofa were two wooden rocking chairs and an Admiral television and radio set combo off in the corner.

"Can I get you some coffee, Mr. Marlboro?" Mrs. Dawson asked.

"Thank you, no. I hope my asking you questions about your daughter won't be too painful. But the more I know, the better."

"Ask us anything you want," Charles Dawson said.

"Tell me about Diana."

"Diana was a sweet, charming young woman. She had a smile that would light up a room when she entered. Our baby was smart and funny, if anything, maybe too trusting of people. She was a good girl, Mr. Marlboro," Mrs. Dawson said as she began to cry.

"I guess it's true what they say, only the good die young," Marlboro said as if to ease her pain.

Mr. Dawson put his arm around his grief-stricken wife.

"How did Diana seem the weeks and days before she was killed? Was there anything bothering her?" Marlboro asked.

"As I remember, she seemed fine, didn't act as if she was troubled about anything, did she to you?" Mr. Dawson looked at his wife for confirmation.

"I didn't notice anything out of the ordinary," Mrs. Dawson agreed.

"Was your daughter seeing anyone?"

"Not that I knew of, Margaret, was she?"

"Well, I don't believe that she was seeing anyone in particular. She did go out on dates occasionally. But I do believe that she was interested in this one fella."

"And do you happen to know his name?" Marlboro asked.

"Nathan Fleckenstein. I think. That's his real name. He's an actor. His stage name is Johnathan Silvers."

"Johnathan Silvers. Did you tell the police about him, Mrs. Dawson?"

"Yes, I believe I did."

"Interesting. I glanced at the police file yesterday, and didn't come across his name, but I may have missed it. I'll recheck it. Can you tell me any girlfriends she may have hung out with?"

"Well, she had two roommates, Skylar Darrow and Robin Summers. Both were very nice girls, weren't they, Charles? We met them a couple of times. They even came out here once for a long weekend. They're successful actresses, too, Mr. Marlboro," Mrs. Dawson explained.

"I'll have to take your word on that, Mrs. Dawson. I'm not much of a moviegoer. To that, how was her career going? Was Diana in many films?"

"Oh, yes. Diana had been in several feature films. In the first couple of films, she was just an extra, but in the last two, Diana had speaking roles and even got screen credit," Mrs. Dawson said proudly.

"Really? What were the names of them?"

"The first speaking role was in the sci-fi film Frankenstein and the Monsters from Outer Space. She was one of the girls who were captured by the space monsters. And her latest, I mean, her last film was called Maximum Overkill. It's a story of a group of young women who went camping in the woods. They were being stalked and killed by an escaped mental patient. Diana was one of the last to die. The movie got panned, but she had gotten good reviews.

Diana said that the head of the studio, Marvin Holmberg, told her that he would see her star in his next film, The Buttercup Decapitator."

"And Marvin Holmberg is the head of which studio?" Marlboro said as he wrote all this down in his small black wire-bound notepad.

"Miracle Studios."

"Who was her agent?"

"Lewis Barrymore of CAM, Creative Arts Management. He's an older man; I'd say he's in his late fifties, a nice man. Don't you think so, Charles?"

"Yes, he did seem nice. He signed Diana when she was just eighteen. He said that she was very talented."

Marlboro finished up taking notes. He closed his notepad and asked, "May I see Diana's room now, if you don't mind."

"Charles, would you mind showing Mr. Marlboro Diana's room? I'm still not ready to go in there," Mrs. Dawson said, teary-eyed.

Mr. Dawson led Marlboro down the hallway to a room where the door was closed. He opened the door and said, "This is Diana's room. We haven't touched it since that day. All her possessions from her apartment are still in boxes, and we still can't bring ourselves to go through them."

"I understand," Marlboro said sympathetically.

"Well, I'll just close the door so you can get on with it. Take your time," Dawson said as he left the room, closing the door behind him.

Aside from all her possessions from when she lived at home before going off to make it big in Hollywood, there were several boxes from her Los Angeles apartment that the police had apparently gone through and released back to her parents.

It was always eerie going through other people's personal belongings. Seeing the things that hold special meaning to them, but to others, they're worthless. Diana's trinkets, doodads, novelties, mementos, and whatnot all had special memories.

Marlboro's job is to find the meaning behind them and interpret them to find any clues that may lead him to her killer or killers.

The ride out to the Dawson's farm proved to be useful. He came across Diana's diary and datebook in the boxes the police had gone through in her apartment. Marlboro was surprised they hadn't kept them; it was either sloppy police work or a surprising lack of interest in solving her murder.

By the time he returned to L.A., it was after seven in the evening. He stopped off at his office to see if there were any messages. He called his service and was told there were three calls, two from his ex-partner Detective Hanson and one from Marvin Holmberg, the big wheel at Miracle Studios.

He called Hanson.

"Jason, Marlboro here; what's the word?"

"Can't talk right now. I'll have to call you back."

"Okay,"

CLICK

He contemplated calling Holmberg when the phone rang. It was Hanson.

"Marlboro, It's Jason. Sorry I couldn't talk before, but I'm feeling a bit hinky since the word got out that you were on the Dawson case."

"Whad'ya mean, you think that someone's tapping your phone?"

"Yeah, after I came back from the library with the Dawson file, I got the feeling I'm being watched. I think someone is afraid you will to be stepping on some people's toes. So, you better watch your back."

"Whose toes should I be watching out for, so's not to step on?"

"I really can't say."

"Well, are we talking high society or politics?"

"Just take it easy, man; I wouldn't want you getting behind the eight ball. You understand?"

"You know, talking to you is exhausting. I'm going to blow."

"Just remember what I said."

Marlboro decided he'd call Holmberg in the morning. He was hungry and tired from the long drive, and talking in circles with Hanson gave him a headache. He figured he could use a drink and some female companionship.

He rang up one of his steady girlfriends, Sergeant Molly Isle, a fifteen-year veteran with the Los Angeles police department.

"Hello, doll. It's Marlboro. Can I interest you in a little dinner and a nightcap? Yeah? Swell, why don't you slip into some glad rags, and I'll swing by in a few."

Molly lived in the Los Angeles suburb of Rampart Village at 435 South Lafayette Park Place, apartment 3F.

When the red Fleetmaster pulled up to the front of the La Fayette Park Place apartments, Molly was coming out the front entrance dressed to the nines.

"Hey, doll, you didn't have to come out. I was planning to come to your door."

"That's okay, Johnny. Where are we headed?" She said as she got into the Fleetmaster.

"I figured we'd go grab a bite."

"Not at some hash house."

"Naw, doll, not when you're looking like a million bucks. I was thinking of us cruising over to

Tom Breneman's for some dinner and dancing. Whad'ya think?"

"Sounds swell," She purred as she slid over to sit on the bench seat next to him.

Tom Breneman's was on Vine just north of Sunset. It wasn't the swankiest joint in Hollywood, still, they got their fair share of the glitterati, movie stars like Rock Hudson, Doris Day, Randolph Scott, and on occasion, members of the Rat Pack, Joey Bishop, Dean Martin, and the Chairman of the Board himself, Frank Sinatra.

The inside was all decked out in a Polynesian motif with lots of palm fronds, tiki torches, and palm trees. The joint was jamming. Marlboro asked for a table in the back so they could keep an eye on the goings-on.

"Can I get you and the lady something to drink?" The waiter asked.

Marlboro ordered. "The lady will have a Pink Squirrel and make mine a Bullshot."

"Excellent, sir. I'll come back for your dinner order."

As they were waiting for their drinks, Marlboro noticed an old adversary.

"Oh, great, Lieutenant Foster."

"Jeffery Foster? Isn't he the one you gave the going-over for sapping a suspect with a phone book?"

"Yeah, that's the mug that put the kibosh on my career. Why I oughta…" Marlboro said as he started to get up from his chair.

"Relax, Johnny. He ain't worth the trouble. Besides, here comes our drinks," Molly said, trying to calm Marlboro down.

"You're right, doll. That creep ain't worth it."

The waiter set their drinks down and asked, "Are you folks ready to order? Ma'am?"

"Yes, I think I'll have the veal."

"Yes, ma'am, and for you, sir?"

"I'll have the T-bone steak raw."

"Very good. I'll get those right in."

"So, Johnny, What are you working on?"

"The Diana Dawson murder. Her parents want me to see what I can dig up since you guys got bupkis."

"Well, the scuttlebutt around the station is that the case went flat when some big muckety-muck pulled some strings downtown to stall the investigation."

"Any idea who's or why they're trying to quash it?"

"No, all I know is that some high pillow wants it buried."

The waiter brought their dinner and asked, "Is there anything that I might get you?"

"No, I think we're Jake. Thank you," Marlboro said to the waiter. He turned to Molly, holding up his drink, and said, "Well, enough shop talk for one night. Here's to you, doll."

"Mr. Holmberg will see you now, Mr. Marlboro," Holmberg's secretary announced. The doll was a real looker with long flowing red Rita Hayworth hair as she wore in "Angels Over Broadway." Her eyes were bright aqua green and a set of gams that went from here to there and back again.

Marlboro got off the couch in the waiting room; as he did, he flung down the Hollywood Magazine he'd been looking at onto a large stack of current movie magazines: Screenland, Movie Life, Silver Screen, and Photoplay. He had been reading all about how Charles Boyer claims that love begins at forty.

As he was making his way to Holmberg's office door, the secretary smiled and asked, "Is it true?"

"What?"

"That love begins at forty."

"I wouldn't know, doll; I've got a couple more years to go. But I'll let you know."

"You do that, Mr. Marlboro," She said with a sexy smile.

"It's Johnny to you, doll. Say, what's your name?"

"Misty. Misty Thompson."

"Well, Misty, whaddya say we go out and grab a bite sometime?"

"You in the business?"

"Me? No, I'm a shamus."

"Oh, a private dick, huh?"

"That's right. Is that against your religion?"

"Oh, yes," She said, laughing. "But for you, I just might convert."

Their flirting was interrupted by a gruff voice over the intercom. "Miss Thompson, is Mr. Marlboro coming in or not? I don't have all day. Thank you."

"Yes, sir, he's on his way in now," She said, grinning.

"Sorry, doll, I'll make it up to you."

"Mmm. You better."

Marlboro entered the movie mogul's office. Holmberg's office was as big as most people's homes. He sat at the very end, behind an exaggerated, oversized desk raised at least two feet higher than the chairs opposite him. So, the occupant would have to look up at him as if Holmberg were a king sitting on his throne.

Behind the desk was the Miracle Studio's logo with its tagline; "If It's Good, It's a Miracle."

"Mr. Marlboro, please have a seat," He said, gesturing to one of the chairs at the foot of his desk.

Marlboro did as he was requested.

"Mr. Dawson called me yesterday and asked that I help you in any way that I can. So, Mr. Marlboro, how can I help you in your investigation of dear Diana's death?"

"I appreciate that. I know that you're a busy man, Mr. Holmberg."

"Well, I will do anything I can to help you find Diana's killer."

"First, let me say that some of these questions might seem a little forward, but I need you to be square with me. I'm not here to pass judgment. Like you, I only want to find out who murdered Diana, okay?"

"Of course."

"How long had you known Diana?"

"About six years."

"You signed her when she was eighteen, is that right?"

"Yes."

"How did you discover her?"

"She was brought to my attention by Lewis Barrymore, Diana's agent. He's the agent for several of our stable of actors. He's kind of like a scouting agent for a baseball team when he spots someone that Lewis thinks has talent; he has my authority to sign them."

"And you believe that she had the makings of a star?"

"Well, Mr. Marlboro, I don't know how much you know about the movie industry or Miracle Studios, but we aren't a giant studio like MGM, Paramount, or Universal. So, our stars aren't on the scale of people like Katharine Hepburn or Ingrid Bergman. You understand."

"Sure. Do you know if Diana was seeing anyone in particular?"

"I understand that she was keeping company with one of our male stars, Johnathan Silvers."

"Was this arrangement of dating something the studio initiated?"

"Yes, we encouraged it. It's good publicity for our stars and the studio."

"So, do you know if they were serious or just playing a role?"

"I think they started out playing the role, but after a while, it began to become serious."

"Do you know of anyone who might have wanted to harm Diana?"

"I can't think of anyone who would have wanted to hurt her. Everyone truly liked Diana."

"Well, thank you, Mr. Holmberg. I appreciate you taking time out from your busy schedule to meet with me," Marlboro said as he made his way to the door.

He stopped halfway and turned around, "Oh, one more question if you don't mind?"

"No, of course. What is it?"

"Did you ever have sexual relations with Diana?"

Holmberg sat silent, getting angry before answering, "Good day, Mr. Marlboro!"

When Marlboro got to the other side of the door, Misty was busy typing a letter.

"How'd it go?" She asked.

Before he could answer, the intercom squawked, "Mrs. Thompson, would you please come here?"

"Coming," She said.

As she passed by Marlboro, she handed him a slip of paper, "Call me," She whispered, smiling.

"Count on it, doll."

Marlboro found Nathan Fleckenstein, better known as Johnathan Silvers, to his adoring fans, sitting, sunning himself poolside in front of cabana number nine at the Beverly Hills Hotel.

Johnathan Silvers, 32 years old, black hair, lean built, clean-shaven, and had that Jimmy Stewart look about him. He was sporting round tortoiseshell sunglasses with dark green lenses.

"Johnathan Silvers?"

"Depends; who wants to know?"

"Marlboro, John Marlboro, I'm a private detective working on the Diana Dawson murder. Got a minute?"

"Sure, have a seat, shamus."

Marlboro sat on the lounge chair next to Silvers, who hadn't moved or even turned his head.

"You got a ticket?" Silvers asked.

Marlboro opened his wallet and flashed his P.I. License.

"So, you know the lingo, kid."

"Yeah, I had a bit part in Double Indemnity with Fred MacMurray."

"Okay."

"What can I do ya for?"

"I understand you and Diana were an item. True?"

"Well, we did go out from time to time, but the studio's publicity department mostly set up. You know, for the fan magazines."

"So, that's all it was? Just for show?"

"Hey, don't get me wrong, she was a sweet kid, and we had a few laughs, but she really wasn't my type."

"Do you know of anyone who might have wanted to harm her?"

"No."

"Was everything good at the studio? No problems there?"

"What? You think someone at the studio had it in for her?"

"You tell me?"

"None that I know of. But there was a rumor floating around that Diana might have been hitting the pipe. Mind you. It was just a rumor. I never saw any evidence that that was true."

"Opium?"

"As I said, it was just a rumor."

"Yeah, but I find that there's usually a hint of truth in every rumor. Any idea if it was true, who she might associate with who'd have connections?"

"No, not really; like I said, we only dated for show. You might ask Diana's roommates, Skylar Darrow and Robin Summers."

"You tell the cops any of this?"

"No, because at the time of her death, I hadn't heard anything about it."

"Here's my card; if you happen to think of anything else, give me a ring."

Marlboro noticed a young, well-built Hispanic cabana boy making his way to Silvers' cabana, carrying some towels and massaging oils out of the corner of his eye.

"Cuse me, mester Silvers: it's time for your massage."

"Ah, thank you, Ramón, I'll be right there. Is there anything else?"

"No, I guess that's all. Say, nice cheaters, where did ya pick them up at?" Marlboro said as he stood up.

"These. Oh, these are from the studio prop department. Here you want them?" Silvers said as he took the sunglasses off and offered them to Marlboro.

"Aw, I couldn't."

"Here, take them. I insist. I can get more. Here."

"You sure?"

"Take them."

"Thanks."

As Marlboro was leaving, he asked, "Say, do you think Diana was having an affair with Holmberg?"

"Holmberg? She could have; he does have a reputation for being a letch. I know for a fact that he uses his casting couch to make or break careers."

"Including yours?"

"Including mine," Silvers said stoically as he went into the cabana, closing the flap behind him.

Skylar Darrow and Robin Summers, Diana Dawson's roommates, lived at 1137 N Genesee Avenue in West Hollywood. The small adobe-style house was made of stucco with a red-tiled roof—very Hollywood. There was a small front porch with two white wrought iron chairs with pink and white stripe cushions and a small teak coffee table.

Marlboro found Skylar sitting on the front porch drinking a beer, reading the latest copy of Silver Screen, and listening to KFI on her RCA Victor portable radio.

"If you're selling, I'm not buying."

"Are you, Miss. Darrow or Miss. Summers?"

"You a cop?"

"No, I'm John Marlboro. I'm a private dick on a case. The murder of Diana Dawson."

"Have a seat. I'm Skylar Darrow."

Marlboro sat down next to the young starlet.

"Would you like a beer?" She said as she drew a cold one out of a tin pail full of ice and bottles of London Tavern Ale.

"Thanks, don't mind if I do."

"Say, I really like those cheaters."

"Thank you, Miss. Darrow."

"Skylar, call me Skylar," She said, smiling in a low, sexy voice.

"Okay. Thank you, Skylar," Marlboro replied with a devilish grin.

Marlboro grabbed the church key and popped the cap off the ice-cold bottle of beer. He held it to his forehead for a moment and then took a long drink, "Aaaah. Nothing like a nice cold brew on a hot summer's day."

"You got that right, Shamus."

He took another swig and began the interrogation.

"So, Skylar, what can you tell me about Diana?"

"Whad'ya want to know?"

"Did she ever confide in you or Robin?"

"Well, we were pretty much just roommates. We were friends, but not girlfriends. Competitors, you know, sometimes for the same roles."

"Was she liked?"

"Overall, people liked her, I guess. There were some people who thought that she got where she did a little too easily. Duck soup if you know what I mean?"

"Are you saying that she skated around?

"It's not nice to speak ill of the dead, but let's just say Diana didn't get leading roles on her acting talents."

"Not a great actress?"

"Well, not on the screen, anyway. Have you ever seen any of her films?"

"Can't say that I have."

"Diana Dawson was no Lana Turner, more like Carole Landis."

"Carole Landis, I know that name?"

"During the war, she made a decent living as a pin-up girl. After the war, Carole was a bit player at Warner Brothers. She started to have an affair with the producer Darryl Zanuck. All of a sudden, she was getting bigger and better roles until she ended her affair with Zanuck. He then made sure she was blackballed."

"So, was Diana sleeping with Marvin Holmberg?"

"Like I said, Diana was no Lana Turner."

"Do you think Holmberg could have had her bumped off?"

"You tell me, you're the gumshoe."

"Do you know if Diana did drugs?"

"Since you ain't a copper, yeah, we used to do a little bit of reefer. Diana would score some from a grip at the studio."

"Grip?"

"Yeah, grip. They work with both the camera and lighting crews."

"Would you happen to know his name?"

"I think it was Chinese. Something like Wang, or Chang, Wong, or Fong. Something. Robin might know."

"What about opium? Did you ever hear that she was doing opium?"

"Funny that you should mention it; maybe that's why, towards the end, just before she was killed,

Diana lost a bunch of weight, and she was always happy-go-lucky but always drowsy."

"Yeah, it could have been Chinese Molasses. If she had been using and got hooked, Diana could have gotten into a jam with the Chinese. That junk ain't cheap, and they've known to blow one down if you get behind the eight-ball with them."

"I'll ask Robin about the Chinese grip when she gets back."

"Well, what can you tell me about Johnathan Silvers? He and Diana were supposed to be an item."

"Fleckenstein? He's a poof. They always team him up with women to keep his image as a leading man, just like they do with Rock Hudson."

"Rock Hudson!"

"You didn't know? Old Rock is as bent as a butcher's hook."

"No, I didn't. That's disappointing. By the way, how's your career going?"

"Oh, you know, strikes and gutters, ups and downs. I'm getting small bit parts, but I'm keeping busy. I'm signed to be in a feature for MGM, The Mighty McGurk. A Wallace Beery boxing flick, it's not going to be any boffo box office."

"At least you're working. I hear the film business is a hard slog. What was your biggest role so far?"

"Last year, I was in a screwball comedy called The Cockeyed Miracle. I played opposite Keenan

Wynn. I was mostly background scenery, but I did have one line."

"Yeah. What did you say?"

"Well, Keenan plays the ghost who comes back to help his son. I play Keenan's son's secretary, Gloria, who sees the ghost and says, "Holy moly, did you see that!""

"Very convincing. Hope you got screen credit?"

"Sure did."

"Well, I appreciate your talking to me. Guess I better hit the bricks."

"What's the rush, peeper? You just got here. Besides, the case can wait; I mean, Diana's been dead for over a year. Can I offer you another oat soda?"

"Yeah, sure. Boy, the beer isn't the only thing that's cold." Marlboro observed.

"Hey, it's a cold, cruel world, am I right? What did I hurt your feelings?"

"Listen, sister. I don't mean nothing by it. Maybe you're the sensitive one."

"What do you get out of all of this?"

"Me? I'm just a guy paid to do other people's laundry."

"Well, shamus, I got some laundry needs doing."

The starlet handed Marlboro a beer as she stood up and went into the bungalow, leaving the front door wide open. He could see her taking her blouse off as she walked down the hall. She wasn't wearing a bra.

When she got to her bedroom, she stopped, turned towards him, unzipped her shorts, let them fall to the floor, slid down her panties, and entered her room.

Benjamin "Bugsy" Siegel is known as one of the most "infamous and feared gangsters of his day." Newspapers described him as handsome and charismatic. He became one of the first front-page celebrity gangsters.

When he moved from New York to Hollywood, Siegel made millions by infiltrating the movie unions and extorting studios and production companies. However, the main reason that he came to California was to organize a horse racing wire service on the West Coast for the National Syndicate.

Early in 1943, Bugsy started introducing himself to the Hollywood elite and movie moguls. Informing them that from then on, they would be in need of protection from certain un-named villains that were out to sabotage their films, destroy their movie sets, and do bodily harm, not only to their actors but to themselves.

Of course, some of the bigger studios tried to resist and soon found out that there were, in fact, ne're-do-wells who sabotaged their films, destroyed their movie sets, and did bodily harm to their actors and themselves. Eventually, every movie studio was under the watchful eye of Bugsy Siegel's security services.

Bugsy didn't bother going to the small studios himself. He sent a couple of his torpedoes, the Costello brothers, Luigi and Anthony, *aka* Fat Tony.

A couple of button men who liked nothing better than to give these rich old geezers a proper working over, a few punches to the gut, and force-feeding them a couple of knuckle sandwiches until they came around to their way of thinking.

One summer evening, Marvin Holmberg pulled his brand new Cadillac Coupe de Ville into the driveway of his Beverly Hills mansion in the company of a lovely young lady, Miss Sheboygan State Fair Queen, just fresh off the bus. Since she was a little girl, her sole dream was to be a movie star, and Marvin was going to give her a personal screen test.

As they got out of the car, they were greeted by two formidable figures, Luigi and Tony "Fat" Costello.

"You, Marvin Holmberg?" Luigi asked.

"I am. What may I do for you, gentlemen?" Marvin said as he looked around for Frank, his personal security guard.

"I see that yous be looking around for that guard of yours. Well, he kinda handed in his resignation after me, and my brother here told him that his services wouldn't be needed no more."

"And why is that?" Marvin asked.

"Cause from now on, you're going to pay 2 G's every week to Mr. Siegel."

"Why would I do that?"

"Cause if'n you don't, my brother Fat Tony will cut off your dick. You capeesh? Now, you wouldn't want that to happen cause this fresh young thing here won't have anything to suck, am I right?"

Fat Tony reached into his pocket, pulled out a ten-inch switchblade knife, snapped it open, and got nose-to-nose with Marvin. Marvin felt the point of the knife blade touch his rapidly shriveling penis and whispered in Marvin's ear, "Capeesh?"

"Capeesh," Marvin uttered.

"Well, nice doing business with you, Marvin. We'll be seeing you next week. Now, yous two go and have a nice time," Luigi said.

Within eighteen months, Bugsy Siegel owned 25% of Miracle Pictures. He could occasionally be seen walking around the studio, movie sets, backlots, and hobnobbing with actors such as George Raft, Jean Harlow, Cary Grant, and Frank Sinatra. His picture was in the Los Angeles Times more than Clark Gable, Rod Taylor, and Edward G. Robinson together.

Marlboro pulled his Fleetmaster into the Brown Derby restaurant parking lot at 3427 Wilshire Boulevard. Originally designed in the actual shape of a derby hat to catch the eye of passing motorists. It had been a popular hang-out for vaudevillians in the 1920s, across the street from the Hollywood night hot spot Coconut Grove. Unlike the Original Pantry Café, the Derby always had the top stars wheeling and dealing, being seen and pretending not to be seen.

It was 11:45 a.m. when he walked in. He was to have a lunch meeting with Diana's agent, Lewis Barrymore.

The hostess approached him as he walked in, "May I help you, sir? Do you have a reservation?"

"I'm here to meet Lewis Barrymore."

"Oh, yes, sir. Mr. Barrymore is expecting you. If you would, please follow me."

The Derby was the kind of place where everyone would stop eating and turn to look to see who had just come in. Once they realize you're a nobody, they return to their eating, drinking, and surveillance. And not necessarily in that order.

Lewis Barrymore was less of an agent for the actors he represented and more of a lackey for the studios. His clients would get jobs other actors wouldn't take because the fees were too low. The studios would kick back a percentage of the money they saved directly to Barrymore. It is a win-win for the studios and Barrymore not so much for the actors.

Marlboro approached Barrymore's table. He was reading the latest issue of Variety, the movie industry insider magazine, on what's going on in the entertainment world. It tells what studios are in production on what films, what actors and actresses are signing for which studios, all business, and very little personal gossip.

"Mr. Barrymore, your guest," The hostess said.

"Thank you, Dottie. Mr. Marlboro, please do sit down."

Marlboro figured Barrymore to be in his late fifties, weighing in at a little over three hundred pounds, wearing a toupee to hide the fact that he's going bald, has a full beard to cover his multiple chins, and he wears expensive hand-made suits that help camouflage his tonnage.

Marlboro sat down across from the big man.

"Thank you for seeing men, Mr. Barrymore. Like I told you on the phone, I'm investigating the murder of Diana Dawson."

"Well, Mr. Marlboro, I will be more than happy to assist you in any way I can. Can I offer you something to eat?"

"That's very kind, yes, thank you."

"I can vouch for just about everything here is fabulous. I'm considering having the Porterhouse Steak, but feel free to have whatever you like."

Marlboro pursued the menu and decided on the Brown Derby Fabulous Super Salad with shrimp.

"A salad? I pictured you as a meat and potatoes man, Mr. Marlboro."

"Well, I've found that when working on a murder case, it's best to eat light, just in case you have to move fast. A heavy meal slows you down, and that could be embarrassing, or worse, you might end up wearing a Chicago overcoat."

"I get ya," Barrymore said with a Cheshire Cat grin.

An elderly waiter dressed in black pants, a white shirt, and a bow tie approached to take their orders.

"Are you gentlemen ready to order?" He asked.

Barrymore took the lead and said, "Yes, I'll have the Porterhouse Steak, rare, with a baked potato and a side of succotash. My friend here will have the Brown Derby Fabulous Super Salad with shrimp."

"Very good, and can I get you anything to drink?"

"I'll have a glass of the Cresta Blanca Red Pinot."

"And for you, sir?"

"I'll have a Bull Shot."

"Thank you, gentlemen. I'll get those orders in right away," The waiter said as he took their menus and headed to the kitchen.

Barrymore asked, "What, pray tell, would you like to know about poor Diana?"

"When did you become her agent?"

"About eight years ago. I saw her doing Shakespeare in community theater."

"Good?"

"I signed her on the spot. I could tell that she had talent."

"What other actors do you represent?"

"Oh, let's see. Bobby Havoc, Earl Storm, Rex Angel, Opel Brown, Helen Coleman, and, of course, the legendary Victoria Reign," He boasted.

"Victoria Reign. She was in that movie, "The Couple in the Grave" with Dirk Spencer."

"That's right. She was nominated for an Oscar. Poor Victoria was robbed. The Academy fixed it, so Joan Fontaine won; it's all politics."

"Did you think Diana Dawson was on the level of Victoria Reign?"

"She would have been a star."

"With films like Frankenstein and the Monsters and Maximum Overkill?"

"Mr. Marlboro, not everyone can step into a starring role in such films as Now, Voyager, Mrs. Miniver, or a Casablanca right out of the box. You have to pay your dues. Diana was starting to get noticed. Those bigger and better roles would have come."

"The Buttercup Decapitator," Marlboro asked.

"Yes. It was another step in climbing the Hollywood ladder. She would have been in the leading female role."

"Isn't it true that most, if not all, of your stable of actors work for Marvin Holmberg of Miracle Pictures?"

"So?"

"So, is that usual?"

"Mr. Marlboro, are you investigating me?"

"No, I'm just trying to get a handle on how the whole Hollywood racket works. That's all."

"I can assure you, Mr. Marlboro, that I am not involved in any racket," Barrymore said, sounding annoyed.

"Mr. Barrymore, you said yourself that Victoria Reign didn't win the Oscar because of politics. That sounds a little bit like a racket to me."

"Oh, I see what you're saying. I guess in that respect, it could be construed as a racket."

"How well did you know Diana, personally?"

"What do you mean?"

"I mean, did you know her friends?"

"Well, she was dating Johnathan Silvers."

"Yeah, but that was really a set up, but the studio for publicity. Diana wasn't involved with him, was she? I mean, from what I hear, he's a bit light in the loafers."

"It's just the Hollywood rumor mill spreading more scandalous gossip."

"So, it's just a bunch of hooey?"

"Nothing but balderdash."

"Do you know if Diana had any enemies?"

"Enemies? Everyone loved Diana."

"Well, not everyone."

"Ah, true, true."

"Was Diana into drugs?"

"Not that I knew of. What kind of drugs?"

"I've heard from reliable sources that she occasionally smoked cannabis. Were you aware of that?"

"Certainly not!"

"Hey, I really don't care. Mr. Barrymore, all I'm interested in is finding out if that might have had anything to do with her death."

"You didn't hear it from me, but once, Diana mentioned that she had to miss an audition because she had to meet some chink or greaser."

"Did she happen to say if it was a grip?"

"Now that you mention it, I recall her saying that."

"Could it happen to be something like Wang, or Chang, Wong, or Fong?"

"Chang, that's it. Chang."

At that moment, the waiter came with their drinks. "A glass of Cresta Blanca Red Pinot and a Bull Shot. Your lunch will be out shortly," He said as he placed the drinks on the table.

"Cheers," Barrymore said as he held up his wine glass.

"Cheers," Marlboro returned the toast.

"Is there anything else?" Barrymore asked.

"Just one more thing. Was Diana having an affair with Marvin Holmberg?"

"You know, Marlboro, you got a lot of moxie."

"I've heard that."

"I don't know if she was or not. You seem to be telling me that Diana was mixed up in some kind of racket. What racket?"

"I don't know. I'm not her agent."

"Marlboro, my sense is that you just go around stirring up the pot to see what boils to the top."

"Or sticks to the bottom."

"Gentlemen, lunch is served," The waiter said as he set their orders in front of them.

Detective Jason Hanson had been Marlboro's partner for five years. They worked out of the Central Division, although they occasionally helped out when needed in both the Rampart and Hollenbeck Divisions.

Their beat went from Chinatown, Little Tokyo, and South Park to the Financial District, Olvera Street, and the Civic Center.

They started as patrolmen in the Juvenile Division until they made detectives. They worked with other detectives in the Narcotics Division and were eventually teamed up when they were transferred to Robbery-Homicide.

Hanson was a couple of years younger than his partner; he was married with two kids. He had a kind face and a gentle disposition, was tall and lanky, had brown hair, and brown eyes, and was always serious, whereas Marlboro was cool and calm under fire but quick to react. Hanson was restrained and reserved, and his response was measured. Together, they made the perfect team. Both respected the other's abilities and judgment.

That afternoon, after lunch with Lewis Barrymore at the Brown Derby, Marlboro found his ex-partner sitting inside his office reading the sports sections of the L.A. Times. He read all about The Brooklyn Dodgers signing the first negro ball player into the majors, some kid named Jackie Robinson.

Inside the Dodger locker room, there was a mutiny brewing until Manager Leo Durocher made a statement to the team, "I don't care if the guy is yellow or black, or if he has stripes like a fucking Zebra. I'm the manager of this team, and I say he plays. What's more, I say he can make us all rich. And if any of you cannot use the money, I will see that you are all traded."

"How did you get in here?" Marlboro queried.

"Are you kidding me? My four-year-old could pick that lock?"

"Would he like a job? I could use the help."

"You couldn't afford him."

"Yeah, you're probably right. So, what brings you down here."

"I understand you're making lots of people nervous. You're not trying to find a Chinese angle on this case, are you?"

"I'm just trying to get to the truth. What, am I starting to get under somebody's skin?"

"Johnny, the people with deep pockets are getting spooked. They don't like being in the hot seat. I suggest you lay off the big-wigs."

"So, are boys upstairs taking some heat?"

"I'll say."

"Hell, Jas, I've only been on the case less than a week. And already, people want to put the kibosh on the investigation. Well, I guess I must be doing something right then."

"So, you're not going to take it easy?"

"No."

"Okay then, watch yourself. I'll try and do what I can, unofficially, of course."

"Of course. I do appreciate it, and tell Sally I send my love."

Marlboro headed over to the Original Pantry Café for some dinner. As he walked in, he heard his usual greeting from the counter gal, Anne, "Hey, Johnny, whaddya know?"

"Hey, Anne, how's it going?"

"Boy, Johnny, you're looking a little ragged."

"Yeah, it's been a rough day."

"Well, my offer still stands, Johnny. I'm available if you need help cracking the case."

"I'm keeping that in my back pocket."

"Swell, now what can I get you?"

"How's the liver and onions today?"

"Fresh."

"I'll take it."

Anne turned to the cook and shouted, "Put the lights out and cry."

"And I'll have a baked potato with butter and a coffee."

"Add a Murphy with axle grease and a cup of joe."

The cook, while beating an egg, gave an unenthusiastic acknowledgment, "Yeah, yeah."

While Anne was off getting the cup of coffee, Marlboro heard a familiar voice from behind, "Hey, handsome." It was Molly.

"Hey, doll. How'd you know where I'd be?"

"You know, you're not the only gumshoe in town; besides, your answering service told me where I could find you."

"Care to join me?"

"You buying?"

"For you, doll? Sure. Whad'ya have?"

"I'll have the beef stew; it's always good here."

"Hey, Anne, the lady will have the beef stew."

Anne placed the cup of coffee in front of Marlboro and shouted over her shoulder, "One Bossy in a bowl!"

"You got it," Came a voice from somewhere in the kitchen.

"Was there anything special that you wanted?" Marlboro asked Molly.

"No, nothing special. It's just that I've been hearing certain things down at the station house."

"Yeah? Like what," He said doggedly.

"Rumors that you're making certain muckety-mucks twitchy."

"Aw. You're breaking my heart," He grinned.

"So, you're not going to ease up?"

"Listen, doll, when people get wired, I know I'm doing my job."

"Just take it easy, Johnny."

"I'm perfectly calm."

Anne came over and set their dinners down in front of them. "Here ya go. If there's anything else you need, just give a shout."

"Thanks, Anne, you're the tops."

They ate their meal in relative silence, making only small talk. Afterward, Molly whispered, "Wanna come over to my place for a nightcap?"

"Sure, but I gotta go back to the office to pick up my car. I'll be over in a jiff."

She winked and purred, "I'll be waiting."

He was a block away from the Brockman Building, where his office was. As he was passing the mouth of a narrow alleyway, a man stopped him, "Hey, Mac, you got the time?"

Marlboro had no time to react. Two men step out of the shadows of the dark alley. One of them saps Marlboro adroitly while the other two goons drag him out of sight into the alley.

Dazed but not out, Marlboro tries to fight back. He leans against one of the attackers; he feels the bulge of a gun under the man's coat. His hand tries to hold on as he sinks downward, but the three thugs give him an expert beat down. Marlboro goes crashing down onto the dirty, wet cement. One of the men kicks Marlboro in the gut, bends down, and gently says, "Lay off Marlboro. Get it, just lay off, shamus."

Marlboro lies there, floating in and out of consciousness for over an hour. He finally came around long enough where he could stand upright. He was dizzy, nauseous, and unsteady but managed to stagger his way back to his office; the streets were as deserted as Hitler's bunker on VE Day.

Marlboro fumbled with his keys as his head was pounding, his mind was cloudy, and he almost passed out but somehow willed himself to stay focused.

Once inside, he teetered into the pitch-black chamber that was his office. He made his way to his desk chair and collapsed.

In the silence of his suite, he began to hear the faint sound of something dripping. He realized that it was the dripping of his bloody head wound onto the floor.

Listlessly, he started to regain his bearings; it was then that Marlboro became aware that he had something clenched in his left hand while he was getting pummeled. He had inadvertently grabbed it when he was trying to steady himself against one of his assailants. Marlboro sluggishly opened his hand to reveal a Los Angeles Police detective I.D. and badge. Badge number 714 belonging to Detective Sergeant John Books.

As Marlboro sat in the dark gingerly, touching the gashes on his head, his body felt like he had just gone ten rounds with Rocky Graziano. He was banged up, bruised, and bleeding. He felt as scuffed-up as an old pair of Florsheim wingtips.

He was jolted into the present when the phone rang; it was Molly.

"Johnny? What's wrong? You were supposed to be here eons ago. I've been calling your house for hours."

"Oh, hey, doll," He uttered.

"Johnny, you alright?"

"Yeah, doll, I'm Jake. I ran into a couple of palookas who jumped me in an alley near my office, gave me the business, and cold-cocked me. They made it very clear that they want me to lay off the Dawson case."

"Any idea who they were?"

"I got a hunch," Marlboro said, looking at the police I.D. and badge.

"Whad'ya going to do, Johnny?"

"I'm gonna play my hand, doll."

"You can't be serious."

"Deadly serious."

"Want me to come get you?"

"No, you stay put. I don't want you to get swept up in this mess. I'll be okay to drive and will call you in a day or so. Now, don't go saying nothing to nobody, okay?"

"Okay, Johnny. You watch yourself."

"Bye, doll."

Marlboro swiveled his chair around opposite his desk and opened the door to the credenza. Built into the cupboard was a small Mosler Ironworks safe with a combination tumbler dial–34 right, 18 left, 44 right.

CLICK

He swung the heavy door open and pulled out three roscoes and ammunition.

The first one he loaded was his Colt – Official Police .38 Special. The second pistol was his .32 caliber Colt Detective Special 'snub-nosed' revolver. And the third was the semi-automatic Colt M1911 .45 caliber just in case things got hairy. Playtime was over.

Marlboro drove to his home at 1626 W. 11th Place in the wee hours of the morning. He drove around in circles and backtracked several times, ensuring he wasn't followed. Once he reached home, he pulled into his driveway and entered through the backdoor. The house was empty of intruders.

Over the years, he has encountered unsavory characters trying to intimidate him by breaking into his home. Since then, he has set up his abode with several booby traps on the windows and doors. Some lethal, some aimed at just causing severe bodily harm.

Not turning on any lights, he went upstairs, opened the bathroom cabinet drawer, pulled out a large bottle of aspirin, shook out three or four, and tossed them in his mouth.

Marlboro walked over to the bedside table, unscrewed the top to a bottle of Scotch that he kept there for just such occasions, and took a big swig to wash little white pills down. He plopped down onto the unmade bed, fully dressed in his bloody clothes, holding the snub-nose pistol in his hand. He rolled onto his left side and fell fast asleep.

Starting that night, he began to sleep with a gun under his pillow.

The distant ringing of the phone brought him slowly stirring out from the middle of a deep dream of smoky Scotch and some blonde doll, naked and laughing.

He didn't want to come out from the fog, but the constant ringing wouldn't stop. Up from the depths of the cloudy, murky bubble, he finally awoke.

"Marlboro here," He rasped.

"Mr. Marlboro, Charles Dawson. Are you all right? You sound terrible."

"Oh, hello, Mr. Dawson. I'm fine; I just got a bit of cold coming on. What can I do for you?"

"It's been a while, and I hadn't heard from you, so I thought I'd call and see if you've made any progress?"

"Well, as I told you, Mr. Dawson, these things take time. I can tell you that I am making some progress, but it's still way too early in my investigation to draw any concrete conclusions."

"I understand."

"I promise that as soon as I know anything, you'll be the first to know."

"Alright, I'm sorry to have bothered you."

"No, bother. I'll be in touch."

"Bye."

CLICK

Marlboro languidly eased himself out of bed. Still unsteady, he made his way to the bathroom one step at a time. As he undressed in front of the mirror, the effects of the assault from the night before were revealed: bruises, swelling, contusions, cuts, scrapes, lacerations, and lesions.

His head was pounding; it felt like a smashed Dewars flask. If he moved it too fast, the shattered pieces would rattle around inside his head. As he examined his battered face in the mirror, he mumbled to himself, "Forget about shaving; I'll kill myself."

Marlboro stepped into the shower, closed the curtain, and turned on the hot water. He aimed the showerhead onto the wall, slowly sank to the floor and, sat there sucking in the steam.

Forty minutes later, he emerged from the shower, less achy and with a clearer head. He dressed in his blue pinstriped suit, white shirt, red power tie, and Colt – Official Police .38 Special shoulder holster. The semi-automatic Colt M1911 .45 caliber would slip into the hidden gun rack installed under the driver's side dashboard. As for the snub-nose, he'd tuck it onto an ankle holster as a backup.

Before heading out, Marlboro went around the house, double-checking all of his break-in deterrents. Everything was locked and loaded.

Marlboro drove to the office, parked in the garage, and headed up to his lair. Once he got settled, he called his service. He had four messages: two from his ex-partner, Detective Hanson, one from Misty Thompson, Holmberg's secretary, and one from Robin Summers, Diana Dawson's other roommate.

"Detective Hanson speaking."

"Jas, Marlboro. What's up?"

"You okay? I heard you had a bit of a kerfuffle last night."

"Yeah, a couple of gorillas gave me the Broderick, but good."

"Did you recognize any of them?"

"No, but I got my suspicions."

"If there's anything I can do, you just let me know."

"Thanks, pal. I'll do that."

"Watch yourself."

CLICK

"Hello, Miracle Studios, Marvin Holmberg's office."

"Hey, doll. It's John Marlboro. Got a message you called."

"Well, I'm free for lunch today. Mr. Holmberg's out of the office all day. Whad'ya say?"

"I'll be by at noon, doll."

"Mmm, can't wait. Bye."

CLICK

"Hello."

"Robin?"

"Yes, this is Robin."

"Hi, this is John Marlboro. I got a message you called."

"I spoke with Skylar about Diana. I might have some information for you."

"Hey, that's swell. Would you be available this evening to meet?"

"What are you thinking?"

"Say six o'clock?"

"Where?"

"I could swing by your place if that's okay?"

"No. There's a lounge that I like, the Crown House on Santa Monica and Fairfax. Do you know it?"

"No, but I'll find it. So, I'll see you there at six tonight."

"Bye."

CLICK

By the time he made his way over to Miracle Studios, it was a quarter to twelve. He passed through the entrance gate to the security station.

"John Marlboro. I'm here to see Misty Thompson, Mr. Holmberg's secretary."

The guard checked the names on the guest list.

"Yes, Mr. Marlboro. I see your name here. Do you know where Mr. Holmberg's office is?" The guard asked.

"As a matter of fact, I do."

"You may pass," He said as he nodded to the guard inside the small station, who raised the gate arm.

As Marlboro drove through the studio backlots, he drove by the sets where they were shooting the westerns. "Pawnee Bill and the battle of Rio Hondo," "The Battle of Monte Cassino," and "Mystery, Mayhem, and Murder."

It was five minutes after the noon hour when Marlboro waltzed into Holmberg's office. Miss Thompson was freshening up her lipstick.

"You don't need that for me, sister. You're quite the looker without it," Marlboro said, lifting his sunglasses.

"Who said I'm doing it for you, smart guy," She said with a devilish grin.

He liked her; she gave as good as she got. Not many dames could handle themselves with such ease and poise.

As he stepped into the light of the office, she saw how bruised and battered he was.

She rushed over to him, "What the hell happened to you?" She asked as she removed his cheaters.

"A couple of thugs mistook me for a punching bag. I kept trying to beat them senseless by ramming my face into their fists. I wish I could say you should see the other guys."

"Ooh, you poor baby," She said as she cradled his face in her hands. They were soft, smooth, and cool to the touch.

"Nice. Makes it almost worth it," He said.

"Are you sure you're up for going out? I don't live too far away, why don't we go to my place. I can fix us something to eat."

"Are you sure?"

"As long as you don't mind leftovers."

As Marlboro drove to Misty's house, he noticed they were being tailed. A couple of guys in a deep blue Buick Model 51 Super 4-door sedan were far enough back for the average Joe not to notice, but Marlboro wasn't any average Joe. He'd been tailed by the best of them and to no avail. It had become second nature to him.

He pulled into a Safeway supermarket parking lot and waited.

"What are we doing here? Do you need something?"

"Yeah, hang on. You'll see."

The Buick pulled into the parking lot and parked several parking spots away. Marlboro said to Misty, "Sit tight. I'll be right back."

He went into the store and came out of the side exit. He looped around the parking lot and came upon the parked Buick from behind, the two men still inside waiting. With his .38 Special in hand, he approached the car.

"Alright, keep your hands where I can see them. What are you mugs tailing me for?"

"I don't know what you're talking about, Mister."

Marlboro cocked the pistol and placed the barrel behind the driver's left ear. "Keep both hands on the steering wheel," He ordered.

He proceeded to pat the man's jacket and found what he had been looking for–a pistol in a shoulder holster.

He pointed his gun at the man in the passenger seat.

"Ease your piece out nice and easy and toss it in the backseat."

The man did as he was told. Marlboro tossed the driver's gun in the back seat as well.

"I can explain," The driver said.

"I'm looking forward to it."

"Can I get my wallet from my back pocket?"

"Sure, but no sudden moves, or I'll drill ya."

The man slowly removed his wallet from his back pocket. He opened the wallet to reveal a police I.D. and badge.

"Detective Jason Hanson asked that we keep an eye on you."

Marlboro uncocked the gun and placed it back into his holster.

"Sorry, fellas, but as you can see by just looking at my face, why I am extremely cautious."

"Man, whoever did that musta been a pro," The passenger said.

"I'm Officer Redding, and this is my partner, Officer Johnson," The driver announced.

"Pleasure to meet you both, but I don't think I really need protection."

"Yeah, well, your face says something different," Redding said.

"I was just caught off guard. Won't happen again."

"Sure. Well, I think we'll report our conversation to Detective Hanson, but don't be surprised if you spot us again," Officer Johnson said.

"Thanks again, fellas. Now, if you'll excuse me, I have a luncheon date."

Marlboro got back into his car, and they drove off to Misty's apartment.

"Man, that's some hot tomato," Johnson said enviously to his partner.

"Yeah, some guys have all the luck.

Misty lived in a small bungalow at 116 Hart Avenue in Santa Monica. From her picture window in the living room, you could see the Pacific Ocean. It was one swanky joint.

"Great view," He said. "And the seascape ain't bad either."

She smiled, and as she left the room, she said, "Pour yourself a drink and make yourself comfortable. I'll be right back."

"Can I make you one as well?"

"Sure. Whatever you're having," She said as she closed her bedroom door.

Marlboro poured two whiskeys. He drank his down, waited, and then poured himself another. He stood looking out the picture window, watching the surf roll in.

He heard her approaching. He turned to see that she had changed into a sheer, soft pink satin lace kimono dressing gown.

"Hope you don't mind. I thought I'd slip into something comfortable. Whad'ya think?"

Marlboro's eyes were on her like metal on a magnet. "You look swell, doll," He said.

He held out the drink he had poured for her, but only far enough out where she would have to come to him to get it. "Care to join me?" He offered.

She took a couple of tentative steps towards him as if she were being lured into the spider's web.

Marlboro reached to take her in his arms. At first, she resisted, pushing him away, but then she yielded. He pulled her close and kissed her passionately. As they separated, she said, "Well?"

"Mmm, I don't know yet," He said as he leaned in and kissed her longer and deeper.

"Yeah. It's even better when you help," He said, grinning.

Misty put her drink on an end table, took his hand, and led him into the bedroom.

As Marlboro was undressing, she saw the true extent of his injuries. His upper torso was one giant bruise; the legs and arms were scraped and abraded. The only portion of his body that didn't seem injured was his manhood.

He stood there naked as she undressed; he noticed that she was staring at his body.

"Disappointed?" He asked.

"Not at all. Are you sure you're feeling up to it? You're pretty beat up."

Marlboro saw her soft naked body standing in front of him; she reached up and unpinned her hair, letting it fall and cascade down past her shoulders. He began to feel himself getting hard. He glanced down, smiled, and said, "Oh, I think I'll be able to rise to the occasion."

They made love twice within an hour. The second time, Marlboro felt lightheaded, as if he might pass out before climaxing. Misty was a voracious lover with an insatiable sexual appetite; she was ready for thirds, but he said, "Misty, I'm not a machine. Gimme some time."

"Mmm, you're wrong; you're quite the machine."

"Well, this machine is pretty beat up, sore, run-down, and drained. I need to shut down for a little while."

"Okay, we'll just lie here."

"Thank you," He murmured before slipping into a deep sleep.

It had seemed to him that he had just fallen asleep when he was slowly being drawn to conciseness by Misty caressing and stroking him, making it hard for him to sleep.

"How long have I been asleep?" He asked.

"Long enough," She purred as she pulled the sheet off him, slid down, and took him in her mouth.

"Just relax and enjoy," She whispered.

Marlboro did as he was told.

"So, Misty, what can you tell me about Diana Dawson? Was she having an affair with Holmberg?" Marlboro asked.

"I don't know for sure. I do know that Diana and several other young girls were often invited to large parties thrown by him and his new associate."

"Who is this associate?"

"Bugsy Siegel."

"Bugsy Siegel, the mobster?"

"The one and only. Apparently, Holmberg was forced into selling a portion of the studio to Siegel because of heavy gambling debts. Every week, a couple of his men would come into his office and collect two thousand dollars, cash."

"Do you know their names?"

"No, and I don't want to know. They are huge and villainous-looking. I get scared every time they come."

"Would you be able to recognize them if I showed you some photographs?"

"Sure. But I really don't want to get involved and end up like Diana Dawson."

"No, doll. This would be strictly on the QT."

"Well, maybe."

"Great, angel. Now, I got to blow. I have to interview one of Diana's roommates to see what she can tell me."

"Aw, do you have to go so soon?"

"I'll be back later, doll. You know, this case isn't going to crack itself," He said as he cupped her face in his hands.

Marlboro slipped out the back way, down the alley, and came out on Barnard Way, crossed over to the opposite sidewalk nearest the beach, looking for anything or anybody out of the ordinary. He found none.

The heavy traffic to the Crown House put him ten minutes behind his scheduled appointment. He parked in the parking lot and entered through the back entrance. There were a couple of fellas playing a spirited game of Eightball, with a rather large crowd watching intently.

He spotted Robin Summers sitting alone at a table by the front window from a photograph he had seen when he met with Skylar at their home. She was nursing a cocktail, staring out onto Santa Monica Boulevard, people watching.

He stopped by the bar, "Bullshot," He ordered.

The bartender, a pudgy middle-aged man who looked like he had seen and heard just about every story a barkeeper could have, nodded and mumbled something that sounded like bullshit, but Marlboro wasn't sure, and it wasn't worth pressing him on it.

When he got his drink before the barman could ask, Marlboro said, "I'm running a tab. I'll be sitting with that young lady up at the front."

"Robin?"

"Yeah, Robin. She's expecting me."

Marlboro walked over to where Robin was sitting.

"Robin. Hi, I'm John Marlboro."

"Sit down, take a load off," She said.

"Thanks for taking the time to see me. As you know, I'm working on the murder of your roommate, Diana."

"Yeah, Skylar told me."

"How well did you know Diana?"

"Not well. We were just roommates. I mean, she was a good kid, you know. But we were never really girlfriends."

"Was there anyone that you knew that she was close to?"

"You mean boys?"

"Well, boys or girls? Anyone that she paled around with?"

"Well, there was that queer the studio forced her to go out with, Johnathan Silvers."

"What kind of guy is he? Was he nice to her, do you know?"

"Oh, Johnathan was a real lady. Diana really liked him as a friend. A girlfriend if you know what I mean."

"But there were no girl, girlfriends?"

"No. She did have Taylor Carter come over to the house a couple of times. Taylor is also under contract at Miracle Pictures. On occasion, the two of them would be required to attend some studio parties thrown by Holmberg and this mobster friend Siegel."

"Whad'ya mean required?"

"There would be these out-of-town BTOs and industry VIPs at these parties."

"BTOs?"

"Big Time Operators."

"Gotcha," Marlboro said.

"Anyway. The girls were expected to be "*nice*" to them. The "*nicer*" they were, the more money they'd make."

"By nice, you mean have sex with these men?"

"Well, most of the time, no one forced them to have sex, but there were times when things got out of hand, and there would have to be big payoffs to satisfy all parties. Ya get the picture?"

"What happened at these parties?"

"A lot of dancing, drinking, drugs, and depravity."

"Did you ever happen to go to one of these parties?"

"Once," She winced.

"Can you talk about it?"

"You have to understand, Mr. Marlboro, that they dangle contracts and movie parts out to you as an incentive to attend. They said that all that is required of you is to come and be social, be a companion to these big shots. That's all."

"What happened?"

Robin's eyes teared up; she started to sob.

"Look, you don't have to tell me if it's too painful. I'll understand," Marlboro said.

"There were these two brothers, gangsters from New York. A couple of real pigs, Luigi and Anthony Costello. This particular party was held on the New York City backlot.

It started off innocently enough. Luigi and his brother, who he called Fat Tony, asked if I could show them around the set. They said it reminded them of their old neighborhood. So, I agreed to give them a tour.

When we reached the end of the New York lot, they dragged me behind one of the buildings and ripped my clothes off. The two of them raped me and forced me to do terrible things for over two hours.

Afterward, they just left me lying on the ground naked as they walked off laughing.

I don't remember how long I laid there until a studio security guard found me and rushed me to the hospital."

"Did the police investigate?"

"Investigate, you're kidding, right? All they did was take my statement and then accused me of making false allegations against the Costello brothers. They said that it was me who lured them into having sex with me.

The studio offered me a starring role in their next feature film and a ten thousand bonus as a way to make things go away."

"What did you do?"

"At first, I told them to shove their contract up their ass. Then, two days later, my dog, Buster, was strangled with piano wire and hung on our front door.

The next day, I signed the contract and collected my bonus."

"Did Diana know what happened to you?"

"Oh, it was no secret. I think Diana felt that she could handle herself. I guess she was wrong."

"Do you know if Holmberg was aware of what these two goons did to you?"

"Either he did and didn't care, or he didn't and is too scared to care."

"What's he got to be scared about?"

"Bugsy Siegel and his torpedoes."

"Hmm, maybe it's time that I have a little talk with Mr. Holmberg and Mr. Siegel."

"Oh, you must be careful, Mr. Marlboro. Siegel and his men are killers."

"I just want to talk, is all," He said with a grin.

Marlboro stood up to leave, "You take care of yourself. I appreciate you talking to me. Oh, one more thing. Can you tell me the name of the Asian grip that Diana bought her drugs from?"

"Bohai Zhang, Z H A N G. Everyone calls him Bo."

"Is there anything that you can think of that might help?"

"A couple of nights ago, our house was broken into."

"Was there anything stolen?"

"No, but whoever broke in was definitely looking for something."

"I assume you called the police?"

"Yeah, they just came out and took a report since nothing appeared stolen. We've since changed the locks."

"Smart move, kiddo. You take care of yourself. Oh, here's my card. Call me day or night if you need anything," He said as he handed her his business card.

As he walked out of the bar, he dropped a sawbuck on the bar and said to the bartender, "Get the lady whatever she wants."

Marlboro decided to go home so he could get some sleep. He knew he would never get any rest if he headed back to Misty's. And it was too soon to call Molly; besides he didn't want her mixed up in this mess. So, he went back to his place.

As he made his way home, Marlboro checked to see if he was being tailed. He didn't spot anyone, good or bad. When he pulled up to his house, there was a black and white parked out front.

He pulled into his driveway. As he was walking to his front door, a figure dressed in LAPD blue exited the squad car and approached him.

"Hey, Marlboro."

Marlboro recognized the voice to be that of his old nemesis, Lieutenant Jeffrey Foster. The man who got him thrown off the force.

"Lieutenant. Always a pleasure," He said sarcastically.

"Marlboro, I heard a nasty rumor that you were investigating the Dawson murder."

"You heard right."

"You're in way over your head, Marlboro. You don't know what you're getting yourself into."

"And you came down all this way to tell me that out of the kindness of your heart?" Marlboro said sneeringly.

"Hey, look, we might have had our differences in the past, but I still consider you a brother police officer."

"Stop it, you're making me cry. What is it you really want, Foster?"

"To tell you that your life is in danger."

"Is that what you want to tell me, that I'm in danger? People have been telling me that for two days now. I don't even give cigars for it anymore."

"Okay, wise guy, suit yourself. Don't say I didn't try and warn you."

"Say, Foster, do you know how I can get in touch with Bugsy Siegel?" Marlboro said to see the Lieutenant's reaction.

Foster's eyes got as big as saucers.

"Are you fucking crazy? What the Hell do you want with him?"

"I just need to ask him a couple of questions. That's all."

"Jesus Christ, Marlboro, you're really starting to gripe my cookies!"

"Gee, I'm sorry, Lieutenant. Didn't mean to jam you up," He said caustically.

"Ah, the Hell with you. I'll just let his boys take care of you," Foster said as he got back into the police car.

"Good night, Lieutenant, and thanks for stopping by," Marlboro said sarcastically.

He watched the squad car drive off before going into the house. Once he was inside, he checked all the entrances to see if there were any attempts of forced entry. Everything looked Jake.

Before going to bed, he took another hour-long hot, steamy shower. Afterward, he felt he was less damaged and more flexible.

As he slid into bed and placed his snub-nose pistol under his pillow, the phone rang.

"Marlboro here," He answered.

"It's Jas; just called to see how you're doing?"

"Swell."

"I heard you had a run-in with Foster."

"Boy, news travels fast. What gives?"

"You free tomorrow night?"

"Why?'

"I got a couple of tickets to the fights. Figure we can talk there."

"Oh, somewhere quiet."

"You wanna go or not?"

"Who's fighting?"

"Topping the card is world bantamweight champion Manuel Ortiz and this new kid from Chicago, Harold Dade, and on the undercard, a couple of middleweights, Jordan "Killer" Johnson and Jackie "The Beast" Cohen."

"Jackie Cohen, the Beast? It's more like "Canvas-back" Cohen? He's been knocked down so many times they're selling advertising on the bottoms of his shoes. I thought he was dead."

"He was. But he's staging a comeback. So, you wanna go? It's going to be at the Grand Olympic Auditorium."

"Sure, it'll be good to see someone other than myself get beaten up for a change."

Jordan Johnson and Jackie Cohen were the scheduled opening card, and at the top of the card, the main event was for the Bantamweight title, a fifteen-rounder between Manuel Ortiz and Harold Dade.

Detective Hanson picked up Marlboro at his home around five in the afternoon.

"Hey, Johnny. How are you feeling? I hope better than you look."

"I'm feeling pretty good, not as aching."

"I heard that you spotted Officer Redding and Johnson."

"Yeah, thanks for the thought, but I'm good. Really."

"Okay, just trying to help."

"And I appreciate it. Oh, and you might want to teach those boys the art of surveillance."

"They musta been sick the day we taught that class. By the way, how's the case going?"

"So, did you guys know about Holmberg and Siegel's after-hours bacchanals?"

"What are you talking about? Who's this Siegel?"

"You don't know? Bugsy Siegel."

"Bugsy Siegel!"

"Holmberg's in Siegel's pocket. Big-time gambling markers. So, now Siegel owns twenty-five percent of Miracle Pictures."

"And the festive after-hours occasions?"

"Holmberg would entice young starlets with the promise of better contracts, larger roles, and big bonuses if they played nice to the so-called VIPs."

"Siegel and his pals."

"Them and, from what I hear, city officials and even some of L.A.'s finest."

"So, you think someone from these parties may have been responsible for Diana Dawson's death?"

"I'd say it's six, two, and even that they had some part in her death. Now, the only question is who."

"Boy, our guys were sure barking up the wrong tree."

Marlboro smiled. "Let me guess. Lieutenant Foster."

"That's right."

"Where was he steering the investigation, towards Barrymore, Silvers, or maybe a Chinese drug gang? I heard that story about her smoking opium, and it's a bunch of hooey. Spread around like a load of manure by Foster to take the heat off of Siegel and Holmberg."

"But why?"

"Why! Because Foster's on Siegel's pad, he's gotta be on the take."

"Can you prove it?"

"Not yet. But I'm working on it."

"What's your next move?"

"Don't know yet. I have a couple of cards up my sleeve."

"Can I help?'

"Yeah, you can buy me a beer and a dog when we get in," Marlboro said as they entered the Grand Olympic Auditorium parking lot.

The fight between Jordan Johnson and Jackie Cohen never went the distance. It was scheduled for twelve rounds; Cohen only made it to the eighth before he lived up to his nickname "canvas-back." He was laid out flat on his back by a series of devastating body punches and a vicious uppercut, sending "the Beast" down for the count.

The Manuel Ortiz and Harold Dade fight was an absolute slugfest. Dade, a relatively unknown twenty-three-year-old 12-to-1 underdog, pounded out a unanimous 15-round decision, ending Ortiz's five-year reign as champion.

"That was a profitable evening. I made 1200 bucks," Marlboro gloated.

"What, you bet on Dade? He was such a long shot."

"Well, that's how you make the big money, my friend. Whad'ya say we go out and celebrate."

"Maybe another night. I got to get back to Alice and the kids."

"You sure?"

"Yeah, let's do it next week. You take Alice, and I'll bring along someone, and we'll go out on the town. My treat."

"I can't let you do that."

"Listen, I wouldn't have placed the bet if it wasn't for you taking me to the match. So, just shut up and show up."

The following day, as Marlboro was walking to his car, his neighbor Glenn Ashley, who was watering his lawn, hollered, "Hey, John. Hope your car's okay."

"Whad'ya mean, Glenn."

"Well, I saw a couple of guys from a garage; they had your hood up and were tinkering with the engine about an hour after you left with your friend."

"Did you happen to catch the name of the garage?"

"Yeah, it was Acme Garage. Everything okay?"

"Glenn, do me a favor; go back into your house and call the police. Tell them to send the bomb squad. And stay inside."

"The bomb squad!"

"If you don't mind."

His neighbor ran into his house and called the police department.

"Hello. Is this Glenn Ashley? I'm calling about a bomb; somebody placed a bomb in my neighbor's car. The address is 1626 W. 11th Place. Hurry!"

The bomb squad, police, and fire department all arrived within minutes of each other. Marlboro was standing outside, waiting for them. He had gone door-to-door to warn the neighborhood of what was happening. Some fled, while others began to gather to watch the show.

The police cordoned off the area, the fire department stood by with hoses, ready for action, and two officers from the bomb squad, Officer Billy O'Riley and his partner, Officer Johnathan Hurley, carefully approached Marlboro's Fleetmaster.

O'Riley slowly opened the hood less than an inch, carefully looking for any tripwires. Finding none, he lifted the hood and locked it into the open position. Both he and Officer Hurley, as they stared into the engine well, spotted the bomb. It was attached by wires just below the battery, tucked away in the lower-left side of the engine well. A wire ran up and over the engine to the ignition switch.

If Marlboro had tried to start the Fleetmaster's 216.5 cubic inch, 3.5-liter engine, he would have been blown to smithereens.

According to Officer O'Riley, if the bomb had gone off, Marlboro and both the neighbors on either side of him would be standing at the pearly gates.

"Marlboro, you're one lucky son of a bitch. Now, I'm just thinking out loud here, but I think somebody really doesn't like you," O'Riley declared, smiling.

"Hmm. you may be on to something."

"You're lucky you have a nosey neighbor and even luckier that he likes you."

"Yeah, that's me, lucky."

"I'm guessing he doesn't know you all that well."

"Thanks, Billy."

"Just give him time."

"Bye, Billy."

"He'll soon hate you like the rest of us."

"Get the Hell outta here, ya fucking Mick." Marlboro laughed gutturally.

"Aye, now I know you're a racist."

"I am not a racist, you stupid Paddy. I hate everyone. Equally." Marlboro said, smiling.

"See ya, Marlboro."

"Bye, Billy."

"I'll give it the once over and let you know what we find," O'Riley said as he held up the bomb.

"Thanks again, and give my best to the misses, Billy."

"Mr. Siegel, there's a man to see you. A shamus, John Marlboro. You want I should get rid of him?" Luigi Costello asked.

"No. Bring him in," Siegel said.

Luigi went out to the reception room, where Marlboro was sitting on the corner of the receptionist's desk, making small talk.

Luigi growled, "Mr. Siegel will see you now. Turn around."

Marlboro turned around, never taking his eyes off the young brunette secretary. Luigi proceeded to pat him down, checking for armaments. Marlboro figured that he would be the subject of a pat-down, so he left all his guns stashed hidden in the Fleetmaster's secret compartment.

What Luigi didn't check was Marlboro's right hand, in which he had a roll of quarters. A faux pas that soon would prove to become apparent.

"Okay, let's move it," Luigi said as he gave Marlboro a bit of a shove on the shoulder. As Marlboro left, he winked at the receptionist and said, "See later, ya doll."

As Marlboro entered the room, he observed Bugsy Siegel sitting behind a large wooden desk, his hands folded. Fat Tony started to walk towards Marlboro. When Fat Tony was within striking distance, Marlboro took a large step forward, swinging a haymaker with all his might, connecting with Fat Tony's jaw. *CRACK.*

Fat Tony collapsed in front of Siegel's desk like the mighty Kong fell in front of the Empire State Building.

Marlboro then swung around, smashing his fist into Luigi's mid-section, bending him over like a pretzel, and finishing him off with an upper cut that was very reminiscent of the punch that laid out old Canvasback Cohen at last night's pugilistic tournament.

He reached into Luigi's coat and retrieved his Colt .45. He proceeded to do the same with Fat Tony. All the while, Bugsy just sat behind his desk, unfazed, watching the show.

"My, my – so many guns around town and so little brains. You wouldn't believe the number of people that I come across every day who think a gat in the hand means having the world by the tail," Marlboro said poetically.

"Very impressive, Mr. Marlboro. They were two of my best."

"You feed them too well. They got fat and lazy. Ya gotta keep them hungry," He said as he revealed the roll of quarters from his hand. He then rolled the roll of quarters toward the mobster on his desk.

"Hmm, I'll remember that," Siegel asked as he picked up the roll of quarters.

"Marlboro. Marlboro. I've heard of you."

"I'm sure. How is Lieutenant Foster?"

Siegel, not giving anything away, said, "What can I do for you, Mr. Marlboro?"

"I'm investigating the rape and murder of a young woman, and I think you might be able to help me."

"Really?"

"Really. Diana Dawson, she was a regular at your soirees down at Miracle Studios."

"I'll admit I attend those parties, but I am unaware of any girl being murdered."

"Oh, I'm not saying that you personally were involved. But maybe one of your torpedoes might have gotten a little rambunctious. I know for a fact that these two mugs brutally raped another young woman at one of those gatherings."

"Did she go to the police?"

"She did, but they were less than enthusiastic about proceeding against any members of the Bugsy Siegel gang, especially when it boiled down to, he said, she said."

"Well, Mr. Marlboro, as you probably know, I deal in gambling, prostitution, extortion, and yes, even murder. But I will not and do not condone rape. I will most certainly look into this matter."

He scribbled an address on a sheet of paper from his note pad handed it to Marlboro.

"Here. This is the address of Miss Virginia Hill, a friend of mine. Come by this evening after eight, and we will talk more."

Marlboro took the note, turned to leave, and as he stepped over the dead to the world bodies of Bugsy's hatchetmen, he said, "Sorry about the mess."

"See you tonight, Mr. Marlboro."

That night, at approximately seven o'clock, Bugsy Siegel sat having drinks with his associates Allen Smiley, a former movie producer turned gangster, and Melvin Holmberg, along with his girlfriend, Virginia Hill, in her Beverly Hills home. An unknown assailant fired at them through the window, hitting Bugsy multiple times, including twice in the head.

By the time Marlboro arrived for his meeting with Siegel, LAPD had closed the whole neighborhood. There were dozens of newspaper reporters, radio crews, and even a Movietone film crew trying to get footage for next week's theater newsreels.

Marlboro parked his car several blocks away at a Sinclair service station and gave the attendant a five-spot to watch his car.

When he reached the police tape barrier, he spotted a friendly face: his ex-partner, Detective Jason Hanson.

"Hey, Jas!" He hollered.

"Marlboro? What the Hell are you doing here?"

"I thought I'd let you know, just in case."

"Just in case, what?"

"Well, I kinda had an appointment to see Mr. Siegel tonight."

"What's this all about?"

Marlboro began to notice that people were starting to eavesdrop.

"Say, maybe we ought to find somewhere quiet to talk," He suggested.

"Stay right here. I'll be right back."

Hanson went over and told several officers that he would be leaving the scene for a short time. While Hanson was away, Marlboro noticed the two gorillas he TKO'd in Siegel's office amongst the crowd of people watching the circus.

Hanson returned, "Let's go."

They began to walk back to the gas station, where Marlboro left his Fleetmaster.

"So, you were going to see Siegel about Dawson's murder?"

"Yeah, I met with him earlier today."

"How'd you get to him? He's always surrounded by muscle."

"You mean Anthony, *aka* Fat Tony and Luigi Costello. They were a couple of real gentlemen."

"You're kidding, right?"

"Right. But Siegel was genuinely disturbed that one of his men would commit rape, gambling, prostitution, extortion, and murder was okay, but not rape. So he was supposed to look into it and asked that we could meet this evening."

"Unbelievable."

"How may I ask was the legendary Bugsy Siegel killed?"

"He was knocked off by an unknown assailant who fired at him through the window with a .30 caliber military M1 carbine. He took two to the puss, splattering his brains all over the baby grand. Not a pretty sight."

"Rival mob?" Marlboro asked.

"Could be. Do you think the Costello brothers could have done it?"

"I doubt it. It wouldn't seem to be their style; they're more the type that just goes in with roscoe's blazing, killing everything in sight. Doesn't seem to be a lot of finesse with tweedled dee and tweedled dumber."

"So, where does that leave your case?"

"I still got a couple of leads to follow up on."

"Say, I heard about the bomb scare today. You're pretty lucky."

"Yeah, that's what they call me, Mr. Lucky."

"Hey, Misty, Marlboro here. How are ya, doll?"

"Johnny, what happened? I thought you were coming back."

"I had to follow up on some leads."

"When can I see you?"

"How about tonight?"

"Where?"

"I'll pick you up at your place around six."

"Mmm. Can't wait."

"Six o'clock."

CLICK

Marlboro was back in the office trying to get a handle on all the ins, the outs, and the what have yous of the case.

He wanted to find out all about this Bohai Zhang character. He had a friend who worked as a stuntman with most of the major studios, Monty Sinclair.

Monty had choreographed hundreds of gags, high falls, low falls, faceoffs, headers, branny's, sword fights, street fights, and hand-to-hand combat scenes for such films as Silent Wind, The Wild Slave, The Abyss of the Pirates, and the Academy Award-winning Master of Termination.

The buzz around Hollywood is that he hurt his back doing a car gag; he drove a car off a three-story garage, crashing on top of a moving dump truck. They call Monty the one-take wonder because when there are dangerous gags that can't be repeated, Monty has the man to call.

They got the shot, and Monty got a broken leg; he's out of action for six weeks, stuck at home.

"Monty. Marlboro here. How're you doing, partner? I hear you're sidelined for a spell."

"Yeah, broke my leg, driving a car off a three-story building."

"Well, that wasn't very smart."

"No, not very smart, but very profitable."

"Well, now it makes sense. Say, I'm working a case that involves you Hollywood types."

"Hey, it wasn't me. I have an alibi."

"I haven't told you anything yet."

"Doesn't matter; I have an alibi."

"Smartass."

"Whad'ya need?"

"Do you know a grip named Bohai Zhang? Goes by the name Bo."

"Yeah, we call him Mr. Bojangles. He's the guy to see if you're interested in buying dope. Why are you looking to get some reefer?"

"No, the girl who got killed is supposed to be getting dope from this Bo character. Any idea where I might find him?"

"Not offhand; let me nose around and see what I can find out."

"Thanks, Monty. Need anything?"

"Yeah, a broad and some booze."

"See what I can do."

"Bye."

CLICK

The following day, the headline in the Los Angeles Herald-Express read, "BUGSY SIEGEL MURDERED" Mobster Rubbed Out in Beverly Hills in a Hail of Bullets.

Benjamin "Bugsy" Siegel, 42, once named as the West Coast brains of the notorious Murder, Inc., cut-rate homicide syndicate, was rubbed out in true gangland style by a hail of bullets from a carbine in a nighttime ambush at a Beverly Hills mansion.

The assassin crept through the dense shrubbery in the darkness and fired nine shots through the window at the unsuspecting racket chief as he sat reading a newspaper.

Two bullets ripped through his head, and two lodged in his body. He died instantly, slumping over the newspaper, which had a tiny advertising sticker that read: "Good night, sleep well."

The article went on to say that neither Miss Virginia Hill, Allen Smiley, or Melvin Holmberg were injured. The police theorize that the triggerman must be an expert shot, according to Police Captain W. W. White of Beverly Hills. It is suspected that a rival gang perpetrated Siegel's death.

After reading the article, Marlboro had to laugh to himself, knowing that all the LAPD top brass that were on the take were shitting themselves, worrying that something was going to surface to point the finger at them.

Marlboro arrived at Misty's six o'clock on the nose. As he parked, he noticed an LAPD black & white parked out front of her building.

When she answered the door, he could see an overweight, somber, detached man in his late thirties, balding with dark, cold eyes. His brown tweed suit wasn't expensive and wasn't well pressed. He looked like he had slept in it.

"Mr. Marlboro, this is Detective Sergeant Books. He came by to ask me some questions about Mr. Holmberg and Mr. Siegel."

Marlboro stepped into the living room and offered his hand, "Detective Sergeant Books, it's a pleasure to meet you."

"So, you're John Marlboro. I've heard a lot about you."

"Nothing good, I'm sure," Marlboro said, half-joking.

"Yeah, nothing good," Books countered.

"Lieutenant Foster, I'm assuming."

"We partner up from time to time on special assignments. He's told me all about you, Marlboro. You know something; you look familiar. Have we met before?" Books asked, smirking.

"Sorry, I can't place the face."

Detective Sergeant Books, Foster's brutish sidekick, then strolled over to Misty and slid his arm around her shoulder, who seemed uneasy.

"Hey, isn't she a cutie?" The pudgy flatfoot said.

Marlboro tapped the brute on the shoulder, "Hey, Books."

He turned and stupidly said, "Huh?" and Marlboro punched him in the nose. Books dropped like a sack of potatoes.

Books touching his bleeding nose hauled his fat ass off the carpet. "You're going to jail for striking an officer, you son of a bitch!"

"You gotta witness?" Marlboro replied.

"Yeah, I got one," Books said, but when he turned around, Misty was gone.

Marlboro put his face into the Detective's and said, "Anytime you want to go at it man to man, and not in an alley with two other gorillas, I'll be more than happy to oblige."

Books grabbed his porkpie hat off the coffee table as he stormed out the door, slamming it shut on the way out.

Apprehensively, Misty returned into the living room after hearing the door slam shut.

"Thank goodness. It's you. That man scares me every time I see him."

"You've seen him before?"

"Yes, he and Lieutenant Foster both were regulars at the studio parties. Every time he came by the studio, he'd always make a play for me."

"Listen, doll, can you get me in to see Holmberg tomorrow? He and I got some unfinished business."

"Sure, Johnny. But we got some unfinished business, too," She said coyishly as she unbuckled his belt.

By the time Marlboro got into the office, it was almost noon. His answering service relayed his eight phone messages: one from Diana's father wanting to know of any updates, one from Misty, telling of his appointment with Holmberg set for 4:30 that afternoon, five from Monty Sinclair about the whereabouts of Bohai Zhang, and one somewhat obscene message from Detective Sergeant Books that the service refused to read aloud.

He returned each call in the order that he received them. He told Mr. Dawson there was some movement on his daughter's death, but he was still days away from any final conclusion on who the actual murderer was.

He called Misty and confirmed the 4:30 appointment with Holmberg, and yes, he also had a wonderful evening.

"Monty, Marlboro here. Whad'ya got for me?" He asked.

"Well, I'm sure you have heard about the scandal between Rex Harrison and Carole Landis…."

"Monty, I'm really not interested in all that Hollywood shit-chat. Just tell me where I can find Bohai Zhang."

"Well, word on the street is that he's looking to take it on the lam."

"Any idea where he's off to?"

"My guess would be San Francisco. They have a big Chinese community up there. Once he's up there, you'd never be able to find him."

"Any idea where he lives?"

"The last address I got was 746 South Central Avenue."

"Zhang's a long way from Union Station. The bus station was only a couple of blocks away, off of Alameda, and buses were cheaper and left more frequently. Thanks, Monty; I owe you one."

CLICK

Marlboro headed over to the Greyhound Terminal to try and intercept Zhang. He parked the Fleetmaster in the adjacent parking lot across the street and entered the massive bus station.

There were hundreds of passengers milling around the terminal, waiting to be called for their bus. He probably would have missed Zhang if the belligerent Asian hadn't gotten into a quarrel with a rather large station security guard about being forced into waiting in the "Colored" waiting room.

"Can't you read panface?" The guard said, pointing to a signposted inside of the "White" waiting room.

NO DOGS – NEGROS – MEXICANS – CHINESE

"I'm not Chinese. I was born here. I'm an American."

"Listen, you little Chink. You get your yellow ass into the colored waiting room before I give you a little chin music!"

"Get your hands off me!"

"Come on. I'm calling the cops," The guard hollered as he grabbed Zhang by the scruff of the neck.

Marlboro approached the guard, flashed Detective Books' ID and badge, and said, "What seems to be the problem here."

"This fucking Ching Chong was trying to sit in the whites-only waiting room. Can you believe it?"

"I'll take care of it. Come with me, and don't try anything foolish. I'd hate to have to shoot you,"

Marlboro said, flashing his .38 Special seated in his shoulder holster to Zhang.

He walked him out of the station by the arm to where his Fleetmaster was parked.

"Get in," Marlboro directed.

"Listen, kid. You play straight with me, and this never happened. You follow?"

"Yes, sir."

"Okay, let's see some ID."

The man showed Marlboro a California Driver's License, Bohai Zhang. And his union card, Local 80, for studio grips.

"Now, Mr. Zhang, I'm investigating the murder of a Miss Diana Dawson. Did you know her?"

"No, I don't know nothing about nothing," He rasped.

"Take it easy. I know that you supplied her with dope, and honestly, I couldn't give a hoot about that. I'm only interested in nabbing the people responsible for her death. Understand?"

Zhang sat silently, giving Marlboro the once over, trying to figure out what his game was.

"You don't care that I was selling her dope?"

"No, I don't."

"Hey, you take me for a chump."

"Bo, tell me what you know, and you can catch that bus to Frisco."

"I ain't no stoolie."

"Did you like Diana?"

"Yeah, she was a good kid."

"Don't think of it as ratting out somebody; think of it as helping a friend get justice. She didn't deserve to die like she did."

"All I know is that that crumb Holmberg found out I was selling. He put the screws on me to supply his parties with blow, smack, and tea."

"Tea?"

"Marijuana."

"I know there were police at these parties. Are you telling me they allowed that?"

"You're kidding, right? Not only did they know about it, but they also participated."

"Do you think the people you got your drugs from had anything to do with Diana's death?"

"My people never even heard of Diana."

"Why are you leaving?"

"You saw what happened to me in that bus station. I'm tired of that crap. At least in Frisco, I'll be amongst my people."

Marlboro looked at his watch, "Go catch your bus."

Zhang got out of the car, shut the door, crossed the street, and was stopped by a LAPD plain clothes vehicle.

Marlboro could see that the driver of the car was Detective Sergeant Books, along with another detective. They forced him into the backseat of the car and sped away.

Marlboro pulled a U-turn and proceeded to tail them. He was a crackerjack in the art of surveillance, spying, and stakeouts.

He followed the car to a vacant warehouse on the corner of Yale and Alpine Street. Marlboro drove past them and parked on the next block; he saw them enter the building in his rearview mirror. He walked towards the warehouse and decided to see if there was a back entrance.

He found an unlocked door and stealthily entered undetected. He slowly advanced to where voices were coming from. He eased into the next room. He couldn't see, but he distinctly heard Books and Zhang's voices.

"Going somewhere?"

"See, my folks in San Francisco."

"I hear you and that Dawson girl were pals. Anything to that?" Books asked.

"Not friends. I just sold her some dope occasionally."

"I heard it was more than that."

"No, it was just business. Besides, that was over a year ago."

"Did she ever tell you about a notebook that she had or any photos?"

"No. Photos of what?"

"Of people who attended private parties at Miracle Studios?"

"No, I was just her fixer, the guy who got her dope. That's all."

"Sure thing. I believe you, kid. But I hear you been talking to people."

"Not people; I was just talking to another cop before you picked me up, that's all."

"Who? What cop?"

"He didn't give me a name."

"What did he look like?"

"Tall, dark hair, muscular."

"Sounds like Marlboro, a peeper. What did you tell him?"

"Nothing, honest."

"I think you talked and talked plenty, and that's why you're taking it on the lam."

"No, really. I didn't say nothing."

"You better talk and talk fast!"

"Detective, put the gun away, please. I didn't say nothing."

"You want me to count to three or something, like in the movies? Talk you little slant-eyed son of a bitch!"

"I swear I didn't…."

POW POW POW

Marlboro heard the sound of a gun being dropped on the ground and footsteps leaving. He waited a few minutes, then went to see if Zhang was still alive. Three shots to the head said no.

Marlboro spotted a Walther PPK pistol that Books discarded on his way out. He carefully picked up the gun using a handkerchief from his inside coat pocket and left the scene.

He looked down at the kid and said, "Don't worry, kid, he'll pay for this. I promise you."

Marlboro drove straight to Miracle Studios for his 4:30 meeting with Holmberg. He was waved through the security gate and drove to the executive office building.

"Good afternoon, Mr. Marlboro. Mr. Holmberg is in a meeting at the moment, but he should be able to see you shortly. Won't you please have a seat?" Misty said.

The reason for her being so formal was that there were several other people in the waiting area scheduled to see Holmberg.

"Thank you, Miss," Marlboro answered as he found a seat adjacent to the sofa where three studio executive types sat, pretending to be reading a movie magazine.

The intercom buzzer sounded as Misty was feverishly typing; she stopped and answered.

"Yes, Mr. Holmberg? Right away, Mr. Holmberg."

Misty hung up the receiver, turned to Marlboro, and said, "Mr. Holmberg will see you now, Mr. Marlboro."

As Marlboro rose from the chair, he could feel the eyes of the three studio suck-ups staring at him as he entered Holmberg's lair.

"Thank you…"

"Misty."

"Thank you, Misty," He said with a wink. Two can play the same game.

He marched into Holmberg's office, sat down, leaned forward, and told him, "You're into this mess right up to your eyeballs, Holmberg! I have a witness who tells me that you and Siegel, your so-called partner, who was shaking you down because of your heavy gambling debts, were involved in forcing women to have sexual relations with movie big-wigs, city officials, and even high-level police."

"You got nothing on me, flatfoot."

"Don't go simple on me, Holmberg. I told you there was a witness. Rape. Murder."

"You're crazy."

"Am I? Do you think Siegel was the only target? Count yourself lucky, Holmberg."

"Why would anyone want to kill me? I just make movies."

"You know, Holmberg. Even if you didn't pull the trigger on Diana Dawson, you could hold your breath for it, just the same."

"They'd kill me if I talk," Holmberg pleaded.

"Don't play the sap. Do you have any idea what they'd do to a weak sister like you in stir?"

"You have no idea who you're dealing with here, Marlboro. Don't let their thousand-dollar suits fool you. They would just as soon kill you as look at you. I can't go to the police because they're in on it, too. If I open my mouth, I'm a dead man."

"Yeah, you're in a jam, alright, but I still need a fall guy. Someone to take the fall for Diana Dawson's murder, and where I'm sitting, you'll fit the bill nicely."

"It was the Costello brothers."

"Why?"

"Diana found out about some girl who had been raped."

"Robin Summers?"

"Yeah, Robin Summers. Diana threatened to go to the police. So, Luigi and Fat Tony whacked her."

"Don't give me that. Luigi and Fat Tony don't act on their own. They only do as they're told. The order had to come from above. So, don't give me that load of hooey that Bugsy ordered the hit. Let's cut the babble and start with the straight talk."

Holmberg sat silent for a minute; his face was wooden, but his eyes were dancing. He looked at Marlboro and muttered, "Books."

"Detective Sergeant John Books?"

"Yeah, him, Foster, and another cop, I don't know his name. They wanted her taken care of because she had evidence. Photographs, and she told them that she had tapes of girls talking about what had happened to them."

"Where is this evidence now?" Marlboro asked.

"I don't know. What I do know is that neither Books nor Foster has found anything. Yet."

"Maybe the reason they haven't found anything is because they aren't looking for anything," Marlboro suggested.

"Hello?" Molly said.

"Hey, doll. It's John. Feel like grabbing a bite?"

"Sure."

"Great, I'll swing by in about fifteen minutes."

CLICK

It had been over a week since he last saw his special lady. He was in desperate need of some intelligent conversation and adult companionship. Sleeping around with these twenty-something chippies was great for the ego, but Marlboro needed something other than his dick to be stimulated, like his brain. Occasionally, you need the blood to flow up to the cerebrum rather than down to the mentula.

Moly was waiting outside when he pulled the Fleetmaster into the apartment driveway.

"Hey, doll. You're quite the looker tonight," He said as he leaned over and kissed her.

"Yeah, well, you're looking pretty sharp yourself," She countered.

"Hungry?"

"Famished. Where we are going like I don't already know."

"The Original Pantry Café."

"Johnny, don't you ever want to try someplace new?"

"Listen, doll. My motto is *go with what you know*."

The Original Pantry Café is usually busy on a Wednesday night. But they always had a table reserved for John Marlboro.

The hostess sat them at a table by the front window. She handed them menus and said, "Anne will be your waitress tonight. Enjoy your dinner."

Marlboro sat facing the door, a habit he had acquired from his many years as a detective. You never sit with your back to the door; you never know who might be coming in looking for you.

Anne Hoppe, who usually worked the counter, decided she needed a change of scenery, so she's waiting tables.

"Hey, Johnny boy and Molly, how you kids doing tonight?"

"We're doing swell, and you?" Marlboro asked.

"Oh, I can't complain."

"Well, you could, but nobody would care," He quipped.

"Right, you are. So, what can I get you two to drink?"

Molly said, "Beer."

"Make it two."

"Two oat sodas coming up," Anne said as she sauntered off.

Marlboro gave a quick glance at the menu, knew what he wanted, and asked Molly, "So, what looks good doll?"

"Mmm, I think I'll have the corned beef and cabbage."

"Okay, that's one Irish turkey for you, and I'll have the Zeppelins in a fog."

"What the hell are Zeppelins in a fog?"

"Sausages and mashed potatoes. Everyone knows that," He said, laughing.

Anne brought two ice-cold bottles of Iron City Beer.

"You ready to order?" She asked.

Marlboro winked at Molly and gave the order, "The lady will have the Irish turkey, and I'll try the Zeppelins in a fog."

Anne stood dumbfounded. She finally said, "Johnny, I think I'm in love." as she walked back towards the kitchen.

Moments later, Marlboro's back stiffened when he spied Luigi and brother Fat Tony walk into the restaurant wearing long duster coats. He could see the tips of the shotgun barrels peeking out from the bottoms of their coats.

"Listen, doll, grab your heater, and get ready."

"What are you talking about?"

"There are two torpedoes coming our way."

The two button men stood just inside the entrance, looking around for their target. Marlboro kept his face hidden behind the menu as he reached inside his jacket to retrieve the Police .38 Special out of the shoulder holster. Molly pulled out her .32 caliber Colt snub-nosed revolver from her pocketbook.

"Wait. Wait. Hopefully, they won't spot us in here. Things could get really messy if they do," Marlboro said.

Anne brought over their meals and set them down in front of them.

"Want I should take those menus?"

"Anne, I need you to go and call the police," Marlboro whispered.

"Whad'ya talking about, Johnny?"

"Anne, those two guys standing by the door are a couple of hitmen. Go call the police now."

Anne winked at Marlboro as she headed straight toward the two brothers.

"Shit!" Marlboro growled.

"Hello, table for two?" Anne asked Luigi with a big smile.

"Beat it. We're looking for someone," He snarled.

"I'm afraid I'm going to have to ask you to leave," Anne demanded.

Marlboro reached down and fetched his snub-nose pistol out of his ankle holster. It looked like Hell is coming to dinner.

"He told you to scram, bitch!" Fat Tony barked.

"You get outta here before I call the police!" Anne hollered.

Luigi, still looking around, not paying attention to the squawking shew, spotted Marlboro.

"There's the son of a bitch!" He bellowed.

Both Costello brothers drew their shotguns from beneath their dusters and started walking toward Marlboro and Molly.

"Now!" Marlboro said calmly.

Molly threw herself onto the floor, firing her weapon at the two goombahs, while Marlboro tipped the table over and began firing from cover.

Pure pandemonium broke out, people rushing out the door, stepping and tripping over each other, screaming and yelling. Marlboro was right; Hell had come to dinner.

Luigi managed to get off three shots.

BOOM BOOM BOOM

Before Molly put a bullet in his 21" neck.

POW

Hitting the carotid artery, causing a geyser of blood to squirt over ten feet in all directions.

As Fat Tony was advancing towards Marlboro, firing his Remington pump-action shotgun at the four-inch thick oak dining table that Marlboro was taking cover behind, Anne attempted to grab his arm.

Fat Tony swung the gun around and fired one round point-blank into the feisty waitress.

BOOM

Marlboro blew up like an overheated engine. He jumped up from behind the table and started firing both pistols, one at a time, at the fat thug as he walked towards him, striking the obese greaser over eight times, five rounds in the torso and three slugs in the head.

POW POW POW POW POW POW POW POW
Felling the big man like a giant sequoia.

Marlboro stepped over the dead gunsels and rushed to Anne; he held her in his arms.

"Stay with me, Anne. The ambulance will be here any second. Come on, doll just stay with me."

"Hey, Johnny, how'd I do?" She breathed.

"You were aces, doll."

"How about a little kiss, Johnny."

Marlboro held her tightly in his arms, leaned down, kissed her softly, and whispered, "I love ya, doll."

"Ah, Johnny, I bet you say that to all the…."

He was still cradling her in his arms when the police and ambulance arrived. Molly was kneeling beside him with her arm around his shoulder. They were both weeping.

"Jesus H. Christ! What Hell happened in here? I haven't seen this much carnage since I landed at Normandy Beach," Sergeant Allister proclaimed.

Marlboro sat in interrogation room two, while Molly was seated in interrogation room four.

"Am I under arrest?" Marlboro asked.

"No, and you're not being charged. We just want to hear what happened at the Original Pantry Café tonight," Detective Wilson from Homicide said.

Marlboro was long gone before Wilson became a homicide detective, which is one reason he was chosen to interview Marlboro. All the long-serving detectives had worked with him in the past. The department didn't want to give any wrong impressions to the public, especially the press.

"Well, Molly, I mean, Officer Isle and I went to the Original Pantry Café for some dinner."

"Did you often go there?"

"I was considered a regular."

"How often would you say you eat there? Once a week, more?"

"On average, about four or five times a week. You see, my office is only a couple of blocks away."

"Sort of a creature of habit, are you?"

"Yeah, and unfortunately, it bit me in the ass."

"So, you and Officer Isle were sitting in the restaurant…."

"So, me and Officer Isle had ordered some beers, and we was chit-chatting, waiting for our dinners when I see Luigi and Fat Tony come strolling in wearing long duster coats."

"That would be Luigi and Anthony Costello, correct?"

"Correct."

"Then what?"

"Well, I got suspicious."

"What made you suspicious?"

"It's 85 degrees outside, and these two jamokes are sporting heavyweight dusters. Plus, I can see the barrels of their shotguns that they have hidden in the coats sticking out."

"Then?"

"I tell Officer Isle that if she has a weapon, be prepared to use it."

"How did you know they were looking for you, these two guys?"

"I'm working on a case, and I had the opportunity to run into them."

"I won't bother asking who your client is; I get the whole confidentiality thing. It's sufficient to say that you had some sort of altercation with the Costello brothers. Am I right?"

"Right."

"So?"

"So, they come in and stand in the entranceway; Anne Hoppe, a waitress, asks them if they would like to have a seat. They become belligerent; she then asks them to leave, and shortly after that, Luigi spots me. That's when all Hell breaks loose."

"How did Miss Hoppe die?"

"Fat Tony was heading my way, popping off round after round of double ought buckshot at me when

Anne attempted to grab his arm. He turned around and shot her once at point-blank range.

That's when I stood up and emptied both guns at the fat pig. Luigi was already down and dying from an expert shot from Officer Isle. Moments later, you guys showed up, and here I am."

"Anything else you'd like to say?"

"No. That about covers it."

"Okay, sit tight," Wilson said as he left the interrogation room.

An hour later, both Marlboro and Molly were released. The ride home was quiet and solemn. When they arrived at Molly's apartment, she asked, "Care to stay the night?"

"That would be nice," Marlboro said sedately.

As they were going into the apartment building, Marlboro noticed the deep blue Buick Model 51 Super 4-door sedan with Officers Redding and Johnson parked at the end of the block.

Marlboro gave a slight wave to them as he went into the building.

"SLAUGHTER ON 9TH STREET" Three people were shot and killed in a downtown Los Angeles restaurant. Two gunmen and a waitress died in a gun battle, read the headline in the Los Angeles Herald-Express.

Last night, a gun battle broke out at The Original Pantry Café in downtown Los Angeles. Two men with shotguns hidden under their raincoats began firing at a Los Angeles policewoman, Officer Molly Isle, and her dinner companion, John Marlboro, a private investigator, while the pair was having dinner.

The two gunmen started shooting at Isles and Marlboro soon after entering the restaurant; a waitress, Miss Anne Hoppe, tried to intervene and was shot at point-blank range, killing her almost immediately.

Officer Isle was able to shoot and kill one of the shooters, while John Marlboro, a private detective, rubbed out the second assailant, blasting him over eight times in the head and torso.

A police officer was overheard to have said, "Last time I saw something as bloody as this place was Iwo Jima."

The identities of the two hitmen were later confirmed to be that of Luigi Costello and his brother Anthony 'Fat Tony' Costello. They were known members of the Bugsy Siegel mob. Their motives for the attack have not yet been disclosed.

Marlboro was still asleep when Molly got up and dressed for work. She was working out of the robbery division. Before leaving, she woke him with a kiss.

"Wake up, sleepyhead."

"Why don't you come back to bed? I'll make it worth your while."

She lifted the blanket and smiled.

"Mmm, I bet you would. Later, gotta go."

And then she was gone.

He rolled over and tried to go back to sleep but kept thinking about poor Anne and the events of last night. Trying to go back to sleep was useless.

He sat at the edge of the bed for a minute before walking to the bathroom. He showered, shaved, and put on the suit and clothes that he kept at Molly's place. The clothes from last night's blitzkrieg were all covered in blood, Anne's blood.

Driving back to his office, Marlboro hatched a plan, a plan of revenge. The Costello brothers were just the tip of the iceberg. Marlboro figured it was time to go deep and get even.

There were still some loose ends to tie up, like interviewing Diana's friend, Taylor Carter, for one. Maybe Misty could help him get hold of her.

"Mr. Holmberg's office," The familiar voice said.

"Hey, doll, Marlboro here. Could I ask you to do a favor for me?"

"Sure, Johnny. What do you need?"

"I'm trying to locate one of Diana's friends, Taylor Carter."

"Okay, let me see what I can find out. Call ya back."

"Thanks, doll. I owe ya."

CLICK

As he was waiting to hear back from Misty, Marlboro retrieved the Walther PPK pistol, the throwaway gun that Books used to kill Zhang, from his safe, cleaned it, wiped all the prints off of it, and carefully placed it in a soft handgun case.

Thirty minutes later, the phone rang.

"Marlboro."

"Hey, Johnny, it's Misty. I got Taylor's phone number. Are you ready?"

"Go."

"Englewood 4-5789."

"Got it, thanks, doll. Dinner?"

"Tonight?"

"Yeah, if you're free."

"Where?"

"How about if I pick you up at seven?"

"How about you stop by at seven, and we eat in?"

"Even better. See you at seven."

CLICK

Marlboro had called Taylor and had arranged to meet her at Clifton's Brookdale Cafeteria on South

Broadway. He spotted her waiting in an unpopulated area of the restaurant, reading the latest issue of Variety.

The restaurant was cavernous. Two stories tall, with an old European feel lots of heavy dark wood paneling, the massive stone fireplace presides over brooks and streams of water. A chapel and assorted nature dioramas, the multilevel forested main dining room, and a grand staircase leading to the upstairs where people dining can look down onto the main dining area. It seemed to Marlboro more like a museum than a restaurant.

"Miss Carter, I'm John Marlboro. May I join you?"

"Please," She said with a smile that could end a war.

"Can I offer you something to eat? I hear the food here is as unique as the décor," Marlboro said.

"Yes, I know. I work here," She said, looking down, ashamed.

"I thought that you were under contract to Miracle Pictures?"

"I am, but I'm still a bit player. I don't make the kind of money that the top stars make. And I only get paid when I'm working. So, between films, I work here."

"Waitress?"

"Hostess."

"Would you like to go somewhere else?"

"No, this is fine. The food here is wonderful."

They went through the cafeteria line; she got the roast beef sandwich, and Marlboro had the smoked salmon platter. After dropping off their plates at the table, Marlboro went to the Monarch Bar and ordered two beers to be brought over to their table.

"Taylor, what can you tell me about Diana?"

"Diana and I were close. We had worked on a couple of films together and became fast friends. We were constantly being harassed by Holmberg and other studio execs to attend these parties that the studio threw."

"I understand that they dangled better parts and contracts to entice you to attend those parties."

"That's right. We could see some of the other girls who went getting the better parts. And it wasn't because they were better actors."

"What exactly did they expect from you at these parties?"

"Sex."

"Did either of you go?"

"We went together once."

"Do you remember any of the men who attended?"

"I remember there were a bunch of mobster types, some local politicians, and some top brass from the police department in uniform."

"Does the names Detective Sergeant John Books or Lieutenant Jeffery Foster ring a bell?"

"Yeah, they were very keen on us. I think because we were the new flavor of the month."

"Did anything happen?"

"They were all over us like a cheap suit. Foster tried to kiss me, and Books tried to put his hands up Diana's dress. Diana slapped Books and scratched his face. He slapped her back, hard. He grabbed her and threw her on the ground. I think he would have raped her right there on the spot if Foster hadn't pulled him off."

"We were both called into Holmberg's office, and each would be given a two thousand dollar "bonus" if we sign a nondisclosure agreement."

"Did you?"

"I did, Diana didn't."

"How soon after that was Diana found?"

"Two weeks. Diana confided in me that she had gotten threatening phone calls, people following her, and notes saying disgusting things."

"Do you know if she kept any of these notes?"

"Notes and some photographs, but I don't know where she kept them.""

"Any ideas?"

"Not really. Although, I do know that she did go home to see her folks days before she was killed."

"Hmm. Interesting, they didn't mention that to me when we met. I'll have to check into that. So, how are you doing these days?"

"I'm still just getting small bit parts. The good news is that my agent has been in talks with MGM. So, I'm keeping my fingers crossed."

"Well, Taylor, I appreciate you spending time with me. Here's my card, if for some reason you either think of anything, or you might need help. Feel free to call anytime."

They shook hands, and Marlboro left the restaurant, and Taylor went back to work as the hostess.

Bugsy Siegel's body wasn't cold when Myer Lansky's "associates" took over Siegel's operation in Las Vegas and Los Angeles.

The story of the LA Mob gets a bit sketchy from here on because of the code of silence and the honor among thieves canon.

But rumor has it that once Siegel was fitted for his Chicago overcoat, a couple of enterprising brothers, Stephon "Little Caesar" D'Adamo and his little brother Tomas "The Fixer," moved into positions of power. Stephon became the Boss of the Los Angeles crime family and named his brother Tom his consigliere. A close friend and supporter of theirs, Girolamo "Momo" Adamo, was named underboss.

After Siegel's untimely death, there was a minor "reorganization" within the mob community. Certain individuals whose positions were considered redundant or threats to the new management were whacked.

The D'Adamo brothers, unlike their predecessors, weren't all that interested in movie studios and hobnobbing with the Hollywood elite. They favored a more monastic approach, preferring anonymity. Rather than them being seen in the spotlight, they elected to stay hidden in the dark, like a rat or a cockroach.

Therefore, it wasn't too long after Siegel's death before Marvin Holmberg was called upon by two of D'Adamo's associates, Gianfranco 'The Weasel' Buonaiuto and Vinicio 'Three Fingers' Fassio, both hitmen from the notorious southside of Chicago.

"Yes, may I help you, gentlemen?" Misty asked.

"Yeah, we're here to see Mr. Holmberg," Gianfranco answered.

"Is he expecting you?"

"I doubt it," Three Fingers said, laughing.

"May I have your names?" She asked nervously.

"Mr. Smith and Mr. Jones. You can tell Mr. Holmberg that he can either see us now, or we can stop by his house tonight," Fassio sneered.

"But you tell him dat Mr. Smith here, he don't like making house calls," Gianfranco rasped.

"Hey, I thought you was Mr. Smith," Three Fingers said.

"If you, gentlemen, wouldn't mind waiting a moment, I'll let Mr. Holmberg know that you're here."

"Sure thing, sweet cheeks," Three Fingers said.

Misty jumped up, ran to Holmberg's door, gave a quick knock, and rushed in before he had a chance to acknowledge her.

"Yes, what is it, Misty? Can't you see I'm busy?" He growled.

Misty could see the top of a woman's head bobbing up and down from below Holmberg's desk.

"Mr. Holmberg, there are two men outside who make those Costello brothers look like pansies. They say they want to see you. Now."

"Give me a couple of minutes, and then let them in."

On her way out, she heard a small voice mumble, "How'm I doing, Mr. Holmberg?"

"Oh yeah, you're doing great, kid."

Misty shut Holmberg's office door, went to her desk, sat down, smiled nervously at the two killers seated on the sofa, and said, "Mr. Holmberg will see you now,"

The two button men walked into Holmberg's office just as the woman was leaving through the back entrance. Gianfranco 'The Weasel' Buonaiuto and Vinicio 'Three Fingers' Fassio walked up to Holmberg's desk; they each opened their suit coat jackets to reveal that they were armed.

"Holmberg, this here is Mr. Smith. I'm Mr. Jones. We were sent to let you know that due to the unexpected death of Mr. Siegel, the new head of the organization is no longer interested in being involved in the motion business industry. Therefore, you have thirty days to pay off your debt in full, or else we will be forced to foreclose. You capeesh?" The Weasel asked.

"Foreclose? Foreclose on what, the studio?" Holmberg asked.

"No, on you."

"On me?"

"I have here an insurance policy that you *will* sign, stating that the beneficiary is Mr. Stephon D'Adamo. You'll notice that the sum of the policy is exactly what you owe Mr. D'Adamo: two million clams."

"But I only borrowed one million," Holmberg pleaded.

"Interest," Gianfranco said deadpan.

The Weasel placed the insurance policy in front of Holmberg.

"But I don't seem to have a pen," Holmberg said apprehensively.

Three fingers flipped open a switchblade knife. "How's about we cut off the tip of a finger, and you can use your blood instead?"

Holmberg quickly found a pen in his coat pocket.

"I…I…I forgot I had it," Holmberg said as he quickly scratched his name on the policy.

"You got thirty days, understand," The Weasel reiterated.

"Yes."

"In full. Say it."

"In full."

Gianfranco picked up the policy, folded it nicely, and placed it in the coat pocket next to his gun.

The Weasel stopped before opening the door, turned, and said, "Oh, and if you get some crazy idea about taking it on the lam, don't. Because when we find you, and we will, it won't be a quick and painless death.

I'll cut your dick off and shove it in your mouth. Then we'll cut each of your fingers and toes off, one by one, and finally, I have Mr. Jones here, take a blow torch and turn you into two hundred pounds of pork rinds."

"See you in thirty days," Vinicio said as he held up the three fingers on his left hand.

Marlboro rang the doorbell at precisely seven o'clock. Misty answered, wearing a black sheer babydoll nightgown, leaving very little to the imagination.

"Hey, doll," Marlboro said with a wolfish grin.

"Hey, Johnny," She said, followed by a deep kiss.

She took him by the hand and led him to the small dining room table where there were two bowls of shrimp linguini, Italian bread, salad, and two glasses of red wine.

"I hope you're hungry. I made it myself." She said proudly.

"Looks delicious, and so does dinner."

"You're terrible!" She said, laughing.

"So, how're things in Movieland?"

"It was scary today."

"Why, what happened?"

"Two gangsters came in to see Holmberg, and after they left, he looked as white as a ghost."

"Any idea what happened?"

"He said that they forced him to sign an insurance policy made out to some mobster named D'Adamo for two million dollars, and if he didn't repay the total amount of his gambling debt, that they would kill him for the insurance."

"What's he going to do?"

"He doesn't know. They gave him thirty days to either pay up or else."

"Can't he go to the cops? He has some top brass connections."

"I'd say it's worth a shot. What does he have to lose? It sounded to me like some of those coppers were in bed with Siegel; maybe they just switched beds."

"I'll mention that to Mr. Holmberg."

"Say, let's eat this before it gets cold. I prefer mine hot, don't you?"

After five minutes, four bites of linguini, and a full glass of chianti, Misty stands up and asks, "Mmm, ready for dessert?"

"What's for dessert?"

"Pie. You like pie, Marlboro?" She said as she slowly walked back towards her bedroom. Marlboro was hot on her heels.

"There's nothing I like better than pie. Especially when it's hot."

"Oh, it's hot, alright." She purred as she took his hand, guided it down into her panties, and forced his hand deep inside her moist mound.

She moaned with delight. She fumbled, removing his clothes. Finally, they stood naked by the side of the bed. He was behind her as she knelt down on the bed on all fours.

He started to move around to her side.

"No, stay there." She whispered.

She reached down between her legs and guided him inside her.

The next morning, Marlboro got up early before the sunrise and walked down to the deserted beach in his boxers for a predawn swim.

By the time he returned, Misty was making breakfast: scrambled eggs, bacon, toast, and coffee.

"Where were you?" She asked.

"Took a swim, quite invigorating," He said as he kissed her.

"Mmm, you taste salty. Still, I think you should go take a shower."

"I'll be right back."

When he returned, breakfast was waiting.

"Say, now that Siegel's dead, does the studio still have those parties?" Marlboro asked.

"They did. Now that Siegel's gone, I don't know what's going to happen."

"Well, does Detective Sergeant Books and Foster still come around?"

"At least once or twice a week. Why?"

"Listen, doll; I need you to do me a favor." He said as he held out the soft gun case containing the Walther PPK pistol used to kill the Chinese grip.

"The next time Books comes into the office, you ask if he could show you how to load this gun. You tell him that your father gave it to you as protection.

Now, it won't be loaded. But I need him to get his fingerprints all over it. Do you understand? Under no circumstances are you to touch it. Let him handle it. You just unzip the case and let him show you how to operate it. If he asks you to hold it, feign like you're scared even to touch it; the only reason you have it is because of your dad."

"What if he persists?"

"Well, maybe you can throw him off his game with a little innocent flirting."

"I don't know. What's in it for me?" She said suggestively.

"A surprise."

"Promise?"

"Promise."

Marlboro was sitting in his office, working the LA Times crossword puzzle, when there was a bang on the door.

"Yeah!" Marlboro yelled.

The doorknob turned slowly; the door swung open revealing, Detective Sergeant Books with the man Marlboro had seen when they kidnapped Zhang.

Marlboro remained seated and asked, "Hey, Books, what's a four-letter word for an unpleasant or contemptible person?"

Books didn't answer; he just grunted, "Ungh." He and his companion came into the office. Books sat down in the chair across from Marlboro, while this other un-named party roamed around the office.

"Oh, never mind. It's F I N K, fink. You know, Books, maybe you should try working the crossword puzzle. It helps build a more robust vocabulary."

"Ugh!" Books snorted as he plopped down on the couch.

"Well, what do I owe the pleasure of your company this morning, Detective Books?"

"Marlboro, I don't like you sucking around bothering our citizens, shaking things up, drudging up the past, and mudding the waters of the investigation of Diana Dawson. You understand?" Books growled.

Still looking at the crossword puzzle, Marlboro asked, "Detective Sergeant Books, aren't you going to introduce me to your partner?"

"That's Detective Hargrove."

"Doesn't say much, does he?"

"He's the quiet type."

"Just exactly what is it you want, Books?"

"I want you to drop the Dawson case."

"But Detective, you never said why."

"Because it's my case."

"But you haven't made any progress as far as I can see in over a year. Aren't you interested in solving the case?"

"Marlboro, you are meddling with the primeval forces of nature, and I promise you, you do not want to get tangled up in that shit storm," Books said as he got up to leave.

"Oh, do stop by anytime, Books, and that goes for you too, Detective Hargrove."

"I warned you, Marlboro. Keep sticking your nose in where it doesn't belong, and one morning, you'll wake up a dead man," Books squawked.

"Hey, Hargrove, how about a five-letter word for a foolish or easily deceived person? Begins with a C."

Hargrove followed Books out of the office.

"Ah, got it, C H U M P, chump."

Hargrove slammed the door on his way out.

"Mr. Dawson. Marlboro here."

"Yes, Mr. Marlboro, what can I do for you?"

"I was hoping that I might come out and see you, folks, again."

"When would you like to come down?"

"Day after tomorrow?"

"Alrighty, I look forward to seeing you again."

"Bye."

CLICK

Detective Sergeant Books and Hargrove arrived at Miracle Studios around one o'clock. They stopped at the gate to announce themselves.

"Good afternoon, gentlemen. Do you have an appointment?" The security guard asked.

"I'm Detective Sergeant Books. I have an appointment with Marvin Holmberg."

"Yes, very good. One moment, please," The guard said as he checked his guest roster.

"Yes, sir, there you are. Do you know how to get to the executive office building?"

"Yes, I've been here before."

The guard waved to his counterpart inside the guard building, who raised the gate.

"Have a good day, gentlemen."

The guard inside the guardhouse called Mr. Holmberg's secretary to alert her that they had a visitor.

Books gave a short tap on Holmberg's door before entering.

Misty had just hung up the phone from informing Holmberg that Books was on his way.

"Hey, Misty," Books said.

"Detective Books. You're right on time. Mr. Holmberg is expecting you. Oh, but could I ask a favor of you before you go in?"

"Anything."

She opened a drawer in her desk and took out the soft black gun case that Marlboro gave her, unzipped it, and showed the pistol to the copper.

"My father sent this to me; he's scared for me living in the big city all alone. I don't know anything about them. In fact, I'm deathly afraid of them. But I promised my dad I'd have someone show me how to use it."

Books picked up the pistol and the unloaded magazine and started to give her a tutorial on the weapon.

"This is a Walther PPK pistol, and this is the magazine that holds the ammunition. The Walther PPK is a blowback-operated semi-automatic pistol developed by the German arms manufacturer Carl Walther. It holds six rounds; this particular model uses

7.65 caliber ammunition. I prefer my Colt Police Positive .38 Special, myself."

He put the magazine into the pistol, pulled the slide back, which cocked the gun, pointed the gun in the air, and pulled the trigger.

CLICK

"And that's all there is to it. Here," Books said with a toothy grin as he held out the gun for her to take it.

Feigning terror, she recoiled, saying, "No, please just put it back in the case. That thing scares me."

"It's empty. There's no danger here."

He held it out to her again.

BUZZZ

The intercom rang.

Misty picked up the phone.

"Yes, Mr. Holmberg, he's right here. I'll send him right in."

Books laughed, put the gun back in the case, and said. "Dames. Go figure."

Books had never seen Holmberg so discommoded. He was as white as a ghost, nervous, stammering, and fidgeting.

"Holmberg! Settle down, what's the matter?"

"You got to help me, Books," Holmberg pleaded.

"Tell me what's going on."

"Yesterday, two gunsels came by. They said that the new mob Boss, some guy named D'Adamo, isn't interested in being in bed with Miracle Studios, so they're calling in the whole nut on my loan.

They said that I have thirty days, or else. These two goons forced me to sign a life insurance policy; if I don't repay the loans in thirty days, they'll put the whack on me and collect on the insurance. You gotta help me!" He begged.

"Take it easy, Holmberg. Let me and Foster have a little chat with this D'Adamo. I'm sure we can work something out. Okay?"

"Oh, thank you, Detective. I don't know how I can ever repay you," Holmberg groveled.

"That's okay, we'll think of something. I'll get back to you when I know something. Until then, relax."

Books walked out the door to where Misty was typing a letter.

"Say, did you happen to see these two mugs who came and scared the bejesus out of old Holmberg?"

"Yeah, they were terrifying. They called themselves Mr. Smith and Mr. Jones."

"Think you'd be able to recognize them if I showed you some mug shots?"

"Probably."

"Maybe I'll swing by tomorrow and show you some. Would that be okay?"

"Ah, sure. But why not ask Mr. Holmberg?"

"Because he's not all that much fun to look at as you are, Angel. See ya tomorrow."

Marlboro parked his Fleetmaster two blocks south of the warehouse where Bohai Zhang's dead body was. It was well after midnight when he came across Zhang's corpse. It lay undisturbed, except for where the rats had begun to gnaw on the exposed flesh of his face, arms, and fingers.

Marlboro carefully placed the items he had brought and placed around Zhang's remains. He then retraced his steps, left the vacant building, and walked the two blocks back to where his car was parked. On the corner was a telephone box. He stepped inside, deposited the twenty cents into the coin slot, and called LAPD homicide.

"Hello, homicide. Yeah, I'd like to report a dead body."

"Who may I ask is calling?"

"Just a concerned citizen. The body appears to have been pumped full of lead."

"Where is this body?"

"801 Yale Street. The vacant warehouse. Up on the second floor. Better hurry before the rats eat all of his face."

CLICK

Marlboro drove around the block so that he would be parked in the dark, between the street lights. He slumped down into his seat when he heard the police coming. He could observe all the comings and goings.

At first, just a couple of officers arrived to make sure the call wasn't bogus. Once they found Zhang's body, they called in the troops.

Looking through a pair of binoculars, Marlboro saw that one of the Detectives on the scene was his ex-partner, Jason Hanson. He saw that Hanson held an evidence bag containing the murder weapon, the Walther PPK pistol that Books had actually shot Zhang with. The police would also find in the dead boy's hand the Wallet containing Detective Sergeant John Books' ID and badge.

Marlboro could tell when they found the ID and badge, all Hell broke loose. Six more squad cars showed up; one was that of the division commander.

An hour later, Detective Sergeant Books showed up, and the circus had begun. Marlboro could see that they were questioning him; they took his police revolver, placed him in handcuffs, set him in the back of a black and white, and drove him off to division headquarters.

Mission accomplished.

Back at division headquarters, Detective Sergeant Books was being interrogated by homicide detectives and internal affairs.

"Detective Sergeant Books, my name is Detective Jason Hanson; this is Detective Vincent Becho; we're from homicide. That man over there is Detective Marc Gerstel, internal affairs."

"This is bullshit. Can't you see I'm being framed!"

"Detective Sergeant Books, can you explain how your ID and badge were found on the body found at 801 Yale Street?"

"No."

"And when we test the gun found at the scene, a Walther PPK revolver, will we find your fingerprints on it?"

"No!"

Then, like a bolt of lightning out of the sky, it all became crystal clear to Detective Sergeant John Books.

"Marlboro." He whispered under his breath.

"Excuse me?" Hanson asked.

"I'm being framed by John Marlboro."

"John Marlboro, the former detective?"

"Yeah, yeah. John Marlboro."

"Why would he want to do that?" Hanson asked.

"Okay, it's like this. A couple of weeks ago, me and a couple of other guys jumped Marlboro in an alley and gave him a pretty good beat down. He must have stolen my ID and badge sometime during the beating."

"So, you're now confessing to aggravated assault against a private citizen," Detective Gerstel said.

"Hey, it beats a murder rap."

"Who were these other assailants that assisted you in this assault?" Gerstel asked.

"Luigi and Anthony Costello."

"You do know they were killed two nights ago?" Hanson queried.

"Yeah, don't you see it was Marlboro that killed them?"

"Well, Mr. Marlboro and Officer Isle were attacked while having dinner in a restaurant; they defended themselves. It was ruled self-defense," Hanson said.

"And why, might I ask, did you beat up Mr. Marlboro in the first place, Detective Sergeant Books?" Detective Gerstel demanded.

"I refuse to answer on the grounds that it may incriminate me."

"Who were you working for at the time when you attacked Mr. Marlboro?" Gerstel pried.

"I refuse to answer on the grounds that it may incriminate me."

"Was the Walther PPK revolver found at the murder scene yours?"

"No, actually, it belongs to Misty Thompson, who is a secretary for Mr. Marvin Holmberg, president of Miracle Studios. She asked me today to show her how to use it, as it was a gift from her father. That's how my fingerprints will be found on it.

Hey, did you do any ballistic tests on the gun?" Books pleaded.

"There weren't any casings left at the scene."

"Don't you find that suspicious? No shell casings left at the scene."

"I'd find it more suspicious if I did. A Detective with your experience would know not to leave any incriminating evidence behind," Gerstel replied.

"Can't you all see she's in cahoots with Marlboro."

"So, let me get this straight. You beat up John Marlboro, who was able to steal your ID and badge during the assault. Marlboro then killed Bohai Zhang with the Walther PPK revolver. Afterward, they tricked you into putting your prints on the gun that killed Zhang in the warehouse. Right?" Gerstel asked.

"Right!" Books said, exasperated.

"Why would Marlboro want this particular man dead in the first place?"

"I don't know. Ask him."

"Oh, we will. In the meantime, John Books, I am placing you under arrest for the murder of Bohai Zhang. Book 'em," Detective Hanson ordered.

"I want to thank you for coming in today, Miss Thompson," Detective Gerstel said.

"I hope I can be of some help. What is this all about, Detective?" Misty asked.

"Just a couple of questions. Do you know Detective Sergeant John Books?"

"Yes, I do."

"How do you know him?"

"He comes to the studio at least once a week to meet with Mr. Holmberg."

"And that would be Mr. Marvin Holmberg of Miracle Pictures?"

"Yes."

"Would you know why a Detective would be meeting with Mr. Holmberg on a weekly basis?"

"At first, I believed that it had to do with the death of Diana Dawson."

"And now?"

"They seem to have become friends. Detective Sergeant Books has been attending studio parties by invitation of Mr. Holmberg."

"Have any other police officers attending these parties that you know of?"

"Yes, Lieutenant Jeffrey Foster."

"Lieutenant Jeffrey Foster?'

"Yes, they usually would attend these parties together."

"What kinds of parties were they?"

"At the studio parties, there would be executives and usually some of our actors and actresses. There were also local politicians and some VIPs."

"Were there any mobsters ever invited to these parties?"

"I believe so, yes, sir."

"Would you know who they might be?"

"The only person I could identify would have been Mr. Siegel."

"Do you know why Mr. Holmberg would have associated with a known gangster?"

"You would have to ask Mr. Holmberg."

"Now, Miss Thompson, do you own a gun?"

"No."

"Did you at any time tell Detective Sergeant Books that your father had sent you a handgun and asked him to show you how to operate it?"

"My father is a Baptist Minister. He would never have given me a gun."

"Thank you, Miss Thompson. I appreciate you coming down. You may go now."

"Goodbye, Detective."

"Mr. Marlboro, I'm Detective Marc Gerstel. I want to thank you for making time to come down and talk to me," Detective Gerstel said.

"Sure. What's this about?"

"Mr. Marlboro, do you know Detective Sergeant John Books?"

"I do."

"How do you know him?"

"Well, as you probably know, I was a Detective with the LAPD about six years ago. I met Detective Sergeant Books on several occasions during that time."

"Did you like Detective Sergeant Books?"

"No, I wouldn't say that either of us liked the other."

"And why is that?"

"I guess you could say we had different styles of operating."

"I understand that you were assaulted several days ago. Is that correct?"

"Yes. I was going to my office late at night when three men attacked me, drug me into an alley a good working over."

"Did you report the incident to the police?"

"I did not."

"And why not?"

"Well, the attackers were long gone, and having been a police officer, I knew that I didn't have any real solid information to give them that would help apprehend them."

"Where you robbed?"

"No. One of the attackers said, "Lay off, Marlboro. Get it, just lay off, shamus.""

"And any idea what he was referring to?"

"I presumed he was talking about the Diana Dawson case. I was hired to look into her death. Her folks are concerned that the police have made no progress. She died over a year ago."

"Any idea who it was that assaulted you, Mr. Marlboro?"

"I wish I did."

"Detective Sergeant Books has confessed to taking part in the assault and that you knew. it"

"I didn't know, but why would he do that?"

"What? Admit to it or assault you."

"Both."

"He hasn't said. During the beating, did you happen to take Detective Sergeant Books' police ID and badge?"

"I did not. Why is he saying I did?"

"Do you know Bohai Zhang?"

"I do. I interviewed him the other day in connection with Diana Dawson's murder."

"Was he a suspect?"

"No, but he did supply Diana from time to time with minor narcotics. I thought that she might have gotten into debt with someone. It turned out not to be the case."

Where did you meet with him?"

"Outside the Greyhound bus terminal. We talked for a few minutes, and I let him go. I did, however, see Detective Sergeant Books stop him and take him away in a car. Books was with another person, a white male."

"Do you know why Zhang was at the bus station?"

"He said that he was planning to go up to San Francisco to see his folks."

"And you're saying you saw Detective Sergeant Books and another police officer pick him up?"

"That's right. You can ask Bohai Zhang if he hasn't left for Frisco."

"Bohai Zhang was found dead last night. Shot to death."

"Jesus."

"Do you know Misty Thompson?"

"I do. We've gone out several times."

"Did you give her a pistol?"

"A pistol? No."

"You didn't give her a Walther PPK."

"No, I had no reason to give her a gun."

"Books is saying that you provided Miss. Thompson with a Walther PPK in order to acquire his fingerprints on the gun."

"And why would I do that?"

"For the purposes of framing him for the murder of Bohai Zhang."

"So, let me see if I got this straight, Books is saying that while he was kicking the shit out of me, I had the foresight to steal his badge and ID, entrap him to handling a gun for his prints, and kill Bohai Zhang so that I could frame him. Do I have it right?"

"Right. Did you?"

"Detective Gerstel, I like to think of myself as a pretty smart guy, but I have to admit that I'm not that smart, calculating, or cold-blooded to kill somebody just to get even with someone who attacked me, even if I did know who he was, which I didn't until you just told me."

"Okay, well, thank you for your time, Mr. Marlboro. Before you go, do you want to press charges against Detective Sergeant Books for assault and battery? He's currently being held for capital murder in the shooting death of Bohai Zhang."

"No, he's in enough trouble without me piling on."

"I see. Not many people would be so understanding."

"Have you ever been up to San Quentin and seen what life is like?"

"No, I can't say that I have."

"It's Hell, Detective Gerstel. Like I said, he's in enough trouble without me piling on."

"Detective Andrew Hargrove, you're partners with Detective Sergeant Books; is that correct?" Asked Detective Gerstel.

"Yes, sir."

"I have an eyewitness who claims that you and Detective Sergeant Books picked up Bohai Zhang outside the Greyhound bus terminal three days ago. Is that correct?"

"Yes."

"What happened once you picked him up."

"I was driving. Detective Sergeant Books put him in the back seat of the car and got in next to him."

"Books told me to drive over to Yale and Alpine Street."

"Did he say why?"

"No, he didn't."

"Go on."

"Detective Sergeant Books starts to hit the prisoner on the way over."

"What did you do or say?"

"Nothing, sir. I'm just a rookie Detective. I didn't feel it was my place to challenge my superior officer."

"Then what?"

"I park in front of this vacant warehouse. Detective Sergeant Books gets out and takes the prisoner into the building. He tells me to sit tight and that he'll be right back."

"How long was Detective Sergeant Books in the building with Bohai Zhang?"

"About fifteen minutes, sir."

"So, he comes back, then what?"

"He comes back alone. He tells me that he left Zhang inside."

"Did he say he killed him?"

"No, sir!"

"Did you hear any gunshots?"

"I can't be certain; I did have the police radio on while I was waiting."

"Detective Hargrove, you're already in a world of shit. I'll ask you one more time: did you hear any gunshots?"

"I heard three shots, sir."

"Did Detective Sergeant Book say anything when he returned to the car?"

"Not right away; he just told me to drive. A few minutes later, I asked where Zhang was. He said Zhang was in Chink Heaven. He then held up a bus ticket that he took from Zhang's pocket, laughed, and said, see Hargrove, no tickee, no washee."

"And what did you think when he said all of that?"

"That he must have killed Zhang."

"Did you report him?"

"No, sir."

"Because?"

"The code, sir."

"What code?"

"The blue code. Protecting fellow officers."

"So, you're telling me that you think it's okay for a cop to kill someone and get away with it?"

Hargrove sat silent, not answering.

Detective Gerstel stood and said, "Detective Andrew Hargrove, you're under arrest for accessory after the fact and for aiding and abetting in covering up the murder of Bohai Zhang."

Marlboro drove over to Misty's apartment, arriving just after six p.m.

"Hey, doll, how'd it go?"

"Fine. Are you sure we did the right thing?"

"Yes, one hundred percent. Books did kill Zhang. I was in the next room when it happened."

"Why didn't you just leave the gun there after Books shot the kid?" She challenged.

"Books wouldn't leave a gun behind with his prints on it. He's too smart for that. Misty, it's not like we framed an innocent man. Books shot Zhang."

"Yeah, I guess you're right," She said

"So, you hungry? Want to go grab a bite to eat?"

"Starving."

"Feel like some seafood. How's Ted's Grill in Santa Monica Canyon sound?"

"Great."

Marlboro put down the top of the Fleetmaster, as it was a glorious night to enjoy driving down to Malibu on the PCH, top down.

Driving north on the Pacific Coast Highway, Marlboro sensed that they were being followed, and this time not by Hanson's men, Officers Redding and Johnson.

They arrived at the restaurant just as the sun was starting to set. He pulled into valet parking, handed the boy a sawbuck, and said, "Park it right up front and keep an eye on it."

"Yes, sir!" the valet said.

Marlboro didn't want another surprise planted under the hood of his car. That reminded him he needed to give a call to O'Riley from the bomb squad in the morning.

Marlboro requested a table in the back overlooking the ocean. He took his seat facing the front entrance like he always did.

It wasn't long after they had ordered their drinks that Marlboro spotted two gunsels enter the restaurant. He leaned into Misty and whispered, "Look towards the entrance. Do you recognize those two mugs?"

"Yes, those were the two men I mentioned to you who came to see Mr. Holmberg." She said anxiously.

"Don't worry, doll, nothing terrible is going to happen."

He saw Gianfranco 'The Weasel' Buonaiuto indicate where they were seated to his partner Vinicio 'Three Fingers' Fassio where they were seated. They started making their way to them. Marlboro had his .38 Police Special close at hand.

The Weasel tipped his fedora to Misty, "Hello, Angel, remember us?" I'm Mr. Smith, and this here is Mr. Jones."

"Yes, I do remember you both," She said demurely.

"That's nice. And are you John Marlboro?" The Weasel asked.

"I am. What can I do for you, gentlemen?"

"We hear that you've been sticking your nose where it don't belong."

"Where did you hear that?"

"Oh, here and there."

"And?"

"And, a guy could get hurt by not minding his business. Know what I mean?"

"No," Marlboro said defiantly.

"Look, you keep asking for it, and you're going to get it. Plenty. I'm telling you to lay off, so lay off."

"And, if I don't?"

"Keep it up, Marlboro, and they'll be picking iron out of your liver."

Marlboro looked at Misty and said sarcastically, "The cheaper the hooligan, the gaudier the patter. Now, you Mr. Jones."

"Mr. Smith."

"Smith, Jones, whatever your alias is this week, I don't scare easy, get it! Just ask your friends Luigi and Fat Tony. Me, I'm not overly worried by you pocket-edition desperadoes waving your guns all around.

Personally, I think you've been watching too many Jimmy Cagney movies. So, you go back and tell whoever is pulling your strings that I'm paid to end trouble, not start it.

Now, as you can see, this is a table for two, so blow," Marlboro said forcefully.

Both the Weasel and 'Three Fingers' Fassio started to reach inside their coats for their guns; as they did, Marlboro had his gun out and pointing at them.

"Go ahead. Let's see how far you get," Marlboro dared.

"This ain't over, Marlboro. Not by a long shot," The Weasel sneered.

On the way back to Misty's apartment, Marlboro again detected that they were being tailed.

"Listen, doll, I'm sorry to have drug you into this mess. I think it best that you stay somewhere other than your apartment tonight. Is there somewhere you can stay?"

"My folks live in Venice Beach."

"Okay, I'll lose the tail and drop you off there."

Through a combination of U-turns, bootleg turns, J-turns, float shifting, and a couple of hand-brake turns, Marlboro was able to shake the tail.

He dropped off Misty at her parents' house.

"I hate to say this, but I think that I got you involved where I shouldn't have. You need to lay low until I sort this whole mishegoss out. Call in sick tomorrow, and don't let anyone know where you're at.

I'm going back to your place now. I got a nasty feeling that those two goons will be headed back there.

I hope I'm wrong. I'll give you a call later. Sorry, doll," Marlboro said and gave her a deep, passionate kiss.

He watched her go inside her folk's house, then drove back to her place. He arrived at 2 a.m., parking several blocks away, he walked in the shadows and alleyways to her apartment building. He didn't see the Weasel's car anywhere. Hopefully, he got there before them.

He waited in her darkened doorway, listening for any telltale signs of intruders. Nothing.

He used the key she gave him; he quietly opened the front door, and with his Colt M1911 .45 caliber semi-automatic pistol in hand, he eased into the entranceway and waited. Again nothing.

He walked through the entire house, making sure that he was alone. Marlboro closed all the blinds and curtains; he unscrewed all the light bulbs to make the room as dark as possible.

He made sure that the light next to the couch was operational before sitting on the sofa in the dark living room. Marlboro sat in the darkness, his eyes adjusting to the absence of light while waiting for the inevitable.

He didn't have to wait long. He heard scratches on the front door lock; someone was trying to pick the lock. The guy was a pro. It took only seconds.

Marlboro knew that he would have a limited advantage in the dark room before the interloper's eyes would eventually adapt to the darkness.

He saw two shadowy figures enter the living room; he could hear them fumbling around, trying to find a light switch.

"Find the light switch," The Weasel whispered.

"Here it is," Three Fingers uttered.

CLICK CLICK CLICK

"What's the matter?" Buonaiuto frantically asked.

"Nothing's happening!" Fassio replied.

When Marlboro felt that he had the advantage, he reached up and turned on the lamp next to where he was seated on the sofa.

The sudden flash of light jarred the two would-be assassins. As they turned, guns drawn, Marlboro emptied the Colt .45 caliber semi-automatic pistol's seven-round clip.

POW POW POW POW POW POW POW

He quickly released the now-empty clip, jammed another full magazine into the gun and fired four more rounds, two into each gunmen.

POW POW POW POW

During Marlboro's career as a police officer, he had witnessed too many killers that the police thought were dead rise up and fire off deadly rounds, striking and killing the officer. He wasn't willing to take that chance.

Marlboro walked over to the telephone and dialed his ex-partner, Detective Jason Hanson.

"Jas. Sorry to call you so late, but I think you need to get over to 116 Hart Avenue. I got a couple customers for the morgue."

"You okay?"

"Yeah, I'm okay."

"Do you know who they are?"

"No, all I know is that they're a couple of pros."

"Okay. Sit tight. I'll be over there as soon with the cavalry."

"Jesus Fucking Christ, Marlboro!" Lieutenant Foster growled. "This makes the Saint Valentine's Day Massacre look like a tea party."

"Sorry, Foster. Next time, I'll try and be more tidy."

"So, who were these guys?" Foster asked.

Detective Hanson, who was first on the scene, walked up to where Lieutenant Foster and Marlboro were standing and said, "We haven't gotten their true IDs yet, Lieutenant. But they're pros; they had unregistered weapons with the serial number filed off the guns, tools for picking locks, and they were wearing gloves."

"I saw them earlier this evening while eating dinner at Ted's Grill in Santa Monica Canyon. They approached me and told me that their names were Mr. Smith and Mr. Jones," Marlboro recounted.

"Probably aliases," Foster said.

"Very good. I bet that's why you're a lieutenant," Marlboro quipped.

"A wise guy, huh? Haul him down to the station and get his statement," Foster barked.

"Come on, John, let's go downtown," Hanson said.

On the ride to the station, Marlboro filled Hanson in on his case.

"I don't know yet who's pulling the strings, but all I know is that it must be someone very high on the food chain," Marlboro confided.

"Well, maybe once we find out who Smith and Jones are, we'll have a better idea."

"Yeah, maybe. My guess is that these two mugs won't draw a direct line to who's really at the top. They're just probably a couple of triggermen that some crime Boss lent out as a favor to Mr. Big."

"Yeah, you're probably right," Hanson agreed.

"You know Jas, I'm getting too old for all this wild west shoot 'em ups. I think from on, I'll concentrate on the more mundane cases, like divorces."

"Hey, don't kid yourself; divorce can get pretty messy. Remember back when you were in homicide, all the butchery and carnage spouses can do to each other?"

"Yeah, now that you mention it."

Marlboro was in and out of the police station by eight a.m. after giving his statement. As Hanson was going to give him a ride back to his car, they got the report from forensics on the ID of the two shooters.

"Hey, Detective Hanson. We just ID'd those two men from this morning's shooting," Officer Kasmin said.

"Who are they?"

"Gianfranco 'The Weasel' Buonaiuto and Vinicio 'Three Fingers' Fassio. They're with the Stephon D'Adamo mob; you know he took over for Bugsy Siegel."

"Thanks, Kasmin. Ever hear of this D'Adamo, John?" Hanson asked.

"As a matter of fact, I have. See, now that Siegel's gone and D'Adamo took over, D'Adamo has decided that he isn't interested in being a part of the movie business. So, he sent Buonaiuto and Fassio to let Holmberg know that he wants his gambling debt all paid in full within thirty days, or else."

"Or else?

"Buonaiuto and Fassio forced Holmberg to sign a life insurance policy made out to D'Adamo."

"How convenient," Hanson sniped.

Hanson dropped Marlboro where his car was parked, blocks away from where the blood bath occurred. He drove back to the scene of the crime. The police warning tape was still up, but there weren't any police stationed there. So, Marlboro used the key and entered. The living room, which he found somewhat ironic; it seems like this one should be referred to as the dying room, looked like a bomb had gone off.

The police never clean up after themselves. They leave behind gloves, fingerprint powder, coffee cups, and assorted other odds and ends on top of all the blood and guts.

He picked up the phone and called Misty.

"Hello."

"Hello, Mrs. Thompson. This is John Marlboro. May I speak with Misty, please?"

"One moment, I'll get her."

"Thank you."

"Hello, John."

"Hey doll, how are you?"

"I'm good, are you alright? I got a call from my neighbor, Mrs. Ward. She told me that there was a big shootout."

"Oh, I'm fine. I wish I could say the same about your apartment."

"What happened?"

"Well, Mr. Smith and Mr. Jones decided to make an unannounced house call. Unfortunately for them, I was waiting for them."

"But, you're okay?"

"Yeah, I'm fine. But I think you should continue to stay with your folks until I can arrange to have your house cleaned up."

"When can I see you again?"

"Probably not until late tomorrow. I have to run out to the Dawson Brothers Dairy in San Jacinto today. Is that okay?"

"Sure, my folks are glad that I'm here."

"Great. I'll see ya soon."

"Bye."

CLICK

Marlboro hung up and called the company that handles all the clean-ups for the LAPD. Epilogue Crime Scene Cleaners' motto is *"There is Life after Death."*

"Epilogue Crime Scene Cleaners."

"Rudy, this is Marlboro."

"Hey, Johnny boy, how ya doing?"

"I got a clean-up. Can you come right over?"

"Jeez, Johnny, I'm up to my neck in stiffs. But for you, no problem. Where you at?"

"Santa Monica. 116 Hart Avenue, apartment 2B."

"Sit tight. We'll be there in thirty."

"Thanks, Rudy, I owe you."

CLICK

Precisely thirty minutes later, Rudy and his crew came knocking at the door.

"Hey, Rudy, thanks for coming over so quickly."

"No problem. Whad'ya got?"

"Right in here," Marlboro said as he brought him in through the entranceway into the living room.

"WHEEEWW!" Rudy whistled.

Rudy Thacker had been cleaning up crime scenes for over twenty years. He got his start in Chicago during the "sinful, ginful" 1920s prohibition era. Between the years of 1920 to 1929, there were 594 mob-related murders in the city of Chicago.

It was after gambling racketeer and "whoremaster" Big Jim Colosimo was gunned down in the lobby of his restaurant at 2126 S. Wabash Avenue on May eleventh, 1920, that Rudy's father, who ran a rug cleaning business right next door to Colosimo's café, got a call from his widow to clean up the mess.

Over the 1920s and 1930s, the Thackers have cleaned up such famous crime scenes as the murders of "Diamond" Joe Esposito, "Machine Gun" Jack McGurn, Frank Capone, Theodore "Handsome Jack" Klutas, and John Dillinger.

After Rudy's father passed away in 1942 and Rudy returned from the killing Nazis with General Patton's 3rd Army, he decided to move out to Los Angeles.

It didn't take too long before Epilogue Crime Scene Cleaners was running on all cylinders. Once the LAPD heard about them, Rudy was busy year-round.

"Did you do this? It looks like the work of Johnny Marlboro," Rudy said with a devilish grin.

"Yeah, unfortunately."

"You know, we just finished cleaning up over at the Original Pantry Café. If I'm not mistaken, that was you, too."

"Yeah."

"Mmm, I like your style, Johnny."

"Thanks."

Rudy started examining the scene and noting what he would need to repair the damage.

"So, how long before it's livable?" Marlboro inquired.

"Nah, six hours max."

Marlboro handed him the key. "Do me a favor, lock up when you leave, put the key under the flower pot by the front door, and send me the bill."

"You got it. I'll be seeing ya, Johnny. You know, I will."

The drive to The Dawson Brothers Dairy was uneventful. Marlboro didn't detect anyone following him. It was a sunny day, just another day in paradise. With the top down on the Fleetmaster, cruising down the highway, and listening to Frank Sinatra on the radio, life was good.

It was eleven-forty-five when Marlboro pulled up to the Dawson farmhouse.

Mrs. Dawson came out to greet him.

"Good morning, Mrs. Dawson. How are you today?" He asked.

"Oh, we're doing as well as can be expected, Mr. Marlboro. And you?"

"I'm doing fine; thank you for asking. Is Mr. Dawson about?"

"He's down at the equipment barn working on something or another. He shouldn't be too long; care to come in and wait?"

"I could go down to the barn."

"No, best not. Charles doesn't like people about when he's working on the equipment; he says he can't concentrate."

"Alright, then, I would love to come inside and wait."

"Can I get you something to drink, coffee or tea?"

"A cup of joe would be nice."

They went inside through the living room into the kitchen.

"Now, you sit right down here and get you a cup. How do you like it?"

"Black is fine, thank you."

"That's how we like it, too. Think I'll pour myself a cup, too," She said.

"How's the investigation going, Mr. Marlboro? Are you finding out who killed my baby?"

"Like I told you and Mr. Dawson, these things take time. I have eliminated several suspects, and I am making progress, but I can't make a rush to judgment. You can appreciate that."

"Yes, of course. It's just the waiting that's the hardest."

"I understand," He said sympathetically.

She set his cup of joe down in front of him and sat across from him with her cup.

"So, what brings you down this way, Mr. Marlboro?"

"I wondered if I might take another look in Diana's room. I'm looking for something like a diary. Have you come across anything like that?"

"A diary, you say? No, I haven't."

"I understand that she visited you a week or so before she went missing."

"That's right. Diana came down for a couple of days with her friend Taylor Carter. Taylor's a nice girl. Have you talked to her?"

"Yes, yes, I did," He answered as he finished his coffee.

"Would you like another?" Mrs. Dawson asked.

"No, thank you, that really hit the spot. Think I'll go look in Diana's room if you don't mind."

"Please."

Marlboro walked down to the end of the hallway to the last room on the right. Diana's room. Nothing appeared to have been moved since the last time he had been there.

He started by going through all of the drawers in her dresser and the drawers at her desk. Marlboro looked under, on top, behind, and in every nook and cranny in her room. He went through all the books in her bookcase, looking inside each. Nothing.

Finally, on his way out, something odd caught his attention. All the pictures hung on the walls in her bedroom were those of famous actresses Ava Gardner, Vivien Leigh, Katharine Hepburn, Hedy Lamar, and Lauren Bacall. All actresses, with the exception of the picture hanging over her bed. An illustration of Jesus Christ reaching out to the viewer.

Marlboro gingerly took the picture off the wall and turned it over. There, taped to the back of the framed picture, was an 8X10 black manila envelope. He carefully removed it and replaced the print over the bed just as he had found it.

He tucked the envelope in his waistband behind his back, hidden by his suit jacket, made sure everything was just as he found it, and went back into the kitchen.

"Did you find what you were looking for?" Mrs. Dawson asked.

"No, I'm afraid not, Mrs. Dawson. But I want to thank you for your hospitality. Tell Mr. Dawson I'm sorry to have missed him. And I promise I will let you both know as soon as I know something."

"Well, I'm sorry you came out here for nothing."

"Oh, it wasn't for nothing. It was good to see you, and I did get a great cup of joe."

"I'm glad you enjoyed it."

"Goodbye, Mrs. Dawson."

"Bye. Bye."

By the time Marlboro got back to Santa Monica to check on Misty's apartment, Rudy and the boys from Epilogue Crime Scene Cleaners were long gone.

He went inside to check on the apartment; as usual, Rudy had outdone himself. To look at it, you'd never know that a slaughter had taken place earlier that night. The walls and rug were spotless, with no sign of blood or brain splatter; there was no smell of death, only that of a fresh coat of paint.

Being satisfied, Marlboro headed downtown to his office to review the contents of Diana's envelope.

Once safely in his office, the door locked, and he broke the seal of the envelope. Inside, he found multiple candid photographs of Los Angeles' political elite, high-ranking police officials, and some of the city's most prominent business captains of industry. Any one of them would not want these images to get out to the public.

Also in the envelope was a list of names and dates, a virtual list of who's who of LA's upper crust.

Marlboro was sure that Bugsy Siegel also had images and was using them to his advantage. But the idea of somebody else having the power was totally unacceptable. As a rule, mobsters don't like competition, hence the great New York, Detroit, Kansas City, and Chicago gangland massacres.

Now that Siegel was gone and Stephon D'Adamo was LA's newly crowned king, he would be contacting all his puppets to dance to his tune.

Marlboro knew he was sitting on dynamite, and if it ever got wind that he was in possession of the dingus, he'd be in a real jam. D'Adamo would be sending out the chopper squad to fit him for a wooden kimono.

He was sure that he was already on D'Adamo's radar since he had bumped off four of the mob's top made men. Until things cooled down, he would be continually looking over his shoulder. He would also have to distance himself from the dolls, Misty, Skylar, Taylor, Robin, and especially Molly.

Marlboro would need some time to figure out what his move would be. He knew he would only have one shot at the golden ring. If he muffed it, he'd be sleeping with the fishes.

He resealed the envelope and addressed it to himself, to be held at the main post office at 506 S. Spring, downtown care of general delivery. He then called Misty, Skylar, Taylor, Robin, and Molly and told them that he was going to cheese it for a couple of weeks. He was getting too hot to be seen with. He said to them that he would be checking in with them from time to time to make sure they were okay.

Marlboro made two calls after touching base with the dolls. His ex-partner, Detective Jason Hanson, and Donald Wilson, a hack for the Los Angeles Herald-Express. Wilson and Marlboro became acquainted while he was a detective working homicide on several sensational murder cases.

He called his partner to check in to see if Hanson had picked up any scuttlebutt buzzing around Central Division about him.

"Marlboro, where are you?" Hanson asked.

"I'm on the lam until the heat blows over. I'm just going to hunker down at my place till things cool down."

"Good thinking. I'm hearing that D'Adamo's not all that happy with you whacking his two top torpedoes, Holmberg called the cops and lodged a personal complaint against you, and the boys in blue aren't all that thrilled with how you ratted out Books."

"Gee. Life's a bitch, ain't it."

"All I'm saying is stay low and keep your head down. Let me know if you need anything."

"Thanks, Jas."

CLICK

"Wilson, of the Herald-Express."

"Donald, Marlboro here."

"Marlboro, you're quite the popular fellow."

"Tell me about it. Listen, I've got an envelope sitting at the main Post Office under my name in general delivery. I wanted you to know about it in case I get rubbed out. There's a lot of dynamite against some very powerful people who will stop at nothing to keep it under wraps. I'm hoping that it's my life insurance policy, and I'm going to try and grift it as far as I can."

"You know you're skating on dangerously thin ice, Marlboro. Word on the street is that D'Adamo has given the go-ahead the moment you surface to start throwing lead.

There are trouble boys cruising all over town looking for you. I hear that the price is 50 large," Wilson relayed.

"Gee, I wonder if I could collect the bounty if I offed myself."

"Interesting concept. Anything I can do?"

"Yeah, make sure they spell my name right in my obits."

CLICK

Marlboro left his car at the office garage, took a taxi several blocks from his house, and carefully made his way home in the dead of night. He canvased the area, making sure that no one saw him enter his house through the alleyway.

He went around and checked the booby traps that he had set up, making sure that they were all functional. He placed some extra weapons in strategic places around the house.

Once he felt everything was in place, he sat in the living room with a Thompson submachine gun, or "Tommy Gun," *aka*, "the Chicago typewriter," on his lap and waited.

One of the more vulnerable spots in the house is the kitchen window at the back of the house. Marlboro strung several strands of exposed electrical wire across the inside of the window while placing a small tray with about an inch of water hidden next to the house. At night, the water wouldn't be visible to anyone trying to enter the house through the window. The result of someone trying to enter that way would be electrocution.

EEYGAAH!!!

The scream came from the back of the house. Marlboro stealthily made his way through the dark house. When he reached the kitchen, the body of a man was standing halfway in the kitchen window. Dead.

He could hear multiple men whispering outside. Moments later, he heard a crash of glass from the side window. Somebody threw a Molotov cocktail into the house. Marlboro had been prepared for such an eventuality; he had placed fire extinguishers near every window. The fire was soon out. While standing in the shadows of the hallway, a man started to enter through that same window. Marlboro waited until the man was halfway in, drew his .38 Police Special, and fired one shot in the man's head.

POW

He went back into the living room and put on a WW2 US Army M3A1 Gas Mask, anticipating a couple of tear gas canisters being lobbed in through the living room glass plate window. Marlboro picked up his Thompson submachine gun and waited.

He didn't have to wait long.

CRASH CRASH THWIP THWIP

The tear gas canisters immediately started to emit their effluvium vapors. Seconds later, a battering ram smashed through the front door. Three men holding extremely bright flashlights came rushing in, firing wildly; unfortunately for them, the torches made them easy targets.

Marlboro gripped the Tommy Gun tightly against his shoulder and let loose several rapid-fire bursts.

RATT RATTTT TRATT RATT TRATTTT TRATT RATTTT TRATT RATTTT TRATT RATT TRATTTT TRATT RATTTT TRATT RATTTT TRATT RATT TRATTTT TRATT RATTTT

Outside, he heard the scrambling footsteps of men running away, then the screeching sound of tires. Off in the distance, were the comforting sounds of police, ambulance, and fire truck sirens.

When the first uniformed police officers entered Marlboro's house, they found him sitting on his sofa in the living room, staring out of the shattered front plate glass window, his gas mask sitting atop his head, holding the Tommy Gun on his lap.

"LAPD! John, I need you to raise your hands! Leave the gun on the ground," Shouted Sergeant Fitzgerald, a fifteen-year veteran of the force who knew and liked Marlboro.

Marlboro did as he was told. He raised his hands over his head after placing the submachine gun on the floor by his feet. He stood up and walked over to Officer Fitzgerald.

"Hey, Pat."

"Hey, John. It looks like you had one Hell of a party," He said, grinning.

"Yeah. You should have been here. Well, I guess there goes the neighborhood."

"Come on, let's get you down to the station for your statement."

"I want all my weapons returned."

"You got a license for all of these?"

"Yes. For every one of them, and I want them all back."

"You have my word on it, John. Any idea who these mugs are?"

"I'd put even money on out-of-town talent. Chicago, maybe New York."

"D'Adamo?"

"That's what I'm thinking."

"Okay, let's take a ride downtown."

Giotto "The Rat" Randolph, Amintore "The Viper" Sella, Anthony "The Nose" Musumeci, Alejandro "The Boot" Gencarelli, and Cristopher "The Butcher" Congleton were all hitmen flown in from Chicago.

"Now, why would all these goombahs come all the way from Chi-town just to try and knock you off?" Asked Lieutenant Foster.

In interrogation room three, Lieutenant Foster sat with Detective Sergeant Morris, head of the homicide division, Officer Fitzgerald, and Marlboro.

"I don't know, Lieutenant. I guess I must be doing something right," Marlboro quipped.

"You're a funny guy, Marlboro."

"I am a funny guy, Lieutenant. I come from funny."

Lieutenant Foster glared disdainfully, "Come on, Marlboro cut the crap! What is it you have that they're afraid of?" He growled.

"You know, Lieutenant, you seem awfully interested in what I might have. Why is that?"

"Now, you listen to me, you two-bit glorified gumshoe. You got more dead bodies stacked up in the morgue than Bonnie and Clyde, and I'm sick and tired of cleaning up after you. You've been lucky so far that no civilians have been killed.

Marlboro, I don't give a hoot in Hell if you get killed or not, but if some poor joker gets killed in the crossfire, I'll see that you take the fall for it.

I never liked you, Marlboro, or your cavalier attitude," Foster snarled.

"I don't much care that you don't like me or my attitude, Lieutenant. I admit my attitude is pretty bad; I grieve over it during these long winter evenings, but instead of hounding me, don't you think your time would be better off looking into why and who sent those torpedoes to kill me?

Funny thing, Lieutenant, I always thought the police were supposed to protect the victim, not the criminal," Marlboro challenged.

Foster jumped up from the table and shouted, "Get him outta here, now!"

"Come on. Can I give you a ride home?" Officer Fitzgerald offered.

"Thanks, Pat," Marlboro said.

As they were headed towards the squad car, Marlboro stopped.

"Hey, my guns!" Marlboro said, alarmed.

"Don't worry. I have them all in the trunk of the car."

"Whew," Marlboro said, relieved.

On the drive back to his home, Marlboro kept checking the side mirror and looking back through the rear window for any sign of their being followed.

"You don't think they'd be foolish enough to try tailing a police car, do you?" Fitzgerald asked.

"Probably not, but better safe than sorry."

"So, John, what is this really all about?"

"The Diana Dawson murder."

"Who?"

"Diana Dawson. She was found murdered over a year ago. Her folks hired me to look into it since they felt you guys have been dragging your feet."

"Have we?"

"Well, in just three weeks, it seems I've touched a nerve that you guys hadn't exposed. Wouldn't you agree by the number of attempts on my life?"

"Why don't you just turn whatever it is that you've got over to homicide and take the heat off yourself?" Fitzgerald asked.

Marlboro said nothing and just looked at Fitzgerald with a questioning gaze. It took a few seconds before the lightbulb went off inside Fitzgerald's head.

"No! You think that somebody on the force is crooked?"

"As a three-dollar bill."

"Whad'ya going to do, John?" Fitzgerald asked.

"Well, first things first. I gotta call Rudy when I get home."

"Rudy from Epilogue Crime Scene Cleaners?"

"Yeah, Rudy, the magician."

"Then what?"

"Then, I go see Stephon D'Adamo."

"DETECTIVE DEATH." Five known mobsters were gunned down while trying to invade the home of

John Marlboro, a private detective, read the headline in the Los Angeles Herald-Express.

Last night, five known hitmen from Chicago, Illinois, tried an assault on the home of a former police detective, now private investigator, John Marlboro.

The attack came around 2 a.m. last night, when Giotto "The Rat" Randolph, Amintore "The Viper," Sella, Cristopher "The Butcher," Congleton, Anthony "The Nose," Musumeci, and Alejandro "The Boot," Gencarelli, tried to enter Marlboro's home on West 11th Place.

They were greeted with a hail of bullets sprayed from Marlboro's Thompson sub-machine gun, reigning death upon these would-be assassins. Reliable sources told the Express that Marlboro is currently investigating the murder of Diana Dawson, a year-old cold case that the LAPD has yet to solve.

There are rumors that the murder of the young starlet may have the involvement of several high political, police, and mob entanglements.

When questioned, we at the Express have received nothing but "no comments." As more and more facts begin to surface, people are...."

At 601 Mountain Drive, Beverly Hills sits a giant mansion, even by Beverly Hills standards. The 27,555-square-foot chateau of Mr. Stephon D'Adamo.

The house was built in the classic French country houses of Louis XIV. Sitting on 1.65 acres, the house was built with Parisian limestone, as was Versailles. The entrance has water cascading down into a series of reflecting pools.

It has sixteen bedrooms, eighteen bathrooms, an indoor and outdoor swimming pool, a tennis court, formal and junior dining rooms, a custom-made artisanal kitchen, a wine cellar, and a ballroom.

When approaching the driveway entrance, there stands a gatehouse. Inside, there are three armed private security guards. The compound has armed guards with dogs constantly patrolling the perimeter, day and night.

Marlboro drove the red Fleetmaster up to the guardhouse and waited. Two armed guards appeared from the shack and approached him.

"Can I help you, sir?" A tall, thin unarmed man dressed as a police officer said. The other guard standing behind him, holding a Browning A5 12-gauge shotgun, stood at the ready.

"Yes, my name is John Marlboro. I'd like to see Mr. D'Adamo, please."

"Just wait here, sir."

The tall guard went inside the guardhouse while the guard with the shotgun stood his ground, showing no emotion.

Marlboro could see that the tall guard had picked up a phone and was talking to someone from the big house. After he hung up the phone, he returned to the car.

"Mr. Marlboro, I need you to step outside the car so that I may frisk you."

"Sure," Marlboro said as he exited the car.

The frisk was very professional, very courteous, and not rough or demeaning.

"You may proceed to the main house; once there, someone will greet you at the entrance," The guard turned and waved at the guard seated in the guardhouse operating the gate.

As Marlboro approached the house entrance, he saw two stocky-looking men in dark suits waiting for him. When he got out of the car, they had him turn around, and one of the men frisked him again, this time not so genteel.

"I got to admit, you sure gotta pair of stones coming in here," One of the goons said.

"Come on, this way," The other hooligan said as he took Marlboro by the arm.

They walked around the outside of the house to where D'Adamo was lying on a lounge chair by the side of the pool. It was obvious that he'd been swimming. He lay on his back, sunning himself, wearing a pair of blue plastic eyecups for tanning.

He was in his mid-fifties, maybe older, with thinning salt and pepper hair that he combed from the left side of his head over the top to the right side. He had more hair on his back than atop his head.

He had an even dark tan, with a paunch of a spare tire around his middle. And although you wouldn't confuse his nose for a zucchini, it didn't hurt that it wasn't green.

"Here he is, boss. Want I should knee-cap him?" The punk holding his arm said.

"Lorenzo, non essere stupido! Go away, you too Angelo. Capeesh?" D'Adamo said.

D'Adamo didn't move, he didn't take his eyecups off, he didn't turn his head towards him, and he didn't offer Marlboro a seat. So, he stood.

"You're one tough son of a bitch to kill, Mr. Marlboro."

"Sorry."

"What is it you want?"

"I want to know who killed Diana Dawson."

"And why do you think that I would know that?"

"Because you're a very powerful man, Mr. D'Adamo, and knowledge is power. And even if you don't know, you could find out who gunned her."

"Why would I want to do that? What's in it for me?"

"What is it you want?"

"Oh, I think you know very well what I want."

"What makes you think that I have it?"

"If you don't have it now, you know where you can get your hands on it. Like you said, Mr. Marlboro, knowledge is power. So, do you want to make a trade?" D'Adamo asked, showing no sign of emotion.

"How soon can you get me the name and credible proof of Diana's killer."

"Proof?"

"A name without proof is worthless."

"Forty-eight hours."

"Forty-eight hours, but none of your gunmen are dogging me. I'm tired of looking over my shoulder, and besides, I think I've bagged the hunting season's legal limit of wise guys."

"Look on the table to my left where I have my towel and a bottle of Coppertone. There's my business card. Take it and give me a call in forty-eight hours. Goodbye, soldier," D'Adamo said.

He raised his right hand, snapped his fingers, and barked, "Angelo, take Mr. Marlboro back to his car."

"Right, boss. Come on," Angelo said as he prodded Marlboro around the house to the driveway where his car was waiting, facing the correct position.

"You know, Marlboro, The Weasel was a friend of mine. This ain't over. Now scram before I finish you off right here."

"Yeah, well, I'll try not to lose sleep over it," Marlboro said as he got into his Fleetmaster and drove off out of the estate.

Lieutenant Foster walked into the Los Angeles Hall of Justice, more commonly referred to as L.A.'s Taj Mahal of Misdeeds. The building houses everything from courtrooms, evidence rooms, coroner tables, HQs for the district attorney, public defenders, Sheriff's department, and the county jail.

Foster rode the elevator up to the fourteenth floor to where ex-Detective John Books sat awaiting trial for murder. The Lieutenant was seated in the prisoner's visitors area, waiting for the guards to bring in Books.

The room was divided into two separate rooms, with a large glass divider running down the middle. The visitors sat on one side of the glass, and the prisoners sat on the other. They spoke through a series of small holes drilled into the glass, large enough to converse but too small to pass anything through to each other. There were wooden partitions between the individual visiting areas that stretched from floor to ceiling for privacy.

While visiting, the guards would stroll back and forth the length of the room behind the prisoners, making sure that nothing irregular was transpiring. Each prisoner had fifteen minutes for personal visitations, and those with their attorneys or law officials were allowed thirty minutes.

When Detective Books entered the visitation room, he had been beaten up pretty badly. Once the word that he was a police officer, especially a homicide detective, he was a marked man. The jail officials placed him in protective custody.

"John? What the Hell happened to you? Are you all right?"

"No, God Damnit! I am not all right," Books shouted.

A guard came over and gave Books a warning.

"Keep it down, or I'll take you back to your cell. Understand?"

"Yes," He whimpered.

Foster couldn't believe what he was looking at. Books had a black eye, a split lip, a broken nose, and a gash on his forehead that required over twelve stitches. He sat slumped in the chair after receiving two bruised ribs, a fractured wrist, and a cracked vertebra.

"It was three days ago. As I was heading into the showers, six guys came out of nowhere and beat the living Hell out of me. You got to get me out of here, Jeffrey; I mean it!"

"Now, take it easy, John. I've already had you moved into protective custody. I'm working on some other angles."

The truth of the matter was that Foster had done nothing to help his colleague or better his situation.

"Jeffrey, unless you do something to get me out of here soon, I'm going to rat out the lot of you. Because as long as I'm in here, I'm a dead man and got nothing to lose."

"Easy does it, John. I'll work something out. I promise."

"You got two days, or I go and drop a dime on the DA. Two days," Books stood up and walked back towards the cells, leaving Lieutenant Jeffrey Foster sitting there looking like he'd just been gut shot.

Marlboro drove past his house on 11th Place, where he saw Rudy and his crew working on the repairs from last night's bloodbath. As he drove down the block, he noticed that all the neighbor's windows were either shuttered closed, or curtains were tight.

He decided to see Molly. He hadn't spoken to her since the shootout at the restaurant. She had been ordered to take some leave time, which was standard police policy after an officer had been involved in a shooting, especially a shooting where someone was killed.

He rang the doorbell of her apartment and waited. As he stood in the hallway, he could hear voices and laughter coming from inside.

Molly was laughing when she swung the door open to reveal that, apparently, she had been entertaining a man.

When she saw it was Marlboro, her cheerful demeanor changed.

"Oh, John. Ah, please come in," She said.

"Hey, Molly. I guess I should have called before coming over. Didn't mean to interrupt."

"No. Don't be silly. John, do you know Ray Chandler? He's a motor, out of Ramparts."

"Pleased to meet you, Ray," Marlboro said as he shook the officer's hand.

"It's my pleasure to meet you, Mr. Marlboro. I've heard a lot about you."

"Nothing good, I bet. And it's John, please. Mr. Marlboro is my father."

"Well, it depends on who you talk to, John."

"Yeah, usually is. Well, Molly, I won't keep you; I just stopped by to see how you're holding up."

"I'm coping. You?"

"Haven't had much time to cope."

"Heard you had some Chicago lightning at your house last night; sorry I missed it," Molly said.

"Yeah, some of D'Adamo's boys tried to stitch me up. They left with a bad case of lead poisoning."

"How many?" Chandler asked.

"Five," Marlboro muttered.

"Is this all about what happened at the restaurant the other night?" Molly asked.

"No. Some powerful people think I have something they fear might hurt them."

"And do you?" She pressed.

"You don't want to know. Say, would you look at the time, I'm gonna drift."

"You take care of yourself, John."

"You too. Ray, it was nice to meet you. I'll talk to you later, doll."

"Bye, John," Molly said.

After dinner, Charles and Margaret Dawson were sitting in their living room listening to You Bet Your Life with Groucho Marx on the radio when they heard a knock on the door.

Charles Dawson got up to see who it might be calling so late at night. He went to the front door; he saw two men wearing suits, claiming to be Los Angeles County Sheriff Detectives, through the small window on the front door.

"Mr. Dawson? I'm Detective Wilson, and this is my partner, Detective Beech. May we come in for a minute, sir?" The man claiming to be Detective Wilson said, without showing any identification.

"What's this about, Detective?" Dawson asked.

"It's about your daughter, sir."

"May I see some form of ID?"

The two men looked at each other.

"Sure," The man claiming to be Wilson reached inside his suit jacket and revealed a pistol.

"Open the door, old man!" Wilson demanded.

"You go to Hell!" Dawson shouted as he turned and ran into the living room to fetch his shotgun from over the fireplace mantle.

"Margie, go upstairs, call Sheriff Trimble, tell him to hightail it over here, now! Then, call Raymond and David and tell them to come armed. Stay upstairs and get my pistol, lock the door, and shoot anybody that tries to come in. Now go!"

As his wife ran upstairs, Wilson and Beech randomly fired shots into the house.

POW POW POW POW POW POW POW

Dawson turned off all the inside lights and switched on the outdoor floodlights, illuminating a swarth area half the size of a football field around the entire house, leaving the two gunmen exposed.

"Come on out, Dawson, and nobody will get hurt," Wilson yelled.

Charles Dawson fired both barrels of his Remington Double Barrel Shotgun.

BAROOM BAROOM

He winged the man calling himself Wilson in the right shoulder, forcing the two assailants to rush for cover.

Over the next twenty-five minutes. A savage gun battle erupted. Wilson and Beech fired over eighty rounds into Dawson's farmhouse.

They split up, trying to attack from different fronts, but every time they tried to advance due to the illumination surrounding the house, they were thwarted.

Mrs. Dawson could see the headlights and flashing red police lights of Sheriff Trimble off in the distance. Soon, the sound of the siren was noticeable, even to the attackers. They tried to make their getaway as soon as they heard the sirens.

As they ran towards their car, Dawson had the forethought of shooting out the front tire, leaving them to escape on foot. The last Charles Dawson saw the gunmen. They were running off into the cow pasture.

Sheriff Trimble arrived just moments before Dawson's brothers Raymond and David who came armed to the teeth. Trimble called for backup; they set up a perimeter around the Dawson farm, all nine hundred acres.

They didn't try to enter the pasture while it was dark; in fear of possibly shooting each other, they decided to wait until sunrise.

Marlboro was spending the night in his office, sleeping at his desk. He couldn't go back to his place; Rudy wasn't finished. Molly seemed to be entertaining Chandler, the motor boy, and physically, he just wasn't ready to try and pleasure Misty three or four times a night. Maybe tomorrow, but after the havoc wreaked upon him last night, Marlboro needed a restful night's sleep, which he did not get.

At eleven that evening, as he was just starting to fall into a deep sleep, the telephone rang.

"Mr. Marlboro, Charles Dawson here. I just wanted to tell you that there has been a shootout at the farm tonight."

"Is everyone all right?"

"Yes, we're fine. I think that you should come down here."

"Would you like me to come now?"

"I think it might be best."

"I'm leaving now."

CLICK

Marlboro made the typically hour forty-minute trip in one hour and five minutes. When he arrived, the area was cordoned off by police; he had to pass through a police roadblock to get to Dawson's farmhouse.

When he drove up to the farmhouse, he spotted Charles Dawson talking to a man dressed in a sheriff's uniform, wearing a tan Stetson 10-gallon cowboy hat. There were dozens of people meandering around: deputies, crime photographers, forensic lab technicians, and Dawson's younger brothers.

Marlboro parked the Fleetmaster and walked over to Charles Dawson.

"Mr. Dawson, are you all right?"

"Fine. Fine. I want to thank you for coming out all this way at such short notice."

Dawson turned to Sheriff Trimble and said, "Sheriff Trimble, this here is Mr. Marlboro. He's the one I told you about."

Trimble tipped his cowboy hat, "Glad to meet ya, Mr. Marlboro."

"Sheriff." Marlboro acknowledged.

"What the Hell happened?" Marlboro asked.

"Well, two fellas came knocking at our door around a little after eight. Margaret and I were listening to the radio.

Said they were L.A. Sheriff's Detectives. When I asked to see their IDs, they pulled their guns and started to shoot up the house.

Luckily, I was able to hit one of them in the shoulder. When they heard the Sheriff coming, they ran to their car; as they started to back up, I was able to get a shot off that flattened their front tire, forcing them to hightail it outta here on foot," Dawson explained.

"And Margaret?" Marlboro inquired.

"Oh, she's fine. She's one tough cookie."

"Thank goodness; you're both okay. Any idea what they wanted?"

"No, They said it had to do with Diana. But they never said what. I think they were looking to rob us; I just don't know."

"Well, the important thing is that you're both safe."

"Looks like a God Damn circus with all these people running around here. I'm Ray. Charles' brother and you must be Marlboro," Raymond Dawson said as he approached.

"That's right. Nice to meet you, Ray. Sorry, it had to be under such circumstances."

"So, shamus, whaddya think these two guys wanted?" Raymond rasped.

"Well, they could have been trying to rob your Charles and Margaret."

"Or?" He pumped.

"Or. Maybe they were looking for something that they felt Diana might have left behind here," Marlboro postulated.

"Like what?"

"I'm more interested in who they are. Once we know that, we might be able to figure out what they were looking for. Excuse me," Marlboro said as he walked over to the abandoned getaway car.

The black and white 1946 Ford Coupe sat like a beached whale in Dawson's driveway, gasping at its last breath as the steam from the radiator succumbed to its fatal wounds. Its right front fender, headlight, and wide whitewall tire looked like so much shredded wheat. That's what two barrels of double-ought buckshot will do to chrome, steel, and rubber.

Sheriff Trimble, standing over on the opposite side of the disabled leviathan, asked, "So, whaddya think, Mr. Marlboro?"

Marlboro gave the Ford a quick once over, then answered.

"She's definitely not a police issue. The license plates are fake; there's no police radio, and the registration has been doctored. Also, the positioning of the City Seal on the side of the car isn't correct, and the type font for the word "police" should be Eurostile Bold, not Helvetica. I'd say whoever fitted her up, although not perfect, was a pro."

"Bravo, Mr. Marlboro. Very Impressive," Trimble said with awe.

"I'm a detective, Sheriff Trimble. I work at it. I don't play at it."

"Yes. I can see that."

Once the sun peaked over the peach-colored tops of the San Jacinto Mountains, the Sheriff's deputies began sending men and dogs in to look for the suspects.

After three hours, they found the man claiming to be Detective Wilson dead. Apparently, he died from the wounds he suffered at the hands of Charles Dawson.

The second man, known as Detective Beech, had escaped. Trimble put out an APB based on Dawson's description.

"Attention. Attention. Attention. The following is an all-points bulletin for all law enforcement officials in the Riverside and Los Angeles Counties.

Be on the lookout for a Caucasian, six-foot-tall, thin, blonde-haired male. He was wearing a blue pinned striped suit, a white shirt, a red striped tie, and a dark grey fedora. The suspect is believed to be on foot. He was last seen in the San Jacinto area. It is thought that he is using the alias of Detective Beech.

Approach with extreme caution. He is considered to be armed and dangerous. That is all."

Sheriff Trimble's men brought the dead man to Dawson's farm, where Trimble had set up his headquarters and base camp. The county coroner was standing by to examine the body.

Marlboro had been expecting the body to be that of one of D'Adamo's assassins, but he was in for a big surprise.

"I know this man," Marlboro confessed.

"This is Detective Scanlon of the LAPD. He works out of the Gang and Narcotics Division," Marlboro said.

"Are you sure?" Trimble asked.

"Positive."

"But why would an LAPD detective try to rob and kill the Dawsons?" The Sheriff asked.

"I don't know, Sheriff. But I might suggest you give a call to the Los Angeles Police Chief, Clemence Horrall, PDQ.

Sheriff, do me a favor if you would. When you talk to the boys in the LAPD, I would appreciate it if you didn't mention my name."

"Shy?"

"No, it's just that, we haven't seen eye to eye lately," He said with a shrug.

"Marlboro, who?" Trimble said with a wink.

"Exactly."

"Right-o! Jenkins, let's head back to the office," Trimble ordered his driver as he got into his squad car.

"Good luck, Sheriff," Marlboro said as Sheriff Trimble drove off with the meat wagon.

Charles Dawson came up to Marlboro, shook his hand, and said, "Thanks for coming all the way out here. We really appreciate it."

"Mr. Dawson, I'm so sorry you had to go through this, but I'm pretty sure I know what happened to your daughter.

I need to be sure, but I should be able to wrap things up in a day or two. Until then, you stay safe, and I'll talk to you soon."

Marlboro strolled back to his car, put the top down, and headed west back to the city of angels.

He got to his office around four in the afternoon. On the ride back from Dawson's farm, he had a feeling that he might have picked up a tail. Marlboro pulled into a Texaco service station on Blaine Street in Riverside for a fill-up; as the attendant checked the oil, his hunch was right on the button.

As hard as they tried, Marlboro was quickly able to spot Officers Redding and Johnson following him.

The question Marlboro was asking himself was why. And how did they know that he was at Dawson's farm? He wasn't followed last night; he was sure of that. Someone must have tipped them off. But who.

Once back at the office, he planned to check with his message service for any missed calls, then call Rudy to check in on the progress of his house, and depending on the status, he might give Misty a ring.

The service reported that he had an urgent message from Officer Bill O'Riley, two calls from Detective Hanson, two calls from Misty at Mr. Holmberg's office, and one message from Rudy at Epilogue Crime Scene Cleaners. The message was, *"The house will be ready tomorrow. Sorry."*

Marlboro called Bill O'Riley first, as it was marked as urgent.

"Bill. Marlboro here. What's urgent?"

"Oh, hi, babe. I really can't say when I'll be home."

"Can't talk?"

"Yes, that's right."

"Want me to come to your place?"

"No, I have a better idea; why don't we go out to dinner? Whad'ya say?"

"How about Canters? Seven o'clock?"

"Deli? Sounds perfect. See you then, babe. Love you."

CLICK

"Jason, Marlboro here. You called?"

"Yeah, I was just checking in to see how you're holding up after that rhapsody in blood out at your place the other night?"

"I have Rudy fixing things up. Should be back in tomorrow night."

"Need a place to stay? We got a spare bedroom."

"Thanks, but I'm good."

"Sure?"

"Yeah. So, what big cases are you working on these days?"

"Oh, nothing new, just tying up some loose ends on some old cases. Nothing exciting."

"Well, keep a good thought. Who knows, tomorrow you could get a double homicide."

"Yeah, something to look forward to."

"Okay, Jas, thanks for checking in. I gotta go and make sleeping arrangements."

"Give her my best."

"Who?"

"Misty."

"How do you know about Misty?"

"Ah… Redding and Johnson must have mentioned her."

"Right, the master surveillance team."

"Hey, give them a break; they're still rookies."

"Yeah, you know, Jas, I could have sworn that they were on my tail this afternoon."

"That's impossible, John. They're out cruising Westwood."

"Oh well, my mistake. I must be getting paranoid."

"Who could blame you," Hanson said.

"Okay. Well, we'll talk soon."

CLICK

The forest green DeSoto Custom sedan stopped at the gate entrance at 601 Mountain Drive, where two armed guards came out of the guard's house and approached the driver.

"Can I help you, sir?" The guard asked while the other guard stood in front of the DeSoto holding the same Browning A5 12 gauge shotgun he had when Marlboro visited.

"Lieutenant Foster, Los Angeles Police," Was the response from the driver.

"May I see some identification, please?"

Lieutenant Foster handed the guard his wallet containing his ID and badge. The guard looked at the items, then said, "One moment."

He walked back into the guardhouse and made a phone call. Foster could see the guard was having a spirited conversation with the party at the other end of the line. Several minutes later, the guard returned, handed Foster his ID and badge, and said, "Sorry for the delay. You may go through."

The guard waved him through. The gates opened, and Lieutenant Foster proceeded to drive up the driveway to the main house, where Lorenzo and Angelo were waiting to meet him.

When Foster got out of the car, Lorenzo said, "Arms up; I need to frisk you."

"Keep your filthy mitts off me," Foster said, holding his hand out in defense.

Lorenzo and Angelo drew Colt .45 semi-automatic revolvers and pointed their weapons at the Lieutenant.

Unfazed, Lieutenant Foster did not back down.

"I suggest you go and ask your Boss if he thinks it would be good business for you to kill an LAPD Lieutenant dressed in full uniform in his front yard," He demanded.

From the front door entrance the voice of Stephon D'Adamo shouted, "Va tutto bene. Lascia passare l'uomo. Idioti!"

The two gunsels lowered their guns and allowed the copper by. Lieutenant Foster walked to the front door and was warmly greeted by the Crime Boss.

"Lieutenant Foster, Benvenuto, welcome to my home. Please come with me," D'Adamo said as he led Foster into his office.

His home office was oak-paneled from floor to ceiling with built-in bookcases stuffed with leather-bound first-edition books. The bed was covered with colorful oriental and Prussian rugs. Against one wall was a great rolltop desk covered with stacks of papers, and next to the desk were two wooden filing cabinets.

On the wall were black and white photographs of D'Adamo standing with his heroes and amici. There was him standing next to Alphonse "Al" Capone, smiling; each of them was holding up bottles of illegal whiskey.

There were other photographs of him with such notable gangsters as Dutch Schultz, Nucky Johnson, Legs Diamond, and Lucky Luciano. There was even one of D'Adamo standing next to a smiling Dillinger holding a Tommy Gun.

"Can I offer you something to drink, Lieutenant? Whiskey?"

"Whiskey would be nice, thank you."

"Lieutenant Foster, I've heard a lot of good things about you and your men. And I want you to know that I always show my gratitude to the boys in blue," D'Adamo said with a raptorial grin.

"And we appreciate it."

"So, what can I do for you, Lieutenant Foster?"

"We have a problem."

"We?"

"I mean, I have a problem that I could use your help with."

"And what problem is that, Lieutenant?" The Mob Boss asked as he handed Foster his Whiskey in a Baccarat crafted cut crystal glass.

Foster nodded thank you and took a sip of one of the world's most expensive single malt Whiskey, Dalmore 64.

"Dear Jesus, I've never tasted anything like this in my life," Foster professed.

"And you never will!" D'Adamo laughed gutturally.

Foster sat in silence, savoring the delicate blend of truffles, sweet sultanas, and figs topped with a slight hint of caramelized Seville oranges. He was in a complete state of dopamine orgasm until D'Adamo said, "The problem?"

"Ah, it's Detective Books."

"Oh?"

"He's been charged with, among other things, capital murder. Now, he's threatening to spill his guts to the DA if we, I mean, if I can't get him off."

"Can you?"

"Can I what?"

"Get him off."

"No. There's too much evidence against him. The DA won't budge."

"Did he do it?" D'Adamo asked.

"Yes."

"Well, how can I help you, Lieutenant?"

"Books have to be silenced."

"And, how exactly do I fit into all of this?"

"I was hoping that you might know somebody on the inside who could get to him."

"You're asking me to have someone kill a police officer. Am I understanding this correctly, Lieutenant Foster?"

"Yes, sir."

"You're asking a lot. What do I get in return for this favor?"

"What is it that I can do for you, Mr. D'Adamo?"

"Nothing… now. But one day, I *will* call upon you to do a service for me. Do you understand?"

"Yes, sir."

D'Adamo finished his drink, walked to the door of his office, and called out, "Angelo, Lorenzo, come here and see Lieutenant Foster off."

He turned to Foster and held out his hand. Foster shook it reverently with a slight bow. "Thank you, Mr. D'Adamo."

"Prego," D'Adamo said with a vulturine smile.

Canters was a hot spot for Hollywood's motion picture icons. It was located across the street from the Samuel Goldwyn Studios. Everybody from Ava Garner to Humphrey Bogart, from John Wayne to Frank Sinatra, could be seen having a meal tucked away in their signature red leather booths or knocking back a few at the plush Chinese red lanterned cocktail lounge.

As Marlboro walked up to the hostess station, he mumbled, "Just looking for a friend, Betty."

"Good to see ya, Johnny. Sure, go on," Betty said.

"Thanks, doll."

Marlboro strolled through the main dining room towards the back, where he saw O'Riley sitting in a dark pocket of the restaurant, nursing a scotch and water.

"What's with the cloak and dagger stuff, O'Riley? Are we being watched by the Nazis?" Marlboro said jokingly.

"Worse," O'Riley whispered as he passed a folded sheet of paper to Marlboro.

"What's this?"

"It's from the FBI forensics unit. I had them send me and only me the results. There were two sets of fingerprints on the bomb that we found in your car."

Marlboro unfolded the official government communique and read it over twice before replying.

"This can't be right!" He rasped.

"I had them check it twice, John."

"I just can't believe it."

"Trust no one!" O'Riley cautioned.

"Has anyone else seen this?" Marlboro asked as he placed the paper inside his coat pocket.

"No one."

"Let's keep this between you and me for the moment. Okay?"

"Sure. Of course."

"Okay, thanks, O'Riley," Marlboro said as he shook O'Riley's hand and then left.

After leaving the Canters, Marlboro felt angry, outraged, and betrayed. He got into the Fleetmaster and started driving west on Sunset Boulevard towards the coast. He found that concentrating on all of the twists and turns was therapeutic, relaxing, and healthful.

By the time he reached PCH, Marlboro felt that he had worked out a plan; whether or not it would work remanded to be seen.

He pulled into the Fiddler's Inn for a drink and to make a call.

The Fiddler's Inn sat across the highway from the Malibu Pier. The Inn was a hot spot on the coast; the owner, Max Amsterdam, the first violinist in the Los Angeles Philharmonic, would bring his fiddle to the Inn and entertain the guests.

The inside of the Inn looked like a hoarder's dream. The eclectic decorations featured everything from autographed photographs of Jean Harlow to a stuffed moose head. Most nights, Max would be sitting next to the cash register, playing his violin and greeting the guests.

"Whad'ya have, young fella?" Asked the old-timer serving drinks at the bar. He looked to have been at least seventy years old, but as it turned out, he was just fifty. He was a self-proclaimed beach bum who worked tending bar at night and spent his days surfing the beaches of Southern California, from La Jolla to Leo Carrillo and up to Pismo. All those years in the sun turned his face into looking like Yogi Berra's old catcher's mitt. Luckily for the people sitting opposite him, his long, bleached out, scraggly hair hid most of his face.

"I'll have a Bullshot," Marlboro said.

"Coming right up. The name's Willie. If you need anything, just give me a shout," The old swagman chuckled.

"Say, Wille. Telephone?"

"Right outside to the left. I'll have your drink waiting for ya," He said with a toothy grin.

Marlboro found the phone booth just where Willie said it would be. He picked up the receiver and dropped two dimes into the slot. He dialed the number.

"Hello, Mr. Thompson; this is John Marlboro. Is Misty there, please?"

"One moment," The man's voice said as he placed his hand over the phone; Marlboro could hear the muffled interaction between a father and his daughter.

"It's that John Marlboro. I don't like him."

"Oh, daddy, you don't even know him. He's very nice."

"He sounds like trouble."

"Daddy, please!"

"Here!"

"Hello, John," Misty said gregariously.

"Hey, doll, is everything all right?"

"Yes, everything is fine."

"I Just wanted to check in on you and tell you that your apartment is all spick and span."

"Can't wait to see it."

"Would you like me to come by and take you back home?"

"That would be great. Tonight?" She inquired.

"Sure. I could be there in a couple of hours, say ten o'clock?"

"Perfect."

"I'll see you then."

"Bye."

"Bye, doll."

CLICK

Marlboro went back into the Anchor Inn to the bar. There waiting for him was his Bullshot. Willie came waltzing by as Marlboro took a drink.

"Well?" The old sea urchin asked with anticipation.

"Damn it, Willie. That's the best Bullshot I think I've ever had. You, sir, are an artist," Marlboro said as he took a big chomp out of the celery stalk.

"Glad you like it," The old windswept mixologist said with a Cheshire Cat smile.

Former Los Angeles Detective John Books, currently Los Angeles County prisoner H-28575, was sitting in his cell in the protective custody ward reading over the legal brief that his public defender had given him earlier in the day.

"Books! Come on; you have a visitor." The guard shouted.

Once again, Books walked past the cells of the general population prisoners, who taunted him, yelled death threats, some threw garbage, and worse, some threw feces.

"You're a dead man!"

"Can't wait to make you my bitch!"

"Eat shit and die!"

"You're dead, copper!"

"I'm waiting for you!"

He spotted Foster sitting dressed in his uniform seated in the back.

"Lieutenant," Books said as he sat down.

"Hey, John, how are you holding up?"

"Not good. Look at me," He said, pointing to his soiled, striped prison uniform.

"You got to get me out of here, Lieutenant. Soon!"

"I just met with someone willing to help."

"Who?"

Foster looked around, making sure that he couldn't be heard, leaned in towards Books, and softly said, "D'Adamo."

Books, looking surprised, asked, "What's he going to do? Bust me outta here?"

"Don't be silly. He's agreed to grease a few palms. He's got the connections that go all the way to the top."

"How long?" Books asked anxiously.

"A couple of days, that's all. You have to hang on for a couple of days more. Then you'll be out. I promise," The Lieutenant said, trying to soothe and relieve Books' fears.

"Okay. I'm supposed to see the DA the day after tomorrow, so it better happen before then. Or else," Books said, with a hint of a veiled threat.

"John, trust me. It will be all over before you know it."

Books was led back through the same gauntlet of jeers, threats, and garbage as before.

He was surprised after the guard opened his cell door and announced that he would have to share a cell with another inmate.

"Hey! I thought I wouldn't have a cellmate since I was in protective custody?" Books questioned.

"Relax! We're overcrowded, okay. This guys in the same boat as you," The guard snapped.

The man entered the cell carrying his pillow and bedding for his bunk. He looked like a fireplug; he was as tall as he was wide, with a neck the size of a telephone pole.

"You take the upper bunk; I've already taken the bottom one," Books announced.

The behemoth stood silent, just looking at his prey. Books stared back, trying not to show fear.

"The names Books. I'm in for capital murder," He said in hopes that he would gain a smattering of respect.

"Bonito Tuminello. Bats," The giant grunted.

"Bats? Why Bats?" Books asked.

"Cause I'm batshit crazy," Bonito said as he lunged for Books.

Twenty minutes later, when the guard made his usual rounds to check on the prisoners in protective custody, he found Bonito "Bats" Tuminello sitting on the bottom bunk.

The body of former Los Angeles Detective John Books, currently Los Angeles County prisoner H-28575, lying on the cell floor with three fingers on his right hand severed, both eyes gouged out, his tongue cut off, and his intestines piled neatly next to his body.

Bats looked at the guard, smiled, and uttered, "He said he wanted to spill his guts to the DA. Well, here they are."

Marlboro rang the doorbell once and stood waiting for someone to answer. He was prepared to be greeted by Mr. Thompson but was pleasantly surprised when Misty's mother met him.

"Hello. You must be Mr. Marlboro. Won't you please come in?"

"Thank you, Mrs. Thompson. I apologize for calling so late."

He was shown into the living room, where Mr. Thompson sat in an overstuffed wingback chair hidden behind a copy of the Los Angeles Times. A cloud of smoke rising from his pipe and the top of his balding head was all Marlboro could see of the man.

He felt like he was seventeen again, calling for his prom date and ready to be grilled by the overprotective father.

"Mr. Thompson, I'm John Marlboro. It's a pleasure to meet you, sir," He said humbly.

There came a *harrumph* from behind the birdcage liner, nothing more.

Feeling that the intruder was still hovering nearby, Thompson eventually started to slowly lower the paper, revealing deep-set hazel eyes behind a thick pair of tortoise-shell readers. As the tabloid was further lowered, it exposed that the man sported a walrus-handlebar mustache while his teeth clenched the stem of a calabash pipe.

Once Thompson was finally in view, Marlboro took a step forward with his hand extended.

Ignoring Marlboro's advances, Thompson gruffly said, "Misty will be down in a minute. Take a seat."

He then brought the paper curtain back up, signaling that no further conversation was expected nor needed.

"Thank you," Marlboro said as he sat across on the sofa.

"Roger, don't be so rude," Mrs. Thompson said, scolding her husband.

Another *harrumph* bellowed from behind the Times.

"Can I offer you something to drink, Mr. Marlboro?"

"Thank you, no. And please, it's John."

"Misty tells us that you're a private detective."

"Yes, ma'am."

"Sounds exciting."

"Sometimes, usually, it's pretty routine."

"Except when you're killing people in my daughter's apartment," Mr. Thompson exclaimed as he crumpled the paper down in his lap.

"I am sorry about that. I am…"

"You could have gotten Misty killed!" Thompson interrupted angrily.

"As I said, sometimes there is danger involved. I'm investigating the murder of Diana Dawson, and there are some very powerful people trying to stop me from telling the truth," Marlboro explained.

"You've become quite the gunslinger, Mr. Marlboro. I've been reading all about your exploits. You've been involved in three shootouts in the last week alone, notching up nine kills. Haven't you?" Thompson challenged.

"Actually, Mr. Thompson, to be accurate, I killed only eight of those men; a police officer killed the ninth man. I didn't go looking for trouble. It came looking for me.

And let me ask you a question. If Misty had been murdered, wouldn't you want to find out who killed your daughter? I believe that the Dawsons deserve that right," Marlboro said defiantly.

Misty rushed into the living room carrying a small suitcase.

"Well, I'm ready. Mom, Dad, I'm going back to my apartment. I'll call you as soon as I arrive to let you know I'm safe. John, are you ready?"

Marlboro stood up, "Mr. Thompson, Mrs. Thompson, it was a pleasure to have met you. Good night."

They were walked to the front door by Misty's mother.

"Goodbye, Mr. Marlboro, thank you. Please watch over our Misty."

"Good night, Mrs. Thompson. There's no need to worry," Marlboro said reassuringly.

"Goodbye. Mom. I love you."

"You be careful, dear."

Marlboro noticed that Officers Redding and Johnson were once again tailing them on their way back to Misty's apartment.

What was once a sense of relief suddenly turned into annoyance and harassment. Marlboro decided that he would have to put a stop to it.

He parked the Fleetmaster in front of the apartment building and walked Misty into the flat. She was surprised at how spotless the apartment was, that there wasn't a hint of the carnage that had occurred days before.

"Listen, doll, as much as I'd like to stay. I think that until I get this case solved, it would be better if we didn't see each other for a while."

"Mmm, you could stay for just a little while, can't you?" Misty moaned softly, then kissed him.

"Well. Maybe just a little while."

Once Misty was fast asleep, Marlboro got dressed, left a note on the kitchen table asking to set up a meeting with Holmberg later in the day, and eased out of the apartment. He made his way through the alley, where he found Officer Redding and his partner, Officer Johnson, sitting sound asleep in their car.

Marlboro walked back to his car undetected and retrieved a pair of workmen's gloves, a twelve-foot length of industrial chain, and two padlocks. He stealthfully returned to the unmarked police car, padlocked one end of the chain to the car's axle and the other to the base of a nearby streetlight.

He walked back through the alley to the front of the apartment and proceeded towards his car, making as much noise as possible. Marlboro slammed the car door shut and gunned the engine.

BBBRRRMMM!!! BBBRRRMMM!!!

Dropped the clutch and peeled out.

SCREEEEEEECH!

Johnson jolted awake and shouted, "Curtis, wake up! Marlboro's on the move."

Officer Redding reached for the keys in the ignition, turned the key, heard the engine rev up, dropped the gear lever into drive, and stomped on the accelerator.

CRASSSHHH!

The car advanced ten feet before the slack in the chain caught, bringing the thirty-foot streetlight crashing down onto the vehicle of Officer Redding and his partner, Officer Johnson. Fortunately, neither one of them was injured.

Lieutenant Foster sat in his office going over manpower reports when he received a call from the warden at the Los Angeles Hall of Justice Jail.

"Lieutenant Foster, here."

"Lieutenant Foster, this is Warden Miller at the Los Angeles Hall of Justice Jail. We've had an incident regarding John Books."

"What kind of incident, Warden?"

"Due to overcrowding, we had placed another inmate in the cell with Mr. Books. Apparently, the other inmate seems to have killed Mr. Books," Miller said apologetically.

"Seems to?"

"Ah, no. He definitely killed Mr. Books."

"And who may I ask was the other inmate?"

"Bonito Tuminello."

"Bats Tuminello! The man's a homicidal maniac. Who authorized that freak being put in with a protective custody prisoner?" Foster demanded.

"Well, now, Lieutenant, we're still looking into that."

"Miller, I'm holding you responsible for this recklessness after this cock-up. You'll be lucky to be picking up dog shit at the animal shelter!" Foster yelled as he slammed the receiver down.

CLICK

Checking to see that no one was looking, Foster breathed a sigh of relief and smiled to himself. He no sooner leaned back into his seat when the phone rang again.

"Lieutenant Foster, here."

"Can you talk?"

Foster recognized D'Adamo's gravelly voice on the other end of the line.

"No, I'm sorry, madam, this isn't a good time. May I call you later?"

"Yeah. And soon," D'Adamo said. It was more of a demand rather than a request.

Foster hung up the phone and left the office. He walked four blocks to a phone booth on the corner of North Spring Street and 1st Street.

"Hello, this is Lieutenant Foster."

"Hold on," A voice said.

"Hello," D'Adamo said.

"This is Lieutenant Foster."

"Did you hear?"

"Yeah, just before you called."

"Okay, here's the thing. You got to come up with fifty large."

"Fifty. For what?" Foster asked, astonished.

"For Bonito Tuminello's family! What do you think? This was going to cost you nothing! Fifty large by the end of the week. Capeesh?"

"Could I have a little more time?"

"By the end of the week."

"Okay, yeah."

"Oh, and more thing. I'm calling in my marker that you owe me for taking care of that dirty cop."

"What can I do for you?" Foster asked, fearing the worst.

"Since that punk detective Marlboro whacked my two top torpedoes, I might need you to arrange for Mr. Holmberg to be fitted for a pair of cement shoes."

"Holmberg, the movie mogul?"

"Yeah, he owes me a gambling debt and has until the end of the month to pay up. If he comes up with the scratch, no problem. If he doesn't, that's where you come in. So, just sit tight until I call."

"Okay, Mr. D'Adamo. Goodbye."

"Hey! Don't I get a thank you?"

"Oh, I'm sorry. Thank you, Mr. D'Adamo."

"That's better."

CLICK

After leaving Misty's, Marlboro returned to his place to check on the renovation that Rudy and his crew did. No matter how many times he has seen the disasters that Rudy walks into, the end product is a thing of beauty.

Marlboro entered the house cautiously since all the booby traps had been unarmed. Holding his Official Police .38 Special at the ready, he turned on every light, searched every room, opened every closet, pulled open every dresser drawer, and checked all the cabinet shelves.

Once he was satisfied that his castle was secure, he reset all the traps and tripwires, took a hot, steamy shower, tucked the snub-nose .38 under his pillow, and went to sleep.

When the phone woke him up at 10:30, his head felt like it was full of cotton candy; he wasn't sure what day it was or where he was. He'd recently slept in so many different beds he began to think he needed a scorecard to tell who's who.

He rolled out of bed naked, drowsy, fumbling around, trying to find where that goddamn ringing was emanating from. He finally stopped, saw the cord coming from the wall, and followed the wire to discover the phone had been buried under the clothes that he had left in a pile on top of the bed stand.

"Hello, Marlboro."

"Hi, Johnny; I missed you this morning," Misty purred.

"Sorry, doll, I had things to do. You know how it is."

"You wouldn't believe it. Early this morning, I was awoken when somebody crashed into a street lamp outside my apartment."

"No kidding. Was anyone hurt?"

"No, but there were a lot of police cars."

"Sorry, I missed it," He smirked.

"Oh, Johnny, I mentioned that you wanted to see Mr. Holmberg, and he said he wanted to see you too. He said anytime is good for him; just stop by."

"Great. I'll be there in a couple of hours."

"See ya, Johnny."

"Bye, doll."

CLICK

The guard at Miracle Studios knew the fire-engine red Fleetmaster and Marlboro well enough that he just flagged him through.

"Have a good day, Mr. Marlboro."

"Thanks, Rick. You, too." Marlboro said as he drove by.

There wasn't anyone in Holmberg's waiting room, just Misty sitting at her desk, typing some correspondence at lightning speed.

"Hey, doll. Am I early?"

"No, He said, as soon as you get here, go right in. Hold on."

She picked up the receiver and pressed the intercom button.

"Mr. Holmberg, Mr. Marlboro, is here to see you."

She hung up the phone, smiled, and said, "You can go on in."

He leaned down and gave her a peck on the cheek before walking into the lion's lair.

"Mr. Marlboro, please come in," Holmberg said cordially.

"Quite the different tone from our last encounter, Holmberg. It wouldn't have anything to do with the new mob Boss, Mr. D'Adamo, would it?"

"Marlboro, I'd like to hire you. You just name your price," Holmberg pleaded.

"Holmberg, I'm a sleuth, not a bodyguard."

"Please, you got to help me, please!"

"The way I figure it, Holmberg, you got many choices. One, don't pay him."

"He'll have me killed and collect on the life insurance policy he forced me to sign."

"Two, you can pay the man."

"I don't have it."

"Three, you can go to the police and testify against him. They'll protect you."

"Protect me, Ha! That's a joke. I'd be killed like that Detective Books."

"No, Books is under protective custody."

"Apparently, you didn't see this morning's papers, Marlboro? Here, read this," Holmberg said as he tossed the front page section to Marlboro.

"Ex-COP TORTURED AND KILLED IN JAIL." *Ex-LAPD Detective John Books, killed while being held in protective custody yesterday, read the headline in the Los Angeles Herald-Express.*

Yesterday, Detective John Books was murdered by his cellmate Bonito 'BATS' Tuminello, a known hitman for the D'Adamo Crime Family.

The Herald-Express has been informed that a guard found Books. It is reported that the ex-cop had his eyes gouged out, fingers ripped from his hand, and his intestines cut out and placed next to his body.

Police officials are still investigating how something like this could have happened. Sources tell the Herald that...."

"This didn't happen by mistake. This was an intentional hit job, and the police let it happen," Marlboro said, more to himself than to Holmberg.

Marlboro looked up from the Herald and said, "Or, four, you can help me get the proof of Diana's killers, and I'll nail the dirty cops who were involved in her death and D'Adamo.

I already know who killed her. I just need you to give me the proof you've been holding on to and make a statement.

Those are your choices, Holmberg. What's it going to be?" Marlboro demanded.

"I don't know! I don't know!" Holmberg howled in frustration.

"Look, Holmberg, face it, your life as you know it is over. The only question is how you will spend what's left of it. You can either spend it somewhere with a new identity, do time in the big house, or you can spend it being dead."

When Marlboro got back into the office, he checked in with his message service; they said that Sheriff Trimble had called at 1:45 and requested that he return the call at his earliest convenience.

"Sheriff's office, how may I direct your call?" The Hispanic woman's voice asked.

"Sheriff Trimble, please."

"Whom may I say is calling?"

"John Marlboro."

"One moment."

Minutes later.

"Marlboro, Trimble here. Thanks for getting back to me so quickly. Mr. Dawson wanted me to call you and keep you abreast of the goings-on."

"I appreciate that, Sheriff. So, what is going on?"

"Well, I called Chief Horrall and told him about the incident that involved the shooting and killing of one of his officers, Detective Scanlon."

"I bet he was none too happy to hear that."

"Boy, you got that right. He went on that since it involved one of his men, the LAPD should be in charge of the investigation. I told him the crime happened here, so the investigation will be done here, but I would keep him apprised."

"I bet he offered to send down some of his best men to help out."

"Yep. I let him know that although I appreciated his kind offer, that we were more than capable of handling it."

"Good for you, Sheriff."

"Well, I had our boys in the crime lab go over that '46 Ford Coupe for clues and prints."

"And?"

"And, in addition to Detective Scanlon's, we found several sets of fingerprints, some unknown and one set belonging to a couple of other LA policemen, Detec…."

"Detective Jason Hanson and Lieutenant Jeffrey Foster," Marlboro said morosely.

"That's right. How did you know?"

"I told you when we met that I'm a detective; I work at it, I don't play at it."

"Other than his prints, we have no other hard evidence that he was, in fact, the other man in the car that night."

"Have you told Horrall yet?

"I have a call into him. But haven't heard back."

"I'd be obliged if you keep me up to date with any new developments, Sheriff Trimble."

"Say, Marlboro, you wouldn't be interested in becoming a deputy, would you?"

"That's very kind of you, Sheriff. But, no."

"Worth a try."

"Talk soon."

"Bye."

CLICK

"Mr. Holmberg's office," Misty answered.

"Hello, doll."

"Hi, Johnny," She cooed.

"Listen, doll. I got some loose ends I have to tie up tonight. I'll try and buzz by later, but since it'll be very late, I might not be able to."

"Come by anytime; I don't mind."

"I'll try."

"Bye, Johnny."

CLICK

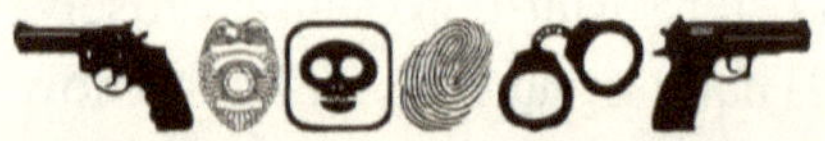

Marlboro went home and got everything set up for the uninvited guests that he figured would be dropping by unexpectedly.

On his bookcase in the living room, he placed the Brush Soundmirror BK-401 Reel-to-Reel Tape Recorder next to his AF-860 AM-FM Pilotuner Radio. Together, side-by-side, they looked to be one unit.

With the tape recorder lid closed, one couldn't tell that it was indeed a recording device.

It was a little after 10 p.m. when he heard the car pull up at his house, 1626 W. 11th Place. Two car doors slammed shut, footsteps approached the front door, ascending the front steps, and there was a knock on the door.

Marlboro opened the door to find Lieutenant Foster standing next to his ex-partner, Detective Hanson.

"Marlboro. Can we come in?" Foster asked.

"Why, Lieutenant Jeffrey Foster and my old partner Detective Jason Hanson, what an unexpected pleasure. Please come in."

Marlboro showed them into his living room and offered them seats.

"Gentlemen, take a load off." He said as he sat with his back to the bookcase facing the front door.

Foster and Hanson sat opposite him on the sofa.

"Business or pleasure?" Marlboro asked.

"Hopefully, both," Hanson said, forcing a smile.

"Look, Marlboro, We know you've been snooping around on the Dawson murder, sticking your nose in places where it doesn't belong. Stirring things up and making certain people very uneasy. What is it exactly that you're trying to prove anyway?"

"I'm just looking to find out who killed Diana Dawson. My question to you is, why aren't you?"

"Drop it, Marlboro, Or else."

"Well, actually, I already know who killed her and why."

"You don't know shit, Marlboro," Foster asserted.

"No?"

"No. And even if you did, who's going to believe you, a disgraced ex-cop? You got no proof. You got nothing, Marlboro. Come on, Hanson, let's go."

"Just one question, Jas. The bomb, why?" Marlboro asked.

"Huh?" Hanson uttered.

"They got your fingerprints on the bomb planted in my car. Why?"

"That doesn't mean anything, so he touched the bomb after it was taken outta your car, that's all." Foster challenged.

"Not according to the FBI and the bomb squad's report."

"He's bluffing," Foster said defiantly.

"Am I? Also, it was very sloppy of the two of you to leave your prints on that '46 Ford Coupe that you left down at Dawson's Farm.

Redding and Johnson followed you and Scanlon down as backup. When Scanlon got popped, you had them pick you up. You got lucky, Jas.

So that you know, Sheriff Trimble has contacted Chief Horrall. So, expect to be called into the clubhouse any day now."

"You're just blowing smoke," Foster sneered.

"Jas, you got to get in front of this! You don't want to go down with these rats," Marlboro urged.

"Let me tell *you* how it is, Marlboro. One of these days, you're going to wake up dead."

"What? Like Books did. You arranged it so he would be doubled up with that homicidal maniac, Bonito Tuminello!"

"You got nothing, shamus; you're grasping at straws," Foster said defiantly.

"Yeah? Well, I've met with both D'Adamo and Holmberg. They're sending you over, Foster. You're taking the fall."

Foster jumped up from the sofa, pulled his revolver, and pointed it at Marlboro. "Stand up, or I'll drill you where you sit, you lousy gumshoe," Foster growled.

"Foster, you ever hear of Donald Wilson, a reporter for the Los Angeles Herald-Express?" Marlboro inquired.

"Yeah, so what?"

"Well, I entrusted him with dozens of documents, photographs, and recordings to be released to the DA's office and the press in the event of my death."

"You bastard! I'll see you in Hell!" Foster gnarled as he cocked his revolver.

"Drop it, Lieutenant," Hanson said coolly as he had his roscoe aimed at Foster.

Foster weighed his options; he could kill Marlboro but couldn't take them both out, so he backed out of the room, pointing his heater back and forth between Marlboro and Hanson. When he got to the door, he holstered his gun, slammed the door shut behind him, and ran to the car.

Moments later, the car engine cranked over, and Foster was gone.

Inside Marlboro's living room, Detective Hanson sat on the sofa, motionless, staring out into nothingness.

"Jas, why? Talk to me," Marlboro asked.

D'Adamo sent Angelo and Lorenzo to meet with Marlboro at the Griffith Park Observatory to make the exchange. Marlboro insisted that the meeting take place at noon in the public parking lot so there would be plenty of people just in case Angelo got rambunctious.

Marlboro had the goods on Bugsy Siegel's drug operation that Diana Dawson had collected. She had compiled photographs and names of L.A.'s power elite buying illegal narcotics and involved in illicit sexual acts with underage starlets. D'Adamo had, by default, inherited Siegel's drug trade and all of his other rackets when he had Bugsy bumped off.

D'Adamo needed Diana's dossier to have complete leverage over the city's kingpins. In exchange, Marlboro would get the weapon used to kill Diana and the names of those involved in her murder.

At noon, Marlboro was leaning against the grill of the fire-engine red Fleetmaster, waiting for the two goons to show. Fifteen minutes later, a black Cadillac Sedan Deville pulls up next to Marlboro. Angelo and Lorenzo step out of the car; Lorenzo is carrying a small blue zippered gym bag.

"You got sumpin for me?" Angelo asked.

"You got the dingus?"

"Show 'em, Enzo," Angelo ordered.

Lorenzo unzipped the small satchel to reveal a Sauer & Sohn 38H Nazi Police 7.65mm semi-automatic pistol with a military blue finish and a folded piece of yellow paper with three names scribbled on it.

"Satisfied, shamus?" Angelo sneered.

"Satisfied," Marlboro said as he took possession of the bag.

"Okay, peeper, where's the file?" Angelo demanded.

Marlboro walked to the rear of the car, followed by D'Adamo's lapdogs, opened the trunk, took out an eight and a half by eleven brown envelope, and tossed it to the hatchetman.

"Here, ya go." He said as he dropped the blue bag into the boot of the car, and then slammed it shut.

Angelo thumbed through the photos and documents. Contented that they got what they came for, he handed the envelope to his associate, turned to

Marlboro, and snarled, "I'll be seeing you soon, pal. This ain't over."

The black Caddy pulled a large sweeping U-turn in the parking lot, almost knocking several people over before zooming out of the park.

Marlboro headed back to the office to complete the file of evidence before turning everything over to the District Attorney.

Marlboro hadn't been back to The Original Pantry Café since the shootout when Anne Hoppe was killed trying to save his life.

Although it looked the same, there was a distinct difference. Marlboro walked up to the counter, sat down on the stool, grabbed a menu, and waited for the counterman.

"Whad'ya have, bud?" The soup jockey asked.

"I'll have the hot dog with sauerkraut and coffee."

"Gimme a bloodhound in the hay and a cup of joe."

Marlboro ate in silence. He finished and somberly went to the cashier's station to pay. As he looked around, there was none of the old staff. Nobody that he recognized. He surmised that after the gun battle, people were too traumatized to continue to work there.

He was walking back to his office, crossing West 8th. Street. Heading north on South Grand Avenue, when screaming up from behind him came a black Cadillac Sedan Deville aimed straight for him.

Marlboro could see that Angelo was behind the wheel; he had only seconds to react. As the black behemoth came bearing down on him, Marlboro drifted effortlessly to the side like a matador in Seville.

Once Angelo realized that he had missed his mark, he slammed on the brakes, jammed the car into park, and jumped out of the Caddy, each hand holding a Beretta Model 1934 seven-shot semi-automatic pistol, firing wildly in all directions.

Anticipating Angelo's actions, Marlboro casually and unemotionally reached into his jacket and pulled out his Colt Police .38 Special. He assumed the position of a shooter's crouch, and sighted down his rigid arm, fired four shots. All of them striking their target, leaving Angelo "Pistol Pete" Corallo dying on the sidewalk in front of Vito's Chicago Style Pizzeria.

Marlboro was taken down to homicide, interviewed, and released. Due to the evidence and multiple eyewitnesses, no charges were ever filed.

When word and circumstances of Angelo's death reached D'Adamo, it was reported that he said to his brother, "Angelo was sfortunato, but a real stronzo."

"A GRAND KILLING." Private detective John Marlboro shot and killed known Chicago gangland hitman Angelo "Pistol Pete" Corallo in a wild west shootout on the streets of downtown, read the headline in the Los Angeles Herald-Express.

Yesterday, private detective John Marlboro, while crossing Grand Avenue, was almost run down by a driver in a black Cadillac Sedan Deville. When the driver, Angelo "Pistol Pete" Corallo, realized that his attempt to run over Marlboro had failed, Carallo stepped out of the car with guns blazing. Carallo's erratic shooting resulted in the casualties of a water cooler, a mimeograph machine, and two female mannequins.

An unnamed police source told the Herald that during the gun battle, Marlboro fired four shots, all four hitting and killing his would-be assassin. This is the fourth shooting incident that the private detective has been involved in, in as many weeks.

Angelo "Pistol Pete" Corallo is believed to be a member of the D'Adamo Crime Family. When reached for comment, D'Adamo's spokesman said, "No comment."

Later that day, Marlboro walked the six blocks from his office to that of District Attorney Andrew Weir.

"May I help you, sir?" The middle-aged spinster asked.

"Yes, I'm John Marlboro. I'd like to see the District Attorney regarding two murders, an organized drug and prostitution ring, and several charges of city officials and police corruption.

<u>EPILOGUE</u>

Lieutenant Jeffrey Foster and Detective Jason Hanson were both charged and convicted of first-degree torture, murder, and rape in the case of Diana Dawson. They were sentenced to life in prison with no chance of parole.

Despite being held in protective custody, both were murdered in prison. Jason Hanson was shanked forty-seven times with inmate-made shivs. He bled to death before guards could reach him.

Jeffery Foster was bludgeoned to death in the prison yard exercise area. Two inmates held him down while others smashed free weights on his head, crushing his skull into a pulp.

Marvin Holmberg was charged with operating a prostitution and drug ring but was granted immunity when he turned state's witness against police officers Foster, Hanson, and Crime Boss Stephon D'Adamo.

Rumor has it that he now lives somewhere in the Midwest, working as a car salesman, selling DeSoto Automobiles. He is married with two children.

Miracle Picture Studios was sold and divided by MGM and Paramount Pictures. The studios renegotiated all the actors' and actresses' contracts. Skylar Darrow & Robin Summers both signed with Paramount Pictures. At the same time, Johnathan Silvers, *aka* Nathan Fleckenstein, quit show business and opened an antique shop in Van Nuys with his partner Arlo Presley.

Stephon D'Adamo was charged and convicted on multiple counts of extortion, prostitution, drug trafficking, gambling, murder for hire, and tax evasion. He was sentenced to two life terms plus 45 years.

No city officials were ever charged, although there were over a dozen resignations within days of District Attorney Andrew Weir's announcement that certain information had come to light and possible charges were being determined.

Due to the sensationalism surrounding the trials and convictions coming from the information that Diana Dawson had collected, District Attorney Andrew Weir ran for and was elected as California state Attorney General.

Marlboro made one last drive to San Jacinto, to The Dawson Brothers Dairy. He came to tell Diana's parents, Charles and Margaret, that their daughter's killers had been apprehended.

"Mr. and Mrs. Dawson, I'd like you to meet Misty Thompson. She was a great help with my solving your daughter's case."

"It's a pleasure to meet you, Misty. Mr. Marlboro, won't you both come in and have a glass of lemonade?" Mrs. Dawson said.

They all sat in the Dawson's living room; once the drinks had been served, Mr. Dawson asked. "So, what can you tell us, Mr. Marlboro."

"Mr. and Mrs. Dawson, your daughter, was killed because she was trying to stop corrupt city officials and police officers involved in drugs and prostitution.

I know it's a little consolation, but Mayor Fletcher Bowron of Los Angeles wanted Diana to be awarded the District Attorney's Courageous Citizen Award for distinguishing herself by conspicuous bravery," Marlboro said as he handed Mrs. Dawson the plaque.

"Thank you, Mr. Marlboro, for all you've done," She sobbed.

"We appreciate everything, Mr. Marlboro. I know that you were in danger at times, and yet you persisted. It means a lot to Margaret and me. And thank you, too, Miss Thompson."

"I'm so sorry for your loss," Misty said, tearing up.

They visited for a while; Marlboro even helped hang the plaque on the living room wall next to a Hollywood glamour photo of Diana.

"Well, I guess we should head back to town and try and beat the traffic," Marlboro said.

"Boy, I don't envy you driving in all that crazy Los Angeles traffic. Can't see how it can get much worse," Dawson said, laughing.

"Now, don't be a stranger, Mr. Marlboro, and you too, Misty. You all come back and see us sometime."

With the top-down, Marlboro put on his favorite cheaters that he received from one-time movie idol Johnathan Silvers, slipped the Fleetmaster into gear, and hit the gas.

"Say, doll, whad'ya say we grab a bite somewhere?"

"How about my place?" She said as she slid over to sit next to him on the bench seat.

"Okay, what's on the menu?"

Misty ran her hand up and down his thigh and whispered in his ear, "Me."

"Sounds delicious."

The End

The Red Queen

"Don't put on the Ritz with me, Rocco. I'm not taking orders from a mug like you!" Marlboro growled.

"You give me any trouble, Marlboro, and I'll fill you full of lead," Rocco sneered as he pointed the Colt Diamondback Revolver at Marlboro.

"Ah, I don't think so," Marlboro chuckled as he dropped six .22 caliber bullets from his right hand down to his left.

"You see, I emptied the cylinder last night."

"You're lying. Eat lead!" Rocco yelled pointing, the roscoe at Marlboro, and pulled the trigger six times.

CLICK CLICK CLICK CLICK CLICK CLICK

Feeling frustrated and foolish, Rocco threw the hefty Colt at Marlboro's head.

Marlboro ducked to his right while drawing his .38 Police Special from behind his back and fired once, hitting his assailant in the right shoulder and dropping him to the ground like a sack of spuds.

"You dirty rat! I trusted you! Who are you working for, the cops, Butch and the gang?" Rocco wailed, holding his wounded shoulder.

"The Knudsen's."

"The Knud…Who the fuck are the Knudsen's?"

"You mean you don't know. You should. You killed their son, Mathias. You robbed him, shot em, and burned his body in his car. Remember?" Marlboro challenged him.

"Ah, you're loco."

"We'll see.

"Listen, I got 5 Gs in my coat pocket; it's all yours. Just let me walk," Rocco begged.

"5 Gs?" The shamus walked over to Rocco, sitting on the ground, holding his shoulder. Rocco opened his coat, let Marlboro reach in and take a roll of hundreds and twenties held together with a blue rubber band.

"It's all yours. Just let me walk."

"I tell you what. Here's what we're going to do. I'm taking the dough, and you're taking the fall."

Off in the distance, the sound of police sirens could be heard getting closer.

"You lousy rat bastard. Whad'ya expect from a crummy gumshoe. I shoulda known better than to trust a dick."

Two LAPD squad cars and an ambulance arrived, sirens wailing and lights flashing.

"Hey, Marlboro, whadd'ya got?" Officer Browning asked.

"Hey, Brownie. This is Tony Rocco. He's responsible for the robbery and murder of Mathias Knudsen, and here's the gun that he used to kill the kid.

A sawbuck says it's a match," Marlboro said as he handed the Colt revolver to the officer.

As the medics were attending Rocco's gunshot wound, he shouted to Officer Browning, "Hey, copper, that creep stole 5 Gs off me!"

Marlboro held up the roll of cash, "I'm giving it to Mathias' folks."

Brownie shrugged and said, "Whatever. Come by the station sometime today and give a statement."

"Will do, Brownie."

"Hey! What about my dough?" Rocco squawked,

"Shut up before I give you a mouthful of Chiclets," Browning said, holding up the butt of his service revolver, threatening to bash Rocco in the mouth.

Marlboro just sat down in his office at the Brockman Building, downtown Los Angeles, when the phone rang.

"Marlboro."

"Mr. Marlboro, my name is Barbra Babcock."

"What can I do for you, Mrs. Babcock."

"Actually, it's Miss Babcock, and I need your help. My brother has been kidnapped."

"Have you called the police?"

"No."

"The FBI?"

"No."

"Well, madam, I recommend that you call them. They are better prepared to handle this situation than I am."

"I can't call the police or the FBI!"

"Why not?"

"Mr. Marlboro, I'm the Los Angeles Party Leader of the California American Communist Party. Whoever kidnapped my brother knows that I can't go to the authorities for help. Will you help me?" She said with a tremble in her voice.

"Have the kidnappers contacted you with a ransom note yet?"

"Yes, I got it this morning."

"Where do you live, Miss Babcock?"

"745 West Mariposa Avenue, Manhattan Beach."

"I'll get down there as soon as I can."

"Thank you, Mr. Marlboro. Goodbye.

CLICK

It was a beautiful day in Southern California; Marlboro drove the thirty-minute drive with the top down on the Fleetmaster, listening to the Jimmy Dorsey Band on KFWB.

Marlboro pulled into the driveway of the two-story white stucco Spanish style red tiled roof home. 745 West Mariposa Avenue was a dead-end street that overlooked Manhattan Beach and the Pacific Ocean. The area was considered to be prime real estate.

Marlboro thought that being a member of the Communist Party must pay pretty good.

Marlboro strolled up the walkway to the front stoop and rang the bell.

DING DONG

When the door opened, Marlboro was face to face with a beautiful woman in her mid-thirties, wearing a red and white thin striped T-shirt with a pair of high waisted, wide leg navy blue cotton pants.

She had shoulder-length light brown hair, and an angelic face resembling Audrey Hepburn. She was gorgeous.

Marlboro was ashamed to say that he thought that Miss Babcock should have looked like Nikita Khrushchev in a dress. Boy, was he wrong.

"Mr. Marlboro?"

"Yes. Miss Babcock?"

"Please, won't you please come in."

Marlboro was once again surprised to see how modern and "American" the house was decorated.

Miss. Babcock could see by his expression that she and the house wasn't what he was expecting.

"Mr. Marlboro, not all communists live like peasants, nor do we look like them either. Disappointed?"

"On the contrary. Let's just say that I'm pleasantly surprised."

"Won't you have a seat?"

Marlboro sat on the sofa while Miss. Babcock sat opposite him on a tan wool fabric Danish lounge chair with a sculpted Beech wood frame.

"Miss Babcock, when was your brother abducted?"

"This morning. I was upstairs getting ready for work when someone rang the doorbell. Dwight hollered up that he would get it. I heard muffled voices and what I now know to be the sounds of a struggle. By the time I got downstairs, the door was open, the ransom note thrown on the floor, and Dwight was gone."

"Does your brother live with you?"

"Yes. This was our parents' home, and when they passed away, they left it to us."

"So, it's just you and your brother, no other siblings?"

"No. Why?"

"I just need to know all the players. Now, do you have the note?"

"Yes, I have the ransom note right here," She said as she handed the note to Marlboro.

He took it and carefully examined it, wearing a pair of latex gloves, so as not to contaminate any fingerprints, fibers, or hairs that might have been left on the note.

The note had been constructed by cutting out parts of words from magazines and newspapers, then pasting them down onto a piece of typewriter paper.

"Has anyone besides yourself handled this note?" Marlboro asked.

"No. Just me."

"And it was just lying on the floor?"

"Yes, I found it when I came downstairs this morning. I didn't notice it right away; it was thrown over there by the sofa," She explained.

"We have your brother. If you ever want to see him alive again, gather two hundred thousand dollars in unmarked non-consecutive twenty-dollar bills. Await instructions. No cops! No funny stuff!"

"What does your brother do, Miss. Babcock?"

"He's works in Hollywood."

"Is he also a member of the Communist Party?"

"Yes, he's a member."

"Is he an actor?"

"No. A screenwriter."

"And aside from being the Party Leader, do you work as well, Miss. Babcock?"

"I work in Hollywood as well."

"Writer?"

"I'm what they call a reader."

"A reader?"

"Yes, I read movie scripts and objectively analyze them to see if they have merit."

"What studio do you work for?"

"I work for many studios. I'm freelance. Much like you, Mr. Marlboro."

"Can you think of anyone who might have a grudge against your brother or even possibly you, Miss.

Babcock? Someone professionally or someone wanting to usurp your position within the Party?"

"Nobody professionally, and I don't believe it's anybody in the Party. I'm thinking it's someone who is against our being communists."

"Anybody come to mind?"

"I'm afraid not."

"Can you raise the ransom?"

"Possibly, but it would take some time. We don't have that sort of money lying around."

"I guess the next step is to wait until you hear from them."

"So, you'll take the case?"

"I still think you should get the authorities involved," Marlboro suggested.

"No, I don't trust them."

"Okay. Then I'll take the case. I get twenty-five dollars a day plus expenses."

"That will be fine."

"Here's my card with my phone numbers. Call me day or night. If they call you, take notes, don't promise anything and stall for time. In the meantime, I'm going to take this note and see if there's any evidence on it that might help us. I'll also need the names of you and your brother's co-workers and a list of the members of the Los Angeles branch of the Party."

"Oh, Mr. Marlboro, I couldn't do that."

"Miss Babcock, do you want your brother back or not? I'm not the FBI; I don't give a hoot what club you're in, but I can't do my job if you tie my hands."

"Fine. I'll have the list ready this afternoon."

"Once we get your brother back, I'll destroy the list."

"Thank you, Mr. Marlboro."

"Well, don't thank me yet. I haven't done anything. Oh, do you have a recent photograph of your brother that I can take?"

She walked over to the fireplace mantle and removed what looked to Marlboro as a Hollywood studio portrait, a framed photograph of a balding, chubby man wearing black-rim eyeglasses.

"He takes after my father," She said as she handed the photograph to Marlboro.

Marlboro, examining the man in the photo and comparing it to the beautiful creature standing before him, said, "I'm not seeing any family resemblance."

"I take after my mother's side."

"Lucky you."

She started to laugh, "Mr. Marlboro, you're wicked."

"So, I've been told."

When Marlboro got back to the office, he placed a call to the FBI, Los Angeles branch.

"Federal Bureau of Investigation. How may I direct your call, please?" The operator asked.

"I'd like to speak to Agent James Beck."

"One moment. I'll see if he's available."

SILENCE

"Hello, Agent Beck."

"James, Marlboro here."

"Oh, hello, Marlboro."

"I need your help. Unofficially, of course."

"Of course."

"I'm working on a kidnapping, and I need your help. Could you have someone give the ransom note the once over for any prints or other evidence?"

"Marlboro, why are you handling this and not us?"

"It's the client. She doesn't feel that she can trust anyone in law enforcement."

"Is she on the other side of the law?"

"She doesn't think so."

"Who was kidnapped?"

"Her brother."

"When was he taken?"

"This morning, around 8 o'clock."

"Whad'ya thinking, Marlboro?"

"I'm thinking you want in on the case."

"Well, I am carrying a light caseload. And not working on anything pressing."

"Okay, but you have to go through me. No stepping into the light, strictly on the QT. Got it?"

"Got it."

"Okay, I'll swing by in a half hour to drop off the ransom note."

"What's her name? Can you at least tell me that?" Beck pressed.

Marlboro thought for a moment, then said, "Umm, let's just call her the Red Queen."

"See you in a half hour."

CLICK

Marlboro took the list of Party members and removed all references to the Party or anyone's titles. He made a handwritten copy and brought it along with the ransom note over to Beck.

Beck was waiting outside in front of the building, having a smoke. Marlboro pulled the fleetmaster into the parking lot area designated for official FBI business.

"You can't park there," Beck said.

"Why not?"

"This is for official FBI business only. See!" Beck announced, pointing to the sign.

"Oh, horse feathers. Come on," Marlboro said as he led the way toward the entrance.

"You know, you are the most irreverent shamus I've ever known."

"Why, thank you, James," Marlboro said with a grin.

"Marlboro, that wasn't a compliment."

After obtaining a guest badge, Beck and Marlboro went up to the third floor to where the Dermatoglyphics Lab was located.

The room occupied the entire floor, with dozens of men and women cataloging, reviewing, classifying, and identifying hundreds of fingerprints. They walked through the maze of dactylographers, each one absorbed in inspecting latent fingerprint analysis until Beck stopped at the desk of a middle-aged, balding man wearing glasses that looked like the bottom of Coke bottles.

"Henry Dopkins. How are you doing, my friend?" Beck asked.

"Very well, Agent Beck and yourself?"

"Great, Henry, just great. Henry, this is my good friend John Marlboro."

"It's a pleasure to meet you, Mr. Marlboro," Henry said, peering up through those jam-jar glasses.

"The pleasure is all mine," Marlboro replied.

"Henry got a favor to ask. Could you give this note a good going over and tell me if you find anything?" Beck asked.

"In a hurry?"

"Fraid so."

Henry took the note, examined it, and said, "Sure thing, Agent Beck. Gimme a few minutes, and I'll call you when I'm done."

"Thanks, Henry. I owe you one."

"Come on, Marlboro, don't keep me in the dark," Beck pleaded as they sat in his office on the fourth floor of FBI headquarters.

"I can't. Aside from the whole client privilege thing, I'm sure that if I told you, it might taint your opinion of her."

"Look, even if she's a wanted criminal, she's a victim right now. I give you my word; it won't affect my performance in any way."

"Okay, I can't tell you her name, but what I will tell you is that she is a card-carrying member of the American Communist Party," Marlboro said, watching to see Beck's reaction.

"A red, huh?"

"Yeah."

"A spy?"

"God, no!"

"How do you know?"

"Spies tend to blend in. There's no way this woman would ever blend in."

"Good looking?"

"Pulchritudinous."

"What?"

"The doll is a knockout."

"Why didn't you just say so?"

"Why don't you try reading something other than the sports section occasionally? You might expand your vocabulary."

"Listen, Marlboro, my vocabulary is just…"

The phone rang, it was Dopkins. Beck held his hand over the receiver and whispered to Marlboro, "It's Dopkins."

"Hello. What did you find?

Really.

That's terrific.

Not in the system?

Okay, thanks again," Beck said as he looked at Marlboro with a broken grin.

CLICK

"So, what's the verdict?"

"Well, we have two good sets of prints. Dopkins thinks that one is your client's and the other probably the perp's. Neither one of them are in the system."

"I'll go and get a set of prints from the Red Queen so we can eliminate hers. Can I borrow a fingerprint kit?" Marlboro asked.

"Come on, we'll stop downstairs, and I'll have Dopkins issue you one and walk you out."

When they were downstairs in the lobby, as Marlboro was turning in his guest pass, a light went off in Beck's head.

"Ah, I get it. Red Queen. Very good, Marlboro. You're always cracking foxy."

Marlboro smiles and gives a short wave on his way out the door.

"I really don't feel comfortable giving you my fingerprints."

"We have to know which prints are yours and which prints are the kidnappers," Marlboro explained.

"*We?*"

"Huh?"

"You said, "*We* have to know." Who's we?"

"We, you know, the royal we. The editorial we. I have to know," Marlboro said, trying to juggle while dancing on the head of a pin.

"It's just that I'm overly suspicious, paranoid, and afraid of the authorities," She said nervously.

"Miss Babcock, I am not the authorities. I work for you. Anything you tell me or confide in me is strictly confidential."

"Alright," She acquiesced.

She took him into the kitchen so he could set up the fingerprint kit. They stood side by side at the kitchen counter as he was setting up; he asked, "Ever have your fingerprints taken before?"

"No, I haven't. Have you?" She said demurely.

"Dozens of times," He said as if he was bragging.

Marlboro smiled, "I promise it won't hurt a bit, Miss Babcock."

"Barbra, call me Barbra." She smiled a perfect set of pearly whites, which almost blinded him.

He took her hand in his; her hand was as soft as a cloud, as soft as a baby's cheek. Her fingers were long and thin with bright red nail polish.

Marlboro cupped his hand over Barbra's fingers while tucking under her fingers, not being fingerprinted. He guided the finger that was being printed with his left hand, rolling the finger on the ink pad, then gently rolling the finger onto the paper tablet.

"Sorry, it is a bit messy. Nothing that a little soap and water won't wash away," He said as he examined the prints.

"Can I offer you something to drink, Mr. Marlboro?"

"Sure, and you can lose the Mister. Mr. Marlboro was my father. Marlboro will do."

"What can I get you?"

"I'll have whatever you're having."

"Vodka?"

"Vodka. Uncle Joe Stalin would be proud," He said with a devilish grin.

"What do you think the chances are of getting Dwight back alive?" She asked.

"Honestly, it's hard to say. It could go either way. I don't want to upset you, but I don't want to fill you with false hope, either."

"I appreciate your candor."

"Well, I better go back and see about eliminating your prints off the ransom note. But first, I want to go around the house to make sure everything is secure."

Marlboro went throughout the house, checking all the windows and doors, making sure they were all locked tight. He found her sitting in the living room, staring out the window.

"You alright?" He asked.

"No. Not really," She said as she began to sob.

He sat down next to her, "I'll do everything I can to get your brother back safely." As he put his arm around her to comfort her, she turned into him crying. The intoxicating bouquet of Channel, the warmth of her body, and the sensuality of her vulnerability put Marlboro in a tight spot that tested his code of ethics. Every fiber of his body wanted to make love to her, but it had to be because she wanted to, not because she was defenseless like a sitting duck.

Marlboro lifted her chin up and softly asked, "Is there someone who can come and stay with you? It's not good staying here alone."

"Not really. Would you be able to?" She asked.

"Let me go and get these fingerprints eliminated, and I'll come back. Until then, don't let anyone in. Do you have a gun?"

"No."

He bent over and pulled his .32 caliber Colt Detective Special 'snub-nosed' revolver from his ankle holster and handed it to her.

"Have you ever fired a gun?" He asked.

"No."

Marlboro emptied the pistol and spent half an hour giving her a quick tutorial.

"Basically, if anyone comes into the house, just point and fire. Got it?"

"Got it."

"Don't answer the door for anyone. I'll ring four times. Long, short, long, short, so you'll know it's me. I'll be back as soon as I can."

As Marlboro opened the door, he noticed a footprint just off the front porch that he hadn't seen before.

"Barbra, could this be your brother's footprint?"

She stepped out onto the porch. "No, he's a size 9, that looks much bigger."

"Don't touch it. When I come back, I'll make a plaster cast impression of it. Okay?"

"Okay."

Marlboro turned in the fingerprints sample from Barbra Babcock, listed under anonymous, to eliminate her prints from the other set.

It didn't take Dopkins long. He held up a copy of the ransom note with Barbra's prints X'd out. There were close to a dozen readable prints from the kidnapper on the front and back of the note.

"Once you hear from the kidnappers, be sure to contact me," Beck said.

"Don't worry, I will. I better get back in case they call."

"You sure you know how to obtain that shoe print?" Beck asked snidely with a slight smirk.

"Breeze off, wise guy," Marlboro snapped with a smile.

Brian O'Bannon was a once-wealthy man accustomed to living a swanky and excessive lifestyle before squandering away his million-dollar inheritance on wine, women, gambling, and his entourage of hangers-on and grifters. Once the money was gone, so were the women and the entourage; that's when O'Bannon found himself all alone and broke.

He was arrested in 1945 for robbing two liquor stores and a taxicab of a total of $63. Although sentenced to seven years in prison, he served just two. While in stir, he began plotting his next get-rich quick scheme. A kidnapping for ransom.

He was broke when he got out of the big house at Folsom State Prison. He got a job washing dishes in a hash house in Culver City. O'Bannon lived in a flop house on Washington Boulevard, not far from MGM Studios. One night, while walking back to his room after work, he stopped into The Crow's Nest for a boilermaker.

It was there he met Nora Muldoon, a recent divorcée and sometime prostitute; they moved in together three days later. He told Nora of his kidnapping plan, and she was a more than willing accomplice. She would provide the car, and she had a gun that she had stolen from one of her "Johns." The die was cast, and the stage was set.

Just by chance, Nora and Brian had attended a meeting at the American Communist Party. Not for any intellectual stimulation, the Party meeting offered a free buffet. It was during that meeting when Barbra Babcock and her brother Dwight stood in front of the dozen or so people sitting in the hall spoke about equality and the rights of the working man, that Brian O'Bannon decided that they would kidnap either Barbra or the brother for ransom. Although they talked of the everyman, they themselves seemed to be part of the bourgeois class, which he found to be hypocritical.

He believed that because they were communists that, the police wouldn't look too hard or put too much effort into finding a dirty, stinking commie.

O'Bannon and Muldoon hadn't counted on John Marlboro.

Not far from the footprint, Marlboro found several cigarette butts thrown into the bushes. They were Gitanes, a French brand of cigarettes, not very popular in Los Angeles. There were only a handful of tobacco shops that even stocked them, which would be in Marlboro's favor.

After taking the cast of the footprint, Marlboro determined that the man who made the impression was a size 11 wide. Given that, Marlboro guessed that the man would probably be around 5 foot 8 to 5 foot 11 and stocky, considering the shoe was a wide.

Barbra had made dinner; not only was she beautiful, but she was also a gourmet cook. She had prepared a mushroom asiago chicken meal, served with a spring mix salad and a bottle of Pinot Grigio.

As they were preparing to sit down to dinner, the phone rang.

Barbra and Marlboro sat next to each other, her holding the phone between them.

"Hello?" Barbra answered.

"Do you have the money?" A man's muffled voice asked.

Marlboro whispered in her ear the answer.

"I'm working on getting it. It will take me at least two days to get it. I have to sell some things."

"Today is Wednesday. You have until Friday morning, or else Dwight dies."

Marlboro gave her the response to say.

"I want to speak to Dwight."

"No!"

"If I don't know he's alright, then no deal," She said in a panicked voice.

Marlboro whispered, "Try and stay calm."

There was a long silence, then, "Hello, Barbra."

"Dwight? Are you alright?"

"Barbra, just do whatever they ask," Dwight begged.

"Okay, lady, You got until Friday morning." The voice demanded.

CLICK

"Oh my God. Oh my God," Barbra said frantically.

"No. No, it's good. Look, we know that Dwight is alive and that we have two days."

"Oh, Marlboro, I'm so terrified."

Marlboro held her face to face and softly said, "Barbra, look at me. We're going to get your brother back. You need to trust me."

She looked at him with tears in her eyes, "Do you promise."

"Scouts honor," He said with a smile.

"Were you ever a scout?"

"No, they wouldn't have me."

Barbra broke into a small laugh easing, the tension. Marlboro took a handkerchief from his coat pocket and wiped her eyes. "There. There, it's going to be alright."

He stood up, kissed her on her forehead, and said, "I don't know about you, but I sure could go for some that Oswego mushroom chicken."

"Silly, it's mushroom asiago chicken," She said, smiling.

"Right, mushroom asiago chicken. That sounds even better."

In the basement of an abandoned warehouse, six blocks from the Hughes Aircraft Company plant in Culver City, Muldoon and O'Bannon held Dwight Babcock hostage. He was bound to a wooden chair and gagged a burlap bag over his head so he couldn't see where he was.

O'Bannon had no intention of letting Babcock go after the abduction, Babcock had gotten a good look at both him and Nora. The plan was to string the sister along until she came across with the dough, then Babcock would be fitted for a wooden kimono.

"Think we should feed him?" Muldoon asked.

"What for," O'Bannon answered.

"Well, the next time we call, she might want to speak to him again."

"Ah, I guess. But nothing special. Go over to the White Castle on Westchester and pick us up some burgers, fries, and a couple of beers. Oh, and while you're out, pick me up a pack of my smokes."

"I'll need some money."

"God damnit. Whad'ya do with the two bucks I gave ya yesterday!" He barked.

"I had to get some gas, remember?" She cringed.

He slapped her hard across the face and growled, "You need money? Go out and blow somebody, but you better come back with the food and my smokes. Got it!"

"Yeah, baby. I promise."

"And make it snappy!"

"I'll be back real soon."

O'Bannon liked playing the tough guy, and he'd smack her around then beg forgiveness, saying he'd never do it again. But he would. She just thought it was the booze making him mean, most of the time it was, since he was drunk the majority of the time. When he wasn't drunk, he was surly and mean. He once broke her arm, knocked out two teeth, and threw her down the stairs for not bringing him the wrong brand of cigarettes.

Nora Muldoon had a hard life; she came from an abusive household. Her father and his brother came home drunk one night and raped the then twelve-year-old Nora in front of her mother. When she tried to intercede, Nora's father stabbed her over forty times with a butcher's knife.

He was convicted of murder and sent to the gas chamber in San Quinten. Nora was sent to live with her grandmother, who owned a small farm outside Torrance.

At the age of sixteen, she ran away with and married a thirty-two-year-old Hudson Automobile salesman, who treated her like a dog. When he got tired of her, he divorced her and left her with nothing. She turned to prostitution and drinking, and that's when she met Brian O'Bannon. The rough years and all the booze had left its mark on Nora; she was thirty-three but looked fifty-three. She was on the chubby side, yet had a sweet face.

Nora left O'Bannon to go get food and cigarettes. Not wanting to waste gas, she walked the six blocks to the Hughes Aircraft Company plant. She strolled around the truck parking lot, looking to turn a trick.

Nora saw a man sitting in the truck cab eating a sandwich. She approached him, "Say, Mister, want to have a good time?"

He looked her over, top to bottom, he asked, "How much?"

"Ten dollars."

"Naw, I ain't time to screw; how much for a hummer?"

"Five."

"I'll give ya two," He said, seeing that she looked desperate.

"How about three?"

"Two bucks, take it or leave it, you old cow." He chuckled.

"Okay, two. Gimme me the money."

"After."

She walked over to the passenger side of the truck and climbed in. By the time she got into the cab, he had his pants down around his ankles.

"Come on," He said as he grabbed her head and forced her down into his lap.

Afterwards, she said, holding out her hand, "Two dollars."

"It wasn't even worth two bucks. Get out of my truck, you fat pig."

"I want my two dollars," She demanded.

He leaned over and smacked her in the face, snarling, "Get the Hell out of my truck!"

Nora had received a bloody nose; she walked back to the warehouse where O'Bannon was waiting, expecting another beating.

"What the Hell happened to you?" He gnarred.

She recounted the story to him, but instead of him getting angry at her, he compassionately said, "That's okay, show me who did this."

They walked back to the truck park. Nora pointed out the driver. O'Bannon walked up to the truck and gnarled, "Hey, you. Did you get a hummer from my old lady?"

"Scram, you bum, before I get out of this truck and kick your ass."

"Well, come on down out of your truck, buddy, and we'll see who kicks whose ass," O'Bannon barked defiantly.

The driver flung the cab door open and jumped down; he was a big man, at least a foot taller than O'Bannon and ten years younger.

"Okay, old man, let's go at it," The driver said, poised to duke it out with the short, pudgy fellow standing in front of him.

O'Bannon pulled out his revolver, pointed it at the driver, and with a smirk said, "That will be twenty-two dollars. Hand it over."

"But the hummer was only two dollars."

"Yeah, that's right. Two dollars for the blow job and twenty bucks for me having to come over here," O'Bannon said as he pulled the hammer back on the revolver.

The driver reached into his blue jeans pants pocket and pulled out a twenty and a five dollar bill.

"All I got is twenty-five," He said.

"Nora, go get the money," O'Bannon ordered.

Nora did as she was told.

O'Bannon smiled as he quipped to the driver, "That's very kind of you to tip the lady. Now, get your ass back into the truck. I'll blow your fucking brains out if I see you trying anything funny."

Nora and Bannon went the long way about to get back to the warehouse where Dwight Babcock was sitting in a puddle of his own urine. When they got back and saw the state of their hostage, O'Bannon said, "You go clean him up, and I'll go get the food and smokes. Gimme the keys to the Ford."

Marlboro had stopped by six of the tobacco shops that he knew of that sold the French cigarettes, Gitanes. There was one last shop on Wilshire Boulevard, the Tinder Box; it touted itself to be an Olde English-style tobacco shop, and it had been around since the late twenties.

He parked the fire-engine red Fleetmaster in front of the shop, got out, and as he was about to walk in, a grubby little man approached the door at the same time.

"Allow me," Marlboro said as he opened the door.

The man said nothing as he stepped in front of Marlboro and walked straight to the counter.

"May I help you, sir?" The old gent behind the counter asked.

"Yeah, gimme a pack of them Gitanes and a box of matches, Mac," O'Bannon said.

Marlboro slowly glanced down at the man's feet. Size elevens. He stared at the man, memorizing his features and voice.

"That'll be twenty-five cents," The counterman said.

The man plopped a twenty-dollar bill on the counter.

"Don't you have anything smaller?"

"Nope," O'Bannon said proudly.

"Just a moment," The counterman said as he went to the back of the store to get change.

Another salesman approached Marlboro and asked, "Are you being served, sir?"

"Could I get a tin of the Half and Half pipe tobacco?"

"Certainly, sir. That will be thirty cents."

Marlboro reached inside of his pocket and produced the exact change. "Here you are."

"Very good, sir. Would you care for a bag?"

"No, thank you," Marlboro said as he took the tin, walked out of the store, and sat in the Fleetmaster, pretending to fiddle around with his pipe while he waited for the grubby man to come out of the shop.

It wasn't more than five minutes when the stranger with the Gitanes came sauntering out the door, opening the pack of cigarettes, not noticing that he was being watched.

Marlboro couldn't believe his luck; he kept thinking what are the odds, which gave him pause. Was this really the kidnapper or just some random person that he wished him to be the culprit? He had to follow it through. He figured he'd know soon enough.

O'Bannon walked halfway down the block to a maroon 1939 Ford two-door Standard coupe. He stood by the driver's door lit and a cigarette before getting into the car and driving off, with Marlboro following. The old Ford didn't have a license plate, so tracing the owner was getting tougher.

Marlboro was a master of the "tail," having worked in the LAPD for six years. He knew how to follow, remaining undetected, and he knew how to detect when he was being followed.

He tailed the Ford coupe to an area of abandoned warehouses on the outskirts of the Hughes Aircraft Company plant when he saw the Ford pull over and park. He motored past, parking the Fleetmaster several blocks south of the warehouses in a neighborhood.

Marlboro waited half an hour; he slipped out of his sports coat and put on his fedora, hoping that the man, if he should encounter him, wouldn't recognize him.

He made his way back to where he saw the Ford parked and cautiously approached the warehouse. He tried the car door; it was unlocked. He peeked inside to check the registration. The name on the registration was to a Richard Muldoon in Inglewood.

The streets weren't deserted, and the way he was dressed, he definitely stood out. He decided to head downtown and hook up with Beck; at least he'd have some backup when he returned.

"Are you sure this is the guy?" Beck asked.?
"I got a pretty good hunch."
"A hunch?"

"Look, the guy smokes Gitanes, the same brand of cigarettes as the ones I found outside the house; he wears a size eleven shoe, like the cast I made outside the house. Come on, you've acted on less; admit it," Marlboro appealed.

"Yeah, okay. Let's go see."

"First, I have to stop by my office and drop my car off and check for messages."

"Why are we dropping off your car?"

"Well, for one thing, we don't need two cars, and for another, he might recognize the Fleetmaster from earlier this afternoon," Marlboro explained.

Beck followed Marlboro to the Brockman Building, where Marlboro's office is. After parking his car, they went upstairs to his office so he could call his message center.

"Hello. This Marlboro, do I have any messages?"

"Okay, what time did she call?" Marlboro said with an edge to his voice.

He began to take down notes.

"Did she say anything else? Okay, thank you."
CLICK

Marlboro held up his left hand to stop Beck from asking while dialing a number with his right.

"Barbra.

When did they call?

Uhuh.

And what did they say?

Did you get to speak with him?

Okay, just sit tight.

Yeah, but I have something to check out first.

I'll get there as soon as I can.

Yeah.

Lock the door and don't answer it.

Okay, I'll get there as soon as I can.

Bye."

CLICK

"What was that?" Beck inquired.

"The kidnappers called. They said they now want 300,000 bucks by Friday. They did let her brother speak to her. She said he sounded weak."

Marlboro said as he armed himself with both his Colt – Official Police .38 Special and a .45 caliber semi-automatic Colt M1911.

"Let's roll," He said to Beck, who was already up and heading towards the door.

They decided to call on the owner of the car, Richard Muldoon. 924 South Eucalyptus Avenue was a modest one-story cream-colored stucco cookie-cutter house. With the exception of the color, each house looked like the other.

The lights were on in the house as Beck and Marlboro knocked on the door. A short, stocky man wearing a wife-beater tee shirt holding a beer opened the door.

Beck held up his FBI ID and said, "Good evening, I'm Special Agent Beck with the FBI; this is my associate John Marlboro. Are you Richard Muldoon?"

"Yeah, so?"

"Mr. Muldoon, are you the owner of a maroon 1939 Ford two-door Standard coupe?" Beck asked.

"No."

"No?" Marlboro challenged.

"No. It's my wife's car."

"Could we speak with your wife?"

"No."

"Why not? We need to speak to your wife." Beck demanded.

"Ex."

"Excuse me?"

"Ex. Nora is my ex-wife. She got the car in the divorce. I haven't seen her since I kicked her ass out to the curb months ago."

"Any idea where we might find her?" Marlboro inquired.

"Don't know. Don't want to know," He said as he shut the door in their face.

"Well, he was rather a pleasant fellow, wasn't he." Beck quipped.

When O'Bannon returned late from his smoke run, he decided they had better move after their altercation with the truck driver. He might have called the cops.

While he was out, he was driving around the Venice Beach area when he remembered that he had a pal, Butch Rigger, who lived a couple of blocks from Muscle Beach on Windward Avenue.

O'Bannon and Butch met up in Folsom State Prison while Butch was doing a three-spot for auto theft. When Butch served his time, he got a job as a mechanic at a boat repair shop in Marina Del Rey.

O'Bannon knocked on the door of this old, run-down, one-story wooden bungalow sandwiched in between a couple of newly built two-story houses. The bungalow was tucked in off the street, with a six-foot-tall wooden fence and lots of bushes and trees—the perfect hide-a-way for keeping a hostage.

The door opened, and Butch was pleasantly shocked to see his old cellmate.

"Brian O'Bannon, what do I owe the pleasure?"

"Butch, you old dog. How are ya?"

"Scrapping by. Got me a job as a mechanic over at Buzz's Boat Emporium. The guy who runs it is a real Palooka. How about you?"

"I'm working a deal, you want in?"

"Maybe."

"There's fifty large in it for you."

"Fifty large! Who do I have to kill?"

"Nah, I just need a place to stash a guy for a couple of days. Whad'ya say?"

"Stash a guy? What guy?"

"I kinda kidnapped this guy, and I need a place to stash him until the ransom's paid on Friday. Whad'ya say?"

"Kidnapping! I don't know, that's big!"

"50 Gs, Butch. Just for letting me keep the guy here."

"Who is it?"

"A big time Hollywood writer, and get this, best of all, he's a Commie! So, the police don't care. Whad'ya say?"

"Okay, for two days, right?"

"Yeah, two days. And then I…"

"Don't tell me what you're going to do. I don't want to know."

"Okay."

"And Friday, I get my 50 Gs."

"Right, so I'm going to go get him, and we'll be right back."

"*We'll*? Who else is involved."

"My old lady, Nora. Problem?"

"No, I guess not."

"Good. We'll be over in about an hour. Thanks again, Butch."

"50 large?"

"50 large."

"Let's head over to the warehouse. See if the Ford is there," Marlboro suggested.

By the time they got to where O'Bannon had parked earlier, the car was gone.

"Damnit!" Marlboro cursed.

"Maybe he just went out for food or something. So, let's go check out some of these old, abandoned warehouses out. Grab your flashlight."

They had gone through three before coming across the basement where Babcock had been held.

It reeked of urine and Gitanes cigarettes. Marlboro figured by the amount of butts on the floor, he would be going back to the Tinder Box soon. They looked around but found no signs of blood.

"Looks like they moved him," Beck surmised.

"I'm thinking that Nora Muldoon is in on it too," Marlboro said, looking around.

"What makes you say that?"

"Well, by the looks and smell of this place, Babcock apparently soiled himself and was attended to. I don't know that many tough guys who would do that, do you?"

"No! So, do you think you still want to handle it ourselves? Or do you think we should call in the troops?" Beck asked.

"If it were left up to me, I'd call in the team, but I'll have to discuss it with her; it's her call. Take me back to get my car, and I'll call you tomorrow after I talk to the Red Queen."

Marlboro parked in the driveway; a living room light was on when he rang the doorbell four times. Long, short, long, short.

She opened the door slowly. When he entered, Marlboro saw that she was holding the snub-nose pistol in her right hand down by her side. She was wearing man-tailored style satin two-piece pajamas with a matching bed jacket. Her hair was down, touching her shoulders, and she had a slight touch of ruby-red lipstick. She smelled the way Paris looked in the moonlight. Marlboro was smitten, trying hard to concentrate.

"Any news?" She asked frantically.

"I almost had him today. As I was closing in, they moved Dwight to a new location."

"Any ideas? Any leads?"

"Leads? Yeah, sure, a few. But Barbra, it's not too late to call in the FBI."

"No. No, FBI. I trust only you, Marlboro," She said as she glided over to him until they were eye to eye. Her lips parted ever so slightly; he could feel her warm breath on his lips. He inched closer until their lips became one, their breath flowing from one to another.

He scooped her up and carried upstairs to her bedroom. The covers were turned down, he set her down next to the bed, and they slowly started to undress each other. He gazed upon her perfect body as he caressed and kissed her breasts while lying her back on the bed. His hands gently moved down between her legs. She eagerly spread them, yearning for him to be inside her. They rocked softly back and forth, embedded as one, bringing each other to a raptured climax.

"Barbra, I have to admit, I've never made love to a communist," Marlboro said with a devilish grin, lying beside her, exhausted, breathing heavily.

"How was it, comrade?"

"If this is what Lenin meant when he said, "Workers of the world unite." Then sign me up."

As she began rubbing him with her hand, getting him hard, she whispered, "He also said, "Workers of the world arise! Mmm, come on, Marlboro, that's it rise up."

Once he was hard, Barbra rolled on top of him, straddled him, and then slowly began rocking back and forth as she was riding him. She looked down on him and softly began singing the Communist Internationale Anthem.

> *"Arise ye workers from your slumbers*
> *Arise ye prisoners of want*
> *For reason, in revolt now, thunders*
> *And at last, ends the age of cant.*
> *Away with all your superstitions*
> *Servile masses arise, arise*
> *We'll change henceforth the old tradition.*
> *And spurn the dust to win the prize."*

Marlboro lay there in ecstasy, thinking to himself, "*USSR, you may have the Red Tsar, but I've got the Red Queen.*"

It was after ten o'clock at night when Nora and O'Bannon brought Dwight Babcock into Butch's bungalow.

"Jeezus Christ, this guy stinks like piss. Take him outside and hose him down," Butch ordered Nora.

Babcock's hands were bound behind his back with nylon cord, his mouth had a gag in it, and his eyes were blindfolded. Nora guided him out into the small backyard blocked by the neighbors with several lemon trees. She removed his shoes, socks, and pants and hosed him off. She dried him off, then led him back into the house.

While O'Bannon left, Butch had emptied a pantry closet next to the kitchen and placed a single mattress on the floor to accommodate their guest.

"Stick him in here," Rigger told Nora.

"Look, Babcock, there's a pail in the corner. You gotta take a leak; use the bucket. You gotta take a shit, you holler. I'm tired of you stinking up the joint," O'Bannon gnarled.

Once inside the closet, Butch pushed the hostage down onto the mattress.

"It ain't big, but it's big enough," Butch said to Babcock, then he shut the door.

"You got something to drink?" O'Bannon asked Butch.

"I got some rye."

"That'll do."

Butch had gone out and bought a bottle of rye whiskey to celebrate.

The three of them sat in the living room, drinking, talking, and laughing for hours about what all they were going to do with their share of the ransom. They were all different degrees of drunk.

"Butch, whaddya going to do with your share?" Nora asked.

"Me? I don't rightly know. I'll probably drink, gamble and whore it all away," Butch replied.

"What will you do with your share, Nora?"

Before she could answer, O'Bannon jumped in, "She ain't got a share; her share is my share."

"That ain't fair," She said.

He reached over, grabbed her by the collar, and slapped her two, three, four times across the mouth, cutting her bottom lip.

"Shut up, you whore. Before I really give you what for," O'Bannon shouted.

Butch was pretty drunk, "Now, that ain't no way to treat a lady."

"Lady? She ain't no lady. She's an old whore. Ain't ya, Nora!" He bellowed.

She didn't respond; she just sat there dabbing her bottom lip with an old tissue.

"Lady? Stand up," He shouted.

Nora did as she was told. "Don't hit me no more, Brian," She whimpered.

"Come here and take off your clothes," O'Bannon commanded.

She slowly started to unbutton her blouse. She took off her bra, slipped off her skirt, and finally removed her underwear.

"Turn around for Butch. Go on!"

She did as she was told, trying to hide herself with some modesty.

"Now bend over and get down on all fours."

She got down on the bare hardwood floor on her hands and knees, sobbing.

"Now, Butch, do you want to screw her? Go ahead. She wants you to. Don't you, Nora?"

Nora remained silent, quietly sobbing.

O'Bannon took his foot and kicked her in the ribs. "I said don't you, Nora! Tell Butch you want him to screw you."

"Butch, I want you to screw me," She said, crying.

O'Bannon was fidgeting with the handle of his pistol when he said, "Butch, go on now. Nora's waiting."

Butch realized at that moment that O'Bannon was crazier than a shit-house rat. And he better do as he was told, too.

He stood up, walked behind Nora, dropped his pants, and mounted her. All the time, she was crying, and Butch was eyeballing O'Bannon, who just sat there drinking and handling his pistol.

Afterward, Butch pulled up his pants and sat back down.

"How wus zat?" O'Bannon asked slurring his words.

"That was great," Butch said, hoping to appease O'Bannon.

O'Bannon leaned over and lovingly patted Nora on her backside, still on all fours, and said, "Yeah, good old Nora, she's a good piece of ass."

"Can I please get up now?" She begged.

"Yeah, get up! And go check on Babcock!" O'Bannon barked.

Marlboro showered, dressed, went downstairs, and made a pot of coffee, all before the sun rose at five o'clock. He had just come in from bringing in the newspaper when he saw Barbra coming downstairs. She was wearing his white button-down oxford shirt and a pair of pink panties.

"Good morning. Care for some coffee?" He asked.

"Mmm, sounds good. How long have you been up?"

Marlboro looked at his watch and said, "Oh, about an hour."

"Why didn't you wake me?"

"You looked so peaceful; I didn't have the heart."

She strolled over to him, put both arms around his neck, kissed him softly with her eyes closed, laid her head against him, and asked, "How is this all going to end?"

"I don't know, doll. But I'll do my best to make it a happy ending."

While they sat and had coffee, the phone rang.

Barbra picked up the receiver on the kitchen wall and held it so Marlboro could listen.

"You got the dough?" O'Bannon asked.

"I have the original two hundred thousand, but I need more time to secure the other hundred thousand," She responded as Marlboro, and she had rehearsed earlier.

"That's your hard luck, lady. You better have all the dough when I call tomorrow morning. You got that?"

"I want to speak to Dwight!" She demanded.

"Yeah. Yeah. Hold on," He snarled.

Marlboro could hear in the background muffled voices.

"Hey, Butch, bring him over here."

"Nora, give him a hand."

"Come on, hurry up!"

Then Dwight's weak voice came on the line.

"Barbra. Just do whatever they ask, please."

"Dwight, are you alright?" His sister asked.

A muffled voice could be heard saying, "*You tell her you're fine, ya hear!*"

"I 'm fine, Barbra. Just a little tired but fine."

"Satisfied! Now you got one day to get the rest of the dough. You better have it when I call tomorrow or else," O'Bannon threatened.

CLICK

Marlboro took the phone receiver and hung it up.

"Look, Barbra, I got a couple of leads to follow up on. There were some good clues off that phone call. They're beginning to tip their mitt. I'm going to blow; I'll call you later. Doll," He said as he kissed her on the cheek.

Marlboro got downtown by 8 a.m. He sat in the FBI lobby until 8:30, when Beck walked in.

"Beck!" Marlboro called.

"Let's get you a visitor's pass."

"Did you hear from them?" Beck asked.

"Yeah. A little after seven this morning. I overheard them talking to each other. I distinctly hear the names Nora and Butch, so now we know there's at least three."

"So, we know Nora Muldoon, some guy name Butch, and the leader."

"Do you think we could get a sketch artist up here?" Marlboro suggested.

"Good idea. I'll start composing a wanted poster with a photograph of Muldoon, and we'll add the composite later."

The artist arrived at Beck's office with a drawing pad and several charcoal pencils.

"Hey, Jimmy. Why don't you have a seat at my desk. I have to go run an errand. Oh, Jimmy Walker, this is John Marlboro. He'll describe the mug we're after. I'll be back soon," Beck said.

Walker opened his pad, got a pencil, looked at Marlboro, and said, "Now, Mr. Marlboro, let's start. What shape was his head, round, square, long, and thin?"

"Square."

Walker drew a squat oval and showed Marlboro.

"Something like this?"

"Yeah, like that."

"Hair?"

"Balding on top with a thin ring of hair encircling the outside of the head."

"Like this?"

"Maybe a little more hair on the sides, a bit unkempt."

"How's this?"

"That's it."

"Great. Describe the eyes. Were they close together, wide apart, average?"

"I'd say slightly wider than average."

Walker did a light indication just for placement.

"Something like this?"

"Not so wide and maybe a little higher on the head."

"Okay," Walker said as he was sketching. When he was through, he turned the pad to show Marlboro.

"Like this?"

"Yeah, that's it."

"Facial hair, mustache, beard?"

"No. Although he did have a five o'clock shadow, but no real facial hair."

"How about his lips, thin, fat, full, average?"

"You know, he had lips like Edward G. Robinson."

"Edward G. Robinson, huh?"

"Yeah, just like Robinson."

"Eyebrows, thin, bushy, straight, curved, what?"

"Straight and bushy."

"And finally, his ears."

"Ears?"

"Yeah, did the lay flat against his head, normal or Dumbo ears?"

"Normal. There wasn't anything that stood out to me about his ears."

"Okay, just give me a minute here," The artist said as his pencil feverishly flashed from the top of the drawing pad to the bottom and from side to side. Once finished, he turned the place around.

"What do you think?" Walker asked.

Marlboro got a big grin on his face, gave a thumbs up to Walker, and said, "Man, you nailed it. That's the guy. That's our kidnapper."

"Terrific," Walker said with a sense of accomplishment.

"How'd we do?" Beck asked as he returned to the office.

Marlboro held up the sketch and said, "This is our guy."

"Excellent. Let me have it, and I'll place it in the wanted poster, and we can start distributing them around town. Thanks, Jimmy, great job," Beck said, nodding.

"Glad I could be of some help."

Marlboro stood up and shook the artist's hand, "Nice job."

"You too. Not too many people are so decisive in their descriptions. You made it easy," He said as he left Beck's office.

Moments later, Beck walked in with a handful of posters.

"I'll have dispatch send this out to our agents in the field and the LAPD, concentrating in the Santa Monica, Culver City, and Venice Beach area.

Hopefully, someone will either recognize this mug or will spot them."

"Fingers crossed. We're running out of time."

"So, what did your client say about calling in the Calvary?"

"No way, she won't budge."

"She sounds very passionate," Beck smirked.

"Extremely."

"Where do you think you're going?" O'Bannon gnarled at Butch.

"I'm going to work. Where do you think I'm going?"

"Naw, you call in sick. We got one more day babysitting this punk, and I'm not taking any chances on something going wrong. Got it."

"But."

"No buts! Look, you got 50 large riding on this, too. So, sit down, shut up, have a drink and wait," O'Bannon rumbled.

"Yeah, you're right. I'll just call and let them know I won't be coming in today. Screw them," Butch said as he picked up the phone.

"Hello, Buzz."

"It's Butch. I ain't feeling so good, so I won't be coming in today."

"Yeah, I know, but I can't. I got a pain in my gut, and I got a real bad case of the squirts."

"Yeah. I should be better by tomorrow."

"Okay, bye."

CLICK

"You know, Butch, after tomorrow, you can probably buy the joint. Butch's Boat Emporium. It's got a nice ring to it, don't you think?" O'Bannon said with a devilish smile.

"Yeah. Butch's Boat Emporium. That sounds swell."

"Say, Butch, you got any coffin nails?"

"Chesterfields."

"No thanks, those taste like old socks."

"Sorry, that's all I smoke."

"I'll be back. I need to get some Gitanes. Keep an eye on Babcock. While I'm gone, have Nora take the rube out and hose him down again. I can't wait to get rid of the sap."

"While you're out, we could use some more hooch."

"Yeah, sure. Be back soon."

"I'm heading down to the Tinder Box to see if our friend has come back for another pack of Gitanes," Marlboro said.

Beck held up the handful of wanted posters. "Okay, I'll get these posters out and about. Give me a call later."

Marlboro drove down Wilshire Boulevard with the top down, the temperature dropping block by block as he got closer to the coast.

He dressed down, no suit, as he was going to a more blue-collar area. Suits would ID him as either a cop or a gumshoe. Marlboro wore a pair of khakis, a long-sleeve chambray shirt, unbuttoned and untucked, with a dark navy blue tee-shirt worn underneath, and a pair of cheaters.

Marlboro parked in the back of the tobacco shop, trying to go unnoticed. He entered through the back door and was surprised to see how busy the shop was at nine in the morning.

He hung out in the back of the shop, looking at a display of Meerschaum pipes, waiting for the place to empty out so he could speak to the owner. While he was waiting, his suspect walked in, grabbed a pack of Gitanes, and stood in line to pay.

Marlboro ducked out the back door, got into the red Fleetmaster and pulled around to the front of the store, parking several cars behind the maroon 1939 Ford. He got out of the car and went into a flower shop, keeping his eye out for the kidnapper.

"May I help you, sir?" The floral sales lady inquired.

Marlboro turned around. "Actually, I'm a shamus keeping an eye for my suspect to exit the

Tinder Box. I hope you don't mind my waiting in here for him to come out. Do you?"

"Ooh, no. Sounds exciting. Can I watch, too?"

"Sure," Marlboro said.

"Is he a bank robber, rapist, or a killer?"

"No. Just an adulterer."

"Oh. Sounds boring," She said as she left to go back to arrange flowers.

It was close to twenty minutes before O'Bannon came walking back to his car. He was carrying what looked to be a brown paper bag with a bottle of booze in it.

"That's him. Gotta run," Marlboro said as he scooted out the door.

He waited until a couple of cars got in between him and the maroon Ford before pulling out into traffic. They drove down Wilshire Boulevard towards the ocean, making a left turn onto Ocean Avenue that parallels the Pacific. When Ocean Avenue divides at Pico Boulevard, O'Bannon stayed left onto Neilson Way, which eventually turns into Pacific Avenue.

When they reached Windward Avenue, O'Bannon turned left, drove halfway around on Windward Circle, and then continued a half a block to 221 Windward Avenue, where he parked. Marlboro drove on past for several blocks, eventually parking in the parking lot of the Venice Foursquare Church.

From where he was parked, Marlboro had an excellent view of the maroon Ford and the bungalow. He was familiar with the area and knew that behind the houses and bungalows, there was a small alley called Granada Court. He knew he needed to be in the alley, keeping an eye on 221.

"Can I help you, my son?" Reverend Alfred Clark asked the stranger at the door.

"Yes, Father," Marlboro replied.

"It's Reverend. Reverend Alfred Clark."

"Oh, sorry, Reverend. I was wondering if I might use your telephone."

"Is there something wrong that I might be able to help you with?"

"No, Reverend. It's a police matter. I need to contact the FBI."

"Why, certainly, my son. Please come in. You can use the telephone in my office."

Reverend Clark led him through the worship hall, behind the altar, pulpit, and choir stand, to his tiny office tucked away in the back of the church.

"It's there on my desk; I'll just leave you be. If you need me, I'll be in the sanctuary."

"Thank you, Reverend."

The Reverend closed the office door on his way out. Marlboro sat at the Reverend's desk; staring at him from across the room was a large picture of Jesus surrounded by the multitudes with arms stretched out. Marlboro picked up the receiver and dialed the number for the FBI under the watchful eye of the Redeemer.

"Federal Bureau of Investigation. How may I direct your call?" The FBI operator asked.

"Agent Beck, please."

"One moment, I'll see if he's in."
SILENCE
"Hello. Agent Beck speaking."
"Jimmy. Marlboro here. I got him."
"You got him!"
"I mean, I followed him to a small bungalow in Venice. 221 Windward Avenue. I'm sitting in a church parking lot down the street from him. I'm watching the car and the front, but there's an alley. Can you get down here, PDQ?"

"Yeah. I'm on my way. What church?"

"Venice Foursquare Church, corner of Windward Avenue and Riviera."

"Where are you calling from?"

"The Reverend's office."

"God. That's gotta be the first time you've ever been in a church."

"Don't start."
CLICK

Agent Beck was on his way out of the building when the receptionist in the lobby stopped him.

"Oh, Agent Beck. Director Woolsey would like to see you right away."

"Now?"

"He said it was important."

"Okay. Let him know I'm on my way up." He said as he headed back towards the elevator bank.

He rode the elevator up to the sixth floor anxious, wanting to get down to Venice Beach to help Marlboro nab the kidnappers.

Director Woolsey's office was located down at the end of the hall. The door was open. Sitting behind his massive wooden desk was Director Woolsey; opposite him sat two chairs, one occupied by Assistant Director Roger Ashley, the other unoccupied.

"Agent Beck. Please come in. Have a seat," Woolsey said as he gestured to the unoccupied seat.

"Thank you, sir," Beck said as he took the seat next to Assistant Director Ashley.

"Beck, it has come to my attention that you're working on a case outside of the FBI purview. Am I correct?"

"Yes, Sir. In a way."

"What way is that?"

"Well, a friend of mine is working a kidnapping case and has asked for my help."

"Is this man a police officer?"

"No Sir, a private investigator."

"A shamus?"

"Yes, Sir. John Marlboro. We worked together when we both were cops on LAPD."

"Marlboro? I've heard that name."

"Yes, Sir. He's known to be one of the best."

"Well, why didn't he come to the Bureau and ask for our assistance?

"It's his client, Sir. She insists on no police or FBI. Apparently, she's concerned, for whatever reason, that she would be treated unfairly."

"I see. So, what exactly what services have you provided Mr. Marlboro?"

"At the moment, just the use of a sketch artist and Dopkins in fingerprints."

"And, where does the case stand at the moment?"

"I just got a call from Marlboro saying that he has located the suspect and what he believes is the kidnapper's lair. I was just on my way over there to assess the situation, sir."

Assistant Director Ashley sat up in his chair and asked, "Sir, do you think it's a good idea to let an agent go on an unauthorized assignment? I mean, what kind of precedent are we setting?"

Director Woolsey sat silent for a moment, looked at Beck, and asked, "Agent Beck, Assistant Director Ashely is right. We can't have an agent go off and work on cases outside the Bureau on Agency time. Beck, do you have any vacation time accrued?"

"Yes, sir. I believe I have a week at the moment."

"Were you thinking of taking some personal time off?"

"As a matter of fact, I was, sir."

"Where are you planning on going?"

"I thought maybe Venice Beach, sir."

"Well, Beck, I hope you have a good time. Now, be sure to drop us a postcard or maybe even call us sometime."

"Yes, sir. I'll do that. Thank you, sir."

Beck found Marlboro sitting in his Fleetmaster with the top up peering through a pair of WW2 U.S. Field Binoculars M17s.

"See anything good?" Beck asked.

"Just a bunch of young twerps, soda jerks, and jitterbuggers. What took you so long?"

"I got called into the Directors office."

"What? The dog ate your homework again?"

"He wanted to know what I was doing, spending my valuable time helping a gumshoe like you."

"Yeah? So…"

"So, I'm officially on vacation, working on my own time."

"Beck, you are one stand-up guy," Marlboro said with a devilish grin.

"I'm going around to Granada Court to keep an eye on things. I brought along a pair of SCR-536s."

"Wow, I haven't used a walkie-talkie since Burma."

"I'll call you when I'm in position," Beck said as he drove off.

Minutes later, Beck radioed in.

"I'm in position."

"Roger, that," Marlboro acknowledged.

"I think I'll mosey down the alley and see if I see anything."

"Be careful."

"Roger."

O'Bannon returned from the tobacco shop and liquor store to find Nora hosing off Babcock in the backyard, naked from the waist down, blindfolded, gagged, and hands bound behind his back. Butch was sitting in a lawn chair, watching to make sure his fifty thousand dollars didn't try anything stupid.

"How's it going?" O'Bannon asked.

"Fine," Nora responded cheerfully.

O'Bannon took a drink from the fresh bottle of whiskey and snarled, "I didn't ask you, bitch."

Butch seeing that O'Bannon was already starting to get drunk, piped up, "It's fine. All fine. Everything is fine."

"Good. Let's keep it that way! Nora, he's clean enough. Go dry him off and put him back in the closet."

While the four of them were in the backyard, none of them seemed to notice a figure outside the back gate listening. Beck had casually sauntered down the alley to 221, pretending to be reading the sports section of the paper. Stopping under the shade of one of Butch's lemon trees, whose branches hung over the fence.

Once Nora and Babcock had gone into the house, O'Bannon sat in a lawn chair next to Butch and offered him the bottle while he lit up a Gitanes cigarette.

"Here, have a swig," O'Bannon said

"Thanks. So what happens next?" Butch asked between gulps.

"Well, tomorrow, we let Babcock talk to his dear, sweet sister to prove that he's still breathing. Then we bop him and go get the dough."

"Whoa. Whoa. Whoa. O'Bannon, you didn't say nothing about knocking this guy off!" Butch yawped.

"Whad'ya turning yella!" O'Bannon bellowed.

"Kidnapping's one thing, but to whack the guy, we'll fry for sure!"

"Shut your yap! Now you listen to me, you mug. You're nuts If you think I'm paying you 50 Gs for room service."

"But you said…"

"Never mind what I said. If you want 50 large, you got to earn it!"

Butch sat there running all the scenarios through his head, and none of them ended up good.

"So, you in?" O'Bannon demanded an answer.

Seeing that his ex-cellmate was drunk and holding the handle of the pistol in his waistband, Butch said, "Yeah, count me in."

"Swell. I knew you were a pal, Rigger."

"So, after he talks to his sister, are you going to shoot him?"

"Naw, don't be a sap. Too much noise. We'll just have to stab him to death."

"We?"

"Yeah, we!"

"But I never killed anybody before."

"Well, welcome to the major leagues, Butch. Where the stakes are high, but so are the rewards. Fifty thousand bucks."

"Fifty thousand bucks," Butch said as he took another swig of hooch for courage.

"Marlboro. You there?" Beck radioed.

"Yeah. Nothing going on out front. Whad'ya know?"

"Plenty. I'll be there soon. Over."

Beck pulled up next to Marlboro, facing the opposite direction so they could talk driver side to driver side.

"What gives?" Marlboro asked.

"I overheard two guys, Butch Rigger and some palooka named O'Bannon, who seems to be the honcho. The plan is after the phone call tomorrow morning confirming that the brother's alive, this guy O'Bannon and Butch are going to stab Babcock to death, dump his body, and go pick up the ransom."

"What about Babcock and Muldoon?"

"Apparently, Babcock is being held in some closet in the house, and Nora is babysitting him."

Marlboro reached behind his seat and produced a Thompson submachine gun with a 100-round Type "C" drum magazine, cocked it, and said, "Well, let's go."

"Hold on. You, being a private investigator don't have to worry about a warrant, but I'm FBI."

"Beck, this is the exception. A warrant is not necessary if in hot pursuit of a felon, or to prevent a felon's escape or ability to harm others."

"You sure?"

"I'm sure. Let's go. You want the front of the back?" Marlboro asked.

"I'll take the back, in case somebody tries to weasel out," Beck said.

"Okay. Let's synchronize our watches. It's 3:14... now!"

"Now!"

"I'm going in blazing at 3:30," Marlboro uttered.

"Whad'ya say, we try not to shoot each other," Beck noted.

"Stay low and get behind something solid."

"Got it."

"What heat are you packing?" Marlboro inquired.

Beck held up an Ithaca 37 pump-action 12 gauge 7-round shotgun, "Say hello to my good friend, Izzy."

"Mmm, nice," Marlboro said approvingly.

"See you on the other side," Beck said as he started to slowly drive off.

Marlboro parked the Fleetmaster one house away from 221, fearing it might get hit by a stray bullet that he could not abide. He got out of the car and walked up to the front gate, holding the Tommy Gun behind him.

The front gate latch was open. He slowly swung the gate open and waited for any reaction. There was none. He peeked inside. There was no sign of any activity, so he proceeded to walk up to the front door. Marlboro stood off to the left and peered down at his watch.

TICK TICK TICK TICK TICK TICK TICK TICK TICK TICK TICK TICK 3:29.

Marlboro knocked on the door with his left hand while raising the submachine gun with his right.

A voice from inside yelled, "Scram!"

Marlboro knocked again.

"Beat it!"

Marlboro knocked a third time.

"Who is it?"

Marlboro held the Tommy Gun with both hands ready for action and said, "It's the Avon Lady."

"You're not serious," The voice said.

"Deadly," He said standing off to the left side of the doorway.

POW POW POW

Three rounds came firing from the inside. Had Marlboro been standing in the center of the door, he would have been killed.

Marlboro raised the Chicago typewriter at the door.

TRATT RATTTT TRATT RATT TRATTTT

The wooden door shattered and disintegrated into a pile of pulp. Marlboro stepped in, Tommy Gun a blazing.

RATT RATTTT TRATT RATT TRATTTT TRATT RATTTT TRATT RATT TRATTTT TRATT RATTTT TRATT RATT TRATTTT TRATT RATTTT TRATT RATT TRATTTT TRATT RATTTT TRATT RATT TRATTTT TRATT RATTTT TRATT RATT TRATTTT TRATT RATTTT TRATT RATT TRATTTT TRATT RATTTT TRATT

He made a sweeping arc from left to right and back to the left. He tapped O'Bannon with two slugs while he was hiding behind the living room couch. One in the shoulder and one in the left side.

The air was filled with debris of fabric, wood, plaster, and metal bits floating in the air like a typical smoggy day in San Pedro. The inside of the house looked like a Swiss cheese factory, with rays of sunshine beaming through the dozens of bullet holes from Marlboro's Tommy Gun.

As Marlboro moved rapidly through the house, he could hear O'Bannon screaming in pain, Nora pleading for mercy in the kitchen, and a shotgun blast from the backyard.

Nora lying on the kitchen floor in a fetal position crying like a baby, "Please, don't shoot. Please don't shoot."

"Where's Babcock?" Marlboro asked coldly.

"He's in there!" She said pointing to a closet door.

"Open it," Marlboro said as he held his weapon at the ready in case it was a trap.

Nora got to her knees and quickly scooched over to the door and opened it up. There on the floor, shivering with fear, blindfolded, gagged, and hands bound behind his back.

"Get him out of there," Marlboro commanded.

Nora helped the hostage out of the closet, untied his hands, took off his blindfold, and removed the gag from his mouth.

"Where's his clothes?" Marlboro demanded.

"Here they are, right here," She said as she took them off the closet shelf.

"Get him dressed. When you're done, you get in the closet and shut the door. Don't come out until I come get you. Understand?"

"Yes. Sir."

Marlboro shouted out the back door, "Everything okay out here?"

"Everything is fine. Me and Butch are just having a little talk," Beck hollered.

Marlboro went to Dwight Babcock, standing wobbly in the kitchen, "Have a seat here while I call the police."

He went into what was left of the living room, looking for a phone. Marlboro saw O'Bannon lying unconscious on the floor, still holding his .38. Marlboro kicked it away, knelt down to see if the gunman was still alive, and he was.

Marlboro picked up the phone, called the police department, and reported the shooting, requesting a patrol car and an ambulance.

After hanging up with the police, he made a quick call to Barbra.

"Hey, doll, I got someone here who wants to say hello."

He handed the phone to Dwight, then went out back to check on Beck.

"What do we have here?" Marlboro asked.

"Marlboro, this is Butch Rigger. He's got a lot to say; he's been most cooperative."

"Did you shoot him?"

"No, I fired one shot in the air. Butch had the good sense to surrender. Didn't you, Butch?"

"I ain't no hero," Butch muttered.

"Yeah, I can see that."

Off in the distance, police sirens were becoming louder. In no time, seven black and white squad cars and an ambulance arrived. Right behind them came a swarm of media and newspaper reporters.

Marlboro thought it better if Agent Beck, the FBI agent, greeted the onslaught of law enforcement coming to the crime scene rather than a shamus standing there holding a Thompson submachine gun.

Police Officer Sergeant John Bridges led the dozen armed police towards the house. Lieutenant Anderson, hidden behind a squad car using a megaphone, squawked out instructions.

"This is Lieutenant Anderson of the LAPD. Come out with your hands on top of your head. We have the place surrounded. So, no funny business."

Beck went out onto the porch first, holding his FBI badge up high, followed by Butch, Nora, Dwight Babcock, and Marlboro.

"I'm FBI Special Agent James Beck; we have foiled and apprehended three suspects in a kidnapping plot." Beck pointed to Marlboro and added, "This here is private investigator, John Marlboro who assisted me. And next to him is the victim, Dwight Babcock. There is a wounded man inside the house, who is one of the masterminds of the kidnapping plot."

The police and the crime scene unit swarmed all over the house, collecting evidence and taking photographs and fingerprints. They took O'Bannon to the prison hospital in County lockup. Nora Muldoon and Butch Rigger were arrested and brought downtown to LAPD headquarters for questioning.

Marlboro, Beck, and Dwight Babcock were also taken downtown to police headquarters for statements.

As Beck and Marlboro were escorted to the police station in the same squad car, Marlboro turned to Beck and sarcastically said, "Assisted *you*?"

EPILOGUE

Brian O'Bannon made a full recovery from his gunshot wounds. He stood trial for kidnapping, abduction, assault with a deadly weapon, domestic violence, and false imprisonment.

After a two-week trial in Los Angeles Superior Court, O'Bannon was found guilty of all charges. He was sentenced to a total of one hundred and fourteen years to be served in San Quentin. He will be eligible for parole in the year 2031.

Nora Muldoon was found guilty of kidnapping, abduction, and false imprisonment. The court found that there were extenuating circumstances of domestic violence that resulted in a lessening of her sentence.

Nora was sentenced to a total of fifteen years in Folsom State Prison. She was released after serving eleven years for good behavior in 1959.

Nora found work as a house cleaner at the Best Western Motel in Fresno, California. She died of cirrhosis of the liver in 1966 at the age of fifty-four.

Butch Rigger was found guilty of aiding and abetting in the act of a felony. After turning state's evidence, he received a sentence of only three years in the California Institution for Men in San Bernardino.

When Butch was released, he was offered his old job back as a mechanic at Buzz's Boat Emporium, where he eventually went on to become general manager.

Dwight Babcock spent years in psychotherapy trying to get over the trauma of his experience of capture and psychological torture.

Four years after his ordeal, he wrote a screenplay that was produced into a full-length feature film based on his experiences called "Secret of the Silent," starring Chaz Torres, Nigel Richards, Art Greenwood, and Olivia Hewitt.

Dwight was nominated for best screenplay, but the Oscar went to Budd Schulberg for "On the Waterfront."

After that, Dwight was blacklisted in Hollywood as he was labeled a communist. He was fortunate to still write under an assumed name but never reached the status that he once had. Dwight died in 1985 at the age of sixty-eight in his home in the Hollywood Hills.

Special Agent James Beck received no special commendations from the FBI for his actions, as he was working outside his official duties. He did receive the Police Commission Unit Citation from the City of Los Angeles.

Beck went on to serve with valor in the FBI, rising to the rank of Executive Assistant Director of the Los Angeles Branch Office.

"You lied to me!" Barbra snapped at Marlboro.

"You promised no police and no FBI," She continued. "I trusted you!"

"Well, you know what Comrade Stalin always says, "I trust no one, not even myself."

Barbra stood silent, thinking, smiled, and said, "Shut up and come here, you capitalistic pig."

She put her arms around his neck and drew him close to her, kissed him passionately, and whispered, "Let's go upstairs and make wild, passionate love."

Marlboro scooped her up in his arms and carried her to the bedroom. They lay on the bed naked, entwined as one. as if in a struggle of one against the other, thrusting and jostling for domination.

When the dance was over, Barbra proclaimed herself the winner, "You see, as a strong communist woman, I can bend your weak capitalist male bourgeois desires to my command."

"Oh, really."

Marlboro softly began to caress and stroke her body; he slowly started kissing her breasts, continuing kissing her down to her stomach; He looked up into her eyes and asked, "What is your command?"

She leaned forward and gently lowered his head between her legs.

"Mmm, down with imperialist. Oh, for the love of God, please stay down." She purred.

The End

1940s GLOSSARY

APB: All Points Bulletin
Axle grease: butter

Babe: Woman
Bangtails: Racehorses
Behind the eight-ball: In a difficult position, in a tight spot
Bent as a butcher's hook: A gay member of society
Big house: Prison
Big sleep: Death
Big-wigs: The rich & powerful
Bloodhound in the hay: Hotdog with sauerkraut
Blow: Leave
Blow one down: Kill someone
Blowing smoke: Lying
Bop: To kill
Bossy in a bowl: Beef stew
Breeze off: Get lost
Broderick: A thorough beating

Bruno: Tough guy, enforcer
BTO: Big Time Operators
Bump: Kill; also, **bump-off**: a killing
Bupkis: Nothing
Business: Work over; beating
Button man: Professional killer

Cement shoes: A method of body disposal
Cheaters: Sunglasses
Cheese it: Hide
Chicago lightning: Gunfire
Chicago overcoat: Coffin
Chicago typewriter: Thompson machine gun
Chin music: Punch on the jaw
Chinese angle: A strange twist or aspect to something
Chinese Molasses: Opium
Chink: Chinese
Chippie: Woman of easy virtue
Chopper squad: Men with machine guns
Church key: Various kinds of bottle openers
Clams: Dollars
Clipped: Shot
Clubhouse: Police station
Coffin nails: Cigarettes
Coldcock: To knock someone down
Contract: A favor
Copper: Policeman

Deep pockets: People with a lot of money

Dewars flask: A vacuum flask, i.e., thermos
Dick: Private investigator
Dingus: A thing or item
Double sawbuck: $20 bill
Drift: Go, leave
Drill: Shoot
Drink out of the same bottle: Close friends
Drop a dime: To inform on someone
Duck soup: Easy, a piece of cake

Five-spot: $5 bill
FRY: To be electrocuted

Gams: Legs (especially a woman's)
Gat: Gun
Geezer: An old person
Get under your skin: To annoy
Glad rags: Fancy clothes
Glitterati: People who love the cameras
Goombah: Member of a criminal gang
Greasers: A hoodlum, thief, or punk
Grift: Swindle
Gripe my cookies: Irritate or disgust
Gum-shoe: Detective
Gunsel: Gunman

Hack: Newspaper reporter
Hash house: A cheap restaurant
Hatchet men: Killers, gunmen
Heat: A gun

Heater: A gun
High pillow: Person at the top, in charge
Hinky: Suspicious
Hitting the pipe: Smoking opium
Hit the bricks: Leave
Hold your breath for it: Taking the rap
Honcho: Leader
Hooch: Whiskey
Hood: Criminal
Hot seat: Under great pressure

Jake: Okay
Jam: Trouble, as in "in a jam."
Jobbie: Man
Joe: Coffee, as in "a cup of joe."

Kerfuffle: A commotion or fuss
Kibosh: To stop
Knock off: Kill
Knuckle sandwich: Punch in the mouth

Large: $1,000; **twenty large:** $20,000
Lead poisoning: To be shot
Loogan: A guy with a gun
Looker: Pretty woman

Made Man: A mobster that has killed someone
Manyak: Bastard
Meat wagon: Coroner's vehicle

Mishegoss: Craziness, lunacy
Moniker: Name
Motor: A police officer that rides a motorcycle
Mouthpiece: Lawyer
Moxie: Guts, nerve
Muckety-muck: a person of great importance
Muff it: Make a mistake
Mug: Face
Mugs: Men (esp. dumb ones)
Murphy: Potato

Oat soda: Beer

PCH: Pacific Coast Highway
PDQ: Pretty Damn Quick
Palooka: Bum
Peeper: Detective
Plug ya: Shoot someone
Pop: Kill
Popped: Killed
Pulchritudinous: Beautiful
Pumped full of lead: Multiple gun wounds
Put the lights out and cry: Liver and onions

QT: In confidence or secretly

Rod: Gun
Roscoe: Gun
Rub-out: A killing
Rube: A bumpkin

Rumble: The news

Sap: A blackjack
Sap: A dumb guy
Sapping: Getting hit with a sap
Sawbuck: $10 bill
Scratch: Money
Scuttlebutt: Gossip
Sfortunato: An unlucky guy
Shamus: Private Detective
Shanked: Stabbed
Shiv: Homemade knife
Skate around: To be of easy virtue
Snooper: Detective
Spick and span: Spotlessly clean
Square: Honest
Stitch up: Put someone in danger
Stir: Prison
Stronzo: Asshole

Take it on the lam: To try and escape
Take the fall for: Accept punishment for
Tea: Marijuana
Three-spot: Three-year term in jail
Throw away gun: An unregistered gun to be
used once and thrown away
Throw lead: Shoot bullets
Ticket: P.I. license
Tip their mitt: Reveal something
Tomato: Pretty woman

Tooting the wrong ringer: Asking the wrong person
Torpedoes: Gunmen
Trigger man: Man whose job is to use a gun
Trouble boys: Gangsters
Twist: A confident, strong woman

Weak sister: A push-over
Whack: Kill
Wheel: An influential person
Wooden kimono: A coffin

Yap: Mouth

GERMAN / NAZI GLOSSARY

Achtung: Attention
Als Flieger in Zwei Kriegen: As an aviator in two wars (Book title) Richard Euringer. An autobiography of combat
Auf Wiedersehen: Goodbye

Badezimmer: Bathroom
Bitte: Please
Blitz: Thunderbolt
Blut und Boden: Blood and soil

Dampfkartoffeln: Steam potatoes
Das: The
Die Fahne hoch: Raise the flag – the Nazi anthem
Der: The
Der Neger macht eien Sklaven gut: The negro makes a good slave

Der Untermensch: The Underman (Book title) Jupp Dehler. Propaganda about subhuman, inferior races
Deutschland Erwache: Germany Awakes
Die Waiküre: Wagner's opera about a Norse female figure who chooses who lives and who dies in war
Dummkopf: Fool

Ein bisschen: A little
Ein Rheinlandbastarde: A Rhineland bastard
Entartete Kunst: Degenerate Art (Book title) Fritz Kaiser. Catalog of unacceptable art deemed by the Nazi Party

Feldwebel: Sergeant
Flaggen: Flags
Frau: Misses
Fräulein: Woman
Führer: Leader

Glorreichen Tage: Glory Days
Großartig: Great
Gruppenführer: Group head
Gruppenleiter: Group leader

Hakenkreuzflagge: Swastika Flag
Hauptsturmführer: *"Head storm leader"* rank of Captain
Heil Hitler: Hail, my leader

Hitlerleute: The Hitler People
Helferinnenkorps: Aid corps – woman's corps of the SS
Herr: Mister
Herzlich willkommen, liebe Freunde: Welcome, dear friends
Hitlerjugend: Hitler youth
Hündin: Bitch

Ich danke dir sehr: Thank you very much
Ist gut: Is good.

Jawohl: Indeed
Jüden: Jews
Judenanwalt: Jew lawyer
Judensterben: Death to Jews
Junger Mann: Young man

Kaffee: Coffee
Kampflied der Nationalsozialisten: Battle song of the National Socialists
Kike: Slang for Jew
komm rein: Come in
Konzentrationslager (KZ): Concentration camp
Köstlich: Delicious
Kräuterlikör: Herbal liqueur

Luftwaffe: Air force

Maschinenpistole 40: Submachine gun
Meisterschaft: Master race
Mutterland: Motherland

Neger: Negro
Nur Männer: Men only

Obergruppenleiter: Senior group leader
Oberst: Colonel
Odessa: Organization of Former SS Members

Prächtig: Gorgeous
Privat: Private

Reich: Empire
Reichsführer: Commanding Officer
Reichskriegsflagge: Imperial War Flag
Rapportführer: Report Leader

SS - Schutzstaffel: Protection squadron
Schlägers: Thugs, goons or hooligans
Schmutziger Jude: Dirty Jew
Schmutziger Schweinehund: Dirty bastard
Schnell: Quick
Schön: Beautiful
Schutzstaffel: The SS *"Protection Squadron"*
Schwein: Swine
Schweinehund: Pig dog
Sicherheitsbeamter: Securty guard
Sieg Heil: For ensured victory

Sonderkommandos: Special work units made up of camp prisoners, usually Jews
Speckfannkuchen: Bacon pancakes
Sprichst du Deutsch : Do you speak German
Sig runes: Double SS lightning bolt symbol for victory
Stiefmütterchen: Pansies
Sturmbannbführer: Major
Sturmführer: Storm leader
Sturmtrooper: Stormtrooper

Übermensch: Higher human
Unterwachtmeister: Sergeant

Vielen dank: Thank you
Viel Glüc: Good luck

Waffen-SS: The military branch of the Nazi Party's SS
Wehrmacht: The German Army
Willkommen: Welcome
Wohngeist: Living Spirit woodworking tools
Wunderbar: Wonderful
Wunderschönen: Beautiful
Würdig: Worthy

Yid: Yiddish word for Jew

M. Ward Leon – the Author

M. Ward Leon is a former advertising creative director who started his career at Doyle Dane Bernbach, New York, during the Madmen era. While at DDB, his writing on the Volkswagen Rabbit campaign won him inclusion in the Smithsonian Institution Advertising Archives. Recently his writing has earned him two Emmy Awards for Public Service advertising.

He is a graduate of California State University Los Angeles and an alumnus of Art Center College of Design.

Other books by M Ward Leon: _Blood of the Beast_ • _Revenge of the Beast_ • _The Strange and Curious Cases of Roscoe Brown, Detective NYPD_ • _Ambush at Fig Tree Gulch_ • _Ishmael. My Life After Moby Dick_